DATE DUE

NOV 2 5 1996		

THE YEAR'S **BEST**
MYSTERY AND
SUSPENSE
STORIES
1993

Other Books by Edward D. Hoch

The Shattered Raven
The Judges of Hades
The Transvection Machine
The Spy and the Thief
City of Brass
Dear Dead Days (editor)
The Fellowship of the Hand
The Frankenstein Factory
Best Detective Stories of the Year 1976 (editor)
Best Detective Stories of the Year 1977 (editor)
Best Detective Stories of the Year 1978 (editor)
The Thefts of Nick Velvet
The Monkey's Clue & The Stolen Sapphire (juvenile)
Best Detective Stories of the Year 1979 (editor)
Best Detective Stories of the Year 1980 (editor)
Best Detective Stories of the Year 1981 (editor)
All But Impossible! (editor)
The Year's Best Mystery and Suspense Stories 1982 (editor)
The Year's Best Mystery and Suspense Stories 1983 (editor)
The Year's Best Mystery and Suspense Stories 1984 (editor)
The Quests of Simon Ark
Leopold's Way
The Year's Best Mystery and Suspense Stories 1985 (editor)
The Year's Best Mystery and Suspense Stories 1986 (editor)
The Year's Best Mystery and Suspense Stories 1987 (editor)
Great British Detectives (coeditor)
Women Write Murder (coeditor)
The Year's Best Mystery and Suspense Stories 1988 (editor)
Murder Most Sacred (coeditor)
The Year's Best Mystery and Suspense Stories 1989 (editor)
The Year's Best Mystery and Suspense Stories 1990 (editor)
The Spy Who Read Latin and Other Stories
The Night My Friend
The Year's Best Mystery and Suspense Stories 1991 (editor)
The People of the Peacock
The Year's Best Mystery and Suspense Stories 1992 (editor)

THE YEAR'S **BEST**
MYSTERY AND SUSPENSE STORIES
1993

EDITED BY **EDWARD D. HOCH**

Walker and Company
New York

First published in the United States of America in 1993 by Walker Publishing
Company, Inc.

Published simultaneously in Canada by Thomas Allen & Son Canada, Limited,
Markham, Ontario

Library of Congress Cataloging-in-Publication Card Number 83-646567

Book design by Ron Monteleone

Printed in the United States of America

2 4 6 8 10 9 7 5 3 1

"Candles in the Rain" by Doug Allyn. Copyright © 1992 by Doug Allyn. First published
in Ellery Queen's Mystery Magazine. Reprinted by permission of the author and his agent,
James Allen.
"A Poisoned Chalice" by Jo Bannister. Copyright © 1992 by Jo Bannister. First pub-
lished in Ellery Queen's Mystery Magazine.
"A Bit of Flotsam" by Jacklyn Butler. Copyright © 1991 by Davis Publications, Inc. First
published in Alfred Hitchcock's Mystery Magazine.
"Louise" by Max Allan Collins. Copyright © 1992 by Max Allan Collins. Ms. Tree is a
trademark of DC Comics, Inc.
"Mother Darkness" by Ed Gorman. Copyright © 1992 by Ed Gorman. First published
in Prisoners and Other Stories.
"The Problem of the Leather Man" by Edward D. Hoch. Copyright © 1992 by Edward
D. Hoch. First published in Ellery Queen's Mystery Magazine.
"The Last Sara" by Susan B. Kelly. Copyright © Crime Writers' Association, 1992. First
published in 1st Culprit, edited by Liza Cody and Michael Z. Lewin, and published by Chatto
& Windus. Reprinted by permission of Susan B. Kelly and Chatto & Windus.
"You May See a Strangler" by Peter Lovesey. Copyright © 1992 by Peter Lovesey. First
published in Midwinter Mysteries 2.
"The Model" by Joyce Carol Oates. Copyright © 1992 by The Ontario Review, Inc. First
published in Ellery Queen's Mystery Magazine.
"Sex and Violence" by Nancy Pickard. Copyright © 1992 by Nancy Pickard.
"The Man Who Was the God of Love" by Ruth Rendell. Copyright © 1992 by Kings-
markham Enterprises Limited.
"A Will Is a Way" by Steven Saylor. Copyright © 1992 by Steven Saylor. First published
in Ellery Queen's Mystery Magazine.
"Mary, Mary, Shut the Door" by Benjamin M. Schutz. Copyright © 1992 by Benjamin
M. Schutz. First published in Deadly Allies, edited by Robert J. Randisi & Marilyn Wallace.
Published by Doubleday/Perfect Crime.
"Love in the Lean Years" by Donald E. Westlake. Copyright © 1992 by Donald E. West-
lake. First published in Playboy, February 1992.

FOR **JANET HUTCHINGS**

CONTENTS

CONTENTS

INTRODUCTION

Having edited this anthology over eighteen years for two different publishers, I'm often asked how the mystery short story has changed during this period. My selection of fourteen of the best stories from 1992 gives me a good opportunity to answer that question.

In the first anthology I edited, covering stories published during 1975, sixteen of the seventeen were chosen from magazines, the other from a weekly newspaper. In the current volume, only seven of the fourteen stories are from magazines. The other seven are from books, anthologies, or single-author collections.

In that first anthology, six series characters were represented. This year there are only four—Max Allan Collins's Ms. Tree, my own Dr. Sam Hawthorne, Steven Saylor's Gordianus, and Ben Schutz's Leo Haggerty. In 1975 we had fifteen men and two women among the authors. This year there are eight men and six women.

Perhaps more enlightening than mere statistics are the themes of many of the stories in this volume. Here the reader will find stories about environmental concerns, violence against women, children in danger, serial killers—all topics that barely existed in short fiction eighteen years ago. These are subjects that do not lend themselves easily to the ministrations of master sleuths, and perhaps it's no accident that two of our four series detectives operate in past times.

Comparing today's mystery and suspense stories with those of the past inevitably leads to the question of which stories are better. It is a question that *does* have an answer. Today's stories are better written than those we remember from the so-called Golden Age of the mystery. It must be said, however, that they are often less well plotted. The very best mysteries today, long or short, have entered the mainstream of fiction. What we have gained in powerful language and evocative images has come at the expense of the intricate plotting and exhaustive investigations so beloved by Christie and Carr and Queen. These authors are gone forever, but happily their books are still with us.

Here, then, is today's model of the mystery and suspense story—not without humor, not without an occasional impossible crime, but with a distinct sense of today, of the way we live now. And die.

My special thanks this year to Doug Greene, Janet Hutchings, Marv Lachman, Percy Spurlark Parker, Bill Pronzini, and especially my wife, Patricia, who read every suspense story published during the year and offered invaluable comments.

—*Edward D. Hoch*

THE YEAR'S **BEST**
MYSTERY AND
SUSPENSE
STORIES
1993

DOUG ALLYN

CANDLES IN THE RAIN

"Candles in the Rain" marks the fourth appearance by Doug Allyn in this series since his first story won the Robert L. Fish Memorial Award from Mystery Writers of America in 1985. You'll find three of his stories listed on the Honor Roll at the back of this book, all different and all of high quality. This story, which won the EQMM Readers Award as their favorite of the year and brought Allyn his fourth MWA Edgar nomination, reflects the environmental and human concerns of Clark Howard, Michael Collins, and other writers who know how to get a message across without ever diminishing the suspense of the telling.

From a distance it looked like a modern-day siege of Rome. A small army of tents and campers was arrayed in a field across from the air-base entrance, and a ragged line of demonstrators was pacing along the shoulder of the road. But as I threaded my battered Chevy van past haphazardly parked cars and strolling protesters, the sense of conflict waned a bit.

The marchers were a mix of scruffy college kids and only slightly less scruffy adults in fashionably frayed denims, working-class duds à la Ralph Lauren. I gave them points for tenacity though. It was a chill, drizzly day but their spirits seemed high and dry.

Their placards were straightforward: No Nukes, No Incinerator. Ban Bombs and Toxic Waste. And on a less enlightened note: Don't Give America Back to the Redskins.

The airfield looked secure enough, protected by a fifteen-foot

1

chain-link fence crowned with coils of bayonet wire. There were air police on duty at the gate, and a county sheriff's black-and-white parked on the shoulder of the road, flashers swirling slowly in the rain. The billboard beside the entrance was as formidable as the fence: lightning bolts clenched in an armored fist. Bullock Air Force Base, Strategic Air Command, Crater Creek, Michigan.

The air-police gate guard, starched and immaculate in white gloves and cap, snapped to attention as I pulled up and gave me a smart salute. I returned it on reflex. Old habits die hard.

"Good afternoon, sir, welcome to Bullock. Can I help you?"

"My name's Delacroix. I have an appointment to see the base commander, Colonel Webber."

"Yes, sir," the sergeant said. "Could I see some identification, please?" He gave my driver's license a quick once over, then peered into an empty van. "Are you alone, Mr. Delacroix? It was my understanding that the Ojibwa Council was sending a delegation."

"They have," I said. "I'm it."

"I see," he said doubtfully. "A delegation of one?"

"You just have the one air base to give away, right?"

"Yessir," he said, frowning. "Still . . ." A bottle arched high in the air from behind the county black-and-white and smashed in the middle of the road, an explosion of beer foam and splintered glass.

"What's going on across the road, Sergeant?"

"The usual weekend demonstration," he said sourly, handing me a plastic visitor's card. "The local peaceniks have been picketing Bullock for years. Now that it's closing, they're griping about the base incinerator staying open. No pleasing 'em, I guess."

"At least they care enough to get wet," I said.

"Or they ain't got sense enough to get outa the rain," the sergeant said. "You'll find Colonel Webber at the base reception center just up the road. Please keep your pass with you at all times. Enjoy your visit, Mr. Delacroix." He waved me past and saluted. This time I didn't return it.

* * *

2

The base reception center was easy to find. It was the only building with cars parked in front of it. The others I passed were all closed and padlocked. On a field that once supported an entire wing of B-52s, only one solitary plane remained on the tarmac, a transport of some kind, with USAF markings. Beyond it, the runway stretched away endlessly into the silvery drizzle, silent and empty as a parking lot on the moon.

The portico in front of the entrance was draped with a red-white-and-blue banner. Welcome Michigan Ojibwa Council. I brushed the road dust off my corduroy sportcoat, straightened my tie, and walked in.

The reception room was jammed, a cocktail conclave in full swing, mostly civilians, men in suits, women in spring dresses, with a smattering of men in USAF blue uniforms scattered through the crowd. A gaggle of reporters and cameramen were clustered near the door and a refreshment table piled with sandwiches and hors d'oeuvres. Conversation died a slow death as I entered. I had a momentary flash of a half-forgotten dream, walking into high school minus my trousers.

A mid-thirtyish Native American woman in a stylish umber suit, her dark hair cropped boyishly short, left her companions and walked over. She had an open, honest face, and an eager smile. "Hello, I'm Eva Redfern. Are you with the delegation?"

"Not exactly," I said. "I am the delegation. My name's Delacroix, tribal constable from Algoma County. Can we talk somewhere for a moment? Privately?"

"I think we'd better," she said, her smile fading. A pity. I followed her back out under the portico. "Now, what's going on? When are the others arriving? We're running late already."

"We're going to run a little later, I'm afraid. The council voted last night to send me down to inspect the facility. If everything checks out, I've been authorized to accept the base on their behalf. Tomorrow."

"Tomorrow?" she echoed, stunned. "Are they out of their minds? I've spent weeks negotiating this arrangement. The transfer is set for this afternoon, and this is *not* a done deal, Delacroix. Not until the papers are signed. If we stall—"

"No one's stalling. Anytime somebody wants to cede land

back to the tribes we'll take it. They just want me to take a last hard look at it."

"No offense, Mr. Delacroix, but this is hardly a police matter. Why did they send a constable?"

"Because I know a little about military bases. I served on a few. Look, I'm not your enemy, Miss Redfern, but I have my instructions. The sooner I carry them out, the sooner we'll get things back on schedule. Unfortunately, since they only called me in on this last night, I barely had time to scan the paperwork involved. Would you be kind enough to brief me? Please?"

Irritation and professionalism skirmished in her dark eyes for a moment. Professionalism won.

"All right. In a nutshell, Bullock is being closed. There was a government auction, and Kanelos Waste Disposal won the bidding. But since all Mr. Kanelos really wants is the base waste incinerator and a few hundred acres of runway for parking, he's offered to cede the base to the Ojibwa Council in return for a permanent lease on the incinerator and parking area."

"Which sounds almost too good to be true. Why should he give us the base?"

"To avoid taxes," she said simply. "Since the state can't tax tribal land, Mr. Kanelos can operate the waste facility tax free, and we get roughly five thousand acres of land, *gratis.*"

"Most of which is covered with concrete," I said.

"Dammit, it's still a good deal for us, Delacroix. Have you ever heard the old saying about looking a gift horse in the mouth?"

"Yes, ma'am. I also remember one about Greeks bearing gifts. Shall we get on with this?"

"I guess we haven't much choice. But by God, you'd better not blow this deal."

Redfern led me through the crush to a corner where the base commander was holding court. There was no other word for it. In his impeccably tailored blue uniform, close-cropped sandy hair, with just a trace of silver at the temples, Webber cut a striking military figure. The granite-faced black master sergeant standing half a pace behind him added to the effect. Webber was chatting with a gaunt vampire of a man, fortyish, with blue jowls, and fluid-filled pouches under his eyes. He was wearing a dark suit and shirt, a single strand of gold chain nestling in the hollow of his throat.

"Colonel Webber, Mr. Kanelos," Redfern said, "I'd like to introduce Mr. Delacroix, of the Ojibwa Council." She gave them a quick briefing on the situation. I expected annoyance, and got it.

"Mr. Delacroix," Webber said coolly, not bothering to offer his hand, "what's the problem? I was under the impression everything was arranged. Some members of the council having . . . reservations, so to speak?"

"As far as I know, everything's a go, Colonel," I said. "Or it will be as soon as I complete my inspection."

"But what kind of a survey can you do in a few hours?" Kanelos said heatedly. "The base is six thousand acres. Look, I've put myself on the line for you people. I stretched myself to my financial limits to win the bidding and I'm even giving hiring preference to Indians at the incinerator facility. Hell, I should think you people might show a bit more gratitude—"

"Easy, Frank," Webber interrupted, "the constable's just following orders, and as a soldier I can relate to that. Sergeant Jenkins, why don't you give Delacroix a tour of the base, show him whatever he wants to see. Frank, we'd better talk to the newspeople. I don't want any bad press over this." He stalked off without a backward glance, sweeping Kanelos along in his wake.

The sergeant shrugged. "Don't mind the boss. He's used to having people jump when he says frog. What do you want to see, Mr. Delacroix?"

"The major facilities, PX, hangars. As much as I can in the time we have," I said, watching the colonel and Kanelos disappear into the mob scene.

"I'm coming too," Redfern said.

"Then we'd better get started," Jenkins said. "The power's already been shut off to the perimeter lighting. When it gets dark out on the field these days, it really gets dark."

"What happened to the command and electronics bunkers?" I asked. We were in a closed Jeep, humming down a rain-slick

5

runway toward the shadowy mountains of a hangar, Jenkins driving, me riding shotgun, Redfern in the backseat.

"All strategic or classified equipment was dismantled and shipped back to SAC headquarters, or destroyed on site," Jenkins said. "We blew the bunkers, filled 'em in, and laid sod on the graves. How do you know about bunkers? You serve on a base?"

"A few," I said. "U Bon, Thailand, and Tan Son Nhut."

"No kidding? I was U Bon during the war. When were you there?"

"When I was too young to know better."

"I know the feeling." Jenkins smiled, relaxing a little. "Okay, if you know bases, then you know there ain't all that much more I can show you. You've seen most of the buildings, there's really nothin' else to see but a lotta open concrete."

"And trucks," I said. "What are all those trucks doing on the far end of the runway?"

"Toxic waste tankers, waitin' their turn at the incinerator. Must be twenty of 'em down there at any given time. They come from all over the state. It's big business, waste disposal. It's closed for the weekend now, but come Monday they'll be humpin'. Pardon my French, ma'am. Sometimes when the wind's right, it smells a little funky, but mostly you can't hardly tell it's there. You want to drive over, take a closer look?"

"No, what Kanelos does with his end of the base is his business. I think I've seen enough. Let's head back."

"Fine by me," Jenkins said, wheeling the Jeep in a quick U-turn. "I served three tours on Bullock. Hate to see it like this. It's like attendin' your own funeral."

"I should think you'd be happy," Eva said. "No more wars, or at least no big ones."

"Oh, I don't miss war, ma'am. Nobody hates fightin' more'n the people who might have to bleed. But soldierin's an honest trade, and not such a bad life. How 'bout you, Delacroix? You ever miss the life?"

"The people sometimes," I said. "Never the life. What's all the hubbub over by the entrance?"

"Antinuke parade." Jenkins grinned, checking his watch.

"Right on time, as usual. Wanna check it out? Way the world's goin', it may be the last one."

Redfern sighed. "I certainly hope so."

"Yes ma'am," Jenkins said, his smile fading, "me too."

Jenkins parked the Jeep in the reception-center lot and the three of us trotted briskly to the portico. The rain had started again, a steady, chilly drizzle, driven by the wind. The media people and some of the party-goers had wandered out to watch, but except for the cameramen filming the march through the fence, no one strayed from shelter. There was no reason to do so.

The local peace movement seemed to be winding down with a whimper, not a bang. A line of demonstrators formed a lopsided ring in the road opposite the gate. They were carrying candles, but except for a few who had umbrellas as well, most of the flames guttered in the first few moments. Still, I had to admire their persistence. They marched in a circle in the blustery dusk and drizzle for ten minutes or so, singing "Give Peace a Chance," out of tune, and out of step with each other. And with the times.

"Not much of a show, is it?" Colonel Webber said, moving up beside me. "Not like the old days. A few years ago there were a couple of hundred every weekend, blocking the entrance, chaining themselves to the fence, and being a general nuisance. Arrogant fools, the lot of them. They simply didn't see the big picture."

"I served a dozen years, in two wars, and I'm not sure I ever saw it either," I said mildly. "Maybe the picture seems clearer up at forty thousand feet."

"Perhaps it does," Webber said. "Sergeant Jenkins tells me you've finished your tour. I take it you're satisfied?"

"Yes, sir. As far as I'm concerned we can finalize the transfer tomorrow. I'll phone the council tonight, and—"

But Webber wasn't listening. He'd turned, frowning, peering into the drizzle. Even the marchers gradually stumbled to a halt, listening. Out on the tarmac, behind the curtain of rain, there was the sound of drumming. Tom-toms. And the chanting of many voices, instantly recognizable as Native Americans. But not a tribe I knew. Not Ojibwa.

"Sergeant," Webber snapped, "get out there and secure that aircraft. I don't know what's—"

WHOOOMP! Suddenly, far out on the runway, a pillar of fire erupted, a hundred-foot geyser of flame. And then there was an unearthly wail, louder than the drums and chanting. And a figure came running toward us out of the rain, a human being, ablaze, engulfed in fire, howling like a beast. He staggered, then fell to his knees, crawling like a smashed insect, screaming.

Jenkins was the first to react, springing for the Jeep. I followed, scrambling into the passenger's seat as he gunned the Jeep out of the lot and raced down the runway toward the burning man.

He jammed on the brakes a few yards short of the figure on the tarmac, and I banged headfirst into the windshield, hard. Jenkins yanked a portable fire extinguisher from its dash clip and ran to the figure cowering on the concrete. I followed on shaky legs. He quickly fogged the man down, then trotted beyond him and killed two smaller fires as well.

I knelt beside the blackened man, dazed, uncertain. His clothes were still smoldering, and he was moaning, in soul-deep agony. And I didn't know what to do. He smelled smoky sweet, almost . . . I recoiled mentally from the thought.

"Mister," I pleaded softly, "please, just hang on, okay? Help's coming. . . ."

The moaning stopped. And the breathing. My God. I tried to roll him onto his back to give mouth-to-mouth, but his body was rigid. His arms were locked over his face as though they were welded to it and I couldn't pull them away. And then a piece of seared flesh peeled off in my hand, and I lurched to my feet, gagging, and stumbled off down the runway, staggering like a gut-shot bear. Fleeing the smoking body. And the horror.

Jenkins caught me after twenty yards or so, grasping my shoulders, steadying me down to a walk, then stopping me. We stood there for a long time in silence, in the rain.

Behind us, the sheriff's patrol car screeched to a halt beside the Jeep. Doors slammed. People were shouting. And still Jenkins and I stood there. Holding each other. Like family at a funeral.

"Are you all right?" he asked at last.

"Yeah," I managed. My voice sounded as weak and shaky as I felt. "Is he . . .?"

"He was dead before we got there," Jenkins said, releasing me cautiously, as if afraid I might fall. "He just didn't know it. There was nothing you could do. Nothing anyone could do."

He turned and trudged slowly back to the crowd gathered around the figure on the field, shrouded now by a blanket.

The sheriff rose slowly from beside the body, carefully unfolding the charred remains of a wallet.

"Buck," he read softly, "Geronimo G. My God, it's Jerry Buck." Eva Redfern paled and turned away, her eyes swimming. I touched her arm.

"You know him?" I said.

"I, ahm, no," she said, swallowing. "Not really. He's Native American but he's not Ojibwa. He's just a side—he came up from Detroit a year or so ago."

"A sidewalk Indian," I said.

"Yes," she nodded. "Lakota, I think. From out West somewhere. Montana maybe. Drank his way out of a line job at Ford. Moved up here, did odd jobs. He was an alcoholic."

"Why would he do this?"

"I . . . don't know. I didn't really know him well."

"When you got to him, did he say anything to you?" the sheriff asked me.

"No, he . . . didn't speak. He couldn't."

"Well, it's apparently a suicide," the sheriff said, glancing around. "Had to be. Nobody else could have been near him out here. Found a gas can back on the tarmac maybe sixty yards away. And what's left of a pile of rags. And a boom box. That's what the Indian music was. Apparently he just turned on the tape, doused himself with gas, and, ahm . . . set himself afire. Crazy. Had to be crazy."

"Maybe not," I said slowly.

"Why not?" Jenkins asked. "You know him?"

"No. But even a crazy wouldn't choose to die like this. It's too . . . horrible."

"But what makes you think—?"

"Dammit, I've seen this before! My first tour in 'Nam, the

9

monks were burning themselves in the damn streets! And people said they were crazy. And nobody listened to them!"

"Easy, bro," Jenkins said quietly. "This ain't no Vietnamese police state. We're in backwoods freakin' Michigan. If the man had a point to make, he didn't have to smoke himself to do it. All he had to do was walk up and speak his piece, right? Nobody woulda stopped him."

"I don't know," I said, swallowing, trying to clear my head. "All I know is, the base was supposed to be transferred to the Ojibwa today. He must have been trying to stop it for some reason."

"You can't be sure of that," Jenkins said.

"You're right, I'm not. But I'm not going to go ahead with the transfer until we know."

"Look, Mr. Delacroix," Colonel Webber said, stiffening, "I know this has been a shock, to all of us. But surely the act of the demented individual—"

"You don't know he was demented," I said.

"But he *was* crazy, or nearly so," Redfern said. "He was borderline retarded and an alcoholic as well. Who knows what was in his mind? Delacroix, the colonel's right, this is too important to our people to stop now. He was just—"

"A drunk," I finished. "And not even Ojibwa. So forget it? Business as usual?"

"That isn't what I meant," she said, flushing. "It's just that—"

"Mr. Delacroix, I've tried to be patient, but I have my orders," Webber interrupted. "I agreed to delay the proceedings until tomorrow, but that's the best I can do. I must have your decision then, or I'll have to withdraw from our agreement. Since the man's death occurred on the base, it's technically a military matter, so if you wish to make inquiries, I can loan you Sergeant Jenkins to give you some official standing. I assume you'd have no objections, Sheriff Brandon?"

Brandon shrugged. "No, sir. It's a straightforward suicide. The decedent's state of mind isn't really a police matter, and frankly I've got my hands full as it is. As long as you don't harass anybody, make all the inquiries you like."

*   *   *

"You don't seem too happy about this," I said to Jenkins. We were in his Jeep, headed toward the main gate. Eva Redfern had stayed behind to try to pacify the colonel and Kanelos.

"I'm not," Jenkins said bluntly, keeping his eyes on the road. "I put up with these peacenik crazies every weekend for years, picketing the base, blockin' the gate to get themselves arrested. Now I'm one day away from gettin' outa here and . . . I got my own job to do, you know?"

"Maybe if you'd done it better we wouldn't be in this mess."

"What's that supposed to mean?"

"You're in charge of base security, right? So how did this guy manage to get out in the middle of the runway?"

"Wouldn't be hard. He couldn't have climbed the fence carrying the boom box and a gas can, so I'm guessin' he just cut the fence and walked in. The electronic barriers were disconnected last month when the last of the classified equipment was shipped out."

"And the fence isn't patrolled?"

"We inspect the perimeter once a shift, about every eight hours. I've only got six men and I need 'em at the gate."

"What about guard dogs? Most bases use them on the perimeter."

"We, ahm, we haven't used the dogs in a while. To be honest, I haven't worried much about security. Hell, there's nothin' left on Bullock worth stealin'."

"Maybe not," I said grimly, "but apparently there was something worth dying for."

Jenkins eased the Jeep cautiously down the lane between the demonstrators' tents and campers. There were only a few dozen left. He parked beside a battered trailer, covered with bumper stickers: No Nukes, Peace Now. The usual.

"This is Doc Klein's trailer," Jenkins said, switching off the Jeep. "He's been organizing peace marches since the sixties, and bugging me for at least ten years. If anybody knows anything about your guy, the doc will."

"Will he talk to me? With you there I mean?"

"No sweat," Jenkins said drily. "Gettin' the doc to talk isn't a problem. It's gettin' him to shut up. Come on."

We jogged through the downpour to the trailer door. Jenkins rapped and after a moment the door swung open, revealing a squat stump of a man, fiftyish, balding, with a fringe of shoulder-length, baby-fine blond hair, and a neatly trimmed blond beard. A bulldog pipe was clamped in the corner of his jaw. "Well, well," he said evenly, "if it isn't my favorite arresting officer."

"Doc," Jenkins said, "can we see you a minute?"

"Of course, come in, come in. I wouldn't leave a dog out on a night like this. Or a sergeant."

Jenkins introduced me to Klein, and we shook hands. The three of us filled the postage-stamp camper like pickles in a jar. I sat on the narrow cot that stretched across one end of the room, Jenkins leaned against the door, while Klein sat in the lone chair at the tiny table for one. A pot was burbling on the small camp stove. The aroma of chili and cherry-blend pipe smoke filled the room like incense in a bazaar.

"Mr. Delacroix, I can't tell you how sorry I am about what happened today," Dr. Klein said earnestly. "We're on opposite sides of this matter politically but, well, I'm sorry. It's a terrible irony that after a dozen years of peaceful demonstrations, such a thing would happen on the last day."

"Did you know the man who died, Doctor?" I asked.

He nodded. "A little. As well as anyone, I suppose. He, ahm, he drank, you know."

"So I understand. You said we're on opposite sides. Why? What have you got against us?"

"Against the Ojibwa? Nothing. My goodness, your people have been my life's work."

"The doc's an archaeologist, specializin' in Native American culture," Jenkins said. "When he's not playin' rabblerouser, that is."

"I see," I said. "Then why is your group opposed to our taking over the base?"

"Because of the way it was arranged. We believe you're being used."

"Used by whom?"

"By Kanelos, and Webber as well. Kanelos didn't win the bidding, you know. The high bidder was a salvage company that intended to dismantle the buildings and tear up the runway for the scrap concrete. Colonel Webber awarded the bid to Mr. Kanelos as being least disruptive to the community."

"Hey, he was right," Jenkins put in. "It'd take a helluva lot of blasting to break up the runway. It's a foot thick, most places."

"More disruptive than flying B-52s loaded with nuclear weapons out of there twenty-four hours a day?" Klein countered. "At least when the blasting was finished, we'd have the land back. As it is, we're trading one hazardous nuisance for another."

"But the incinerator isn't new, is it?" I asked.

"No," Klein said, "but it's never been operated on the scale it is now. And by trading you the land in return for a lifetime lease, Kanelos not only avoids paying taxes, he also avoids federal EPA inspections. Did you know that?"

"No," I said, glancing at Jenkins. "I didn't. And Jerry Buck? Was he strongly against the transfer too?"

"Jerry? No, not that I know of," Klein said, puzzled. "He was hardly the political type."

"You mean he wasn't part of your—group?"

"No. Not at all."

"But you said you knew him."

"I did, but not from the movement. We're doing an archaeological dig at an old Anishnabeg burial ground just west of the base. Jerry worked for me there, doing manual labor, catch as catch can. For beer money, really."

"Look, I don't understand, Doctor," I said. "If he wasn't political, why on earth would he have done what he did?"

"I honestly don't know. I've been asking myself the same thing since they told me it was Jerry. Joe Gesh might be able to tell you more."

"Joe Gesh?" I noticed that Jenkins stiffened at the mention of the name.

"He's a local character, an Ojibwa, lives in a shack on the edge of Bullock swamp near the burial ground. Jerry was staying with him out there, learning what he could."

"About what?"

"How to live in the past." Klein smiled. "Old Joe's an atavism, a throwback, the last of the wild Indians. He helps me at the dig occasionally, identifying tufts of decorative fur or animal tracks. He's incredibly knowledgeable."

"Oughta be," Jenkins said. "He eats most anything that walks or crawls back there."

"I guess we'd better talk to him," I said, rising. "One last question, Doctor Klein, could Buck's death have anything to do with this burial-ground dig you're doing? Will the transfer affect it in any way?"

"Nothin' to affect," Jenkins snorted. "I been back there, ain't nothin' *to* see."

"He's right on both counts," Klein said, smiling. "There is very little to see. Cracked stones from fire pits, a few pottery shards, discarded tools. The Anishnabeg lived on this land for nearly fifteen hundred years, and left almost no traces. I wish we could say the same. But the dig won't be affected by the closing of the base. And I doubt that it mattered much to Jerry anyway. He wasn't really serious about the work."

"Maybe not," I said, "but he was damn serious about something."

"Yes," Klein nodded soberly, "I guess he must have been."

"You know this Gesh character, don't you?" I asked. We were in the Jeep, following the narrow track along the outside of the perimeter fence.

"I know him," Jenkins said grimly. "Tangled with him more'n once. And if Buck was livin' with that ol' man, it might explain a lot about him goin' off the deep end."

"Why?"

"'Cause Gesh is nuts, that's why. Lives back in the swamp like the last damn Apache or somethin'."

"Or Ojibwa," I said. "Why did you tangle with him?"

"Because base security is my job, and every now and then we hear gunfire back in that swamp. And we have to check it out. And that old man ain't heavy into hospitality, I'll tell ya."

"Maybe he was poaching, thought you might be the law."

"No," Jenkins said positively, "it wasn't that. He knew damn well we were air force. Even recognized my rank. Kept his gun on me the whole time anyway."

"And you just—let that pass?"

"Yeah, well, maybe I shouldn't have." Jenkins sighed, peering past the wipers into the downpour. "But I didn't figure it was worth gettin' anybody killed over, and that's what would've happened if we'd tried to disarm him. He was scared to death of us, and crazy as a loon."

"Why do you say he was crazy?"

"He was talkin' crazy. And he kept throwin' tobacco at me."

"Tobacco?"

"That's right. Held his rifle in one hand, aimed at my belly, and kept tossin' bits of loose tobacco at me, little pinches out of a can. Prince Albert, I think it was. And talkin' right out of his head."

"About what?"

"Ghosts," Jenkins said, glancing over at me with a fox's grin. "You know, I'm a black man in a white man's country, and I been called a lotta things in my time, but never a ghost. He kept callin' me a ghost. You sure you want to talk to him?"

"No." I sighed. "But I guess I have to. And maybe I'd better see him alone, if you don't mind."

"Hell no, I don't mind. Best news I've had all day," Jenkins said, easing the Jeep to a halt. He shrugged out of his raincoat and gave it to me. "There's a flashlight in the glove box. See that path up ahead to the left? It'll take you back to old Joe's shack, half a mile or so back in the swamp. Seems like it goes forever, but stay on it. And bro? You watch your ass, hear? If that ol' man wastes you, I'm gonna have to fill out a godawful stack of paperwork."

I didn't bother to reply. The rain was on me in an icy torrent the moment I stepped out of the Jeep, like standing under a waterfall. Jenkins's raincoat was little help. I was soaked to the bone before I'd stumbled fifty yards down the muddy track.

I've hunted all my life, so the trail wasn't all that hard to follow. Rough going though, sodden, slippery with uncertain footing. Tag alders and cedar saplings clawed at me out of the

15

darkness, as if asking me to bide awhile, to share their loneliness. I spotted the faint glow of a lamp ahead.

Gesh's shack wasn't a shack exactly. It was a hogan, a rectangular log hut roofed with sod. It was crude, but not totally primitive. It had glass windows, and tar paper had been tacked over a patch where the sod had washed away.

"Hello," I shouted. "Mr. Gesh?"

No answer. The lamp in the cabin winked out. "Mr. Gesh, my name's Delacroix. I'd like to talk to you."

"What do you want?" The voice was a low rasp, barely louder than a whisper.

"For openers, to come in out of the rain. I have news for you."

After what seemed like a month, a match flickered in the cabin and a lamp glowed to life. The door swung slowly open on leather hinges. "Come ahead. But move slow."

Even after the darkness of the forest, the hogan was dim, lit by a single kerosene lamp hanging from a sapling rafter. The air was thick with the stench of tallow and rancid suet from the hides stretched over ash hoops hanging on the walls, raccoon, lynx, muskrat. Gesh watched me from the shadows in the far corner of the room. He was smaller than I expected, a wiry little gnome of a man, gray hair tied back in a ratty ponytail, a brown, seamed face, carved from mahogany. He was wearing a green-and-black plaid flannel coat, faded jeans, worn moccasins. Even his rifle was small. A bolt-action Marlin .22. A trapper's gun. After a moment he lowered it, and leaned it in the corner.

"You're from up north someplace, aren't ya?" he said.

"Yes, sir. From Algoma. Bear Clan. How did you know?"

"Because your eyes don't get big. The young ones come out here from town, they always look around like my house is a museum or somethin'. But you know what things are," he said, gesturing at the hides, the hogan.

"I trapped for a few years, after I got out of the army," I said. "Lived with the Cree, up in Ontario."

"What was it like, that country?"

"Empty," I said. "And hungry. Winters last a hundred years."

"Here too, sometimes." He nodded. "Sit. Sorry it's cold in here, I'm outa kerosene for the stove. Here, wrap up in this, you'll be warm after a while." He handed me a frayed army blanket. I draped it over my shoulders and sat on a tree-stump stool that obviously doubled as a chopping block.

"You bring anything to drink?" Gesh asked.

"No," I said. "Sorry. I didn't know I was coming."

"It's okay." He shrugged. "You said you had news. Bad, right?"

"I'm afraid so. They tell me Jerry Buck was staying with you."

"A few months. Tried to dry him out, straighten him out. Didn't work. What happened to him?"

"He, ah, he's dead, Mr. Gesh. Soaked himself with gasoline, and . . . he burned."

"On the base," the old man said. It wasn't a question.

"Yes."

"Sweet Jesus," Gesh said, swallowing hard. "I told him. Stupid bastard."

"What did you tell him?"

"To stay off there. That they'd kill him."

"Who would?"

"The dead pilots, or whatever they are. The ghosts. They kill everything out there. All them planes, loaded with bombs. With death. Death is all they know. They killed themselves, now they kill everything else."

"I don't understand," I said.

"Maybe you can't," he said. "Do you know about ghosts?"

"I'm—not sure. I've never seen one."

"You won't see these either," the old man snorted. "They're dead. A long time ago. Fifteen, twenty years maybe. They died in the spring, in the rain. Now when it rains, they come back."

"Who comes back?" I asked.

"The dead flyers. The ones who died in the plane. Big one. I heard it fall in the night. Shook the ground. Thought it was the end of the damn world. I snuck over by the field, watched from the woods. There were a lotta bodies around, in them rubber bags, you know? Maybe a dozen. Maybe more. Nothing left of the damn plane. Junk. Pieces of it scattered half a mile. It was all gone the next day. The other airmen picked everything up, made it look like nothing happened. Like it had all been a dream. But it wasn't. I saw the dead men all right. And a few years later, their ghosts came back. They killed the dogs first, the ones that guarded the fence. Other animals too sometimes, coons, possums."

"Why do you think ghosts killed them?"

"Because they wasn't touched. No wounds, no blood. They just—take their souls. Leave the bodies behind. Dead all the same. Maybe the flyers weren't buried right. Maybe their souls are trapped out there and need food. I don't know. All I know is, they come back in the rain. And hunt."

"But Jerry Buck didn't just die. He was burned to death."

"Jerry was a man." Gesh shrugged. "Maybe he was harder to kill than the dogs."

"Maybe." I nodded, glancing around the hogan, inhaling the aroma of curing hides, and tobacco, and blood. A primeval scent that evoked a hazy memory of other lodges, in other places, long ago. Before I was born.

"Do you know what Jerry was doing out there?" I asked.

"Celebrating," the old man said. "Someone told him the air force is giving the base to the Ojibwa. Is that true?"

"Something like that," I said.

"But why? We don't have no planes."

"We'll make something out of it," I said. "We're good at that. You said Jerry went there to celebrate?"

"Yeah. He wasn't from here, he was Lakota Sioux from Montana. Knew a dance he learned in reservation school. Buffalo dance. Did it pretty good too. Had a tape of the drums and everything. He said he was gonna dance out on the runway, put on a show for the people. Maybe make a few dollars."

"I see," I said. "Jesus. He, ahm, he had a gas can with him."

"Not gas, kerosene," Gesh said. "He needed a fire for the dance. Took my kerosene and wet down some rags so they'd burn in the rain. Musta screwed it up. He was drinkin'. He was always drinkin'. It's all the young people know these days."

"Not so many," I said. "Not anymore. Are you sure it was kerosene he took? Not gasoline?"

"I don't keep no gas here. Got no car or nothin'. Just use kerosene for the lamp, the stove."

"Yeah," I said. "Right. Look, there's going to be a ceremony at the base tomorrow. Would you like to come?"

"No," he spat. "No way. It's a bad place. Haunted. I won't go there."

"Suit yourself. Maybe I could come back here, sometime."

"Why?"

"To talk. I'll tell you how the Cree breed wolves. Maybe I'll even bring a couple beers."

The old man stared at me a long time, reading me. Then he shook his head. "I don't think so," he said quietly.

"No? Why not?"

"Because you ain't comin' back, Delacroix. I ain't stupid, just old. You don't believe me about them ghosts. I read it in your eyes. So you're gonna go see for yourself. Ain't you?"

I didn't want to lie to him. So I didn't answer.

"Thought so," he said, not bothering to conceal the contempt in his tone. "You got some education, I can tell by the way you talk. Jerry didn't know nothin'. Just a sidewalk Indian. But if you go out on that field, you'll be as dead as him. As dead as them dogs."

"I can take care of myself," I said. "I'll be back."

"No," he said. "You won't." And he turned his back on me, shutting me out. As though I were dead already.

"Took you long enough," Jenkins said as I climbed into the Jeep. "You find the shack?"

"I found it. The old man said Buck took a can of kerosene to soak some rags and start a small fire out on the runway. He was going to put on a little show. To celebrate the tribe taking over the base."

"But something went wrong?" Jenkins asked, his tone neutral.

"He'd been drinking. My guess is, he spilled some of the kerosene on himself. And when he lit the fire . . . he burned."

"Yeah." Jenkins nodded warily. "That must've been how it happened. It wasn't suicide, then?"

"No. He didn't go out there to die. He went out there to dance."

"So we can go ahead with the transfer ceremony tomorrow?"

"I don't see why not. Do you?"

"No," Jenkins said, visibly relaxing. "What happened was a damn shame. But we have to move on."

"Yeah, I guess we do. The old man said something odd, though. He said the field's haunted. By the ghosts of flyers who cracked up a plane a long time ago. That the ghosts killed Jerry somehow. That they killed your dogs too."

"I told you he was crazy."

"Is he? If the dogs had been patrolling the perimeter, Buck never could have gotten on the field."

"Yeah, well, they weren't. We had no reason to think anyone would try to penetrate the field, so we shipped the dogs out. Transferred 'em back to Offutt. Wish to hell I'd gone with 'em."

"What about the plane? Was there a crash?"

"Bullock was a Strategic Air Command base," Jenkins said warily. "We flew nuclear missions out of here twenty-four hours a day, seven days a week, for nearly thirty years. There was a cold war on, remember? Even if there were crack-ups, I couldn't tell you about 'em. It'd still be classified information. You were a soldier once. You know how it is, right?"

"Yes," I said. "I think so."

Jenkins dropped me off at my van and drove off to report to his colonel. I trotted to my Chevy through the rain and scrambled in. And started as a figure sat up in the backseat.

"Hi," Eva Redfern said. "Sorry. I wanted to make sure I didn't miss you. Must've fallen asleep. What did you find out?"

"That Jerry Buck's death was an accident," I said, starting the van. "Sort of."

"I don't understand."

"Neither do I, exactly. Have you got time to take a short ride with me?"

"I suppose so. Where are we going?"

"To the dogs," I said. "Or to where they used to be."

The kennels had been removed, but the chain-link dog runs were still in place, probably more trouble than it was worth to tear down. The concrete runs had been swept clean. But I found what

I was looking for in the grass that had grown up beneath the edge of the fence. A chalky white pebble, not much bigger than a marble. I bounced it in my palm a moment, thinking. Then carried it back to the van.

"Well?" Redfern said. "What did you find?"

"A lump of truth," I said, passing her the pebble. "You've got fingernails, see if you can dent that."

"I can . . . scrape it a little," she said, "but I can't dent it. What is it? Chalk?"

"Nope, it's crap. A dog turd, to be specific. Hard as rock. Calcified."

"What?"

"Don't worry, it won't contaminate you. It's old. Probably a dozen years or so. And it was the only one I could find."

"And is this thing—" she tossed the turd into my ashtray and dusted off her hands. "Is this supposed to mean something?"

"Maybe. It might mean that what old Joe Gesh told me about the dogs was true," I said, slipping the van into drive and heading out onto the tarmac. "That they were killed a long time ago. As near as I can tell, no dogs have used those kennels for years."

"But why should that matter?"

"I'm not sure it does, but it makes me wonder if the rest of what he told me is true. About dead flyers. And ghosts that kill in the rain."

"You're not making much sense."

"I'm about to make even less," I said, easing the van to a halt on the runway. "Look, I'm going out there to look around. I'll leave the headlights on, but since I may lose track of them in the rain, I want you to blow the horn in exactly ten minutes. And keep blowing it, once a minute for fifteen minutes or so. If I'm not back by then, go to the air-police barracks, find Sergeant Jenkins, and tell him what happened. He'll know what to do. Understand?"

"No! I don't understand any of this."

"Maybe there's nothing to understand," I said. "Maybe the old man really is crazy. It shouldn't take long to find out. One last thing. If I don't come back, whatever you do, *don't* come looking for me. I want your word on it."

"All right, I promise I won't look for you. But why?"

"Because if I'm not back in half an hour, you can offer tobacco to the spirits who haunt this place. I'll be one of them. The stupid one. The one who wouldn't listen to his elders."

I closed the van door on her objections, turned up the collar of Jenkins's raincoat, and trotted off into the rainy dark. I tried to move in a straight line, keeping the headlights directly behind me, but it was impossible. The third time I glanced over my shoulder to get a fix on the van, I couldn't see the lights anymore.

I chose to follow a seam in the concrete instead, hoping it would keep me moving in a more-or-less straight line down the tarmac, away from the van. I didn't meet any ghosts. At least, not at first. There was only the solitary slap of my boots in the puddles, as I trotted along in the sickly glow of the flashlight.

Big airfields have their own special reek, *eau de* exhaust fumes, scorched rubber from rough landings, the acrid stink of wing and windshield de-icer and fuel spills. The stench was strong at first, but seemed to fade as I jogged on. Bullock hadn't been used much for a while, perhaps the rain was rinsing the perfume away. Just as well.

It didn't sound like an airfield either. They're never silent. Always there's the scream of jets, taking off, landing, or just warming up, mingling with the constant rumble of support vehicles. Here there was nothing. Just the whisper of the drizzle. And the occasional whistle of the wind in the wire of the perimeter fencing.

It seemed oddly peaceful, running along in a halo of light, alone, hidden from the world of men by the gunmetal curtain of the rain. No ghosts, no dead dogs, nothing to see. . . . I checked my watch to see how long I'd been running, but the dial was wet and blurry and I couldn't quite make it out.

And then I fell. Hard. I tucked and rolled instinctively, skidding along in the water like an otter on a slide. The flashlight clattered away from me in the dark.

I lay there a few minutes, dazed, trying to catch my breath, gather my wits. God, I was tired, exhausted, heart pounding, head splitting. If I could just rest a bit. . . .

Sweet Jesus. The dogs. They'd died out here. In the rain. Just like this. I forced myself to my hands and knees and crawled toward the faint glow of the flashlight. It was lying beside a puddle, its light diffused, scattered into swirling rainbow bands, by the water, and the nearly invisible turquoise liquid floating on it. I tried to sniff it, but couldn't get a sense of what it was. And realized I couldn't smell anything at all, not the water or the wind. Nothing. And then I recognized the floating slick. Knew it for what it was. It was Death. In the rain. For the guard dogs. And Jerry Buck. And now for me.

I picked up the flashlight, but it was oily, slippery, and I fumbled it away, watched frozen with horror as it tumbled slow-motion down on the tarmac. And winked out.

I turned slowly in a circle, knuckling the rain out of my eyes, trying to get a sense of where I was. It was hopeless. I could only see a few feet. It didn't matter. I had to move, to get away, so I started walking, dazed and aching, stumbling along like a wino, lost in the belly of the beast.

I don't know how long I walked. Years. Then off to the left, I caught a glimpse of a monstrous shape. A ghostly aircraft? It wasn't real. Couldn't be. So I ignored it, and stumbled on. But then I saw a second silhouette, as huge as the first.

I turned and reeled toward them. And found the fence. And the trucks. Toxic-waste tankers, a line of them, a few yards beyond the fence. Waiting their turn at the incinerator. They seemed ugly and misshapen in the rain, foam streaming down their sides like lather, sizzling as the rain reacted to the specks of toxic sludge spatters.

I peered blearily through the fence for a night watchman, anyone. But there was no light, and the exit gate was locked. The tankers might as well have been on the moon. In the shape I was in, there was no way I could climb a fifteen-foot fence and fight through the bayonet wire. And if I got hung up there, I'd die as surely . . .

I heard a groan. A low moan from behind me. I turned, trying to place it . . . and realized what it was. The horn. Redfern had started blowing the horn.

And without thinking, I started running toward it, shambling across the tarmac, a puppet without strings. Veering, stumbling, called on by the horn. And each time it was a little closer. Fifteen. She would blow it once a minute for fifteen minutes. How many had I heard? I couldn't remember. I only knew that to stop running was to die. Like the dogs.

I saw the van. Spotted the faint halo of the headlights ahead, off to the right. I swerved toward them. And fell, tumbling along on the concrete runway, knocking what breath I had out of me. And then Redfern was there, helping me crawl.

I couldn't make it through the van door. I vomited, head down, still on my hands and knees in the rain. I retched and spewed until there was nothing left to give, and then I lost that too.

But it helped. And the drive back toward the gate helped more. I hung my head out the window, drinking the night wind and the rain, purging my lungs, and my soul.

"Do you have a car here?" I asked. It was the first thing I'd said since she found me.

"We'll leave it. You're going to the hospital in Crater Creek."

"No," I said, coughing. "I can't. If I go there we'll lose everything. And we've already paid too much. Jerry Buck paid for it. We can't back off now. Just stop at your car."

"No. I'm staying with you."

"You can't. There are arrangements you have to make for tomorrow. I want you to talk to Dr. Klein. He'll help us, I think."

"Klein? Why should he help?"

"Because at heart, he's basically a decent man," I said, managing a weak smile. "But more important, he has a . . . warped sense of humor."

"What are you talking about?"

So I told her, and she said I was crazy. And she was right and I knew it. But I was so coldly enraged that I didn't care. I asked for her promise. And she gave it. Probably just to humor me. But she gave it. And that was enough.

"If you won't go to the hospital, at least come home with me," she said. "You can't stay here."

"I'll be all right. I'll rest. But I have one last bit of business to take care of first."

"This time of night? What kind of business?"

"Private," I said. "And personal. Very personal."

In the end she left me alone. She didn't like it, but she did. And I was sorry she did. I was sick and miserable and exhausted, and the only thing that kept me going was the thought that if I stopped for even a moment, I wouldn't get up for a week.

That, and the anger, of course. It was like a fire in my belly, a cold blaze of killing rage. For what had been done to Jerry Buck, and to me. And what they were trying to do to my people.

So I sat in my van, with the windows open, and the radio on, and waited. And thought. And I must have dozed off. Because the next thing I knew there was a wan hint of gray light on the horizon and the deejay was babbling about breakfast. I checked my watch. A little after four A.M. Time enough.

I fired up the van and drove over to the air-police barracks. There was a light in the day room. No others. I unlocked the van's glove compartment and took out my revolver, a Smith and Wesson .38. I checked it, and slipped it into my waistband.

I'd hoped they were too shorthanded to post a guard, and there was none. I just walked in. The day room was immaculate, tiled floors gleaming, every magazine aligned. Something clicked in the corner, and I realized the large coffee urn had switched itself on automatically. They'd be up and about soon.

His room was easy to find. It was the largest, and his name was on the door. Chief Master Sergeant Purvis L. Jenkins.

It wasn't locked. I eased the door open, stepped in, and closed it behind me. I waited a moment for my eyes to adjust to the dimness, until I could make out his form on the bed. He was lying on his back, snoring softly, his fingers laced behind his head. I peeled off his sodden raincoat and draped it over him. Then I drew my weapon and switched on the lights.

He blinked instantly awake and alert. I was impressed. He glanced at me, and the gun, and the raincoat. And his eyes widened a fraction. But he didn't flinch.

"Shit," he said softly. "You went out there, didn't you?"

"That's right. I nearly died. Suffocated. Like the dogs."

"What, ahm, what are you going to do?"

"I'm going to ask you some questions. And you're gonna tell me the truth. Because if I even *think* you're lying to me, I'm going to fire this weapon in your general direction. I won't even have to hit you. And your raincoat will explode, and you'll burn. Just like Jerry Buck. Do you understand?"

He nodded, swallowing.

"The plane the old man told me about, the one that crashed. What was it?"

"Look, for God's sake—"

I eased back the hammer of the .38. He read my eyes, and saw his own death there. "It was a tanker," he said, grudgingly, as though each word was an agony. "A KC 135 Stratotanker."

"My God," I said softly. "And it crashed on takeoff?"

"Right. Spilled its whole payload. Nearly twenty thousand gallons of jet fuel. Just dumb luck it didn't explode on impact. But it was raining, and—it didn't."

"Why didn't you recover it?"

"Because by morning, most of it was gone," he said simply. "Drained away, soaked into the gravel bed under the runway. It's low land at that end of the field, next to the marsh. There was no way to recover it short of tearing up the whole damn field, and we couldn't do that. Hell, there was a war on and we had to keep B-52s in the air twenty-four hours a day. Anyway, it was gone. So we went on flying missions, and figured we'd got off lucky. Until it showed up again three years later. And the guard dogs all died."

"In the spring," I said. "In the rain. From the fumes. Gasoline, not kerosene. Buck might have burned himself with kerosene, but it wouldn't have exploded the way it did."

"That's right. Basic physics, jet fuel's almost two pounds a gallon lighter than water, so when the water table rises high enough, we get seepage onto the field. More this year than most. Usually we don't get much, and not for long."

"It was long enough for Jerry Buck," I said. "It was forever."

"Yeah." He nodded. "Look, I'm—"

"Don't!" I snapped, cutting him off. "If you say you're sorry, I swear to God I'll blow you away just for the hell of it. Now, maybe you couldn't clean up the fuel while the base was operational, but it's closing. Why not do it now?"

"Budget," he said bitterly. "With peace breakin' out, they've cut us to the bone. We've barely got money enough to keep a third of our force active. It'd cost millions to tear up the field to clean up the spill. We just don't have it anymore."

"But why us? Why dump it on the Ojibwa?"

"Two reasons. One, because you're broke, and wouldn't have the money to develop the field. We figured you'd open a gift shop or a bingo hall and that'd be it. You'd probably never come across the spill at all. And if you ever did, you likely wouldn't report it and risk losing the land."

"I see. And where does Kanelos fit in?"

"He's a front. If we'd just ceded the base to you, you might've had it inspected. This way it's maybe not the nicest deal in the world, but at least everybody gets something out of it."

"Everybody but Jerry Buck."

"That was an accident. He shouldn't have been out there."

"Maybe he wouldn't have been, if the area was posted as hazardous. And he sure as hell wouldn't have started that fire. Would he?"

"No, I suppose not. What are you going to do?"

"What I have to. Take the deal. Maybe it's a bad deal, but my people have never gotten any other kind. And as you said, at least there's something for everybody. Even for us."

"Good." He nodded. "You're doing the right thing. I'm sorry—"

I pulled the trigger. A reflex. The hammer clicked on an empty cylinder. Jenkins winced, then his eyes narrowed. "You bastard!"

"Easy," I said. "Maybe just forgot to load one cylinder. Thanks for your—cooperation, Sergeant."

"Look, please try to understand. I was just doing my damn job. Trying to protect my own people."

"Your people?"

"The air force. It's the only family I've ever had. But for what it's worth, I really am sorry. About Buck. And the rest of it."

"I think you know what that's worth," I said.

"Yeah," he said, "I guess I do."

* * *

The rain paused briefly at first light, just long enough to reveal a pallid sun, bled white by the storm. But then the sky darkened and the torrent resumed with a vengeance, an icy, wind-driven drizzle, the kind you only see in northern Michigan, or Seattle, or Nome.

Jenkins had told the colonel about my visit. I could tell by the wariness in his eyes as he greeted Eva Redfern and me at the reception center. None of us spoke of it, still the tension was there, like a fuse smoldering just below the surface. An explosion only a word away.

The gathering was almost a repeat of the day before, reporters, a few cameramen, and a gaggle of local politicians. But there were no hors d'oeuvres, no air of gaiety. It was less a celebration than a wake. A vigil for a sidewalk Indian who'd traded the poverty of the reservation for an ugly death, far from his home and his people. A wake for Jerry Buck.

Another difference was the presence of Dr. Klein and a half dozen of his neo-hippie students. I'd thought Colonel Webber might object when they arrived, but I made it clear they were the honored guests of the Ojibwa Nation. Klein and his raggedy clan of peaceniks had protested the presence of nuclear death on this land for years. They'd been ridiculed, harassed, and arrested. Right or wrong, they'd paid their dues, they'd earned admission to this last matinee.

Jenkins surprised me by greeting Klein warmly, and openly. Shaking his hand. Webber's mouth soured in disapproval, but Jenkins's action seemed to defuse some of the tension in the room. If there was going to be trouble, it would have been between these two old adversaries. But there was no animosity left between them. They were like two fighters who go the distance, savaging each other until the final bell, and then embrace. Gladiators, with more spiritual kinship to each other than to those who never bled, no matter what their politics.

The actual transfer was almost an anticlimax. Colonel Webber made a brief speech of welcome, then introduced Mr. Kanelos and his attorneys, Eva Redfern, and me. He then transferred title to the property formerly known as Bullock Air Force Base, Strategic Air Command, to Mr. Frantzis Kanelos, head of Kanelos Waste Disposal. Kanelos in turn transferred the title to the legal representatives of the Ojibwa Nation in exchange for a permanent lease of the waste incinerator and four hundred acres of land adjacent to it. I'd suggested Redfern change the wording of his lease to read: for as long as the sun shall rise, but she said sarcasm had no place in a legal document.

And she was right. The stakes were too high. Native Americans have been swept into the corners of our continent by a tidal wave of history. Our past is over, we can only press on, and struggle to survive in the present. And sometimes that means eating the dirt of injustice and making the best of it.

But not always.

Kanelos signed the final documents with a grin and a flourish, to a smattering of polite applause. And I met Redfern's eyes and they were brimming, with joy or pain, I couldn't tell. Both, perhaps. But there was steel in her glance too. The land was ours again. We had a done deal.

"Ladies and gentlemen," I said, raising my voice, "on behalf of the Ojibwa Nation and its ruling council, I thank you for coming to witness this historic event. But as all of you know, the proceedings were marred by a tragedy, the—accidental death of Geronimo Gall Cobmoosa, known to us as Jerry Buck. To honor Jerry's memory, and to exemplify the brotherhood that now exists between us, we would like to invite Mr. Kanelos to lead a candlelight procession to lay a wreath where Jerry Buck died. Doctor Klein will pass out candles and umbrellas at the door—"

"Wait a minute," Kanelos said, glancing at Webber, "you mean go out there on the runway now? With candles?"

"What's a little rain?" I said. "With a prosperous future—"

"Forget it, Frank," Webber broke in. "Jenkins told me Delacroix was out on the runway last night, damn near got himself killed. This is just his idea of a little joke. He knows it's not safe out there."

"It's not a joke," I said. "It was a fishing expedition. I needed to be sure Mr. Kanelos knew about the fuel spill."

"Even if I did, it won't make any difference to our agreement," Kanelos said uneasily. "My lawyers—"

"Assured you it's rock solid," I finished for him. "I certainly hope so. In any case, since it *is* a little damp for a candlelight procession we've arranged alternate entertainment. Ladies and gentlemen please step to the observation window to view a small display . . ."

Far down the perimeter road, there was a blast of white smoke and three solitary shafts of light flashed into the gunmetal over-cast above the runway. And burst into red flowers of flame, sputtering gamely in the darkness. Candles in the rain.

". . . of fireworks," I finished.

"What?" Webber said, his face going gray. "You can't—"

But it was too late. In slow motion, the flares continued their arc across the sky, and began to fall, raining petals of fire down on the tarmac. There was a deep *chuff,* like a sharp intake of breath, and the runway burst into flame, in scattered spots at first, but quickly dancing across the surface of the water, until the fires united in an inferno a half mile across, howling into the sky as though the gates of hell had opened.

I moved quietly back and stepped out onto the portico, joining Redfern and Dr. Klein at the railing. Reporters and cameramen streamed past us, drawn like moths to the flames. A few minutes later Jenkins sauntered out and stood behind Dr. Klein. Jenkins's face was a carved, ebon mask. I could read nothing in it.

"Quite a bonfire," he said at last.

"Not so bad," Klein said. "Compared to Kuwait, this one's a marshmallow roast. By my calculations, it should burn between five and six hours, depending on how much fuel has evaporated over the years. And that will be the end of it."

"And of the runway, and the incinerator," Jenkins said. "Ain't you worried Kanelos will sue your tails off?"

"I hope he tries," Redfern said grimly. "I'd love to take his deposition under oath, about what he knew and when, about the fire hazard that killed Jerry Buck."

"Good point," Jenkins conceded. "Doubt the government will bother you either. Might try though. The colonel's in there ravin' about sabotage. Ordered me to arrest all three of you, in fact."

"So?" I said. "Are we under arrest?"

"Hell no," Jenkins said wryly. "It just shows how shaky his

grip on reality is. We've got no authority to arrest anybody. This isn't a military base anymore. Won't even look much like one in a few hours. Won't be anything left on that runway but gravel and ash. A couple years, you won't even be able to tell it was there."

"There'll always be traces of it," Klein said. "When you cauterize the earth, it leaves scars. I wonder what archaeologists will make of them a thousand years from now?"

"Maybe if we're real lucky, Doc," Jenkins said quietly, "they'll look around and scratch their heads. And won't even be able to guess what it was used for."

Out on the perimeter of the field, the blaze was already burning low, the concrete sizzling and cracking in the drizzle. But on the tarmac near the spot where Jerry Buck died, the inferno still raged on, furiously roiling plumes of oily smoke into the sky. The flames leapt and twisted and writhed, like a ring of ghostly dancers, carrying candles in the rain.

JO BANNISTER

A POISONED CHALICE

Jo Bannister, a journalist currently living in Northern Ireland, has had several mystery novels published by Doubleday. During 1992 she demonstrated that she can be equally skilled and prolific in the short form, producing four stories for EQMM. One of these, a ghost story titled "Howler," was especially popular and earned its author an MWA Edgar nomination. Ghost stories are a bit outside the range of this volume, and we preferred her tale of a clash between archaeologists and power developers in a quiet Irish valley.

Mountains gathered about the road where the Land Rover died. Their craggy heads inclined forward, like witnesses at an accident. Then, as if moved by what they saw, they began to cry.

David Grace, hunched over the wheel, watched them through the rain-lashed windscreen and reflected that motor-mechanics ought to be a fundamental element in the study of archaeology. He could distinguish between Beaker and Bronze Age potsherds at ten paces, but he had no idea what was wrong with his Land Rover and could not have fixed it if someone had told him. When it began its death-rattle five miles back he knew only two things: that the vehicle would never reach civilization, and that when he finally had to get out and walk it would be raining.

He studied the map. Small-scale maps were more use to him professionally, but in this part of Ireland a small-scale map would have had nothing on it. This was a compromise: when he unfolded it on his knee it showed three villages and two roads.

Ballynaslieve was the closest, eight miles away if he stuck to the road. If he left the road and cut between the mountains, he could halve that. It was a choice between two unattractive alternatives, but he opted for the sheep-trod through the heather. He pulled on boots and waterproofs and committed himself to the fell.

In Ballynaslieve they were celebrating. In the saloon bar of Kavanagh's, Pat Kavanagh had tapped a fresh keg in honor of the occasion and the assembly were helping themselves freely. There was also a cake, which Mrs. Pat had made and iced artistically with the legend "Slieve Crum Power Scheme."

For Ballynaslieve was about to join the twentieth century. A power scheme would bring work. The sons of shepherds need not now be shepherds: some could be builders, some could be engineers. The people who came here to run the scheme would need houses, and groceries, and drink, and some of them might need wives. There would be a bus service. The price of land, that for generations had been less than the value of the sheep it fed, would soar.

Ballynaslieve was about to become an abode of rich men.

A mile away down the long valley, the sheep-trod crested the gap between Slieve Crum and Slieve Diuran. A fast-scurrying little stream tumbled through the narrow place as a waterfall. Archaeologists keep fitter than most scientists, and Dr. Grace was still a young man, but he was panting by the time the path leveled out. The way up had been steeper than it looked from the road, but now all that lay between him and Ballynaslieve was a small lough lying in the cup of the hills.

The day was ending. But before the last of the light went, a maverick ray pierced the leaden sky and lit a cluster of stones close by the lough-shore. Grace broke his stride and stared down at them. Then he left the trod and began to walk toward them. After a moment he began to run.

In Kavanagh's the cake had been cut and the glasses recharged for a toast to the Slieve Crum Power Scheme when the door banged open and in with the night and the rain came something upholstered in mud and PVC. It padded, squelching, to the bar and ordered a hot whiskey. It pushed back the hood of its cagoule and fixed the landlord with a glittering eye, and inquired if he was aware that he was serving alcoholic beverages within a mile of a Neolithic passage grave unknown to archaeology.

"Passage grave? Passage grave?" The words ran through the assembly without striking any chord of familiarity. No one in Ballynaslieve had heard of Knowth or Dowth, and Willie John Savage thought Newgrange was a Gaelic football team.

Dr. Grace asked for the telephone. Kavanagh, who was astute in many ways, was apologetic. "The line's down again." He went outside for another keg, and when Grace tried the instrument behind the bar he met only silence.

When Kavanagh returned he respectfully sought a fuller explanation and Grace, now into his third whiskey, was happy to oblige.

He was on his way to address a conference in Dublin, took a shortcut through the mountains, and broke down. Walking across the moor he chanced upon the bones of a Neolithic passage grave of the seminal, though geographically remote, Boyne Valley group. The significance of the find among these barren hills could hardly be overstated. Once he got through to Dublin, his colleagues would descend on Ballynaslieve with every device known to archaeology. They would pick their way through the site inch by inch and map its history minutely, should it take them years to do it.

Kavanagh understood. He understood the implications of any such excavation for the Slieve Crum Power Scheme. When the archaeologists had had their say there would be nowhere on all that barren mountain moor where a power station could be built without first being picked over by old men with trowels. When Mrs. Pat showed her guest to his room, Kavanagh called a council of war.

In the morning the phone was still not working, but at least the rain had stopped. Grace said he was going to examine the grave in daylight. Kavanagh offered to accompany him.

There was much activity on the sheep-trod: a tractor, a team of chestnut horses, any number of bulky young men mopping

sweat from their brows as they ambled back toward Ballynaslieve. Grace was surprised at such industry so early in the day,
but his mind was too full of his discovery to give it much
thought.

When they got there, there was no sign of the grave. Kavanagh,
watching covertly, saw shock and horror and disbelief chase
through Grace's face. The monument was gone. Where it had
stood, its tall stones buried to their shoulders in the rubble of the
collapsed cairn, now there was only mud rutted with the tracks
of tires, horses, and men. Nearby stood a brand new dry-stone
wall.

Kavanagh laid a paternal arm around the younger man's
shoulders. "What—was that it? Man dear, that was only Willie
John Savage's mammy's old house. Fifty years ago it fell down
and he's been meaning to shift it ever since."

"It was a passage grave," whispered Grace, stricken. "It was
four thousand years old."

"No, no," said the big man kindly, steering him back toward
the village. "Old Mrs. Savage's wee house. It's been an eyesore
all my life."

Later and alone, Grace returned to the lough-shore to grieve.
There was nothing left. He examined the new wall stone by
stone, looking for the carvings typical of the Boyne group, but
there were none. They were only stones, timeless and impervious
to inquiry.

Turning his back on the disaster, he wandered numbly up the
hill. Already he was losing his grip on the reality of what he had
seen. Perhaps his grave had been no more than a tumbled farmhouse and trick of the light.

The sunlight fell obliquely into the valley and, as he looked
down on them, suddenly the humps and ridges he had trudged
across last night began to take on a pattern. He blinked. Tired-
ness and disappointment were deceiving him. But the pattern
was still there, straight lines and circles that had no place in nature, and slowly he recognized what it was he was seeing.

Back at Kavanagh's, he pinned Pat to the wall with one strong
finger. "I'm telling you this so there'll be no repetition of this

morning's performance. Close by that passage grave—sorry, Ma Savage's old house—are a series of Bronze Age earthworks. There are the shapes of huts there, and hearths, and post-holes, and maybe a cistcairn. When we excavate we'll find pottery and metal and cooking-sites and burials. Stay away from it."

As luck would have it, the mechanic from Tamnahogue called by. He drove Dr. Grace round the mountain to his Land Rover, but he could not start it so they towed it into Ballynaslieve. The mechanic promised to return with parts.

Grace set out once more to walk to the little lough. Once more Kavanagh fell into step beside him. "Tell me again what this thing looks like."

"Like nothing. Like a few bumps and ruts in the ground. Never mind what it looks like, it's two thousand years old and when we excavate we'll find a center of political power comparable with the Hill of Tara. Some great chieftain must have ruled from here, and what he left behind will extend immeasurably what we know about the period."

Before they rounded the shoulder of Slieve Crum, a deep throaty roar of machinery reached them, and Grace's eyes widened in dread. He kicked into a run down the track. Kavanagh followed at his own pace, and just round the shoulder found Grace rooted to the spot. On the shore of the lough a giant tractor was ploughing the peat.

"You did this," said Grace, his eyes hating. "Why?"

"The forestry? It's nothing to do with me."

"I found a passage grave and you cleared it. I found earthworks and you ploughed them. Why?"

Kavanagh looked down the hillside. "Is that where your earthworks were? Sure, that was nothing more than drainage ditches Peter Savage dug. They never worked, the valley's too wet for a few ruts to make a difference. But the trees should do well enough."

"You are destroying your own heritage," said Grace in his teeth. "Why?"

"Heritage? An old cottage and some field drains?"

Grace said again, "Why?"

Kavanagh considered for a moment. He was not an unkind

man. He sat down heavily beside the archaeologist. He said, "It's a good job it was only the light playing tricks on you, for if there was anything here that warranted a proper investigation it would be a terrible tragedy for Ballynaslieve.

"I've lived here all my life. It was a one-horse town until the horse died. There were no evictions here during the famine—the landlord didn't want it back. Cromwell marched through and never noticed it, and while Fiach MacHugh O'Byrne spent a night here he could find nothing worth fighting over.

"Now, finally, somebody's found a use for Ballynaslieve. They're going to build a power station in the valley here. After all this time the place has a future. But if you'd been right, they'd have had to hold off building until you finished your digging. Long before that, our power station would be up and running in somebody else's valley. We need that scheme. We need a future more than we need a past."

David Grace was still there two hours later when the great tractor finished ploughing and trundled away. The valley floor was like corduroy. Nothing of its ancient contours survived. He walked down to the lough-shore but could no longer be sure where the earthworks had been.

A shape in the furrow caught his eye. It was dull and gray, and might have been a stone turned up by the plough except that its lines were sharp and regular. Before his fingers touched it he knew what it was. He picked it carefully out of the earth and rinsed it in the waters of the lough, and the bowl took on a gunmetal glow.

It was a silver chalice, turned up by a forestry plough a thousand years after a monk fleeing from Vikings had dropped it. The peat had held it safe through ten centuries while armies and sheep had marched overhead. Even the plough had not damaged it.

This little valley was an archaeological time capsule. Monuments and artifacts leapt out of the ground to ambush the passerby. Whatever Kavanagh had destroyed, more must remain safe and unsuspected under the protecting peat.

"This site has got to be dug," Grace swore to himself. A radiance like religion was in his eyes and, up to his knees in the lough, he held up the chalice in an almost Arthurian pledge.

The men watching from the mountainside saw nothing heroic about him. He looked to them like a bird of evil omen, and from the reverent way he clutched his new discovery he was not finished yet.

Grace looked up and saw the watchers on the skyline. Fear—for himself but more for his treasure—stabbed at him. He waded ashore. The men above him had not moved, but they must have seen what he carried. It was too late to hide it. So he ran. Weighed down by water and mud, the ploughed peat sucking at his steps, the chalice under his arm an awkward burden, he headed down the valley toward the gap between the mountains and the road three miles beyond.

He was never going to make it. It was too far, the going was too rough, and he was an archaeologist, not a fell-runner. The advantage of the high ground enabled the men of Ballynaslieve to cut his path before he reached the gap. Sweat-blinded, his blood pounding in his ears, he turned back along the far side of the lough.

But the end was never in doubt, and when the slower men turned aside to close the top end of the valley as well, Grace had nowhere left to go. He ground to a halt and the surging wave of the pursuit broke over him.

Kavanagh, hurrying down from Ballynaslieve, arrived moments too late to preserve Dr. Grace from violence. But he waded into the scrum bellowing, "Leave off now—leave off when I tell you!" And by the time he reached the heart of the melee, much of the fury had gone out of it and, a little shamefaced, the men fell back. One of them handed him a gunmetal-gray bowl.

David Grace was curled in a muddy ball, the prints of cleated boots plain on his dirty clothes, and could have been dead. Kavanagh knelt beside him, lowering his big body cumbrously, and touched his shoulder. After a moment Grace unwound. His nose was bleeding and his lip was split.

Kavanagh sighed and tried to apologize. "I never meant for that to happen. We had to stop you, but I never wanted you hurt. Oh, I know you'll talk about this. We'll have the police to deal with. But as long as you've no proof, nothing to show the museum people, there'll be no dig. They may be inclined to believe you, but they won't risk large sums of public money on your word alone."

He was right and Grace knew it. He gave it one last try. "This site has been in continuous occupation from Neolithic times to the present day. It would be the most important in Ireland. It has to be excavated. Please, give me the chalice."

Kavanagh stood up. The crowd round them parted and he walked thoughtfully toward the lough, weighing the silver bowl in his hands. Grace guessed what he intended and his battered body responded to the surge of furious adrenaline. He got to within a pace or two of the publican before hands from the crowd dragged him to a halt. He shouted, "No!"

Kavanagh looked back at him, his eyes mild. "I'm sorry." Then he hurled the chalice from him with all his strength, and it tumbled for a moment in the clear air before the lough received it with barely a splash. A small ragged cheer went up.

"Damn your eyes, Pat Kavanagh," whispered Dr. Grace, sinking to his knees in the mud.

Someone said, "Who's that?" and they all looked up the valley.

It was a man in green wellies and a bright blue anorak. He had driven down the track from Ballynaslieve in his new blue four-by-four, and had now got out and was watching them.

Kavanagh said, "That's Mr. Hiram Bernstein of the Slieve Crum Power Scheme." And he waved the man toward them.

Grace, too tired to stand up, looked at the engineer, hating him. He hated his new blue car. He hated his clean green wellies. He hated his flash blue jacket with the words "Slieve Crum Hydroelectric Scheme" emblazoned on the front.

Hydroelectric? On reflection, Grace thought he could make his peace with that jacket.

When Bernstein reached them, he looked doubtfully at Grace and said, "What's going on here?" He was an American.

The hands still holding Grace withdrew guiltily. Kavanagh said, "A little misunderstanding, just." He hurried on: "Are you here to survey for the power scheme?" and the American nodded.

Grace hauled himself to his feet. "Where will you build the dam?"

Bernstein pointed down the lough away from Ballynaslieve, to the gap where the stream became a waterfall. "There."

"How big a flood-back do you expect?"

"All this bog between the mountains," said the engineer, "as far as you can see and then some."

They all turned toward Ballynaslieve, just visible toward the head of the valley. Then they looked at Kavanagh, and Kavanagh looked at David Grace and understood why, under the mud and the blood, he was smiling. He said, very carefully, "You're going to flood the valley?"

Bernstein looked surprised. "Of course. How else do you make hydroelectric power?"

"There must be some misunderstanding. We all live there. In Ballynaslieve."

"Don't worry about it," Bernstein said briskly, "that's all been taken care of. They're building you new homes in a nice modern housing estate, with bathrooms and a bus every half-hour."

If he had announced his intention of machine-gunning them, the men of Ballynaslieve could hardly have looked more shocked.

"But—I was born in that house."

"You'll be compensated," said Bernstein.

"What about our sheep?"

"You'll be compensated."

"Will they build me another pub?"

"No, but you'll be compensated," said the American.

The full horror of it was sinking in. After the dam was built and the level of the lough rose, Ballynaslieve would cease to exist. Its community of displaced souls in a city's suburbs could be paid for that, but not compensated. Everything that Kavanagh had told Grace about Ballynaslieve was true, but no one wanted to leave it.

All eyes turned then toward Pat Kavanagh. It was Pat who had brought the American here; Pat who persuaded him of the valley's suitability, of the residents' cooperation; Pat who got the backing of the area's political representatives. No use now for

Pat to claim that nobody mentioned flooding, that he had expected the power station to burn peat.

Desperation fueling inspiration, he seized Grace like a brother. "I'm sorry, Mr. Bernstein, but I don't think you'll be allowed to flood. Not now. Dr. Grace here is an archaeologist, he's been checking the place over for the National Museum in Dublin. He's found all sorts of interesting things. Haven't you, Dr. Grace?" He shook the smaller man by the sleeve. "Haven't you?"

"Have you?" Alarmed, Bernstein looked round him. He saw nothing.

"Oh yes," insisted Kavanagh. "A passage grave. From the Boyne group. Some Bronze Age earthworks."

The American was still looking. "Where?"

"And a chalice," cried Pat. 'Would you credit that?—a silver chalice, left by the first Christians who settled here. Ballynaslieve has been in continuous occupation from Neolithic times to the present day. Dr. Grace is going to organize the most important excavation ever carried out in Ireland. Isn't that right, Doctor?" Again he shook the archaeologist urgently.

Bernstein too was watching him with concern. "Is that right? You found a chalice here?"

David Grace looked up the valley toward Ballynaslieve. The place was at his mercy. Every house there would disappear unless he stopped this scheme. Every man here would be a refugee, unless he came to their rescue.

He looked at the anguish in Pat Kavanagh's face and sighed. "It's like Mr. Kavanagh said. There was—"

"A passage grave? Earthworks?" The engineer knew exactly what that would mean, staggered under the implications. "My God, a chalice?"

"No, a misunderstanding," said Grace, without a flicker of conscience. "I found something, all right. I found old Mrs. Savage's teakettle. Who'd be interested in a thing like that? I threw it in the lough."

JACKLYN BUTLER

A BIT OF FLOTSAM

*This is Jacklyn Butler's first published story, a fine little tale of
a boy who saw a body in Lake Michigan one day—or did he?*

I stood and watched birds forage in the shallows of Lake Michigan while a policeman talked to the kid. The afternoon sun was warm, but I was glad I'd worn my windbreaker. The breeze blowing off the lake was full of fish and rotting wood. The cop wasn't getting anywhere; a good fifteen minutes of hand-waving jawboning and the boy kept shaking his head. My job would start after he admitted defeat.

I'd just been hired as the psychologist for a suburban school system. The president of the school board came to see me while I was moving into my office. I expected him to question me about my plans for the fall quarter, but instead he presented me with a personal problem concerning his son.

"Business is off this year anyhow," he'd explained to me. He owns and runs one of the large hotels on the north beach. "Our resort has been about forty, forty-five percent occupied. Worst season in years. I need rumors of a body washed up on the beach like I need another hole in my head."

He described how he had tried to reason with his son. First he asked him to admit he just made it up. "I know you're not tellin' a real lie," he'd told the kid. "It's just a fantasy like any of us would think up after a day all alone on the beach. A dream, like."

"But I didn't make it up," the boy said. "And it wasn't a dream."

"So you were mistaken. A lot of people will be better off if you admit it."

"I wasn't mistaken."

"Just say you aren't sure."

The kid insisted he *was* sure. He'd seen a body in the water near the shore. He knew it would come back.

"I could never get him to change his mind, even when he was little enough to spank," his father admitted. "He's hopeless when he gets his back up."

So I had a chance to show what I could do. It was up to me to make friends with this kid, get him to trust me, and talk him into backing down so the local papers could announce it was all a hoax in time to save the Labor Day rush to the beach resorts.

Finally the cop gave up and walked over to me.

"You the shrink?" he asked. He was a young fellow, new on the job like I was. "He's not gonna budge. He insists he saw it, and he's gonna sit there until it comes back so he can prove it."

"Is there any possibility he's telling the truth?" I asked.

"No way. We haven't had a drowning reported in over a month. If there is a corpse, it'll cost more'n it's worth to identify what's left. Another John Doe to get rid of." The police didn't need a body, either. "That kid made it all up because he needs attention." He jerked a thumb over his shoulder at the boy. "You really think you can talk him into admitting he lied?"

"That's my job," I said.

"Lots of luck."

I watched the boy a while longer. He was thirteen years old, short and skinny. Probably had always been the littlest kid in his class, the one left out when they chose up sides, so he'd learned to play alone and he'd learned to be tough. He sat on a dune and took off his sneakers and socks, walked through the warm sand down to the edge of the lake, where the tiny waves broke and receded and left patches of sand slick. East winds carry warm surface water to the edge; the lake is like a warm bath on days like this, but when his foot touched the water the kid drew back like it was cracked ice, or maybe too hot.

He walked back and sat on a dune, and I walked over and stood beside him. The wind and the surf made enough noise so he didn't hear me until I spoke; he let out a little yip and drew away. He was scared, all right. Defensive.

"I didn't make it up," he said right away.

I sat down beside him. "I'd like to be here when it comes back."

I was the first person who seemed to believe him. After a few minutes of silence he decided to trust me a little. "It might come today," he said. I could read his mind. He couldn't back down after all this, he believed the story himself. He waved down the beach, toward a little inlet. "See that log? It washed up close to shore five different times. I counted. Finally it got stuck."

"Wind's right today. Lots of stuff blowing in," I said. I began to take off my own shoes. "You picked a good spot here. We can run in and grab it before the next wave breaks." I rolled my slacks up a couple turns.

"I—I got scared, the first time," he admitted. "At first I thought it was just some junk washing up. When I saw what it was, I shoulda grabbed it, pulled it up on the beach a little. But I've never touched a dead body."

"I would've been scared, too," I told him. I put my shoes beside his.

"I'll know what to do next time," he said.

We stared at the edge of the lake while the sun moved behind us toward Iowa and Kansas. Little sailboats and a few big yachts headed for home and it got colder; the kid would get tired of his game before long. Just before five o'clock a white Mercedes parked up on the road, and a woman came down the steps and walked toward us through the dunes. She looked familiar. She was dressed in designer beach stuff, her earrings were huge anchors that looked like real gold. Probably staying in the new Inn at two hundred a day, or maybe owned one of the big private homes farther up the beach. Before she got to us, a man arrived in a black Cadillac and followed her down the stairs. He looked familiar, too, a little too heavy but his blue linen suit fit perfectly and his red tie was pure silk. By the time they got close, I knew I'd never met either of them, they just reminded me of a whole lot of people I don't like. The man spoke first.

"Has it come back yet?" His voice was deep and resonant.

"Not yet," I said.

"It will," the kid said.

Close up, the lady was tanned and skinny. Under her hat her hair looked dry; she'd spent a lot of time sailing, swimming, and sunning herself. "I've been praying ever since I read about it in the paper," she said, and her voice rasped; her throat must have been as dry as her hair. "My husband disappeared about six months ago."

"You're afraid this might be his body?" I asked, watching the boy. He wasn't a bad kid. Maybe he'd back down on his story if he saw somebody getting hurt.

"I wish it were," she snapped. "It's unlikely that he'd drown himself. He managed to take most of our money. Left me a virtual pauper. I expect he's started a new life somewhere. But there's an insurance policy waiting for me to prove he's dead."

The man's voice rumbled again; I could tell he had trained it to cajole juries.

"I'm here on behalf of a client," he said. "Her husband disappeared, too, just a couple of weeks ago."

I realized who he was. There'd been a lot in the papers about it. "You're talking about the mysterious disappearance of Mr. Franley?" I suggested.

The man nodded. "Yes. Mr. Franley."

"Mrs. Franley is the one who is shacked up with the family lawyer, isn't she?" I asked. The man bobbed his head toward the boy, as if a thirteen-year-old wouldn't know about things like that. "I can see how important it is to your client," I continued. "She needs proof of death so she can marry her lover."

"I've told her that this is all a hoax . . ."

"No, it isn't!" The kid spoke quickly. "It'll be back. Then you'll see!"

We sat and watched the waters and waited for nothing to happen. I couldn't reason with the kid while these two hung around, but I didn't think it was all bad. I could tell he didn't like them either, so maybe they'd do some of my work for me.

After a while a man approached from the south. His shirt was buttoned up, his tie tucked safely into the vest of his three piece suit; those shiny shoes had never touched sand before. He introduced himself as a counselor at one of the medical schools in Chicago.

"One of our students is missing," he said. "I had a premonition when I saw the story in the paper this morning." The doctor stopped, embarrassed. "I'm broadminded on the whole. But medicine is a profession; we have to maintain some kind of standards. Mohawk styles! And now green hair. That's going too far." He turned to the kid. "Was the body a young man, about one sixty pounds?"

"Don't know," the kid said. "Didn't see any green hair."

"I suppose the dye might wash out." The doctor smoothed his own wind-rumpled hair with both hands. "I know that Joseph has no close family. I should have considered that before I threatened to recommend expulsion." He looked at the lake. "Hasn't sent for his clothes or books . . . ."

As we let the waves hypnotize us, I knew I was the only one who even remembered the kid was present.

"It seems to me you hope the body is not your Joseph," the lady said.

"Well, Joseph has no wife or mother staying awake nights wondering what happened to him." He sighed. "But I felt I had to investigate."

The lady went on. "In that case, why not just go away? If the body does come back, and it's my husband's, everything will be fine. If it's Joseph's, I'll just claim it anyhow. I doubt they'll question my identification."

The doctor hesitated. "I'd hate to leave Joe without a decent burial . . ."

"Oh, I'll see that he has a decent burial. I'll even say a little prayer for him at the funeral if that's the way it goes."

The doctor hesitated. "I could never lie, but if I never knew . . . everybody would benefit. . . . Don't forget, a decent burial." He hurried off.

"Aren't you afraid your husband might come back if he hears you've declared him dead?" I asked.

"Hah! I wish he would come back. I'd love to go through a real divorce. When I tell a judge how that monster made me suffer, I'll get everything he has."

"You and I seem to be the only ones who are interested in that kid's story," the attorney said.

"What can I do to persuade you to leave the field to me?" the lady asked.

"What do you offer?" he asked.

"This is no time to be funny," she chided, smiling into his eyes.

"Of course," he said. "I hope my client's husband is alive and well and on his way home."

"How come?" I asked him. "I thought *you* were particularly anxious to help her clear up her marital status . . ."

"Not exactly." He nudged me with his elbow. "Sometimes the game loses its kick when you realize it's not a game."

"Well!" The lady opened her hands out, palms up, as if everything was settled. "All you have to do is follow the other gentleman off the beach."

"I don't think you can get away with it." The attorney turned to me. "Can't the police make absolute identification nowadays? DNA, dental records, stuff like that?"

"They only do that if nobody claims the corpse," I said. "It's easier and cheaper to let somebody identify a body."

"Hey!" the kid shouted and suddenly started to run toward the lake. "I told you!" he shouted over his shoulder as he ran. "I didn't make it up!"

I was right behind him—splashing into the water with him. We each grabbed at an arm, and the "body," a tree limb with old clothes, a piece of tire, rope, garbage stuck to it, came apart in our hands. Rotting fish drifted off with the rest of the junk.

"I don't see how you could be so blind." The lady was standing on the edge of the breakers. A wave broke over her sandals, gold thongs attached to soles made of coiled rope. "Anyone could see it was just a pile of flotsam."

I felt sorry for the kid. I stayed around to talk to him while the others strolled off; the attorney to tell his "client" that everything remained as it always had, and the lady to fret because she couldn't take all the trips she wanted.

"Sure did look like a real body," I said, picking up my shoes. "Fooled me completely. I ran in after it—right up to my knees!" I unrolled my slacks to show how wet they were. He sat silently, unmoving; he was wiped out. "You see, it's really all for the best that you didn't find a body," I said. "Your father will be happy when we tell him." I detected a slight nod. "Come on, let's go talk to your dad."

He shook his head. "I'll stay here awhile," he said.

It had become absolutely quiet on the beach. That time of day, those stiff east winds die just before the wind from the west picks up. "It's getting dark," I warned him.

"I know. I'll have to go to dinner." I doubted he had much appetite, but he'd get cold. He'd go inside soon.

His father was delighted.

"I can't thank you enough," he said, giving me full credit.

"Just be sure not to rub it in," I warned him. "He'll be sensitive about it."

"Oh, I'll be careful. Where is he, anyhow?"

"I guess he's still down on the beach. I'll stop by, send him home."

When I got to the edge of the beach, I climbed up on one of the dunes to look for the kid. I had a shot of fear when I saw him running pell-mell toward the lake. I started to run after him, but I stopped when I saw that he was pulling something out of the water. He had an arm, hauled a body up to the edge of the beach.

He'd said he'd know what to do this time, so I waited for a minute to give him a chance to prove to himself that he wasn't a coward. He reached down and touched a cheek. Then he put his whole thirteen years on the line, gave a big heave that sent it out into deeper water.

The wind from the west had sprung up by then, the kind that gives Chicago its nickname. Blows everything, smog, junk, away. When I shouted to him to stop, my words were lost.

There was no sign of a body when I got there.

"Probably will wash up in Michigan someday," the kid said. He hesitated for a second, then reached for my hand.

MAX ALLAN COLLINS

LOUISE

I hate to weigh down Max Allan Collins with the title of mystery's Renaissance Man, but the facts are these: since 1973 he has published more than thirty detective novels with about five different series characters; for fifteen years he wrote the "Dick Tracy" comic strip and also helped create two other comic book sleuths, Mike Mist and Ms. Tree; he has collaborated on books about mystery writers Jim Thompson and Mickey Spillane (an Edgar nominee); he has edited a collection of Spillane's short stories and is collaborating with him on a series of hard-boiled anthologies; he has produced numerous short stories of his own and occasionally collaborates with his wife, Barbara, herself an increasingly skilled mystery writer; he is a musician and songwriter, and has been entertaining at mystery fan conventions with his classic rock group, Cruisin'. But that's enough to give you the general idea. Let me just add that the best of Collins's novels are the Nathan Heller historical private eye books, especially True Detective *(1983) and* Stolen Away *(1991), both winners of Shamus Awards from Private Eye Writers of America. During 1992 PWA and another writers' organization, Sisters in Crime, got together to produce a joint anthology of new stories,* Deadly Allies. *Collins's contribution was one of his rare stories about Ms. Tree, the comic book character he created with Terry Beatty. It's a pleasure to welcome Collins to these pages, with a memorable story that earned an Edgar nomination from MWA.*

Her face was pretty and hard; her eyes were pretty and soft.

She was a waif in a yellow-and-white peasant dress, a Keane-painting child grown up, oval freckled face framed by sweeping blond arcs. She wore quite a bit of makeup, but the effect was that of a schoolgirl who'd gotten into Mommy's things. She stood with her purse held shyly before her, a guilty Eve with a brown patent-leather fig leaf.

"Miss Tree?" she asked tentatively, only half stepping inside my private office, despite the fact that my assistant had already bid her enter.

I stood, paying her back the respect she was showing, and tried to put her at ease with a smile. "I prefer 'Ms.,' " I told her, sitting back down, and gestured toward the chair opposite me.

She settled gradually into the chair and straightened her skirt primly, though her manner was at odds with the scoop neck that showed more bosom than modesty would allow.

"I never been to a office on Michigan Avenue before." Her big blue eyes took in the stark lines of my spacious but austere inner chamber. "You sure have a nice one."

"Thank you, Miss Evans."

Pretty as she was, she had the sort of countenance that wore more suffering than even heavy makeup could hide; so it was kind of a shock when her face brightened with a smile.

"Louise," she said, and she extended her tiny hand across the desk, with a deliberation that revealed the courage she'd had to summon to behave so boldly, "call me Louise. Please."

"My assistant tells me you were quite insistent about seeing me personally."

She nodded and lowered her head. "Yes. I'm sorry."

"Don't be sorry, Miss Evans."

"It's Mrs. Evans. Excepting, I'd like you to call me Louise. I need us to be friends."

"All right," I said. This wasn't going to be easy, was it? "You said this is about your daughter. That your daughter is in trouble."

I was too busy for this, with Gold Coast divorce cases, legal work, and corporate accounts, but hers hadn't been the kind of plea you could turn down.

"Terrible trouble," she said, and her lower lip trembled; the blue eyes were filling up. "My husband . . . I'm afraid of what he might—"

Then she began to weep.

I got up, came around, and bent beside her as she dug embarrassedly for Kleenex in her purse. She was so much smaller than me, I felt like an adult comforting a child as I slipped an arm around her.

"You can tell me," I said. "It'll be all right."

"She's gone," she said. "He took her."

"Your husband took your daughter?"

"Months ago. Months ago. God knows what he done to her, by this time."

"Tell me about it. Start at the beginning. Start anywhere."

But she didn't start. She grabbed my arm and her tiny fist gripped me hard. As hard as the life that had made the sweet features of her young face so old.

"I wish I was like you," she said. Her voice had an edge.

"Louise . . ."

"I've read about you, Ms. Tree. You're a strong woman. Nobody messes with you. Nobody pushes you around."

"Please . . ."

"You're big. You killed bad men before."

That was me—a cross between King Kong and the Lone Ranger, in a dress. Frankly, this petite if buxom woman did make me feel big; at five ten, one hundred forty pounds, I sure wasn't small. My tombstone would likely read: "Here Lies Michael Tree—She Never Did Lose That Ten Pounds."

And so I was to be Louise's savior; her avenger. I sighed, smiled, and said, "You really should tell me about your daughter, Louise—and your husband."

"That's why I come here. I need somebody like you to go get Maggie back. He took her, and the law can't do nothing."

I got a chair and sat next to her, where I could pat her reassuringly when necessary, and, finally, she told me her story.

Her husband Joe was "a good man, in lots of ways," a worker in a steel mill in Hammond. They met when she was working in a McDonald's in South Chicago, and they'd been married six years. That was how old Maggie, their only child, was.

"Joey's a good provider," she said, "but he . . . gets rough sometimes."

"He beat you?"

She looked away, nodded. Battered women feel ashamed, even guilty, oftentimes; it makes no logical sense, but then neither does a man beating on a woman.

"Has he beaten your daughter, too?"

She nodded. And she started to weep again.

She was out of Kleenex; I got up and got her some.

"But that . . . that's not the worst part," she said, sniffling. "Maggie is a pretty little girl. She got blond hair, just like mine. And Joey was looking at her . . . you know. *That* way. The way my daddy done me."

"Do you think your husband ever . . .?"

"Not while I was around. But since he runned off with her, that's what I'm afraid of most."

I was a little confused; I had been assuming that this was a child custody situation. That the divorced husband had taken advantage of his visitation rights to disappear with his daughter.

"You haven't said anything about divorce," I said. "You and your husband *are* divorced?"

"No. We was talking about it. I think that's why he done it the way he done."

"What do you mean, Louise?"

"He knew that if we was divorced, the courts'd give Maggie to me. And he didn't want me to have her. Ms. Tree, when I was Maggie's age, my daddy beat on me. And he done other things to me. You know what kind of things."

I nodded.

"Ms. Tree, will you take my case? All I got is two hundred dollars I saved. Is that going to be enough?"

"It's going to be like McDonald's, Louise," I said.

"Huh?"

"You're going to get back some change."

*   *   *

Louise had reported her husband's disappearance to the police, but in the five months since Joey Evans and his daughter vanished, there had been little done. My contact at the police department confirmed this.

"The Missing Persons Bureau did what they could," Rafe Valer said, sitting on the edge of his desk in his small, cluttered office at Homicide.

"Which is what, exactly?"

Rafe shrugged. Darkly handsome describes him, but considering he's black, saying so may be in poor taste. Thirty, quietly ambitious, and as dependable as a pizza at Gino's, Lieutenant Valer had been my late husband Mike's partner, before Mike went private.

"Which is," he said, "they asked around Hammond, and South Chicago, talking to his relatives and friends. They found that one day, five months ago, Joe Evans quit his job, sold his car for cash, packed his things, and left."

"With his six-year-old daughter."

"With his six-year-old daughter. The assumption is, Evans has skipped the state."

I almost shouted. "Then this is an FBI matter!"

"Michael," Rafe said, calmly, smoothly, brushing the air with a gentle hand as if stroking an unruly pet, "it isn't kidnapping when a natural parent takes a child along when they take off."

"This is a case of child abuse, Rafe. Possibly sexual abuse!"

"I understand that," Rafe said, his voice tightly patient, "but Louise Evans never filed charges of any kind against her husband, before or after he ran off. Nor has she filed for divorce."

"Goddammit. So what does that leave her with?"

"You," Rafe said.

As if I were dealing a hand of cards, I tossed a photo of rugged, weak-jawed Joe Evans onto the conference-room table; then a photo of blond little Maggie, her mother's cute clone; then another of the family together, in what seemed happier times, unless you looked close and saw the strain in the faces of both adults.

"Sweet-looking child," Dan Green said, softly, prayerfully.

Dan, not yet thirty, was the younger of my two partners, a blond, mustached, good-looking kid whose regular features were slightly scarred from a fire an arsonist left him to die in. He'd lost an eye in that fire, too, and a hand; a glass eye and a hook took their place.

"Right now," I said, "she's very likely enduring hell on earth."

"Sexual abuse at any age is a tragedy," Roger Freemont said, taking Maggie's photo from Dan. His deep voice was hollow. "At this age, no word covers it."

Roger, balding, bespectacled, with a fullback's shoulders, was the rock of Tree Investigations, Inc. He'd been my husband's partner in the business; like Rafe Valer, Roger had worked with Mike in the Detective Bureau.

"I accepted a retainer of fifty dollars from Louise Evans," I said.

The two men gave me quick, searching looks, then shrugged and gave their attention back to the photos spread before them.

"Of course I did that for the sake of her self-respect," I said. "She works at a White Castle. She had two hundred bucks she'd saved and wanted to give it all to me."

"Fifty bucks will cover it," Roger said.

"Easily," Dan said. "So—where do we start?"

"They've been gone five months," Roger said, "and that's in our favor."

"Why?" Dan asked.

Roger shrugged. "He's settled in to his new life. Enough time has passed for him to think he's gotten away with something. So he gets careless. Enough time has passed for him to start seriously missing family and friends. So he makes phone calls. Writes letters."

Dan was drinking this in.

"Evans has a big family," I said, referring to my notes from several conversations with Louise. "They're a tight-knit working-class bunch. Two brothers and three sisters, all grown adults like Joey. One brother and two of the sisters live in the area—Hammond, Gary, South Chicago. Another brother lives in Dallas."

"*That* sounds like a good bet," Dan said. "I bet Joey's deep in the heart of you-know-where."

"Maybe. He also has a sister in Davenport, Iowa."

Roger perked up. "What is that? A three-hour drive?"

"Around," I said.

"Close to home," Roger said, eyes narrowing, "but far enough away."

"Where do we start?" Dan asked.

"You're going to go by the book, Dan. And Roger—you aren't."

Dan said, "Huh?" while Roger only nodded.

I assigned Dan to check up on Evans's last place of employment—the steel mill—to see if Evans used the place as a reference for a new job; ditto Evans's union—that union card would be necessary for Evans to get a similar job elsewhere.

"If Evans wanted to drop out," Dan said, "he wouldn't have used the mill as a reference, or maintained his union card. . . ."

"Right," I said. "But we can't assume that. He may not be using an assumed name. Maybe he's still living as Joe Evans, just somewhere else. Also, Dan, I want you to go over Louise Evans's phone bills for the six months prior to her husband leaving. Find out what, if any, out-of-town calls he was making."

Dan nodded.

"Any credit-card trail?" Roger asked.

I shook my head. "The only credit card the Evanses had was an oil company card, and Louise received no bills incurred by her husband after he took off."

"Any medical problems, for either the father or child?" Roger asked.

"No."

"Damn," Roger said.

"Why 'damn'?" Dan asked him.

"Prescription medicine would give us a trail," Roger said. "And we could check the hospitals and clinics in areas where we suspect they might be staying."

"They're both in fine health," I said. "Except, of course, for whatever physical and mental traumas the son of a bitch is inflicting on that child."

The two men shook their heads glumly.

"Roger," I said, "you talk to Evans's family members—his father's deceased, but mother's still alive. She may be the best bet. Anyway, after you've talked to them all, keep Ma under surveillance. Go through all their trash, of course—phone bills, letters."

Roger nodded, smiled a little. This was old hat to him, but Dan was learning.

"Better cook up some jive cover story for when you talk to the family," Dan advised him. "Don't tell them you're a detective."

Roger smirked at him. But he let him down easy: "Good idea, kid." There was no sarcasm in his voice; he liked Dan. "I'll tell 'em I'm trying to track Joey down for a credit union refund. They'll want to help him get his money."

Dan grinned. "I like that."

"Make it a fifty-dollar refund check," I said.

"I like that figure, too," Roger said.

Dan made it unanimous.

Three days later, we had something.

It hadn't come from Dan, not much of it anyway. The by-the-book route had only confirmed what Missing Persons found: one day, Joe Evans quit and took off, abandoning if not quite burning all his bridges behind him. His boss at the steel mill had not been called upon for a reference, nor had his union card been kept active. And his friends at the mill claimed not to have heard from him.

"None of his pals saw it coming," Dan said. "Or so they say."

"What about the phone records Louise provided?"

Dan checked his notes. "Joey talked to both his brother in Dallas and his sister in Davenport a number of times in the six months prior to his disappearance. They're a close family."

"Which sibling got the most attention? Texas or Iowa?"

"Iowa. That's where little sister is. Agnes, her name is. He must've called her twenty times in those six months."

Roger fleshed out the picture.

"They're a close family, all right," he said. "Even when a businesslike stranger comes around with fifty bucks for their brother, they clam up. Nobody wanted the refund check except the gal in charge—Loretta Evans, the matriarch, a tough old cookie who could put the battle in battle-ax. Come to think of it, she could put the ax in, too."

"She took the check?"

"She did. And she mailed it out the same day. I saw her do it. Speaking of mail, I checked trash cans all over Indiana, seems like. I got to know the Evanses better than the Evanses know the Evanses. I could save 'em some money."

"How's that?"

"They should share a copy of the *National Enquirer*. Just pass one around, instead of all picking it up."

"Speaking of inquiring minds, what did yours find out?"

"Exactly what it wanted to know," Roger said. "The family seems close in general, but in particular, they seem to want to keep in touch with Agnes."

"Joe's sister."

"His baby sister. She's only twenty-two. Anyway, they been calling her a lot. All of 'em."

"Interesting."

"There's also a bar in Davenport, called Bill's Golden Nugget, where they call from time to time. Maybe she works there."

"It's a lead, anyway," I said. "Damn—I wish I knew where that letter Loretta Evans mailed went to."

"It went to Agnes," Roger said. He was smiling smugly.

"How do you know?"

"Because I waited around on the corner where she mailed it till a postman came around to empty the box and told him I slipped an important letter in that I thought I forgot to put a stamp on. I had a hysterical expression on my face and a stamp ready in my hand, and the bastard took pity on me and let me sort through, looking for my letter."

"And you found one addressed to Agnes Evans."

"Sure."

"What did you do with it?"

"Left it right there," he said. "You don't think I'd tamper with the U.S. mail, do you?"

* * *

MAX ALLAN COLLINS

A foul, pungent odor from Oscar Mayer permeated the working-class neighborhood the massive plant bordered; but nobody seemed to notice, on this sunny June afternoon, or anyway to care. Ragamuffin kids played in the streets and on the sidewalks, wearing dirt-smudged cheeks that knew no era, and housewives hung wash on lines strung across porches, apparently enjoying a breeze that to me only emphasized the slaughterhouse stench.

The address I had for Agnes Evans was 714½ Wundrum; it turned out to be a paint-peeling clapboard duplex in the middle of a crowded block.

My Buick was dirty enough to be at home in the neighborhood, and in my plaid shirt, tied into a halter top, and snug blue jeans, I fit in, too. I felt pretty much at home, actually; with a cop for a father, I had grown up in neighborhoods only a small step up from this—minus the slaughterhouse scent, thankfully.

I knocked at 714½ and then knocked again. The door opened cautiously and a round-faced woman in her early twenties peeked out at me. She had permed dishwater-blond hair, suspicious eyes, and her brother's weak jaw.

"Yeah?"

Pleasant, not at all pushy, I said, "I'm looking for Doris Wannamaker."

"No Doris anybody here," Agnes Evans said. She eased the door open somewhat; not all the way, but I could get a better look at her. She wore tight jeans with fashion-statement holes in the knees and a blue T-shirt with "Quad Cities USA" in flowing white letters. She was slim, attractive, and wore no makeup.

I said, "Isn't this 714½?"

"Yeah."

I could hear a TV inside; a cartoon show.

"Wundrum Street?"

"That's right."

I sighed. "She's gone, huh. I guess that's the way it goes these days. Wonder how much I missed her by."

"I lived here six months," she said. "I don't know who lived here before me."

I shrugged, smiled. "We was in beauty school together, Doris

58

and me. I was just passing through town and wanted to surprise her. Sorry to bother."

Agnes Evans finally smiled. It was an attractive smile. "I went to beauty school. At Regent."

Of course I'd known that.

I said, "I went to the University of Beauty Science in Cedar Falls."

"Supposed to be a good school," Agnes allowed. "I graduated Regent. I didn't keep my certificate up, though."

"Me neither," I said.

The door was open wider. I could see the little girl, wearing a red T-shirt and underpants, sitting like an Indian in front of the TV, watching Tom bash Jerry with a skillet.

"Sure sorry I bothered you," I said.

"No problem."

"Look, uh . . . is there any chance I could use your phone? I want to try to catch my boyfriend at the motel, before he goes out."

"Well . . ."

"I thought I was going to have the afternoon filled with seeing Doris and talking old times, but now . . . could I impose?"

She shrugged, smiled tightly, but opened the screen and said, "Come on in."

The house was neat as a pin; neater. The furniture was the kind you rented to own, but it was maintained as if owning it was the plan. The TV was a big portable on a stand, and there was a Holiday Inn–type landscape over the plastic-covered sofa. A window air conditioner chugged and the place was almost chilly, and the smell of whatever-goes-into-weenies wasn't making it inside.

"Hi, honey," I said, stopping near the little girl.

She didn't look up at me; she was watching Jerry hit Tom with a toaster. "Hi," she said.

Maggie looked older than her picture, but not much. A little child with almost white-blond hair, and a lot of it, a frizzy frame around a cameo face that was blank with TV concentration.

I pretended to use the phone in the kitchen—which was tidy and smelled of macaroni and cheese—while Agnes stood with her arms folded and studied me as she smoked a cigarette. She was still just a little suspicious.

"I'll see you later, then," I told the dial tone, and hung up and smiled at Agnes and shrugged. "Men," I said.

She smirked and blew smoke and nodded in mutual understanding.

As I walked out she followed. I said, "So you're not in hair anymore?"

"No. My boyfriend Billy runs a bar. I work there most evenings."

"Really? Who looks after your little girl?"

"That's not my little girl. Cindy is, uh, a friend of mine's kid. I look after her, days."

"Sweet little girl," I said.

"She's a honey," Agnes said.

I left them there, in the neat house in the foul-smelling neighborhood. I wasn't worried about leaving Maggie in Agnes's care. It was someone else's care I was worried about.

The someone who was with Maggie, nights.

Bill's Golden Nugget was a country-western bar on Harrison, a one-way whose glory days—at least along this saloon-choked stretch—were long gone. I parked on a side street, in front of a natural-food co-op inhabited by hippies who hadn't noticed the sixties were over. The Nugget was between a pawnshop and a heavy-metal bar.

It was midafternoon and the long, narrow saloon was sparsely populated—a few out-of-work blue-collar urban cowboys were playing pool; a would-be biker played the Elvira pinball machine; a couple of guys in jeans and work shirts were at the bar, having an argument about baseball. Just enough patrons to keep the air smoky and stale. A Johnny Paycheck song worked at blowing out the jukebox speakers. The room's sole lighting semed to be the neon and/or lit-up plastic signs that bore images of beer, Marlboro men, and *Sports Illustrated* swimsuit models, none of which had the slightest thing to do with the Nugget. Except for the beer.

A heavyset, bearded, balding blond man in his late twenties

was behind the bar. He wore a plaid shirt that clashed with mine and red suspenders that clashed with his. I heard somebody call him Bill.

He semed pleasant enough, but he was watching me warily; I was new, and maybe I was a hooker.

I took a stool.

"What'll it be, sweet thing?" he said. There was nothing menacing about it. Not even anything condescending. But he was eyeing me carefully. Just a good on-top-of-it bar owner who was probably his own bouncer.

"What have you got on tap that I'd like, big guy?"

"Coors," he said, and it was sort of a question.

"You kidding, Bill? Drinking that stuff is like makin' love in a boat."

"Huh?"

"Fucking close to water," I said, and I grinned at him.

He liked that.

"I also got Bud," he said.

"Bodacious," I said.

He went away smiling, convinced I was not a hooker, just available. Even a guy with a good-looking girl like Agnes at home has his weaknesses.

I milked the Bud for fifteen minutes, tapping my toes to the country music, some of which was pretty good. That Carlene Carter could sing. Nobody hit on me, not even Bill, and that was fine. I just wanted to fit in.

There was a room in back that was at least as big as the front, with tables and a dance floor and a stage for a band and a second bar; it wasn't in use right now, but some beer-ad lighting was on and somebody was back there working, loading in boxes of booze or whatever, through the alley door.

When the guy finished, he came up front; he was in a White Sox sweatshirt with cutoff sleeves and blue jeans. He was a brawny character, maybe twenty-five, good-looking except for a weak chin.

He was Joey Evans.

* * *

I had a second Bud and eavesdropped as Evans—whose voice was high-pitched and husky, not suited to his rather brutish build—asked if he could take a break.

"Sure, Freddy," Bill said. "Take five, but then I need you with me behind the bar. It's damn near happy hour, kid."

Freddy/Joey went behind the bar and got himself a can of diet Coke. He went to a table, away from any patrons, and sat quietly sipping.

I went over to him. "You look like you could use some company. Hard day?"

"Hard enough," he said. He took my figure in, trying to be subtle; it was about as successful as McGovern's run at the presidency.

"Have a seat," he said, and stood, and pushed out a chair.

I sat. "Hope you don't mind my being so forward. I'm Becky Lewis." I stuck out my hand. We shook; his grip was gentle. Right.

"You're from Chicago, aren't you, Becky?" he said. He smiled boyishly; his eyes were light faded blue, like stonewashed denims.

I was supposed to be the detective. "How did you gather that?"

"The accent," he said. "I'd know that flat nasal tone anywhere."

He should: he had it himself.

"I figured you for Chicago, too. South side?"

"Close," he said. "How . . .?"

"You're not wearing a Cubbies sweatshirt, now, are ya?"

He grinned. "Hell, no! Screw them and their Yuppie fans."

"You got that right. Let me buy you a beer . . . Freddy, is it?"

"Freddy," he said. "No thanks. I'm workin'. But I'll buy you one."

"I already got one. Let's just get to know each other a little."

There was not much to know, he said. He was fairly new to the area, working as a bartender for Bill, who was a friend of a friend.

"You got strong hands, Freddy," I said, stroking one. "Working hands. Steel-mill hands."

His eyes flared. Maybe I'd gone too far.

"I . . . I got tired of factory life. Just too damn hard. I need to be sharp, not wasted, when I spend time with my kid. I'm a single parent, you know. I'm trying for that quality-time thing, you know."

I bet he was.

"How many kids you got, Freddy?"

"Just the one. Sweet little girl. Cindy. Starts first grade next year. You got any kids?"

"I'm divorced, but I never had any kids. Didn't think I was cut out for it."

"Oh, you should reconsider. There's nothing like it. Being a parent—it's the best thing that ever happened to me."

Really.

"I don't know," I said, "I'm afraid I might lose my temper around 'em or something."

"That can be a problem," he admitted. "But I'd never lay a hand on Cindy. Never."

"Spare the rod and spoil the child, Clyde."

His brow knit. "I don't believe in that shit. Look—I used to have a bad temper. I'll be honest with you, Becky. I used to . . . well, I used to get a little rough with the ladies sometimes."

I stroked his hand, and almost purred, "I like it a little rough."

Gag me, as they say, with a spoon.

"I don't mean that. I don't mean horseplay or nothing. I mean, I hit women before. Okay? See this diet Coke? It's not just 'cause I'm workin'. I don't drink anymore. I get nasty when I drink, so I don't drink."

"It's a little rough, being a recovering alcoholic, isn't it, working in a bar?"

"Being somebody who don't drink is a valuable commodity when you work in a bar-type situation. That's what Bill likes about me."

"You're not . . . tempted?"

"No. I haven't had a drink in five years."

"Five years?" Was he lying, or crazy? Or both? Was this a trick question?

He swirled the diet Coke in the can. "Five years sober. Five years dry. Besides, Becky—this job was all I could get."

"A strapping boy like you?"

His expression darkened. "I got my reasons. If you want to be my friend, you got to respect my privacy, okay?"

Funny, coming from a guy I just met who already had admitted he was a reformed drunk and supposedly reformed woman-beater. Was there something psychotic in those spooky faded blue eyes?

"Sure, honey," I said, "I'll respect your privacy. If you respect me in the morning."

He grinned again, shyly. "I got to get behind the bar, 'fore Bill tears me a new you-know-what."

"Can we get together after you get off work?"

"I got to spend the evening with my little girl."

"Right. Quality time."

"That's it. But I ought to have her in bed by nine o'clock."

I bet.

"You could stop over after that," he said. "I can give you the address. . . ."

Louise sat next to me in the front seat. She wore the same peasant dress she'd worn to my office; clutched the same patent-leather purse. Her heavy makeup, in the darkness as we sat in the car at the curb, gave her a Kabuki-like visage.

I had phoned her long distance, right after my encounter with Joey at the Nugget. She'd been standing by for my call, as I'd primed her that if I found Maggie, I'd need her to come immediately. I couldn't take Maggie without Louise present, and not just because the child would rightfully resist going with a stranger.

The fact was, with Louise along, taking Maggie would not be kidnapping. Without her, it would.

"Are you all right, Louise?"

She nodded. We were in my Buick; we had left her Datsun in a motel parking lot near the interstate. That's where we had met, after she made the three-hour drive in two and a half hours. It was now approaching 9:30 and the sky was brilliant dark blue with more stars than any child could ever hope to dream upon.

Moving clouds seemed to rise cotton candy-like, but it was only smoke from Oscar Mayer.

We were several blocks from Agnes Evans's duplex, but the meat-packing smell still scorched the air. Joey Evans and his daughter lived in a single-family, single-story clapboard, smaller and newer than his sister's place. Built in the fifties sometime. I lived in a house like this when I was six.

"He's expecting me," I told her. I'd already told her this, but I'd been telling her a lot of things and I wasn't sure anything was sticking.

She nodded.

"I'll go up, and knock, and after he lets me in, I'll excuse myself to go to the rest room, I'll find the back door, unlock it, and you come in and I'll keep him busy while you find your way to Maggie's room."

She nodded.

"Then you slip out the back door with her. When you're in the car with her, safe, honk twice. Short honks. Then I'll get out of there on some excuse, and we're outta here. You girls will be on your way home."

She smiled wanly. "Ms. Tree—thank you. Thank you so very much. I knew you could do it. I knew you could."

"I haven't done it yet. *We* haven't. Now, you need to have a clear head about you, Louise! I want to get you in and out, with Maggie, without him knowing till we're taillights. I don't want *any* violence going down—that husband of yours looks like he could bench-press a grand piano."

She nodded.

"Wait five minutes after I go to the door; then go around behind the house and find the back door. How long?"

"Five minutes."

"When you're safe in the car, how many times will you honk?"

She raised two fingers, as if making the peace sign. "Short honks."

"Good, Louise." I patted her shoulder. I felt confident about this. About as confident as you feel when you make your first dental visit in five years.

He answered my first knock. He was wearing a blue-and-white-checked sport shirt and jeans; he looked nice. He asked me to come in, and I did. He smelled like Canoe cologne; I didn't even know they still made that stuff.

"It's not much, Becky," he said, gesturing about, "but it's enough for Cindy and me."

Whether he and his sister had similar decorating styles, or whether one of them had done the other's home, I couldn't say; but it was the same rent-to-buy decor, just a tad sparser than sis's place. The TV was a console, apparently an old used model, with a Nintendo unit on the floor in front representing the only visible extravagance. Over the couch was another discount-store oil painting, this one a sad-eyed Gacy-like clown handing a red balloon to a little girl who looked disturbingly like Maggie.

"You really keep the place neat," I said, sitting on the couch.

"Cindy helps me. She's really the strong one in the family."

"I'd love to meet her."

"Maybe next time. She's asleep. Besides, I don't like her to see me with other ladies."

"Other ladies?"

"Other than her mommy."

"But you're divorced."

"I know. But she's only six. She doesn't understand stuff like that. Of course, then, neither do I."

What sort of sick relationship did this son of a bitch have with little Maggie? Had he turned her into a "wife"? A six-year-old wife? This guy was lucky I wasn't armed.

"Look," I said, smiling, trying to maintain the pretense of warmth, "I need to use the little girls' room. Where . . . ?"

He pointed the way. It was through a neat compact kitchen, which connected to a hall off of which was Maggie's room. Or Cindy's room. At least she didn't sleep with her daddy.

She sure looked angelic right now, blond hair haloing her sweet face on the overstuffed pillow. Her room was the only one that wasn't spare—even in the meager glow of the night-light, I could see the zoo of stuffed animals, the clown and circus posters, the dolls and their little dresses. Daddy gave her everything.

The sick bastard.

When I returned, having flushed a toilet I really had had to use, I left the back door, off the kitchen, unlocked.

I sat down next to Joey—keeping in mind I needed to call him Freddy—and he said, "I can get you a beer, if you like."

The last thing in the world I wanted was for him to go traipsing through the kitchen while Louise was sneaking in.

"No thanks, I'm fine. I just got *rid* of a beer, honey."

He laughed embarrassedly.

I nudged him with an elbow, gently. "What are you doing with beer in the house, anyway? You haven't had a drink in five years, right?"

A smile creased his pleasant face. "You're sure a suspicious girl. I keep a few brews in the fridge for company."

"You entertain a lot?"

"Not much. My si—"

He started to say "sister," I think; then shifted gears.

"My friends Bill and Agnes both like their beer. In fact, Bill sometimes likes it too much." He shook his head. "A guy who runs a bar shouldn't drink up the profits."

"He's lucky to have you around."

"Actually, he is. I only hope he can stay in business. I sure need this job."

The child's scream shook the house.

Evans and I both bolted off the couch, and then, framed in the archway of the hall leading to the kitchen, there was Louise, pulling the unwilling little girl by the arm. The child, wearing an oversize, man's white T-shirt with Bart Simpson on it, was screaming.

Louise, her eyes crazed, her Kabuki face frozen with rage, slapped the little girl savagely; it rang like a gunshot off the swirl-plaster walls.

That silenced the little girl's screams, but tears and whimpering took their place.

"Louise!" Evans said, face as white as a fish's underbelly. "What—"

Her purse had been tucked under one arm. Now, still clinging to the little girl with one hand, she dug her other hand into the brown patent-leather bag and came back with a snout-nosed black revolver.

"You bastard," she said, "you sick bastard . . ."

Those had been my thoughts, exactly, earlier, but now I was having new thoughts. . . .

"Louise," I said, stepping forward. "Put the gun down."

"You did it to her, didn't you?" she said to him. "You did it to her! You fucked her! You've been fucking her!"

The little girl was confused and crying.

Evans stepped forward, carefully; he was patting the air gently. "Louise—just because your father—"

"Shut up!" she said, and she shot at him. He danced out of the way as the shot rang and echoed in the confined space; the couch took the slug.

I wasn't waiting to see who or what took the next one: I moved in and slapped the gun out of her hand; then I slapped her face, hard.

I had a feeling I wasn't the first one to do that to Louise.

She crumpled to the floor and she wept quietly, huddling fetally; her little girl sat down close to her, stroking her mother's blond hair.

"Mommy," Maggie said. "Don't cry, Mommy. Don't cry."

I picked up the gun.

Evans was standing looking down at his wife and child. He looked at me sharply, accusingly.

"I'm a private detective," I explained. "She hired me to get Maggie back."

"She told you I beat Maggie, right?" he snapped. "And worse?" I nodded.

"Why the hell do you think I ran from her?" he said, plaintively; his face was haunted, his eyes welling. "*I* wasn't the one beating Maggie! But the courts would've given Maggie to her mommy. They would never have believed me over her. How *else* could I have stopped this?"

I didn't have an answer for him; he wasn't necessarily right—the courts might have realized Louise was the abusing parent. But they might not have. I sure hadn't.

He knelt beside his wife; the little girl was on one side of her, and he was on the other. They were mostly in the kitchen. Louise didn't seem to notice them, but they tried to soothe her just the same.

"Her father did terrible things to her," he said softly. "She got me all confused with him. Looked at me and saw her daddy— thought I'd do the same things to Maggie he done to her."

"But the only one imitating her father," I said, "was Louise."

"Mommy doesn't mean to hurt me," the little girl said. "She loves me." It was almost a question.

Sirens were cutting the air; responding to the gunshot.

"I was wrong," he said, looking at me with eyes that wanted absolution. "I shouldn't have run. I should have stayed and tried to fix things."

Who could blame him, really?

Something in Louise had been broken so very long ago.

But as I watched them there, the little family huddling on the cold linoleum, I had to hope that something at long last could start being mended.

ED GORMAN

MOTHER DARKNESS

*Ed Gorman, mystery novelist, short story writer, and founder
of the fan publication* Mystery Scene, *has appeared twice before in this series. His stories have a harder edge than most, as
he explores some of the unpleasant social questions of our day.
This one is from his collection* Prisoners and Other Stories,
*and was also published last year in Maxim Jakubowski's Brit-
ish anthology* Constable New Crimes I.

The man surprised her. He was black.

Alison had been watching the small filthy house for six mornings now and this was the first time she'd seen him. She hadn't
been able to catch him at seven-thirty or even six-thirty. She'd
had to try six o'clock. She brought her camera up and began
snapping.

She took four pictures of him just to be sure.

Then she put the car in gear and went to get breakfast.

An hour and a half later, in the restaurant where social workers
often met, Peter said, "Oh, he's balling her all right."

"God," Alison Cage said. "Can't we talk about something
else? Please."

"I know it upsets you. It upsets me. That's why I'm telling you
about it."

"Can't you tell somebody else?"

"I've tried and nobody'll listen. Here's a forty-three-year-old
man and he's screwing his seven-year-old daughter and nobody'll listen. Jesus."

Peter Forbes loved dramatic moments and incest was about as

dramatic as you could get. Peter was a hold-over hippie. He wore defiantly wrinkled khaki shirts and defiantly torn Lee jeans. He wore his brown hair in a ponytail. In his cubicle back at Social Services was a faded poster of Robert Kennedy. He still smoked a lot of dope. After six glasses of cheap wine at an office party, he'd once told Alison that he thought she was beautiful. He was forty-one years old and something of a joke and Alison both liked and disliked him.

"Talk to Coughlin," Alison said.

"I've talked to Coughlin."

"Then talk to Friedman."

"I've talked to Friedman, too."

"And what did they say?"

Peter sneered. "He reminded me about the Skeritt case."

"Oh."

"Said I got everybody in the department all bent out of shape about Richard Skeritt and then I couldn't prove anything about him and his little adopted son."

"Maybe Skeritt wasn't molesting him."

"Yeah. Right."

Alison sighed and looked out the winter window. A veil of steam covered most of the glass. Beyond it she could see the parking lot filled with men and women scraping their windows and giving each other pushes. A minor ice storm was in progress. It was seven thirty-five and people were hurrying to work. Everybody looked bundled up, like children trundling to school.

Inside the restaurant the air smelled of cooking grease and cigarettes. Cold wind gusted through the front door when somebody opened it, and people stamped snow from their feet as soon as they reached the tile floor. Because this was several blocks north of the black area, the juke box ran to Hank Williams, Jr., and The Judds. Alison despised country-western music.

"So how's it going with you?" Peter said, daubs of egg yolk on his graying bandito mustache.

"Oh. You know." Blond Alison shrugged. "Still trying to find a better apartment for less money. Still trying to lose five pounds. Still trying to convince myself that there's really a God."

"Sounds like you need a Valium."

The remark was so—Peter. Alison smiled. "You think Valium would do it, huh?"

"It picks me up when I get down where you are."

"When you get to be thirty-six and you're alone the way I am, Peter, I think you need more than Valium."

"I'm alone."

"But you're alone in your way. I'm alone in my way."

"What's the difference?"

Suddenly she was tired of him and tired of herself, too. "Oh, I don't know. No difference, I suppose. I was being silly I guess."

"You look tired."

"Haven't been sleeping well."

"That doctor from the medical examiner's office been keeping you out late?"

"Doctor?"

"Oh, come on," Peter said. Sometimes he got possessive in a strange way. Testy. "I know you've been seeing him."

"Doctor Connery, you mean?"

Peter smiled, the egg yolk still on his mustache. "The one with the blue blue eyes, yes."

"It was strictly business. He just wanted to find out about those infants."

"The ones who smothered last year?"

"Yes."

"What's the big deal? Crib death happens all the time."

"Yes, but it still needs to be studied."

Peter smiled his superior smile. "I suppose but—"

"Crib death means that the pathologist couldn't find anything. No reason that the infant should have stopped breathing—no malfunction or anything, I mean. They just die mysteriously. Doctors want to know why."

"So what did your new boyfriend have to say about these deaths? I mean, what's his theory?"

"I'm not going to let you sneak that in there," she said, laughing despite herself. "He's not my boyfriend."

"All right. Then why would he be interested in two deaths that happened a year ago?"

She shrugged and sipped the last of her coffee. "He's exchanging information with other medical data banks. Seeing if they can't find a trend in these deaths."

"Sounds like an excuse to me."

"An excuse for what?" Alison said.

"To take beautiful blonds out to dinner and have them fall under his sway." He bared yellow teeth a dentist could work on for hours. He made claws of his hands. "Dracula; Dracula. That's who Connery really is."

Alison got pregnant her junior year of college. She got an abortion of course but only after spending a month in the elegant home of her rich parents, "moping" as her father characterized that particular period of time. She did not go back to finish school. She went to California. This was in the late seventies just as discos were dying and AIDS was rising. She spent two celibate years working as a secretary in a record company. James Taylor, who'd stopped in to see a friend of his, asked Alison to go have coffee. She was quite silly during their half hour together, juvenile and giggly, and even years later her face would burn when she thought of how foolish she'd been that day. When she returned home, she lived with her parents, a fact that seemed to embarrass all her high school friends. They were busy and noisy with growing families of their own and here was beautiful quiet Alison inexplicably alone and, worse, celebrating her thirty-first birthday while still living at home.

There was so much sorrow in the world and she could tell no one about it. That's why so many handsome and eligible men floated in and out of her life. Because they didn't *understand*. They weren't worth knowing, let alone giving herself to in any respect.

She worked for a year and a half in an art gallery. It was what passed for sophisticated in a midwestern city of this size. Very rich but dull people crowded it constantly, and men both with and without wedding rings pressed her for an hour or two alone.

She would never have known about the income maintenance job if she hadn't been watching a local talk show one day. Here sat two earnest women about her own age, one white, one black, talking about how they acted as liaisons between poor people and the Social Services agency. Alison knew immediately that she would like a job like this. She'd spent her whole life so spoiled and pampered and useless. And the art gallery—minor traveling art shows and local ad agency artists puffing themselves up as artistes—was simply an extension of this life.

These women, Alison could tell, knew well the sorrow of the world and the sorrow in her heart.

She went down the next morning to the Social Services agency and applied. The black woman who took her application weighed at least three-hundred-and-fifty pounds, which she'd packed into lime green stretch pants and a flowered polyester blouse with white sweat rings under the arms. She smoked Kool filters at a rate Alison hated to see. Hadn't this woman heard of lung cancer?

Four people interviewed Alison that day. The last was a prim but handsome white man in a shabby three-piece suit who had on the wall behind him a photo of himself and his wife and a small child who was in some obvious but undefined way retarded. Alison recognized two things about this man immediately: that here was a man who knew the same sorrow as she; and that here was a man painfully smitten with her already. It took him five and a half months but the man eventually found her a job at the agency.

Not until her third week did she realize that maintenance workers were the lowest of the low in social work, looked down upon by bosses and clients alike. What you did was this: you went out to people—usually women—who received various kinds of assistance from various government agencies and you attempted to prove that they were liars and cheats and scoundrels. The more benefits you could deny the people who made up your caseload, the more your bosses liked you. The people in the state house and the people in Washington, D.C., wanted you to allow your people as little as possible. That was the one and only way to keep taxpayers happy. Of course, your clients had a different version of all this. They needed help. And if you wouldn't give them help, or you tried to take away help you were already giving them, they became vocal. Income maintenance workers were frequently threatened and sometimes punched, stabbed, and shot, men and women alike. The curious thing was that not many of them quit. The pay was slightly better than you got in a factory and the job didn't require a college degree and you could pretty much set your own hours if you wanted to. So, even given the occasional violence, it was still a pretty good job.

Alison had been an income maintenance worker for nearly three years now.

She sincerely wanted to help.

An hour after leaving Peter in the restaurant, Alison pulled her gray Honda Civic up to the small house where earlier this morning she'd snapped photos of the black man. Her father kept trying to buy her a nicer car but she argued that her clients would just resent her nicer car and that she wouldn't blame them.

The name of this particular client was Doreen Hayden. Alison had been trying to do a profile of her but Doreen hadn't exactly cooperated. This was Alison's second appointment with the woman. She hoped it went better than the first.

After getting out of her car, Alison stood for a time in the middle of the cold, slushy street. Snow sometimes had a way of making even run-down things look beautiful. But somehow it only made this block of tiny, aged houses look worse. Brown frozen dog feces covered the sidewalk. Smashed front windows bore masking tape. Rusted-out cars squatted on small front lawns like obscene animals. And factory soot touched everything, everything. It was nineteen days before Christmas—Alison had just heard this on the radio this morning—but this was a neighborhood where Christmas never came.

Doreen answered the door. Through the screen drifted the oppressive odors of breakfast and cigarettes and dirty diapers. In her stained white sweater and tight red skirt, Doreen still showed signs of the attractive woman she'd been a few years ago until bad food and lack of exercise had added thirty pounds to her fine-boned frame.

The infant in her arms was perhaps four months old. She had a sweet little pink face. Her pink blanket was filthy.

"I got all the kids here," Doreen said. "You all comin' in? Gettin' cold with this door open."

All the kids, Alison thought. My God, Doreen was actually going to try that scam.

Inside, the hot odors of food and feces were even more oppressive. Alison sat on the edge of a discount-store couch and looked around the room. Not much had changed since her last visit. The old Zenith color TV set—now blaring Bugs Bunny cartoons—still needed some kind of tube. The floor was still an obstacle course of newspapers and empty Pepsi bottles and dirty baby clothes. There was a crucifix on one wall with a piece of faded, drooping palm stuck behind it. Next to it a photo of Bruce Springsteen had been taped to the soiled wallpaper.

"These kids was off visitin' last time you was here," Doreen said.

She referred to the two small boys standing to the right of the armchair where she sat holding her infant.

"Off visiting where?" Alison said, keeping her voice calm.

"Grandmother's."

"I see."

"They was stayin' there for a while but now they're back with me so I'm goin' to need more money from the agency. You know."

"Maybe the man you have staying here could help you out." There. She'd said it quickly. With no malice. A plain simple fact.

"Ain't no man livin' here."

"I took a picture of him this morning."

"No way."

Alison sighed. "You know you can't get full payments if you have an adult male staying with you, Doreen."

"He musta been the garbage man or somethin'. No adult male stayin' here. None at all."

Alison had her clipboard out. She noted on the proper lines of the form that a man was staying here. She said, "You borrowed those two boys."

"What?"

"These two boys here, Doreen. You borrowed them. They're not yours."

"No way."

Alison looked at one of the ragged little boys and said, "Is Doreen your mother?"

The little boy, nervous, glanced over at Doreen and then put his head down.

Alison didn't want to embarrass or frighten him anymore.

"If I put these two boys down on the claim form and they send out an investigator, it'll be a lot worse for you, Doreen. They'll try and get you for fraud."

"God damn you."

"I'll write them down here if you want me to. But if they get you for fraud—"

"Shit," Doreen said. She shook her head and then she looked at the boys. "You two run on home now, all right?"

"Can we take some cookies, Aunt Doreen?"

She grinned at Alison. "They don't let their Aunt Doreen forget no promises, I'll tell you that." She nodded to the kitchen. "You boys go get your cookies and then go out the back door, all right? Oh, but first say goodbye to Alison here."

Both boys, cute and dear to Alison, smiled at her and then grinned at each other and then ran with heavy feet across the faded linoleum to the kitchen.

"I need more money," Doreen said. "This little one's breakin' me."

"I'm afraid I got you all I could, Doreen."

"You gonna tell them about Ernie?"

"Ernie's the man staying here?"

"Yeah."

"No. Not since you told me the truth."

"He's the father."

"Of your little girl?"

"Yeah."

"You think he'll actually marry you?"

She laughed her cigarette laugh. "Yeah, in about fifty or sixty years."

The house began to become even smaller to Alison then. This sometimes happened when she was interviewing people. She felt entombed in the anger and despair of the place.

She stared at Doreen and Doreen's beautiful little girl.

"Could I hold her?" Alison said.

"You serious?"

"Yes."

"She maybe needs a change. She poops a lot."

"I don't mind."

Doreen shrugged. "Be my guest."

She got up and brought the infant across to Alison.

Alison perched carefully on the very edge of the couch and received the infant like some sort of divine gift. After a moment the smells of the little girl drifted away and Alison was left holding a very beautiful little child.

Doreen went back and sat in the chair and looked at Alison. "You got any kids?"

"No."

"Wish you did though, huh?"

"Yes."

"You married?"

"Not so far."

"Hell, bet you got guys fallin' all over themselves for you. You're beautiful."

But Alison rarely listened to flattery. Instead she was watching the infant's sweet white face. "Have you ever looked at her eyes, Doreen?"

" 'Course I looked at her eyes. She's my daughter, ain't she?"

"No. I mean looked really deeply."

" 'Course I have."

"She's so sad."

Doreen sighed. "She's got a reason to be sad. Wouldn't you be sad growin' up in a place like this?"

Alison leaned down to the little girl's face and kissed her tenderly on the forehead. They were like sisters, the little girl and Alison. They knew how sad the world was. They knew how sad their hearts were.

When the time came, when the opportunity appeared, Alison would do the same favor for this little girl she'd done for the two other little girls.

Not even the handsome Doctor Connery had suspected anything. He'd just assumed that the other two girls had died from crib death.

On another visit, someday soon, Alison would make sure that she was alone with the little girl for a few minutes. Then it would be done and the little girl would not have to grow up and know the even greater sadness that awaited her.

"You really ain't gonna tell them about Ernie livin' here?"

"I've got a picture of him that I can turn in any time as evidence. But I'll tell you what, Doreen; you start taking better care of your daughter—changing her diapers more often and feeding her the menu I gave you—and I'll keep Ernie our secret."

"Can't afford to have no more money taken from me," Doreen said.

"Then you take better care of your daughter," Alison said, holding the infant out for Doreen to take now. "Because she's very sad, Doreen. Very very sad."

Alison kissed the little girl on the forehead once more and then gave her up to her mother.

Soon, little one, Alison thought; soon you won't be so sad. I promise.

EDWARD D. HOCH

THE PROBLEM OF THE LEATHER MAN

This story of mine attracted favorable comment from several readers and writers. It's nice to know there's still an audience for the traditional whodunit, complete with "impossible crime."

Ever since I'd moved to southern New England in the early 1920s (Dr. Sam Hawthorne told his guest, lifting the glass for a sip of brandy), I'd heard occasional stories about the Leather Man. At first I thought it was a mere legend to frighten the children at night, but later I learned that there really was such a person—a laconic wanderer dressed in a homemade leather suit who toured Connecticut and eastern New York State for some thirty years until his death in 1889.

The summer of 1937 was when the Leather Man returned, and in Northmont we weren't ready for him.

It was Sheriff Lens who roused me with a phone call at three in the morning on the first day of August. "Hawthorne," I mumbled into the bedside phone.

"Doc, I got a bad accident out on Turk Hill Road, near Putnam. You were the closest one to call."

"I'll be there," I answered shortly and hung up. My head was back on the pillow when I jerked myself awake and clambered out of bed. I wiped my face with a wet washcloth, dressed quickly, and hurried out to my car. Except for an occasional patient in labor, it was rare for me to be called out at that hour. Although automobiles had become more numerous on the roads around Northmont, accidents were infrequent.

I reached the scene of this one within fifteen minutes of the sheriff's summons. A black Ford had run off the road and turned over in a ditch. Sheriff Lens's car was on the road about ten feet away and the sheriff himself was doing the best he could with the badly injured driver. A woman from a nearby farmhouse stood watching from a safe distance.

"How bad is it?" I asked the sheriff.

"Bleedin' from the head, Doc," he answered quietly, standing up to greet me in the glare of his car's headlights. "It's March Gilman."

I knew Gilman from the Rotary meetings, though he'd never been a patient or close friend. He was a man around forty with a successful feed grain business in town, and a reputation of chasing after the ladies.

"Bad wound," I said, dropping to my knees beside him. "Have you called the ambulance?"

"Right away, but they were having some engine trouble. That's when I phoned you."

I leaned closer to the bleeding man. "March! March, can you hear me?"

His eyes flickered open for just an instant. "What—?"

"You've had an accident, March."

"Leather . . . the Leather Man—"

"What's that?" I asked. I'd heard him clearly enough but I didn't understand the words.

"Leather Man . . . in the road. Tried to avoid him and . . . went into ditch."

"What Leather Man, March? Who was he?"

But that was all he said, and in the distance I could hear the clanging of the ambulance bell along the dark dirt road. I tried to stanch the flow of blood from his head until it arrived, but I knew the life was draining out of him.

As they were loading him into the ambulance, the woman who'd been watching moved closer. When she stepped into the light I recognized her as one of the teachers from the Northmont grammar school. "Miss Whycliff—I didn't realize it was you."

"I still live here in the homestead," she replied, arms folded across her breasts as if to protect herself from the mild night air.

She was an attractive but plain woman in her late thirties, unmarried and carrying on with life after the death of her parents. There were women like her in most rural communities.

"What happened here?" I asked as Sheriff Lens saw the ambulance on its way.

"I don't really know. He must have been driving fast. I heard the car go by the house and then skid and go into the ditch. I think it woke me up. I threw on some clothes and when I saw he was injured I phoned the sheriff at once."

"Did you see anyone else?" Sheriff Lens asked as he joined us. "This Leather Man he mentioned?"

"No one. But of course the road was dark." She hesitated. "There was a Leather Man in these parts long ago. I don't know much of the legend, but our local historian could tell you."

"I don't believe in ghosts," the sheriff told her. "The fella you're talkin' about's been dead nearly fifty years."

"Some people have seen him this summer," she replied. "I've heard talk that he's back."

"Rubbish!" Sheriff Lens told her. He was not one to believe in things he hadn't seen for himself.

Hannah Whycliff shrugged. "Will you send someone to tow this car out of my front yard?"

"First thing in the morning," he promised.

He drove to Pilgrim Memorial Hospital then, and I followed in my car. March Gilman was dead by the time we arrived.

Mary Best was busy with her office chores, getting out the August first billing, when I arrived a little before ten. "I just phoned you, Sam. I was worried when you weren't here at nine."

"I had a three A.M. emergency, so I decided to sleep an extra hour."

"The accident that killed March Gilman?"

I nodded. "I suppose the news is all over town."

"Pretty much. I gather he was someone important."

"Small-town important," I told her. Mary had taken over as my nurse after April married and moved to Maine. Sometimes I forgot she'd only been in Northmont two years and didn't yet know everyone. "What's my schedule for today?"

"It's pretty slow. Mrs. Ritter at ten-thirty and Douglas Greene at eleven, and then you're free for the day."

At noon I drove over to see Sheriff Lens. "Just looking at the hospital report on March Gilman," he said. "Died of massive head injuries. No surprise there. He had a bad bleeding wound and a lesser one that probably caused a mild concussion."

"I'm sorry I couldn't do anything to save him." I sat down by his desk. "But this business about the Leather Man still bothers me. Hannah Whycliff said the town historian would have information about the legend. Would that be Spencer Cobb?"

"Only one I know, and he's sorta unofficial."

Spencer Cobb had an office in our little library building on the far side of the town square. I found him on a short stepladder, checking an atlas of old New England maps in a leather-bound volume with a scuffed and disintegrating cover. "Hello, Sam," he greeted me. "What can I do for you?" He was white-haired, though barely fifty, and smoked a pipe almost constantly.

"I've got a historical question for you, Spencer. Ever hear of the Leather Man?"

"You're really going way back now. Come—sit down while I dig out some old references." He was actually the county surveyor, but since the job only occupied a small part of his time he'd taken on the additional duties of Northmont's historian.

Presently he laid an old photograph before me on the desk. It showed a scruffy man in his fifties seated on a wooden bench eating a piece of bread or a bun. He was clad entirely in a bulky, shiny garment with crude stitching plainly visible. The pants and coat seemed to be made of the same patchwork material—leather scraps held together by thongs. He wore a visored cap and boots that seemed to have wooden soles. Resting next to him was a leather bag perhaps two feet square.

"This was the Leather Man," Spencer Cobb said. "The photograph was taken not long before his death in 1889."

"Tell me about him."

Cobb struck a match and relit his pipe. "He first appeared in this area in the late 1850s, dressed as you see him here. For the next thirty years, summer and winter, he followed a particular route, walking along country roads from the Hudson River on the west to the Connecticut River on the east. It took him about thirty-four days to complete each circuit of three hundred sixty-five miles. He came as regularly as the full moon, though every thirty-four days instead of the moon's twenty-nine or thirty days. Once they established his route, some thought it had a mystic significance, with the three hundred sixty-five miles standing for the days of the year."

"Who was he? Did anyone know?"

"He rarely spoke—only a few words in broken English. Though he had his regular stops, if anyone questioned him too closely he would abandon that stop in the future. People were frightened of him at first, but they came to know him as a peaceful man who wanted no trouble. It was believed from his accent that he was French."

"What happened to him?"

"In December of 1888 someone noticed a sore on his lip that appeared to be cancerous. He was taken to a hospital in Hartford, but promptly ran away. The press identified him as a Frenchman named Jules Bourglay who'd fled his homeland following business losses and a tragic love affair. However, none of this was ever proven, and when the Leather Man died of cancer the following March, his meager belongings offered no clue to his identity."

"A fascinating story," I agreed. "But there have been recent reports—"

Spencer Cobb nodded. "I know. The Leather Man is back. I've been hearing stories all summer. Since I don't believe in ghosts I can only assume that someone is retracing the old route, for reasons of his own."

"I have a road map in the car. If I bring it in, could you outline the route for me?"

"Certainly. I have it in one of these old newspaper clippings. There's a great deal of material available because so many people at the time kept scrapbooks of his comings and goings."

I watched while he carefully copied the route of the Leather Man. If this new traveler was retracing the old route, I figured I should be able to locate him without too much difficulty. I'd become fascinated by the story, and curious about what he knew regarding the accident that killed March Gilman.

"Thanks, Spencer," I told him. "You've been a big help."

I went back to the office and plotted the distances on the map. "Why are you doing all this?" Mary Best asked. "What happens if you find him? Are you going to walk with him?"

"Maybe."

"That's the funniest thing I've heard!"

"Look, he's covering three hundred sixty-five miles every thirty-four days. That works out to better than ten and a half miles a day, every day. Why should anyone in his right mind do such a thing?"

"The original Leather Man did it. Maybe this is his grandson or something."

I could see she was laughing at me, but I wanted to find him. With the unfolded map beside me on the seat, I set off in my car along his route. Hannah Whycliff's house was as good a starting point as any, and I drove up there to begin my search. Her car was gone, and Gilman's wrecked vehicle had been towed away as promised. I parked in the drive and walked back to the road, looking for traces of the accident. The gravel in front of her house was unmarked, and only a broken piece of bumper remained in the ditch as evidence of the accident.

I tried to imagine where the Leather Man might have been crossing, then decided he'd have stuck to the road, especially at that hour of the night. But why had he been walking at all? Apparently he slept overnight with people, or in fields in good weather. What was he doing up at three in the morning?

I got back into my car and started driving.

After twenty miles of slow and careful searching over the next hour, I came to the conclusion that the Leather Man was nowhere to be found. Perhaps he'd given up his trek, if he'd ever begun it. Maybe the whole thing had been a myth. I stopped in a filling station that had a public telephone and called Mary back at the office.

"I can't find him," I told her. "I've covered the twenty miles between Northmont and Shinn Corners and he's nowhere on the road. Any emergencies back there?"

"All quiet."

"I guess I'll give up and head back in."

"Maybe you've been going the wrong way," she suggested.

"What?"

"You've been driving in a counterclockwise direction around his route. Maybe he walks in a clockwise direction."

"Damn!" I tried to think why I'd driven the way I did, and decided it was because March Gilman had been going in this direction when he went into the ditch and killed himself. Of course that proved nothing. If there had been a man in leather on the road last night he might have been walking in either direction. "Thanks, Mary. You could be right."

Next I phoned Spencer Cobb and asked him the crucial question. "You never told me which way the original Leather Man walked. Was it clockwise or counterclockwise?"

"Let's see—clockwise, I believe. It's not stated as such in the papers I have, but that seems to have been the case."

"Thanks, Spencer."

"Have you found him?"

"I'm on the trail."

I retraced my route and then kept on going past the Whycliff house, skirting Northmont and heading back east. I took it especially slow this time, and before I'd gone three miles I spotted a slim, brown-clad figure walking ahead of me in the road. He moved to one side as I drew up next to him, but I didn't drive past.

"Want a ride?" I called out the open window.

"No, mate. I'm walking."

He spoke with a strange accent, not quite British, and there was no arguing with his words. I made a quick decision and pulled up behind him, parking my car off the road. I hurried to catch up with him and asked, "Don't mind if I walk with you, do you?"

"Suit yourself, mate."

I fell into step beside him. Up close, I could see that he was indeed wearing a leather suit, not made of separate pieces held together by thongs like the original Leather Man, but one that fit him quite well and reminded me a bit of the buckskin garments one associated with Daniel Boone and other frontiersmen. He carried a knapsack of the same material, with a few possessions bundled into the bottom of it.

"Headed anywhere in particular?" I asked.

"I'm on a trek."

"That's a nice leather suit you're wearing. I hear people call you the Leather Man."

He turned his head in my direction and I got my first good view of his sandy hair and weathered face. He was probably in his forties, but I could have been off by ten years either way. His eyes were the palest blue I'd ever seen. He looked nothing like the picture of the old Leather Man that Spencer Cobb had shown me.

A car appeared over the hill ahead, traveling at a good speed, raising a small cloud of dust behind it. "Who calls me that?" the man asked.

"People who've seen you on your route."

The car slowed to pass us and I saw Hannah Whycliff behind the wheel, heading home. I waved and she waved back. "Haven't seen many people," he muttered. "Just when I stop occasionally for food or a night's rest."

"That woman who just passed us—you were in front of her house at three this morning."

"Might have been," he acknowledged. "When there's a moon I like to walk for part of the night and sleep through the morning. It's cooler that way."

"What's your name? Mine's Sam Hawthorne."

"Zach Taylor." He extended a bronzed hand and we shook.

"Zach as in Zachary?"

"That's right."

"We had a president by that name. Long ago."

"So they tell me."

We were setting a steady pace, a bit faster than I liked to walk. "You're not from around here. Are you British?"

"Australian, mate. Ever hear of a place called Alice Springs?"

"Vaguely. I might have seen it on a map once."

"It's real outback country there. Nothing but desert."

"What brought you to New England?"

"Just decided to see the world. Got this far and thought it was nice enough to stay awhile. I spent the spring in New York and then came up here."

It was getting late in the day, almost dinnertime, but we kept walking. "Your trek is following the route of the original Leather Man, more than fifty years ago," I observed. "That's more than coincidence."

"Well, I was wearing this leather outfit and someone mentioned your Leather Man up in these parts. I looked up his route at the library and decided to follow it."

"You've been doing this all summer?"

"Yes."

"If you were out at three this morning you must have seen an automobile accident. A Ford tried to avoid you and went into a ditch."

Now he eyed me with suspicion. "Is that what this is all about? Are you a policeman, Sam Hawthorne?"

"No, I'm a doctor."

We were approaching a railway crossing where I knew the crossing guard. He was an elderly squinty-eyed man named Seth Howlings, and as we approached he came out of his shed to lower the gate across the grade crossing. "Hello, Seth," I called out.

He turned toward me. "Dr. Sam! Haven't seen you in a long time. And on foot, too! What happened to your car?"

"I'm getting some exercise today. Is there a train coming?"

"Sure is! Can't you hear it?"

I could then. It sounded a distant whistle and in another moment it came into view. It was a twenty-car freight train, traveling at moderate speed. "You've got good ears to hear it coming that far away," I told Seth after the train had passed.

"Best there are," he said with a toothless grin as he raised the gate. "I could hear a cow mooing in the next county."

I chuckled and fell into step beside Zach Taylor. "How late you working tonight, Seth?"

"Till my wife picks me up. She keeps track of my hours."

"See you later."

We crossed the tracks and set off down the highway again. "You know a lot of people in this area?" Zach asked.

"Quite a few. I've been a doctor here for fifteen years."

"You hungry? I've got some sourdough bread in my sack here, and a little whiskey to wash it down."

"You're tempting me."

The whiskey burned going down, but the bread had a nice original taste. We paused only about ten minutes before we were off again. Another car passed us, but the driver was no one I knew. Traffic was sparse on this section of the road.

"I was asking you about that accident with the Ford," I reminded him after a time of walking in silence.

"Yes. You were, weren't you?"

"You saw it?"

"I never saw the car until it was on top of me. Don't know where he came from. I dove to one side and he ran off the road. I could see he was dazed but he didn't seem badly hurt, and I'm not one to get involved in those things."

"So you just kept going."

"Sure. I walked for another half-hour and then found a haystack to sleep in. How's the bloke in the car?"

"He's dead."

"God, I'm sorry to hear that."

"You should have stopped to help him, Zach."

He took out the whiskey again and downed another healthy shot, passing the bottle to me. "Last time I stopped to help someone at an accident, I spent a couple nights in jail. Damned cops thought I was a hobo."

"Aren't you, in a way?"

"Not a chance, mate! I've got money on me. Sometimes I even pay for my lodging and food, when I can't get it free."

"But you're wandering the back roads of New England."

"Man, I'm on walkabout!"

"What?"

"Walkabout. I don't suppose you know the word. It's an Australian custom—an Australian aborigine custom, really—meaning an informal leave from work during which the person returns to native life and wanders the bush, sometimes visiting relatives."

"So this is your walkabout."

"Exactly."

"What is it you've left back home?"

"A wife and family, actually. I hope to return to them someday."

We walked on as night fell, and I realized that it must be after eight-thirty. Where had the day gone, and how far had I walked with this man? More important, how many shots of his whiskey had I drunk? "Won't you be stopping for the night?"

"Soon," he agreed. "Soon."

He told me more about his wife and children as we walked, and about life in Australia. He recounted exploits of the legendary bandit Ned Kelly, who wore a suit of homemade armor in his battles with police. After a time the whiskey bottle was empty and he hurled it into the brush along the road.

"I am too tired to go further," he finally admitted. Up ahead, a lighted sign announced a house that offered beds and breakfast for travelers. "I'll stay here for the night," he told me.

"Then I'll be leaving you and going back to my car." As soon as the words were out of my mouth I realized how foolish they were. We'd been walking for hours. It would take me half the night to return to my car.

"That's too far. Stay the night with me, mate."

I thought about phoning Sheriff Lens for a ride, but I'd drunk more whiskey than expected and I didn't want him to see me wavering a bit as I walked. Maybe it would be best to sleep for a few hours.

A fat, middle-aged woman greeted us at the door of the big house. "Welcome, travelers," she greeted us. "I'm Mrs. Pomroy. Looking for a place to spend the night?"

"That we are," Zach Taylor told her. "Can you accommodate us?"

"I've got two nice beds right at the top of the stairs. Ten dollars each and that includes a sturdy breakfast in the morning."

"We'll take them," I agreed, feeling sleepier by the minute.

"Glen!" she called out, and almost at once a small man with

gray hair and a slight limp appeared. "This is my husband, Glen. He'll show you to your room. Glen—number two, top of the stairs."

He smiled at us halfheartedly. "Good to have you folks stop. Any bags?"

"No mate," Zach told him. "Just us."

He led us up the stairs and his wife called out, "You can pay in the morning. I'll wake you at eight for breakfast if you're not up yet."

The room was large and cheerful, even by the uncertain light from a single floor lamp. There were two beds covered with flowery spreads, and a water pitcher and bowl. "Bathroom's down the hall," Pomroy told us. "We leave a little light on all night."

I shed my outer clothes and fell into bed, exhausted. The combination of all that walking and the shots of whiskey had proven to be too much for me. I had a glimpse of Zach climbing into the other bed, and then I was asleep.

It was daylight when at last I opened my eyes. I was aware that someone was knocking on my door and I looked at the pocket watch I'd left on the table next to the bed. It was five minutes after eight. Then I noticed that Zach's bed was empty, the spread pulled neatly into place. It looked undisturbed.

"Just a minute!" I called to the knocker, pulling on my pants.

I opened the door to find Mrs. Pomroy standing there. "Time for breakfast, if you want it."

"I'll be right down. Where's the other man?"

She looked blank. "What other man?"

"Zach Taylor, the fellow who was with me."

Mrs. Pomroy stared me straight in the eye. "You were alone, mister. There was no one with you."

Sheriff Lens arrived within a half-hour of my call. Mrs. Pomroy's place was across the county line, so he was officially outside his jurisdiction, but that didn't stop him from asking Mrs. Pomroy a few questions.

"Doc here says he came in last night with another man. You say he came alone."

She glared at me and then back at the sheriff. "Alone he was."

"Then why'd you give me a room with two beds?"

She shrugged. "It was empty. You were the only guest we had."

Sheriff Lens shifted uneasily. "I've known Doc a good many years, Mrs. Pomroy. If he says he came here with someone—"

"It was obvious he'd been drinking heavily, Sheriff. He couldn't even walk straight. Maybe he was with someone else, but not here."

The sheriff glanced at me inquiringly. "Is that true, Doc?"

"This fellow, the Leather Man, had a bottle of whiskey. We had a few shots while we walked."

The woman's husband came in from outside and she immediately lined up his support. "Tell them, Glen. Tell them this man was alone."

The short man glanced at me. "Sure was! I was glad to see he wasn't drivin', the shape he was in."

I sighed and started over again. "There was a man with me. He went to sleep in the other bed. His name is Zach Taylor and he's wearing a leather suit, almost like buckskin."

They both shook their heads, unwilling to budge from their story. Maybe they killed him for his few meager possessions, I thought, but then why wouldn't they have killed me too? "Come on, Doc," the sheriff said, his arm on my shoulder. "I'll give you a ride back to your car."

As I turned to leave, Mrs. Pomroy reminded me, "That'll be ten dollars for the room."

Back in his car, Sheriff Lens was silent until I spoke. "I found this so-called Leather Man, and when he wouldn't stop to talk with me, I parked my car and walked with him. He's Australian, on something called a walkabout. Trying to find himself, I guess. He saw the accident but didn't think Gilman was seriously hurt. He was afraid of getting involved so he kept on walking."

"What about the drinkin', Doc? Is that part true?"

"He had a bottle with him. After a while I took a couple of swigs from it. I'll admit it hit me harder than I'd expected, but I knew what was going on at all times. Zach Taylor was with me when we took the room at Mrs. Pomroy's place."

"Did you sign a register or anything?"

92

"No. She rents rooms and gives you breakfast, that's all. She's not operating a hotel."

"You think they killed him or something?"

"I don't know what to think. The last I saw of him, he was climbing into the bed next to mine."

"But the bed was made this morning."

"I slept so soundly Mrs. Pomroy could have brought a parade of elephants in there and I wouldn't have known it. She could easily have come in and made the bed."

"The door wasn't locked?"

I tried to remember. "I don't think so. I'm sure we had no key."

He stared hard at the highway ahead. "I don't know what to think, Doc."

"Well, I can at least prove he was with me. When we get to the railroad crossing back across the county line, stop the car."

We reached it in another ten minutes, and I saw old Seth Howlings coming out of the crossing guard's little shed. "Hello, Seth."

"It's Dr. Sam again! But in a car this time."

"Howdy, Seth," Sheriff Lens said, getting out to join me.

"Hello, Sheriff. Beautiful day, isn't it?"

"Sure is!"

I walked closer to him. "Remember when I came by yesterday afternoon, Seth?"

"Sure do! Just as the five thirty-five was passing through."

"Remember the man who was with me?"

He looked blank. "You was alone, Dr. Sam. Are you trying to trick me?"

"Alone?" the sheriff repeated. "Are you certain of that?"

"Certain as I can be. Dr. Sam walked up and we chatted some while the train passed. Then he crossed the tracks and went on his way."

"Alone?"

"Alone."

I was in the middle of a nightmare from which there was no awakening.

* * *

Sheriff Lens and I drove on. "I'm not crazy, Sheriff."

"I know that, Doc."

"And I wasn't drunk enough to have imagined the whole thing. In fact, I never would have had any whiskey at all if Zach Taylor hadn't given it to me."

"Still, that old coot would have no reason to lie. You can't think he's in some sort of conspiracy with the Pomroys! They probably don't even know each other."

"I don't know what to think at this point. But I'm damned if I'm going to let it rest! I have to prove I wasn't imagining this Leather Man."

Sheriff Lens thought about it. "Someone must have seen you on the road together."

"There were only a few cars, and no one I knew except—"

"What is it?"

"Hannah Whycliff. She passed us in her car and waved. I'd forgotten about her."

We drove on to the Whycliff house, where the image of the Leather Man had made its first appearance in March Gilman's headlights. Hannah Whycliff's car was in the driveway and she came to the door when the sheriff rang the bell. She greeted us both and then asked, "Is this more questions about the accident?"

"Not exactly, Miss Whycliff," the sheriff said. "Doc here has a problem. He was with this so-called Leather Man yesterday, but now the man has disappeared and two different people deny seeing him with Doc."

"I remember you passed and waved when I was walking with him. It was late yesterday afternoon."

She turned to look at me. "I remember seeing you, Dr. Sam. I wondered what had happened to your car, but I was in a hurry and couldn't stop."

"Then you saw the Leather Man?" Sheriff Lens prompted.

"No, Dr. Sam was alone. I saw no one else."

The thing was so fantastic I simply shook my head and gave a humorless chuckle. It defied the laws of logic. "Tell me, do you know Seth Howlings, the railroad crossing guard? He's just this side of the county line."

"I may have seen him but I'm sure I've never spoken to him. Why do you ask?"

"And how about a couple named Mr. and Mrs. Glen Pomroy, over in the next county? They rent out rooms in their house for overnight guests."

"I never heard of them. What are all these questions for?"

"We're tryin' to find witnesses who saw Doc with this Leather Man," the sheriff told her. "The man might have been responsible for that accident in front of your house."

"I never saw any Leather Man. The doctor was alone."

"Thank you, Miss Whycliff," the sheriff said. We walked back to the car.

I settled into the front seat and said, "She's lying."

"Sure, and so are the Pomroys and old Seth. But why, Doc? These people don't even know each other."

"I don't know," I admitted. "I only know they're lying."

"Do you think the Leather Man could have hypnotized them so they didn't remember seeing him?"

I snorted at that suggestion. "Hannah Whycliff drove past us in a car. The best hypnotist in the world couldn't have done it that fast."

"Then there's only one other explanation, Doc. Do you believe in ghosts?"

When I told Mary Best about it the next morning, she saw things a bit more clearly than I did. "We have to find the Leather Man, Sam. We have to locate this Zach Taylor and learn the truth."

"He's probably dead and buried somewhere out behind the Pomroy place."

"But maybe he isn't! Maybe he just went away!"

"Then why are they all lying about it? The sheriff even raised the possibility he was the ghost of the original Leather Man, but that one was French, not Australian."

"Can you get along without me today? I'm going out looking for him."

"You're wasting your time, Mary. Even if you find him, that won't explain why everyone lied."

"Everyone didn't lie. Only three people lied—four, if you count Mrs. Pomroy's husband. There has to be a reason."

I let her go. There were patients to be seen, but I handled them all without her. I spent most of the day thinking about Zach Taylor and my walk with him. He'd appeared there on the road, and then he'd disappeared. Maybe I'd never walked with him at all. Maybe I'd imagined the whole thing.

It was only later, toward the end of the day, that I realized what I'd done. March Gilman had been alive in that ditch after the car went off the road. After causing the accident, Zach Taylor had killed and robbed him. Deciding I might be suspicious of him, he bribed the Pomroys to deny his existence. Then he walked back and bribed old Seth and Hannah Whycliff too. That was the only answer.

And I'd let Mary Best go out alone in search of a murderer.

It took me less than a minute to realize that I was getting foolish in my middle age. If Zach had killed Gilman and thought I suspected him, he had more than enough opportunity during our walk to leave me dead in a ditch too. There'd be no need to try bribing four people who might later blackmail him.

I thought about it some more, and remembered something I'd read not too long before. I reached into the bookcase in my waiting room and selected a volume of essays, *While Rome Burns*, by Alexander Woollcott. One of them, "The Vanishing Lady," deals with the legend of a young Englishwoman and her frail mother, recently returned from India, who visit the Paris Exposition in 1889 on their way back to England. The mother vanishes, and the hotel staff denies she ever existed. Their room has different furnishings and wallpaper. All traces of the mother are gone. In the end, a young man from the British Embassy establishes that her mother died suddenly of the black plague, contracted in India. The conspiracy of silence was necessary to prevent panic from driving visitors out of Paris and ruining the Exposition. In a footnote at the end, Woollcott says that he traced the original story to a column in the *Detroit Free Press*, published during the 1889 Paris Exposition. But the author of the column could no longer remember whether he had invented the story or heard it somewhere.

All right, was there any possibility the Australian had suffered from some illness? Had he died during the night and his death been hushed up by the Pomroys, who'd then bribed the others?

But Zach Taylor hadn't appeared ill at all. He was the picture of health, in fact. And the Pomroys would have had no way of knowing that Seth Howlings and Hannah were the only persons who'd seen us. Old Seth hardly seemed the sort to be bribed, anyhow.

By late afternoon I'd had no word from Mary and I was beginning to worry about her. I went out to my car after the departure of my last patient, thinking I should begin searching for her. Just then I saw the familiar little roadster pull into the parking lot. The Leather Man was next to her in the front seat.

"I thought you were dead," I told him. "Where'd you find him, Mary?"

"On his route, just where he was supposed to be. If he wasn't dead, I knew he'd be there."

"Good to see you again, mate," Zach said as he got out of the car. "Your little girl here is certainly persuasive. Once she found me she insisted I had to come back with her. This disrupts my whole route."

"We'll drive you back to where she picked you up," I assured him. "Or anywhere else you want to go. Just tell me what happened at the Pomroys' place last night."

"You mean where we stayed? Nothing happened. I got up early and left. I wanted to be on the road, and you were still sound asleep. Sorry I didn't say goodbye."

"Did you talk to Mrs. Pomroy?"

"It was too early for breakfast so I just paid her and left."

A small, sharp idea was gnawing at my brain. "How much did you pay her?"

"Twenty dollars, mate. I paid for your bed too!"

I went back inside and called Sheriff Lens.

When we returned to the Pomroy house, Glen Pomroy was on the front porch, scrubbing the steps. He looked up expectantly as we approached, but his expression soured when he recognized me. "Is your wife around?" I asked.

"We don't want trouble."

"Neither do I. We just want to see Mrs. Pomroy."

She appeared at the screen door then, pushing it open slowly. "I'm here," she said.

"We found the Leather Man," I told her. "He paid you for both our beds."

"Yeah, I forgot that," she answered glumly. "Guess we owe you ten dollars." The denials had gone out of her.

"You figured I was too drunk to remember clearly, so you made up the bed after he left and lied about his ever being here. That way you got an extra ten dollars out of me. It may have seemed like a minor swindle to you, but it caused me a great deal of trouble."

"I'll be contacting your sheriff to keep an eye on you," Sheriff Lens told them. "If there are any more complaints from your guests you'll both be makin' your beds at the county jail."

When we were back in the car he turned to me and said, "That takes care of the Pomroys, but it doesn't explain the other two. They both claimed you were alone too."

"Seth Howlings is our next stop. When we get there, don't say anything at first. Let me do all the talking."

Seth was seated in the crossing guard's little shack, dozing, but he came awake instantly as I approached. "How are you, Seth?"

"Back again, Dr. Sam? I've seen more of you the past two days than I usually do in a month."

"I doubt that, Seth. I doubt if you've seen me at all. Who's this standing with me now?"

My question seemed to unnerve him, and he shifted his gaze from my face to a point just to the left of me where no one stood. Then he seemed to look in the other direction, but his eyes skipped quickly past Sheriff Lens.

"Seth," I said quietly, "you're blind, aren't you?"

His hands began to shake. "I don't need eyes for this job. I can hear them trains comin' from the next county! The sound travels along the rails, and their steam whistles can be heard for miles."

"How did it happen, Seth? Why didn't you go to a doctor?"

"I never had no pain, just halos around the lights, and my vision kept narrowing down till it was just like looking into a tunnel. After a while even that was gone. I figured at my age it didn't make no difference. My wife drove me to work here every day, and picked me up. So long as I could hear the trains comin' and lower and raise the gate, what difference did it make?" His face wore an expression of utter sadness. "Will they take my job away from me, Dr. Sam?"

I knew it was glaucoma, and there was nothing anyone could do for him. "Probably, Seth. I'm sure you're good at it, but you wouldn't want to cause an accident, would you? Suppose some little child wandered onto the tracks and you didn't hear him."

"I wouldn't want that," he agreed.

"This is Sheriff Lens with me. He'll see about getting a replacement for you right away."

The sheriff put a reassuring hand on Seth's shoulder. "I'll have someone out here within an hour, and we'll arrange with your wife to pick you up."

Back in the car, I shook my head in wonder. "To think we had a blind man guarding that railroad crossing—"

"How'd you know, Doc?"

"He answered people when they talked to him, but he never spoke first to someone. When I asked about the man who was with me, his immediate reaction was that I was trying to trick him. What did he mean by that? It was an odd choice of words if he had seen me alone at the crossing. And both times I saw him he mentioned my coming on foot or in a car, as if to convince me he could see. Then I remembered Zach never spoke while we were there. And Seth emphasized hearing the train, not seeing it. With his wife to pick him up, and relying on his ears, he could do the job."

"Blind people's hearing is supposed to be very sensitive," Sheriff Lens pointed out. "He must have heard the footsteps of two people if he knew you arrived on foot."

"We approached just as a train was coming, and that distracted him. Only I spoke, and after the train passed I remember falling into step with Zach Taylor. If he listened then, he'd have heard only one set of departing footsteps. When we questioned him, he feared I suspected something about his blindness so he stuck to the story he thought was true—that I was alone."

"So Seth Howlings and the Pomroys had their own entirely different reasons for denying the existence of the Leather Man. But what about Hannah Whycliff? Isn't it stretching coincidence a bit far to have a third person who didn't see him for some reason?"

"We'll call on Miss Whycliff next," I answered grimly.

It was almost evening when we turned into her driveway once more. This time it took her a while to answer the ring. "I hope we're not interrupting your dinner," I said.

"No, no. What is it this time?"

"I'm afraid it's still about the Leather Man. We've located him at last."

"How does that concern me?"

"You lied about not seeing him with me on the road yesterday. You see, the sheriff here started out his questioning by telling you that two other people had already denied seeing the Leather Man with me. That was a mistake. You quickly decided it was to your advantage to agree with them, to tell the same lie. You wanted the Leather Man to be gone, to never have existed."

"Why would I want that?" she asked.

"Because you were afraid he saw you murder March Gilman."

Her gaze shifted from me to the sheriff and back again. "Whatever gave you that idea?"

"Zach—the Leather Man—saw the accident and didn't think Gilman had been hurt badly at all. He hadn't seen the car coming until it was almost upon him. You told me you heard the car skid on the road as Gilman tried to apply the brakes, yet when I examined the road yesterday morning, just hours after the accident, the gravel was unmarked by any trace of skidding. Zach didn't see the car coming because it came out of your driveway, Miss Whycliff. It didn't skid. It wasn't going fast at all, but it went off the road to avoid the Leather Man. March Gilman was thrown clear and dazed. Before he became fully conscious you saw your chance. You came down to the road and hit him with something—perhaps a hammer. He was barely able to speak by the time I arrived, and he died soon after. There was evidence of two blows to the head."

"Why would I kill March Gilman?" she asked.

"I don't know. He had a reputation as a ladies' man. What went on between the two of you—"

"Get out of here, both of you! Get out this instant!"

I turned back toward the driveway, just as Mary pulled her car in behind the sheriff's. "We have a witness," I said softly.

Her eyes widened as she saw the Leather Man step out of the car and walk toward us. "No! No, keep him away from me!"

"He really exists, much as you wanted him not to. He's going to tell us what he saw."

"Keep him away!" she shouted. "I'll tell you! I killed March Gilman. And I'll tell you what he did to deserve it!"

"What's the matter with her, mate?" Zach asked as the sheriff led her away.

"She thought you were someone else," I told him. "She thought you were the avenging angel."

"No," he said with a grin. "I'm just a chap on walkabout."

SUSAN B. KELLY

THE LAST SARA

To the dismay of librarians and bibliographers, it seems there are two very good mystery writers named Susan Kelly, one British and one American. This is the British one, who publishes in America as Susan B. Kelly. A resident of London, she's had three novels published here by Scribner's. We're at the halfway point in our selection, a fitting place for the light touch of this charming little tale from the annual anthology of the Crime Writers Association, 1st Culprit. It has not previously been published in the United States.

I'm Stephanie Lawless; my friends call me Steve. I was with the City of London Police until a year ago and I was good at it. I was all set to take my sergeant's exams when I upped and quit.

It was the name. I was sick of taking suspects into the interview room; putting on my toughest expression; switching on my tape recorder; saying, "I'm Detective Constable Lawless"—and recording their mindless sniggering.

So I resigned, just like that; ignored the protests of my long-time boyfriend Detective Sergeant Jim Smith—who even offered me the marital protection of his own anonymous surname—and went freelance. I became the boss and sole employee of the Lawless Detective Agency.

The name brought people in: they still thought it was a joke. Well, most of them did. Some of them thought it meant I'd do things that shaded into the area of the criminal. They were quickly shown the door, as were would-be clients who insisted offensively that anyone called Steve Lawless had to be a man and a big one at that.

Lately I'd begun to specialize. It was a sad sign of the times—
a trend which, like Mutant Ninja Turtles and Madonna, had
flown supersonically across the Atlantic. My clients were young
women: stockbrokers, merchant bankers, barristers. They came
to me by word of mouth, through the City Women's Network
where it was whispered over the coffee and brandy that Ms. Lawless was efficient, discreet, and fairly cheap.

This young woman—I thought of her generically as "Sara"—
had a good address although she was reluctant to give it at first.
She lived in Docklands if she was trendy or in Islington if more
conservative. She had a car with electric windows and real leather
seats. She owned shares—not just in British Telecom or London
Electricity but a carefully balanced portfolio built up over the
years. She had PEPs and a TESSA and a pension scheme.

She was in her early thirties and single, having spent the last
dozen years building her career. Just lately she'd found herself
peering into prams and thinking how lovely the cribs in John
Lewis were with their stenciled sides and floating draperies. Then
Mr. Possible came along. Sometimes he was Mr. Wonderful but
mostly he was just Mr. Might-Be-Right. She was ready to take
the plunge.

Except . . . that she had so much to lose.

There *was* usually something. She was bright, Sara, often brilliant. And then there was her woman's intuition, which had
brought her to that back street in the unfashionable part of
Wandsworth in the first place. Bisexuality, maybe, or promiscu-
ity—so risky these days. More usually it was just petty fraud, bad
credit records, debts. In one case it was a woman in Stockwell
with a prior claim: she was his wife.

Sara would come back at the end of a week: full of hope, a
little nervous, looking for reassurance. She would examine the
photos or the credit references without comment; pay her bill
without quibble; and leave without pride. She never seemed very
grateful for all my hard work—for the cold nights outside his
flat, for the boring hours spent in St. Catherine's House or the
Land Registry.

I longed to tell her how very far from unique she was: how

many other lonely Saras there were in this city. But I knew that Sara hated to be pitied.

But to get to the Last Sara.

One morning about two weeks ago, I'd just put the kettle on and happened to glance out of the window to the street two floors below. A taxi had drawn up outside the Midland bank opposite and a Sara got out and looked round. I knew she was a Sara—it was something in the suit and the briefcase and the look of disbelief that such slums still existed in south London in 1991.

I rinsed the spare mug at the corner sink. Sometimes, browsing in the remnant china shops, I considered buying a mug with the name "Sara" on it for occasions like these. I put a bit more water in the kettle and waited for the knock at the door.

"And then there's AIDS, of course." The Last Sara reddened slightly as she reached the end of her confused but brief justification ten minutes later. "Not that . . . I mean, of course, no one one knows . . ."

"It's seventy-five a day plus expenses," I said. "You should allow a week to ten days, average. Two hundred and fifty deposit. I'll take a check. Is that all right?"

Sara nodded. "Money's not a problem." She began to write out a check. I noticed that she wore a rather nice diamond and sapphire engagement ring. So we were playing for high stakes here.

"More coffee?"

"No thanks." I suspected she had been about to say "No fear." That cheap powdered stuff from Budgens was false economy. Definitely.

"I need a name and address for him, his place of work, car registration would be helpful otherwise make and color. If you have a photo that would be great, otherwise I'll take a full description."

My businesslike attitude seemed to relax Sara. We were talking the same language: money and facts. It made checking up that the man you loved wasn't a gold-digging, pox-ridden bigamist that much more bearable.

* * *

Two years earlier I could not have said for certain what Future Options were. Now half the men I investigated claimed to be in them. I knew it was the sharp end of the City—the one where you were a paper millionaire on Monday and looking at the wrong end of a bankruptcy court on Friday. Future options traders were, by definition, gambling men. It always boded ill for Sara.

My heart sank as I followed Adam Scott and another muscular Adonis to the nearest wine bar. There was always a moment at the start of a case when I wanted to pack it in; to retreat into the waiting arms of Sergeant Jim Smith who had shared my Surrey childhood. There was nothing unknown in Jim's past; nothing sinister beyond a little innocent trespass in the grounds of the local manor house on the night of my sixteenth birthday.

I can still remember the texture of the lawn beneath my naked—and shivering—body.

Adam Scott was a golden boy—his photograph didn't do him justice. At twenty-nine he had to be some years younger than Sara. He was also in another sexual league: Sara was smartly turned out, even elegant; she had intelligent eyes, neat features, nice figure. But her best friend wouldn't have called her beautiful. Adam Scott was beautiful. Every female eye followed him round the room and the assistant in the Golden Grape flirted with him relentlessly.

No, there had to be something although it wasn't, on the face of it, money. Adam had a BMW and a penthouse on New Crane Wharf, which was, according to the Land Registry, not only legitimately his but unencumbered by any mortgage. A painstaking afternoon at St. Catherine's House had not turned up a wife hidden in the wardrobe. It looked like being a long, hard case.

Occasionally I would find nothing. Even then it didn't mean that there was nothing to find, just that I maybe hadn't been smart enough to find it. Besides, once the seeds of doubt were sown in Sara's mind, once she'd climbed the thirty steep steps up to my office and fished in her briefcase for her checkbook . . . you might as well write the relationship off.

*　*　*

By the weekend, it was beginning to look as if Sara had decided to give him . . . whatever the opposite of the benefit of the doubt was, anyway. I had yet to see the lovers together—rather a low-key social life, I thought, before remembering that I myself had been too busy with this case to see Jim all week.

City fraud was Jim's and my area of expertise back in the days when we made a cracking team working out of Wood Street police station. I remember the day I handed in my notice. I can still hear the grief in Superintendent Talbot's voice:

"You've got a nose for it, Stevie. You could catch Mother Teresa out fiddling her tax returns. You always know when people are lying to you."

It was the best unsolicited testimonial I was ever likely to get and Bill Talbot was right, of course. I could smell an insider dealer, could smell the cockiness mixed with fear in the sweat on his Armani suit. Steve, the sniffer dog.

And Adam Scott smelled like last week's kipper.

I'll get you, I thought. I was sitting in a dark corner at Tramps, nursing a Coke, wondering how soon I could leave and watching him jiggling about with a mammiferous redhead. I'd get him for the sake of all the poor, deceived Saras.

"I'm so very grateful," the Last Sara said, to my amazement. We were sitting in the Wandsworth office again ten days after her first visit. "Now, how much do I owe you?" I did some rough sums on the back of an envelope and told her. As Sara began to write out the check, I said, "You realize I have to take it to the police?"

"I'll go to them myself." She ripped out the check with a satisfactory tearing noise and handed it across the table.

"I dunno," I said. She might warn him, give him a chance to do a bunk. "If you still feel . . . you know."

"I assure you I don't feel the least bit 'you know' about him anymore," Sara said crisply. "Let me shop him. It'll be my way of getting my own back."

I hesitated but said at last, "I'll give you twenty-four hours." I trusted her. I always knew when people were lying to me.

Business had tailed off again and I was on my way home to my flat in Battersea the following lunchtime when the first edition of the *Standard* caught my eye.

INSIDER DEALING ON FUTURE OPTIONS—DAWN ARREST

I bought a copy and found myself staring at an unflattering front-page picture of Adam Scott, looking a good deal more disheveled and a lot paler than he had at Tramps. But Adam didn't keep my attention for long. A smaller picture at the bottom of the page grabbed at my eyes as did another headline:

PERSONAL TRIUMPH FOR CITY FRAUD SQUAD INSPECTOR

Grimly, I read on.

> *Senior police officers were full of praise today for Detective Inspector Sara Crook of the Wood Street Fraud Squad. Weeks of painstaking undercover work by vivacious Inspector Crook, 34, resulted in the arrest of insider dealer, Adam Scott, in the early hours of this morning. Mr. Scott is being held on charges believed to involve millions of pounds.*
>
> *"She's only been with us six months but she's got a real nose for it," said Superintendent William Talbot, who heads the squad. "She could catch Mother Teresa out fiddling her tax returns. She always knows when people are lying to her."*
>
> *Inspector Crook was assisted in her undercover operation by her colleague and fiancé Detective Sergeant Jim Smith, pictured with her here.*

I held the pictures up in the early spring sunlight. There was Jim—dear dependable Jim Smith, my childhood sweetheart—with his arm tightly round Sara Crook, who, unlike me, had not let her name get in the way of her ambition.

Unlike me, the Last Sara was not a quitter.

> *"We've been after Scott for ages," Superintendent Talbot said. "But he'd covered his tracks well. Then just yesterday*

Sara and Jim came up with the crucial bit of evidence we needed."

"I suppose we could become a sort of sleuthing couple," *said Inspector Crook, displaying her diamond and sapphire engagement ring for the camera, "like Peter Wimsey and Harriet Vane, or Tommy and Tuppence Beresford."*

I turned to the back of the paper and began to leaf through the Situations Vacant.

I told you: I'm a quitter.

PETER LOVESEY

YOU MAY SEE A STRANGLER

Here's another story from a British anthology, Midwinter
Mysteries 2, *having its first American publication. But Peter
Lovesey is no stranger to these pages, having appeared here
five times previously. His novels are often fine examples of the
historical mystery, though he has recently launched a highly
successful new series about a modern sleuth with* The Last
Detective *(1991). The story that follows, about a serial killer
of young women, is told almost entirely in dialogue. It would
have made a great radio thriller in the days before television.*

Helen's mind was made up. Three times today she had got to
the point of picking up the phone to call the police. She had
pressed the first two numbers of the emergency code, then
stopped, her finger poised over the third. Some loss of nerve had
impelled her to hang up.

This time she would not falter. She stretched out her hand.

The phone bleeped before she touched it. Reacting as if she had
disturbed a snake, she backed against the wall.

Outside in Carpenter Avenue, the kids from next door were
skateboarding. Bees were plundering the lavender bush. Her
neighbor Sally walked by on her way to the art class. Sally modeled nude for five pounds an hour and thought nothing of it. She
was Helen's closest friend, a free spirit, unencumbered by her
four kids. Before the firstborn arrived, Sally had organized a
baby-sitting circle. Helen could discuss anything with her. Or

almost anything. Cool, liberated Sally wouldn't fathom how any woman could be afraid to pick up a phone.

She braced herself. "Yes?"

"Helen?"

"Speaking."

"So you don't know who this is." The voice was difficult to place. Female, youngish, with a trace of the north. There was background noise of voices laughing and talking animatedly, and music.

"I . . . I'm sorry. Your voice is familiar, but . . ."

"Come on, you can do better than that, love. Picture a blowsy dame with pink-rimmed specs and a blond ponytail."

She dredged the name from her troubled mind. "Immy." Imogen had been her mainstay through that dreary history course at university. "It's over ten years. It must be."

"Eleven this June since we chucked our course-notes into the Avon and got totally Brahms and Lizst. Remember? How are things with you, Helen? You don't sound too chipper from here."

"It's nothing."

"An off-moment? What's your news? I know there's a man in your life now. Nelson, am I right?"

"How do you know that?"

"From the Christmas card you sent one year. You caught me out. I didn't think we were the sort who sent cards."

"That was the only year I sent."

"Properly hitched, are you?"

"Yes."

"Kids?"

"No." Helen made an effort to switch the questioning. "How about you, Immy? Did you marry?"

"Me? Can you imagine it? I lived with a footballer for a bit. He was the striker for Manchester City Reserves, whatever that means. All the training kept him really warm, specially on those freezing nights in January. Talk about cozy. I didn't use the electric blanket all winter. But he got sweaty when the weather improved so I blew the whistle. That's meant to be a joke, sweetie. You're supposed to fall about laughing."

"Sorry."

"You would have laughed in the old days. You *are* down. It isn't your health, is it?"

"I'm fine." Helen was trying to decide whether this call from Imogen was just for the chat or whether a visit was imminent. In her present crisis she couldn't face doing the hostess bit, not even for Immy. "Where are you calling from?"

"Got you worried, have I?" Imogen said, laughing.

"Of course not."

"Go on—you've got a mental picture of me standing on your doorstep with two enormous suitcases and a dog."

"Normally I'd love to see you, but—"

"It's all right, kiddo, you can relax. Put your feet up, wash your hair, have nooky with Nelson on the bearskin rug. I'm not about to descend on you."

"You're just as daft as ever," Helen said, trying to sound matey and not succeeding. "Where *are* you speaking from? It sounds like a party there."

"The mental picture gets worse—two suitcases and a dog, a carload of drunks with funny hats. I said relax. There's no way I'm going to make a nuisance of myself."

"The last I heard you were back in the north."

"And so I am. Granadaland. Back to my roots. I'm a television researcher. The history degree got me in, but I make sod all use of it. I don't know why they keep me on."

Manchester. At least two hundred miles away. While Imogen was outlining the pleasures and perils of TV research, Helen's thoughts became less guarded. The voice from the past, chattering freely, confiding failure as readily as success, revived that time in their second year when they had opened their minds to each other. Talking to Immy had been a balm at that vulnerable stage of her life. She had kept nothing back.

Then wasn't this a God-sent opportunity? All the reasons she had for not confiding in Sally next door didn't apply to Imogen. Immy was remote now, eleven years and two hundred miles away. Remote, yet close in spirit. A sympathetic ear. No, that wasn't the point—it wasn't sympathy she wanted. An understanding ear. Immy understood her. She might even know what to do.

"Now what about you, poppet?" Imogen ended by saying. "What's your news?"

"Mine?" In her anguish Helen covered her mouth with her hand and pressed her fingers into the flesh under her cheekbones.

"Helen, it's bloody obvious I must have got you at a difficult time," Imogen said. "Typical of me, wittering on like that. Look, I'll call you back another day."

"No. No, I want to talk," Helen managed to say. "God knows, I want to talk. It must be fate that you called."

Concern flooded into Immy's voice. "Darling, what is it?"

Helen started by saying, "What would you do if . . .?" and then switched to a blunt statement. "Immy, I believe Nelson is a murderer."

She heard the intake of breath from Imogen. The background voices shrilled and giggled inanely.

"I know it must sound crazy spoken cold like this. You must have seen all that stuff in the papers about the Surrey Strangler, the man who killed those women. I think it's Nelson."

When—after another pause—the voice at the end of the phone responded, it was compassionate, but skeptical, with the tone of a mother attempting to coax the truth from her child. "Helen, how do you know?"

Helen made an effort to sound rational. Now that she'd confided her appalling suspicion she had to convince Immy that she was still sane. For a start she needed to convey something of Nelson's personality. She described how she had met him four years ago in the cinema queue for the latest James Bond, how he had offered to keep her place when the rain started tipping down, just when she was about to give up for the sake of her hair. He'd got drenched, along with the others who'd kept their positions, but she'd been able to shelter in the cinema entrance. And when they'd finally got their tickets he hadn't done the expected thing and used his gallantry as a ploy to sit beside her. (She was doing her best to be just to Nelson.) He hadn't forced the pace of their relationship at all. He'd found a seat a couple of rows behind her and they'd only spoken in the foyer as they came out. She'd caught his eye and smiled and only then had he asked her to join him for a coffee in the pub across the street. That was how tentative his first approach had been.

"He isn't dishy, or anything. I mean, he isn't ugly, but you wouldn't look twice at him. He's about average height, dark, with a dent in his nose from falling off his bike when he was a boy. What appealed to me was his personality. Immy, he gave me this wide-eyed look—his eyes are brown, by the way—like he'd just arrived from another planet and never seen a woman before. It made me quite dopey. From the beginning he treated me like someone special, as if I was the first girl he'd ever known. He still does. That's what makes this so creepy. He's never hurt me, or anything, never been violent in any way. If we have a row, as everyone does from time to time, he just goes out of the room until we both see how ridiculous it is to fight."

"What makes you think he . . .?" Immy declined to supply the rest.

"The dates, the places. Each of those women was killed within thirty miles of here. It's happened each time on a night when Nelson got in really late—I mean well after midnight. He spends ages in the bathroom showering—I hear the tank filling in the loft—and then he sleeps downstairs on the sofa. When I ask him about it in the morning he says he didn't want to disturb me after getting in so late."

"Do you ask him why he got in late?"

"Clients, he says. He's a sales rep for a firm that makes computer games. Sometimes he has to see people in the evenings."

"Does he tell you which client he's been with? Maybe you could check in some way."

"It's not so simple as that. He doesn't go in for talking about his work."

"And you say all the dates fit?"

"Yes."

"Listen, I never read things like that in the papers. How many women has this guy killed?"

"Three."

"It could be coincidence. Has Nelson been out other evenings when a woman wasn't killed?"

"Never so late. Generally he's back by eleven at the latest. And he hardly ever takes a shower before going to bed."

"But is that all you've got to go on? Just the dates? I mean, these poor women must have fought the guy who attacked them. They were raped as well as strangled, weren't they? Have you noticed scratches, marks, any signs?"

"There was a scratch down the side of his face a few months ago, but I can't say exactly when it got there. I didn't have these suspicions then. Nelson said he got clawed by a cat."

"A cat?"

"In a pub. He picked it up and it scratched him."

"Have you looked at his clothes? What about spots of blood, hairs and so on? Scent?"

"I tried to find his shirt last Wednesday, after that nurse was killed in Dorking. He got in terribly late, like the other times. Next morning when I heard on the radio what had happened, I looked in the laundry basket, feeling really sick at what I was doing, and found that the shirt he'd been wearing wasn't there. It wasn't in his room either. Nor were his underpants. I think he must have got rid of them somehow. They weren't in the rubbish sack. Immy, did you see the detective on the television news speaking about it? He said someone must be withholding information, someone who suspects that the man they live with could be this murderer. He said by remaining silent they could have the deaths of more women on their conscience. I've got to speak to them, haven't I?"

Imogen sidestepped the question. "You won't mind if I ask a personal question?"

"What is it? Go ahead."

"What's the sex like with Nelson?"

Helen had always found it difficult to talk about such things. If anyone but Imogen had asked her that question she would have slammed down the phone. "He's never tried to force me, if that's what you're getting at."

"But you do allow him to make love to you?"

She saw the drift. "I'm not frigid, for God's sake. I mean it was never *that* passionate, and when it happens it's sometimes more like a duty than a pleasure, or it is for me, but we do sleep together, yes."

"So the satisfaction isn't there?"

"Did I say that? I suppose it's true." Not for the first time, Helen found herself wondering whether she was partly to blame. She wasn't experienced or comfortable as a lover. She hadn't the confidence to be anything but passive. Since the latest episode she couldn't imagine herself wanting Nelson ever again.

Through the net curtains she could see the accountant who lived at the end house. He always got back from the city about this time. Several paces in the rear came his Vietnamese wife. Each day she walked to the station to meet him and trail respectfully home behind him, carrying his briefcase. Most couples' relationships aren't paraded so obviously.

"If you go to the police, that's the end of your marriage," Imogen said. "Even if he's totally innocent, the point is that you believed this ghastly thing was possible. That's a betrayal in itself."

Helen was silent.

"Do you really want my advice, love?"

"Immy, I do."

"You're sure he wouldn't hurt you?"

"He never has."

"Then I think you owe it to Nelson to talk to him."

"Tell him what I believe?"

"If I were faced with this, I hope I'd have the guts to do the same."

"They issued one of those photofit pictures," Helen said, shrinking from the advice. "I don't think it looks much like him apart from his eyes and hair."

"So you want to be certain, and the only way is to find out the truth from Nelson."

She wavered. "How can I say such a terrible thing to him?"

"You mean you'd rather say it to the police?"

Inwardly, Helen admitted the truth of this. Until Immy had suggested confronting Nelson, such a course of action had been too hideous even to contemplate. The most she had been prepared to do was to turn Nelson in. Faced with the biggest crisis in her life she had looked for the easy solution, the coward's way.

"Where is he right now?" Imogen asked.

"Out on the road somewhere. He should be back in the next hour or so."

"Then why don't you talk to him when he gets in? If he's innocent—and he could be—it's the only way to save your marriage, if that's what you want."

"I don't know if I can face it."

"You must, poppet, you must. You asked for my advice and that's it." Having delivered it, Immy steered the call to an end with a promise that she would phone back next day to find out what had happened. Helen thanked her and managed to say that they must meet sometime. She put down the phone.

It was seven-fifteen. Generally Nelson got in by eight. Immy had convinced her. Helen started rehearsing what she would say. She could broach it indirectly, claiming that she'd looked for his pink shirt with the red stripes—the one he'd been wearing Tuesday—to put in the washing machine. She could remind him that Tuesday was the night he'd got in really late. His responses might give him away. He might even be willing to talk about what had happened. If only it could be so simple. . . .

The hour of eight passed. It was getting dark, but she didn't draw the curtains. She stood waiting, staring out of the window. A red Toyota like Nelson's slowed as if to stop, then turned into the drive of one of the neighbors.

She went to make herself some tea and realized when she handled the warm pot that she'd already had two mugs since Immy's call. She'd be awash with the stuff. Instead she did something quite out of character by going to the cupboard where they kept the drinks and pouring herself a gin and tonic. With growing intimations of dread she took up her vigil at the window again.

Another hour went by.

For distraction she dusted the surfaces in the front room, still in darkness, looking out intermittently for the gleam of headlights in the street. She dusted everything twice, moving the ornaments by touch, like a blind person.

It must have been getting on for ten when she heard the heavy tread of a man in the street. She couldn't see enough to tell if it was Nelson, but her pulse raced faster when she saw the shape of someone coming up the garden path. An explanation leapt into her brain: the car had broken down and he'd had to come home by train.

She waited for the sound of his key in the latch. What she heard instead was the doorbell. He was never without his key.

The light in the hall dazzled her when she switched it on. She blinked as she opened the door.

"Sorry to disturb you, Helen," the man on the doorstep said. He was a neighbor, Gerald. She stared at him blankly.

"I'm slightly puzzled," he told her. "Sally isn't back. She's always in by now. I wondered if she said anything to you about what she was doing tonight."

Her thoughts had been so focused on Nelson that it was an effort to register Sally's existence, let alone her movements that day. Finally she succeeded in saying, "I thought she was modeling at the tech. I saw her go past at the usual time."

"Have you spoken to her at all today?"

"Er—no."

"Maybe she's gone for a drink with somebody in the class," said Gerald. "I wouldn't think twice about it normally, but you can't be too careful these days, you know?"

She gave a nod. She knew what was on his mind. There was no need to say more.

Gerald repeated his apology and left. After she'd closed the door, Helen wondered whether she should have offered to babysit, giving Gerald a chance to walk down to the tech and inquire about Sally. Maybe that had been his real reason for calling. She could have gone after him, but she didn't want to be out when Nelson got back. Besides, she told herself in justification, if Sally *was* having a drink with someone from the class, she might not be overjoyed at her husband turning up. Not that Sally was wayward; simply that she'd balk at being treated as if she were in moral danger.

If the unspeakable had happened, and Sally had met the strangler, what could Gerald do? What could anyone do?

More than three hours had passed since Helen had been on the point of calling the police about Nelson. The appalling thought occurred to her that if Sally had met Nelson as she was leaving the tech, she might easily have accepted a lift. Sally knew Nelson. She'd assume she was safe with him. The words of that detective on the television taunted Helen. *"Someone out there knows this man. By remaining silent, they put more women in danger. If they have any conscience at all they should come forward and prevent another murder."*

Instead of listening to Immy, she should have spoken to the police. Immy had been wrong, catastrophically wrong. She hadn't considered the possibility that if Nelson was the strangler he might kill again tonight.

But it was wrong to blame Immy. The responsibility was her own. She, Helen, should have sensed the dangerous flaw in the advice.

Nelson finally got in at ten to one. He hadn't abandoned the car, apparently. He closed the garage doors quietly—furtively, Helen thought—and let himself in. He was clearly startled when she turned on the light.

"I thought you'd be in bed."

"I thought I'd wait," she said in a flat voice.

"Is something the matter?"

"You tell me, Nelson. Look at you. Your hand is bleeding."

Two long scratches were scored across the back of his right hand. He covered them with his left. His tie was twisted askew and there were buttons missing from his shirtfront. "I need a drink," he said.

She followed him into the front room and watched him help himself from the whiskey bottle.

"You haven't even pulled the curtains," he remarked. It seemed to matter to him that they should not be seen from the street. His right hand went up to the cord and tugged at it, displaying the scratches.

Helen said, "I was looking out for you. I didn't expect you to be so late."

"I can't predict what's going to happen."

She found herself saying, "Maybe a psychiatrist could."

The hunted look that was already in Nelson's eyes gave way

first to horror, then, unexpectedly, to tears. He bowed his face and covered it with his hands. He was sobbing.

Helen had no need of her strategies, the questions about the times he'd been late before, and the missing clothes. She had tapped the truth.

And now she had to find out all of it. She still felt safe with him; some instinct told her that he wouldn't attack her, whatever he'd done to those other women. "Where is she, Nelson? Where did you leave her?"

He said in a broken voice, "The river, in the park."

"Ashdown Park?"

He nodded, still sobbing. The local park was just a ten-minute walk away. Sally's children played there often.

"Is she dead?"

"Yes." After a pause he added, "You're right—I'm mentally ill. I was locked up for six years before I met you. I should have told you."

Stunned, she still knew that he was telling the truth. She understood why he'd so often stared at her as if she belonged to another species. She'd allowed herself to be flattered instead of sensing what that wide-eyed regard really meant.

Nelson said, "I'm going to call the police. I've been wanting to call them. Believe me, I planned to call them. That's why I did it so close to home tonight. I was making sure they'd get me, if you can understand."

She took the phone to him and waited while he dialed the number and spoke. He told them who he was and where he lived and what he had done. Then he replaced the phone and told Helen, "They're sending a car."

She said, "I knew it was you. I should have turned you in. I'm always going to blame myself. How could you, Nelson, knowing she had four young children?"

He looked at her without a spark of comprehension. "Who?"

"Sally."

"Sally?"

"Sally next door."

"What are you talking about? It wasn't Sally," he said. "It was some north country woman staying in the King's Arms. That's where I picked her up."

Helen registered first that Sally was spared; she must after all have gone out with some people from the art class. Then she played Nelson's words over in her mind. "This woman—what did she look like?"

"About your age. Blond hair and glasses. She didn't know the town. She was something in television. Said she was at a loose end tonight. She'd planned to drop in on an old college friend, only it wasn't convenient."

JOYCE CAROL OATES

THE MODEL

There can be little doubt that Joyce Carol Oates is one of the half-dozen best writers in America today. Since her first book of short stories was published in 1963 she has enthralled (and sometimes appalled) two generations of readers with her un-flinching view of the human condition. Novels like them *(1969),* Bellefleur *(1980),* You Must Remember This *(1987), and* Because It Is Bitter, and Because It Is My Heart *(1990) are only a few of the high points in her vast body of work. Oates's first appearance in a mystery anthology came in 1973 when Marie Reno included her novelette "Norman and the Killer" in* A Treasury of Modern Mysteries. *Since then she has appeared in mystery magazines and anthologies, and published* Mysteries of Winterthurn *(1984), a novel concerning three cases in the career of late-nineteenth-century detective Xavier Kilgarvan. In the novelette that follows, she shows us how the suspense story can be raised to the level of true literature. I believe it is a story that will rank with her early classic, "Where Are You Going, Where Have You Been?"*

1. The Approach of Mr. Starr

Had he stepped out of nowhere, or had he been watching her for some time, even more than he'd claimed, and for a different purpose?—she shivered to think that, yes, probably, she had many times glimpsed him in the village, or in the park, without really seeing him: him, and the long gleaming black limousine she would not have known to associate with him even had she noticed him: the man who called himself Mr. Starr.

As, each day, her eyes passed rapidly and lightly over any number of people both familiar to her and strangers, blurred as in the background of a film in which the foreground is the essential reality, the very point of the film.

She was seventeen. It was in fact the day after her birthday, a bright gusty January day, and she'd been running in the late afternoon, after school, in the park overlooking the ocean, and she'd just turned to head toward home, pausing to wipe her face, adjust her damp cotton headband, feeling the accelerated strength of her heartbeat and the pleasant ache of her leg muscles: and she glanced up, shy, surprised, and there he stood, a man she had never knowingly seen before. He was smiling at her, his smile broad and eager, hopeful, and he stood in such a way, leaning lightly on a cane, as to block her way on the path; yet tentatively too, with a gentlemanly, deferential air, so as to suggest that he meant no threat. When he spoke, his voice sounded hoarse as if from disuse. "Excuse me!—hello! Young lady! I realize that this is abrupt, and an intrusion on your privacy, but I am an artist, and I am looking for a model, and I wonder if you might be interested in posing for me? Only here, I mean, in the park—in full daylight! I am willing to pay, per hour—"

Sybil stared at the man. Like most young people she was incapable of estimating ages beyond thirty-five—this strange person might have been in his forties, or well into his fifties. His thin, lank hair was the color of antique silver—perhaps he was even older. His skin was luridly pale, grainy, and rough; he wore glasses with lenses so darkly tinted as to suggest the kind of glasses worn by the blind; his clothes were plain, dark, conservative—a tweed jacket that fitted him loosely, a shirt buttoned tight to the neck, and no tie, highly polished black leather shoes in an outmoded style. There was something hesitant, even convalescent in his manner, as if, like numerous others in this coastal Southern California town with its population of the retired, the elderly, and the infirm, he had learned by experience to carry

122

himself with care; he could not entirely trust the earth to support him. His features were refined, but worn; subtly distorted, as if seen through wavy glass, or water.

Sybil didn't like it that she couldn't see the man's eyes. Except to know that he was squinting at her, hard. The skin at the corners of his eyes was whitely puckered as if, in his time, he'd done a good deal of squinting and smiling.

Quickly, but politely, Sybil murmured, "No, thank you, I can't."

She was turning away, but still the man spoke, apologetically, "I realize this is a—surprise, but, you see, I don't know how else to make inquiries. I've only just begun sketching in the park, and—"

"Sorry!"

Sybil turned, began to run, not hurriedly, by no means in a panic, but at her usual measured pace, her head up and her arms swinging at her sides. She was, for all that she looked younger than her seventeen years, not an easily frightened girl, and she was not frightened now; but her face burned with embarrassment. She hoped that no one in the park who knew her had been watching—Glencoe was a small town, and the high school was about a mile away. Why had that preposterous man approached *her?*

He was calling after her, probably waving his cane after her—she didn't dare look back. "I'll be here tomorrow! My name is Starr! Don't judge me too quickly—please! I'm true to my word! My name is Starr! I'll pay you, per hour"—and here he cited an exorbitant sum, nearly twice what Sybil made baby-sitting or working as a librarian's assistant at the branch library near her home, when she could get hired.

She thought, astonished, He must be mad!

2. The Temptation

No sooner had Sybil Blake escaped from the man who called himself Starr, running up Buena Vista Boulevard to Santa Clara, up Santa Clara to Meridian, and so to home, than she began to consider that Mr. Starr's offer was, if preposterous, very tempting. She had never modeled of course, but, in art class at the high school, some of her classmates had modeled, fully clothed, just sitting or standing about in ordinary poses, and she and others had sketched them, or tried to—it was really not so easy as it might seem, sketching the lineaments of the human figure; it was still more difficult, sketching an individual's face. But modeling, in itself, was effortless, once you overcame the embarrassment of being stared at. It was, you might argue, a morally neutral activity.

What had Mr. Starr said—*Only here, in the park. In full daylight. I'm true to my word!*

And Sybil needed money, for she was saving for college; she was hoping too to attend a summer music institute at U.C. Santa Barbara. (She was a voice student, and she'd been encouraged by her choir director at the high school to get good professional training.) Her Aunt Lora Dell Blake, with whom she lived, and had lived since the age of two years eight months, was willing to pay her way—was determined to pay her way—but Sybil felt uneasy about accepting money from Aunt Lora, who worked as a physical therapist at a medical facility in Glencoe, and whose salary, at the top of the pay structure available to her as a state employee, was still modest by California standards. Sybil reasoned that her Aunt Lora Dell could not be expected to support her forever.

A long time ago, Sybil had lost her parents, both of them together, in one single cataclysmic hour, when she'd been too young to comprehend what Death was, or was said to be. They had died in a boating accident on Lake Champlain, Sybil's mother at the age of twenty-six, Sybil's father at the age of thirty-one, very attractive young people, a "popular couple" as Aunt Lora spoke of them, choosing her words with care, and saying very little more. *For why ask,* Aunt Lora seemed to be warning Sybil,—*you will only make yourself cry.* As soon as she could manage the move, and as soon as Sybil was placed permanently in her care, Aunt Lora had come to California, to this sunwashed coastal town midway between Santa Monica and Santa Barbara. Glencoe was less conspicuously affluent than either of these towns, but, with its palm-lined streets, its sunny placidity, and its openness to the ocean, it was the very antithesis, as Aunt Lora said, of Wellington, Vermont, where the Blakes had lived for generations. (After their move to California, Lora Dell Blake had formally adopted Sybil as her child: thus Sybil's name was Blake, as her mother's had been. If asked what her father's name had been, Sybil would have had to think before recalling, dimly, "Conte.") Aunt Lora spoke so negatively of New England in general and Vermont in particular, Sybil felt no nostalgia for it; she had no sentimental desire to visit her birthplace, not even to see her parents' graves. From Aunt Lora's stories, Sybil had the idea that Vermont was damp and cold twelve months of the year, and frigidly, impossibly cold in winter; its wooded mountains were unlike the beautiful snow-capped mountains of the West, and cast shadows upon its small, cramped, depopulated, and impoverished old towns. Aunt Lora, a transplanted New Englander, was vehement in her praise of California—"With the Pacific Ocean to the west," she said, "it's like a room with one wall missing. Your instinct is to look out, not back; and it's a good instinct."

Lora Dell Blake was the sort of person who delivers statements with an air of inviting contradiction. But, tall, rangy, restless, belligerent, she was not the sort of person most people wanted to contradict.

Indeed, Aunt Lora had never encouraged Sybil to ask questions about her dead parents, or about the tragic accident that had killed them; if she had photographs, snapshots, mementos of life back in Wellington, Vermont, they were safely hidden away, and Sybil had not seen them. "It would just be too painful," she told Sybil, "—for us both." The remark was both a plea and a warning.

Of course, Sybil avoided the subject.

She prepared carefully chosen words, should anyone happen to ask her why she was living with her aunt, and not her parents; or, at least, one of her parents. But—this was Southern California, and very few of Sybil's classmates were living with the set of parents with whom they'd begun. No one asked.

An orphan?—I'm not an orphan, Sybil would say. *I was never an orphan because my Aunt Lora was always there.*

I was two years old when it happened, the accident.
No, I don't remember.
But no one asked.

Sybil told her Aunt Lora nothing about the man in the park—the man who called himself Starr—she'd put him out of her mind entirely and yet, in bed that night, drifting into sleep, she found herself thinking suddenly of him, and seeing him again, vividly. That silver hair, those gleaming black shoes. His eyes hidden behind dark glasses. How tempting, his offer!—though there was no question of Sybil accepting it. Absolutely not.

Still, Mr. Starr seemed harmless. Well-intentioned. An eccentric, of course, but *interesting*. She supposed he had money, if he could offer her so much to model for him. There was something *not contemporary* about him. The set of his head and shoulders. That air about him of gentlemanly reserve, courtesy—even as he'd made his outlandish request. In Glencoe, in the past several years, there had been a visible increase in homeless persons and derelicts, especially in the oceanside park, but Mr. Starr was certainly not one of these.

Then Sybil realized, as if a door, hitherto locked, had swung open of its own accord, that she'd seen Mr. Starr before . . . somewhere. In the park, where she ran most afternoons for an hour? In downtown Glencoe? On the street?—in the public library? In the vicinity of Glencoe Senior High School?—in the school itself, in the auditorium? Sybil summoned up a memory as if by an act of physical exertion: the school choir, of which she was a member, had been rehearsing Handel's *Messiah* the previous month for their annual Christmas pageant, and Sybil had sung her solo part, a demanding part for contralto voice, and the choir director had praised her in front of the others . . . and she'd seemed to see, dimly, a man, a stranger, seated at the very rear of the auditorium, his features distinct but his gray hair striking, and wasn't this man miming applause, clapping silently? *There. At the rear, on the aisle.* It frequently happened that visitors dropped by rehearsals—parents or relatives of choir members, colleagues of the music director. So no one took special notice of the stranger sitting unobtrusively at the rear of the auditorium. He wore dark, conservative clothes of the kind to attract no attention, and dark glasses hid his eyes. But there he was. *For Sybil Blake. He'd come for Sybil.* But, at the time, Sybil had not seen.

Nor had she seen the man leave. Slipping quietly out of his seat, walking with a just perceptible limp, leaning on his cane.

3. The Proposition

Sybil had no intention of seeking out Mr. Starr, nor even of looking around for him, but, the following afternoon, as she was headed home after her run, there, suddenly, the man was—taller than she recalled, looming large, his dark glasses winking in the sunlight, and his pale lips stretched in a tentative smile. He wore his clothes of the previous day except he'd set on his head a sporty plaid golfing cap that gave him a rakish, yet wistful, air, and he'd tied, as if in haste, a rumpled cream-colored silk scarf around his neck. He was standing on the path in approximately the same place as before, and leaning on his cane; on a bench close by were what appeared to be his art supplies, in a canvas duffel bag of the sort students carried. "Why, hello!" he said, shyly but eagerly, "—I didn't dare hope you would come back, but—" his smile widened as if on the verge of desperation, the puckered skin at the corners of his eyes tightened, "I *hoped.*"

After running, Sybil always felt good: strength flowed into her legs, arms, lungs. She was a delicate-boned girl, since infancy prone to respiratory infections, but such vigorous exercise had made her strong in recent years; and with physical confidence had come a growing confidence in herself. She laughed, lightly, at this strange man's words, and merely shrugged, and said, "Well—this *is* my park, after all." Mr. Starr nodded eagerly, as if any response from her, any words at all, was of enormous interest. "Yes, yes," he said, "—I can see that. Do you live close by?"

Sybil shrugged. It was none of his business, was it, where she lived? "Maybe," she said.

"And your—name?" He stared at her, hopefully, adjusting his glasses more firmly on his nose. "—My name is Starr."

"My name is—Blake."

Mr. Starr blinked, and smiled, as if uncertain whether this might be a joke. " 'Blake'—? An unusual name for a girl," he said.

Sybil laughed again, feeling her face heat. She decided not to correct the misunderstanding.

Today, prepared for the encounter, having anticipated it for hours, Sybil was distinctly less uneasy than she'd been the day before: the man had a business proposition to make to her, that was all. And the park *was* an open, public, safe place, as familiar to her as the small neat yard of her Aunt Lora's house.

So, when Mr. Starr repeated his offer, Sybil said, yes, she was interested after all; she did need money, she was saving for college. "For college?—really? So young?" Mr. Starr said, with an air of surprise. Sybil shrugged, as if the remark didn't require any reply. "I suppose, here in California, young people grow up quickly," Mr. Starr said. He'd gone to get his sketch pad, to show Sybil his work, and Sybil turned the pages with polite interest, as Mr. Starr chattered. He was, he said, an "amateur artist"—the very epitome of the "amateur"—with no delusions regarding his talent, but a strong belief that the world is redeemed by art—"And the world, you know, being profane, and steeped in wickedness, requires constant, ceaseless redemption." He believed that the artist "bears witness" to this fact; and that art can be a "conduit of emotion" where the heart is empty. Sybil, leafing through the sketches, paid little attention to Mr. Starr's tumble of words; she was struck by the feathery, uncertain, somehow *worshipful* detail in the drawings, which, to her eye, were not so bad as she'd expected, though by no means of professional quality. As she looked at them, Mr. Starr came to look over her shoulder, embarrassed, and excited, his shadow falling over the pages. The ocean, the waves, the wide rippled beach as seen from the bluff—palm trees, hibiscus, flowers—a World War II memorial in the park—mothers with young children—solitary figures huddled on park benches—bicyclists—joggers—several pages of joggers: Mr. Starr's work was ordinary, even commonplace, but certainly earnest. Sybil saw herself amid the joggers, or a figure she guessed must be herself, a young girl with shoulder-length dark hair held off her face by a headband, in running pants and a sweatshirt, caught in mid-stride, legs and swinging arms caught in motion—it *was* herself, but so clumsily executed, the profile so smudged, no one would have known. Still, Sybil felt her face grow warmer, and she sensed Mr. Starr's anticipation like a withheld breath.

Sybil did not think it quite right for her, aged seventeen, to pass judgment on the talent of a middle-aged man, so she merely murmured something vague and polite and positive; and Mr. Starr, taking the sketch pad from her, said, "Oh, I *know*—I'm not very good, yet. But I propose to try." He smiled at her, and took out a freshly laundered white handkerchief, and dabbed at his forehead, and said, "Do you have any questions about posing for me, or shall we begin?—we'll have at least three hours of daylight, today."

"Three hours!" Sybil exclaimed. "That long?"

"If you get uncomfortable," Mr. Starr said quickly, "—we'll simply stop, wherever we are." Seeing that Sybil was frowning, he added, eagerly, "We'll take breaks every now and then, I promise. And, and—" seeing that Sybil was still indecisive, "—I'll pay you for a full hour's fee, for any part of an hour." Still Sybil stood, wondering if, after all, she should be agreeing to this, without her Aunt Lora, or anyone, knowing: wasn't there something just faintly odd about Mr. Starr, and about his willingness to pay her so much for doing so little? And wasn't there something troubling (however flattering) about his particular interest in her? Assuming Sybil was correct, and he'd been watching her . . . aware of her . . . for at least a month. "I'll be happy to pay you in advance, Blake."

The name Blake sounded very odd in this stranger's mouth. Sybil had never before been called by her last name only.

Sybil laughed nervously, and said, "You don't have to pay me in advance—thanks!"

So Sybil Blake, against her better judgment, became a model, for Mr. Starr.

And, despite her self-consciousness, and her intermittent sense that there was something ludicrous in the enterprise, as about

Mr. Starr's intense, fussy, self-important manner as he sketched her (he was a perfectionist, or wanted to give that impression: crumpling a half-dozen sheets of paper, breaking out new charcoal sticks, before he began a sketch that pleased him), the initial session was easy, effortless. "What I want to capture," Mr. Starr said, "—is, beyond your beautiful profile, Blake,—and you *are* a beautiful child!—the brooding quality of the ocean. That look to it, d'you see?—of it having consciousness of a kind, actually thinking. Yes, *brooding!*"

Sybil, squinting down at the white-capped waves, the rhythmic crashing surf, the occasional surfers riding their boards with their remarkable amphibian dexterity, thought that the ocean was anything but *brooding*.

"Why are you smiling, Blake?" Mr. Starr asked, pausing. "Is something funny?—am *I* funny?"

Quickly Sybil said, "Oh, no, Mr. Starr, of course not."

"But I *am*, I'm sure," he said happily. "And if you find me so, please *do* laugh!"

Sybil found herself laughing, as if rough fingers were tickling her. She thought of how it might have been . . . had she had a father, and a mother: her own family, as she'd been meant to have.

Mr. Starr was squatting now on the grass close by and peering up at Sybil with an expression of extreme concentration. The charcoal stick in his fingers moved rapidly. "The ability to *laugh*," he said, "is the ability to *live*—the two are synonymous. You're too young to understand that right now, but one day you will." Sybil shrugged, wiping her eyes. Mr. Starr was talking grandly. "The world is fallen and profane—the opposite of 'sacred,' you know, *is* 'profane.' It requires ceaseless vigilance—ceaseless redemption. The artist is one who redeems by restoring the world's innocence, where he can. The artist gives, but does not take away, nor even supplant."

Sybil said, skeptically, "But you want to make money with your drawings, don't you?"

Mr. Starr seemed genuinely shocked. "Oh, my, no. Adamantly, *no*."

Sybil persisted, "Well, most people would. I mean, most people need to. If they have any talent"—she was speaking with surprising bluntness, an almost childlike audacity—"they need to sell it, somehow."

As if he'd been caught out in a crime, Mr. Starr began to stammer apologetically, "It's true, Blake, I—I am not like most people, I suppose. I've inherited some money—not a fortune, but enough to live on comfortably for the rest of my life. I've been traveling abroad," he said, vaguely, "—and, in my absence, interest accumulated."

Sybil asked doubtfully, "You don't have any regular profession?"

Mr. Starr laughed, startled. Up close, his teeth were chunky and irregular, slightly stained, like aged ivory piano keys. "But, dear child," he said, *"this* is my profession—'redeeming the world'!"

And he fell to sketching Sybil with renewed enthusiasm.

Minutes passed. Long minutes. Sybil felt a mild ache between her shoulder blades. A mild uneasiness in her chest. *Mr. Starr is mad. Is Mr. Starr 'mad'?* Behind her, on the path, people were passing by, there were joggers, bicyclists—Mr. Starr, lost in a trance of concentration, paid them not the slightest heed. Sybil wondered if anyone knew her, and was taking note of this peculiar event. Or was she, herself, making too much of it? She decided she would tell her Aunt Lora about Mr. Starr that evening, tell Aunt Lora frankly how much he was paying her. She both respected and feared her aunt's judgment: in Sybil's imagination, in that unexamined sphere of being we call the imagination, Lora Dell Blake had acquired the authority of both Sybil's deceased parents.

Yes, she would tell Aunt Lora.

After only an hour and forty minutes, when Sybil appeared to be growing restless and sighed several times, unconsciously, Mr. Starr suddenly declared the session over. He had, he said, three promising sketches, and he didn't want to exhaust her, or himself. She *was* coming back tomorrow—?

"I don't know," Sybil said. "Maybe."

Sybil protested, though not very adamantly, when Mr. Starr paid her the full amount, for three hours' modeling. He paid her in cash, out of his wallet—an expensive kidskin wallet brimming with bills. Sybil thanked him, deeply embarrassed, and eager to escape. Oh, there *was* something shameful about the transaction!

Up close, she was able—almost—to see Mr. Starr's eyes through the dark-tinted lenses of his glasses. Some delicacy of tact made her glance away quickly but she had an impression of kindness—gentleness.

Sybil took the money, and put it in her pocket, and turned, to hurry away. With no mind for who might hear him, Mr. Starr called after her, "You see, Blake?—Starr is true to his word. Always!"

4. Is the Omission of Truth a Lie, or Only an Omission?

"Well!—tell me how things went with *you* today, Sybil!" Lora Dell Blake said, with such an air of bemused exasperation, Sybil understood that, as so often, Aunt Lora had something to say that really couldn't wait—her work at the Glencoe Medical Center provided her with a seemingly inexhaustible supply of comical and outrageous anecdotes. So, deferring to Aunt Lora, as they prepared supper together as usual, and sat down to eat it, Sybil was content to listen, and to laugh.

For it *was* funny, if outrageous too—the latest episode in the ongoing folly at the Medical Center.

Lora Dell Blake, in her late forties, was a tall, lanky, restless woman; with close-cropped graying hair; sand-colored eyes and skin; a generous spirit, but a habit of sarcasm. Though she claimed to love Southern California—"You don't know what paradise is, unless you're from somewhere else"—she seemed in fact an awkwardly transplanted New Englander, with expectations and a sense of personal integrity, or intransigence, quite out of place here. She was fond of saying she did not suffer fools gladly, and so it was. Overqualified for her position at the Glencoe Medical Center, she'd had no luck in finding work elsewhere, partly because she did not want to leave Glencoe and "uproot" Sybil while Sybil was still in high school; and partly because her interviews were invariably disasters—Lora Dell Blake was incapable of being, or even seeming, docile, tractable, "feminine," hypocritical.

Lora was not Sybil's sole living relative—there were Blakes, and Contes, back in Vermont—but Lora had discouraged visitors to the small stucco bungalow on Meridian Street, in Glencoe, California; she had not in fact troubled to reply to letters or cards since, having been granted custody of her younger sister's daughter, at the time of what she called "the tragedy," she'd picked up and moved across the continent, to a part of the country she knew nothing about—"My intention is to erase the past, for the child's sake," she said, "and to start a new life."

And: "For the child, for poor little Sybil—I would make any sacrifice."

Sybil, who loved her aunt very much, had the vague idea that there had been, many years ago, protests, queries, telephone calls—but that Aunt Lora had dealt with them all, and really had made a new and "uncomplicated" life for them. Aunt Lora was one of those personalities, already strong, that is strengthened, and empowered, by being challenged; she seemed to take an actual zest in confrontation, whether with her own relatives or her employers at the Medical Center—anyone who presumed to tell her what to do. She was especially protective of Sybil, since, as she often said, they had no one but each other.

Which was true. Aunt Lora had seen to that.

Though Sybil had been adopted by her aunt, there was never any pretense that she was anything but Lora's niece, not her daughter. Nor did most people, seeing the two together, noting their physical dissimilarities, make that mistake.

So it happened that Sybil Blake grew up knowing virtually nothing about her Vermont background except its general tragic outline: her knowledge of her mother and father, the precise circumstances of their deaths, was as vague and unexamined in her consciousness as a childhood fairy tale. For whenever, as a little girl, Sybil would ask her aunt about these things, Aunt Lora responded with hurt, or alarm, or reproach, or, most disturbingly, anxiety. Her eyes might flood with tears—Aunt Lora, who never cried. She might take Sybil's hands in both her own, and squeeze them tightly, and looking Sybil in the eyes, say, in a quiet, commanding voice, "But, darling, *you don't want to know.*"

So too, that evening, when, for some reason, Sybil brought up the subject, asking Aunt Lora how, again, exactly, *had* her parents died, Aunt Lora looked at her in surprise; and, for a long moment, rummaging in the pockets of her shirt for a pack of cigarettes that wasn't there (Aunt Lora had given up smoking the previous month, for perhaps the fifth time), it seemed almost that Lora herself did not remember.

"Sybil, honey—why are you asking? I mean, why *now?*"

"I don't know," Sybil said evasively. "I guess—I'm just asking."

"Nothing happened to you at school, did it?"

Sybil could not see how this question related to her own, but she said, politely, "No, Aunt Lora. Of course not."

"It's just that out of nowhere—I can't help but wonder *why,*" Aunt Lora was frowning, "—you should ask."

Aunt Lora regarded Sybil with worried eyes: a look of such suffocating familiarity that, for a moment, Sybil felt as if a band were tightening around her chest, making it impossible to breathe. *Why is my wanting to know a test of my love for you?— why do you do this, Aunt Lora, every time?* She said, an edge of anger to her voice, "I was seventeen years old last week, Aunt Lora. I'm not a child any longer."

Aunt Lora laughed, startled. "Certainly you're not a child!"

Aunt Lora then sighed, and, in a characteristic gesture, meaning both impatience and a dutiful desire to please, ran both hands rapidly through her hair and began to speak. She assured Sybil that there was little to know, really. The accident—the tragedy—had happened so long ago. "Your mother, Melanie, was twenty-six years old at the time—a beautiful sweet-natured young woman, with eyes like yours, cheekbones like yours, pale wavy hair. Your father, George Conte, was thirty-one years old— a promising young lawyer, in his father's firm—an attractive, ambitious man—" And here as in the past Aunt Lora paused, as if in the very act of summoning up this long-dead couple, she had forgotten them; and was simply repeating a story, a family tale, like one of the more extreme of her tales of the Glencoe Medical Center, worn smooth by countless tellings.

"A boating accident—Fourth of July—" Sybil coaxed, "—and I was with you, and—"

"You were with me, and Grandma, at the cottage—you were just a little girl!" Aunt Lora said, blinking tears from her eyes, "—and it was almost dusk, and time for the fireworks to start. Mommy and Daddy were out in Daddy's speedboat—they'd been across the lake, at the Club—"

"And they started back across the lake—Lake Champlain—"

"—Lake Champlain, of course: it's beautiful, but treacherous, if a storm comes up suddenly—"

"And Daddy was at the controls of the boat—"

"—and, somehow, they capsized. And drowned. A rescue boat went out immediately, but it was too late." Aunt Lora's mouth turned hard. Her eyes glistening with tears, as if defiantly. "They drowned."

Sybil's heart was beating painfully. She was certain there must be more, yet she herself could remember nothing—not even herself, that two-year-old child, waiting for Mommy and Daddy who were never to arrive. Her memory of her mother and father was vague, dim, featureless, like a dream that, even as it seems about to drift into consciousness, retreats farther into darkness. She said, in a whisper, "It was an accident. No one was to blame."

Aunt Lora chose her words with care. "No one was to blame."

There was a pause. Sybil looked at her aunt, who was not now looking at her. How lined, even leathery, the older woman's face was getting!—all her life she'd been reckless, indifferent, about sun, wind, weather, and now, in her late forties, she might have been a decade older. Sybil said, tentatively, "No one *was* to blame—?"

"Well, if you must know," Aunt Lora said, "—there was evidence he'd been drinking. They'd been drinking. At the Club."

Sybil could not have been more shocked had Aunt Lora reached over and pinched the back of her hand. "Drinking—?" She had never heard this part of the story before.

Aunt Lora continued, grimly, "But not enough, probably, to

have made a difference." Again she paused. She was not looking at Sybil. "Probably."

Sybil, stunned, could not think of anything further to say, or to ask.

Aunt Lora was on her feet, pacing. Her close-cropped hair was disheveled and her manner fiercely contentious, as if she were arguing her case before an invisible audience as Sybil looked on. "What fools! I tried to tell her! 'Popular' couple—'attractive' couple—lots of friends—too many friends! That Goddamned Champlain Club, where everyone drank too much! All that money, and privilege! And what good did it do! She—Melanie— so proud of being asked to join—proud of marrying *him*— throwing her life away! That's what it came to, in the end. I'd warned her it was dangerous—playing with fire—but would she listen? Would either of them listen? To Lora?—to *me*? When you're that age, so ignorant, you think you will live forever—you can throw your life away—"

Sybil felt ill, suddenly. She walked swiftly out of the room, shut the door to her own room, stood in the dark, beginning to cry.

So that was it, the secret. The tawdry little secret—drinking, drunkenness—behind the "tragedy."

With characteristic tact, Aunt Lora did not knock on Sybil's door, but left her alone for the remainder of the night.

Only after Sybil was in bed, and the house darkened, did she realize she'd forgotten to tell her aunt about Mr. Starr—he'd slipped her mind entirely. And the money he'd pressed into her hand, now in her bureau drawer, rolled up neatly beneath her underwear, as if hidden. . . .

Sybil thought, guiltily, I can tell her tomorrow.

5. The Hearse

Crouched in front of Sybil Blake, eagerly sketching her likeness, Mr. Starr was saying, in a quick, rapturous voice, "Yes, yes, like that!—yes! Your face uplifted to the sun like a blossoming flower! Just so!" And: "There are only two or three eternal questions, Blake, which, like the surf, repeat themselves endlessly: 'Why are we here?'—'Where have we come from, and where are we going?'—'Is there purpose to the Universe, or merely chance?' These questions the artist seems to express in the images he knows." And: "Dear child, I wish you would tell me about yourself. Just a little!"

As if, in the night, some changes had come upon her, some new resolve, Sybil had fewer misgivings about modeling for Mr. Starr this afternoon. It was as if they knew each other well, somehow: Sybil was reasonably certain that Mr. Starr was not a sexual pervert, nor even a madman of a more conventional sort; she'd glimpsed his sketches of her, which were fussy, overworked, and smudged, but not bad as likenesses. The man's murmurous chatter was comforting in a way, hypnotic as the surf, no longer quite so embarrassing—for he talked, most of the time, not with her but at her, and there was no need to reply. In a way, Mr. Starr reminded Sybil of her Aunt Lora, when she launched into one of her comical anecdotes about the Glencoe Medical Center. Aunt Lora was more entertaining than Mr. Starr, but Mr. Starr was more idealistic.

His optimism was simpleminded, maybe. But it *was* optimistic.

For this second modeling session, Mr. Starr had taken Sybil to a corner of the park where they were unlikely to be disturbed. He'd asked her to remove her headband, and to sit on a bench with her head dropping back, her eyes partly shut, her face uplifted to the sun—an uncomfortable pose at first, until, lulled by the crashing surf below, and Mr. Starr's monologue, Sybil began to feel oddly peaceful, floating.

Yes, in the night some change had come upon her. She could not comprehend its dimensions, nor even its tone. She'd fallen asleep crying bitterly but had awakened feeling—what? Vulnerable, somehow. And wanting to be so. *Uplifted. Like a blossoming flower.*

That morning, Sybil had forgotten another time to tell her Aunt Lora about Mr. Starr, and the money she was making— such a generous amount, and for so little effort! She shrank from considering how her aunt might respond, for her aunt was mistrustful of strangers, and particularly of men. . . . Sybil rea-

soned that, when she did tell Aunt Lora, that evening, or tomorrow morning, she would make her understand that there
was something kindly and trusting and almost childlike about
Mr. Starr. You could laugh at him, but laughter was somehow
inappropriate.

As if, though middle-aged, he had been away somewhere, se-
questered, protected, out of the adult world. Innocent and, himself, vulnerable.

Today too he'd eagerly offered to pay Sybil in advance for
modeling, and, another time, Sybil had declined. She would not
have wanted to tell Mr. Starr that, were she paid in advance, she
might be tempted to cut the session even shorter than otherwise.

Mr. Starr was saying, hesitantly, "Blake?—can you tell me
about—" and here he paused, as if drawing a random, inspired
notion out of nowhere "—your mother?"

Sybil hadn't been paying close attention to Mr. Starr. Now she
opened her eyes and looked directly at him.

Mr. Starr was perhaps not so old as she'd originally thought,
nor as old as he behaved. His face was a handsome face, but
oddly roughened—the skin like sandpaper. Very sallow, sickly
pale. A faint scar on his forehead above his left eye, the shape of
a fish hook, or a question mark. Or was it a birthmark?—or,
even less romantically, some sort of skin blemish? Maybe his
roughened, pitted skin was the result of teenaged acne, nothing
more.

His tentative smile bared chunky damp teeth.

Today Mr. Starr was bareheaded, and his thin, fine, uncannily
silver hair was stirred by the wind. He wore plain, nondescript
clothes, a shirt too large for him, a khaki-colored jacket or smock
with rolled-up sleeves. At close range, Sybil could see his eyes
through the tinted lenses of his glasses: they were small, deep-
set, intelligent, glistening. The skin beneath was pouched and
shadowed, as if bruised.

Sybil shivered, peering so directly into Mr. Starr's eyes. As into
another's soul, when she was unprepared.

Sybil swallowed, and said, slowly, "My mother is . . . not living."

A curious way of speaking!—for why not say, candidly, in normal usage, *My mother is dead.*

For a long painful moment Sybil's words hovered in the air between them; as if Mr. Starr, discountenanced by his own blunder, seemed not to want to hear.

He said, quickly, apologetically, "Oh—I see. I'm sorry."

Sybil had been posing in the sun, warmly mesmerized by the sun, the surf, Mr. Starr's voice, and now, as if wakened from a sleep of which she had not been conscious, she felt as if she'd been touched—prodded into wakefulness. She saw, upside-down, the fussy smudged sketch Mr. Starr had been doing of her, saw his charcoal stick poised above the stiff white paper in an attitude of chagrin. She laughed, and wiped at her eyes, and said, "It happened a long time ago. I never think of it, really."

Mr. Starr's expression was wary, complex. He asked, "And so—do you—live with your—father?" The words seemed oddly forced.

"No, I don't. And I don't want to talk about this anymore, Mr. Starr, if it's all right with you."

Sybil spoke pleadingly, yet with an air of finality.

"Then—we won't! We won't! We certainly won't!" Mr. Starr said quickly. And fell to sketching again, his face creased in concentration.

And so the remainder of the session passed in silence.

Again, as soon as Sybil evinced signs of restlessness, Mr. Starr declared she could stop for the day—he didn't want to exhaust her, or himself.

Sybil rubbed her neck, which ached mildly; she stretched her arms, her legs. Her skin felt slightly sun- or wind-burnt and her eyes felt seared, as if she'd been staring directly into the sun. Or had she been crying?—she couldn't remember.

Again, Mr. Starr paid Sybil in cash, out of his kidskin wallet brimming with bills. His hand shook just visibly as he pressed the money into Sybil's. (Embarrassed, Sybil folded the bills quickly and put them in her pocket. Later, at home, she would discover that Mr. Starr had given her ten dollars too much: a bonus, for almost making her cry?) Though it was clear that Sybil was eager to get away, Mr. Starr walked with her up the slope in the direction of the Boulevard, limping, leaning on his cane, but keeping a brisk pace. He asked if Sybil—of course, he called her Blake: "dear Blake"—would like to have some refreshment with him in a café nearby?—and when Sybil declined, murmured, "Yes, yes, I understand—I suppose." He then asked if Sybil would return the following day, and when Sybil did not say no, added that, if she did, he would like to increase her hourly fee in exchange for asking of her a slightly different sort of modeling—"A slightly modified sort of modeling, here in the park, or perhaps down on the beach, in full daylight of course, as before, and yet, in its way—" Mr. Starr paused nervously, seeking the right word, "—experimental."

Sybil asked doubtfully, " 'Experimental'—?"

"I'm prepared to increase your fee, Blake, by half."

"What kind of 'experimental'?"

"Emotion."

"What?"

"Emotion. Memory. Interiority."

Now that they were emerging from the park, and more likely to be seen, Sybil was glancing uneasily about: she dreaded seeing someone from school, or, worse yet, a friend of her aunt's. Mr. Starr gestured as he spoke, and seemed more than ordinarily excited. "—'Interiority.' That which is hidden to the outer eye. I'll tell you in more detail tomorrow, Blake," he said. "You *will* meet me here tomorrow?"

Sybil murmured, "I don't know, Mr. Starr."

"Oh, but you must!—please."

Sybil felt a tug of sympathy for Mr. Starr. He *was* kind, and courteous, and gentlemanly; and, certainly, very generous. She could not imagine his life except to see him as a lonely, eccentric man without friends. Uncomfortable as she was in his presence, she yet wondered if perhaps she was exaggerating his eccentricity: what would a neutral observer make of the tall limping figure, the cane, the canvas duffel bag, the polished black leather shoes that reminded her of a funeral, the fine thin beautiful silver hair, the dark glasses that winked in the sunshine. . . ? Would such an observer, seeing Sybil Blake and Mr. Starr together, give them a second glance?

"Look," Sybil said, pointing, "—a hearse."

At a curb close by there was a long sleekly black car with dark-tinted, impenetrable windows. Mr. Starr laughed, and said, embarrassed, "I'm afraid, Blake, that isn't a hearse, you know—it's my car."

"Your car?"

"Yes. I'm afraid so."

Now Sybil could see that the vehicle was a limousine, idling at the curb. Behind the wheel was a youngish driver with a visored cap on his head; in profile, he appeared Oriental. Sybil stared, amazed. So Mr. Starr was wealthy, indeed.

He was saying, apologetically, yet with a kind of boyish pleasure, "I don't drive, myself, you see!—a further handicap. I did, once, long ago, but—circumstances intervened." Sybil was thinking that she often saw chauffeur-driven limousines in Glencoe, but she'd never known anyone who owned one before. Mr. Starr said, "Blake, may I give you a ride home?—I'd be delighted, of course."

Sybil laughed, as if she'd been tickled, hard, in the ribs.

"A ride? In that?" she asked.

"No trouble! Absolutely!" Mr. Starr limped to the rear door and opened it with a flourish, before the driver could get out to open it for him. He squinted back at Sybil, smiling hopefully. "It's the least I can do for you, after our exhausting session."

Sybil was smiling, staring into the shadowy interior of the car. The uniformed driver had climbed out, and stood, not quite knowing what to do, watching. He was a Filipino, perhaps, not young after all but with a small, wizened face; he wore white gloves. He stood very straight and silent, watching Sybil.

There was a moment when it seemed, yes, Sybil was going to accept Mr. Starr's offer, and climb into the rear of the long sleekly black limousine, so that Mr. Starr could climb in behind her, and shut the door upon them both; but, then, for some reason she could not have named—it might have been the smiling intensity with which Mr. Starr was looking at her, or the rigid posture of the white-gloved driver—she changed her mind and called out, "No thanks!"

Mr. Starr was disappointed, and Mr. Starr was hurt—you could see it in his downturned mouth. But he said, cheerfully, "Oh, I quite understand, Blake—I *am* a stranger, after all. It's better to be prudent, of course. But, my dear, I *will* see you tomorrow—?"

Sybil shouted, "Maybe!" and ran across the street.

6. The Face

She stayed away from the park. *Because I want to, because I can.*

Thursday, in any case, was her voice lesson after school. Friday, choir rehearsal; then an evening with friends. On Saturday morning she went jogging, not in the oceanside park but in another park, miles away, where Mr. Starr could not have known to look for her. And, on Sunday, Aunt Lora drove them to Los Angeles for a belated birthday celebration, for Sybil—an art exhibit, a dinner, a play.

So, you see, I can do it. I don't need your money, or you.

Since the evening when Aunt Lora had told Sybil about her parents' boating accident—that it might have been caused by drinking—neither Sybil nor her aunt had cared to bring up the subject again. Sybil shuddered to think of it. She felt properly chastised, for her curiosity.

Why do you want to know?—you will only make yourself cry.

Sybil had never gotten around to telling Aunt Lora about Mr. Starr, nor about her modeling. Even during their long Sunday together. Not a word about her cache of money, hidden away in a bureau drawer.

Money for what?—for summer school, for college.

For the future.

Aunt Lora was not the sort of person to spy on a member of her household but she observed Sybil closely, with her trained clinician's eye. "Sybil, you've been very quiet lately—there's nothing wrong, I hope?" she asked, and Sybil said quickly, nervously, "Oh, no! What could be wrong?"

She was feeling guilty about keeping a secret from Aunt Lora, and she was feeling quite guilty about staying away from Mr. Starr.

Two adults. Like twin poles. Of course, Mr. Starr was really a stranger—he did not exist in Sybil Blake's life, at all. Why did it feel to her, so strangely, that he did?

Days passed, and instead of forgetting Mr. Starr, and strengthening her resolve not to model for him, Sybil seemed to see the man, in her mind's eye, ever more clearly. She could not understand why he seemed attracted to her, she was convinced it was not a sexual attraction but something purer, more spiritual, and yet—why? Why *her*?

Why had he visited her high school, and sat in upon a choir rehearsal? Had he known she would be there?—or was it simply accident?

She shuddered to think of what Aunt Lora would make of this, if she knew. If news of Mr. Starr got back to her.

Mr. Starr's face floated before her. Its pallor, its sorrow. That look of convalescence. Waiting. The dark glasses. The hopeful smile. One night, waking from a particularly vivid, disturbing dream, Sybil thought for a confused moment that she'd seen Mr. Starr in the room—it hadn't been just a dream! How wounded he looked, puzzled, hurt. *Come with me, Sybil. Hurry. Now. It's been so long.* He'd been waiting for her in the park for days, limping, the duffel bag slung over his shoulder, glancing up hopefully at every passing stranger.

Behind him, the elegantly gleaming black limousine, larger than Sybil remembered; and driverless.

Sybil?—Sybil? Mr. Starr called, impatiently.

As if, all along, he'd known her real name. And she had known he'd known.

7. The Experiment

So, Monday afternoon, Sybil Blake found herself back in the park, modeling for Mr. Starr.

Seeing him in the park, so obviously awaiting her, Sybil had felt almost apologetic. Not that he greeted her with any measure of reproach (though his face was drawn and sallow, as if he hadn't been sleeping well), nor even questioned her mutely with his eyes *Where have you been?* Certainly not! He smiled happily when he saw her, limping in her direction like a doting father, seemingly determined not to acknowledge her absence of the past four days. Sybil called out, "Hello, Mr. Starr!" and felt, yes, so strangely, as if things were once again right.

"How lovely!—and the day is so fine!—'in full daylight'—as I promised!" Mr. Starr cried.

Sybil had been jogging for forty minutes, and felt very good, strengthened. She removed her damp yellow headband and stuffed it in her pocket. When Mr. Starr repeated the terms of his proposition of the previous week, restating the higher fee, Sybil agreed at once, for of course that was why she'd come. How, in all reasonableness, could she resist?

Mr. Starr took some time before deciding upon a place for Sybil to pose—"It must be ideal, a synthesis of poetry and practicality." Finally, he chose a partly crumbling stone ledge overlooking the beach in a remote corner of the park. He asked Sybil to lean against the ledge, gazing out at the ocean. Her hands pressed flat against the top of the ledge, her head uplifted as much as possible, within comfort. "But today, dear Blake, I am going to record not just the surface likeness of a lovely young girl," he said, "—but *memory,* and *emotion,* coursing through her."

Sybil took the position readily enough. So invigorated did she feel from her exercise, and so happy to be back again in her role as model, she smiled out at the ocean as at an old friend. "What kind of memory and emotion, Mr. Starr?" she asked.

Mr. Starr eagerly took up his sketch pad and a fresh stick of charcoal. It was a mild day, the sky placid and featureless, though, up the coast, in the direction of Big Sur, massive thunderclouds were gathering. The surf was high, the waves powerful, hypnotic. One hundred yards below, young men in surfing gear, carrying their boards lightly as if they were made of papier-mâché, prepared to enter the water.

Mr. Starr cleared his throat, and said, almost shyly, "Your mother, dear Blake. Tell me all you know—all you can remember—about your mother."

"My mother?"

Sybil winced and would have broken her position, except Mr. Starr put out a quick hand, to steady her. It was the first time he had touched her in quite that way. He said gently, "I realize it's a painful subject, Blake, but—will you try?"

Sybil said, "No. I don't want to."

"You won't, then?"

"I *can't.*"

"But why can't you, dear?—any memory of your mother would do."

"*No.*"

Sybil saw that Mr. Starr was quickly sketching her, or trying to—his hand shook. She wanted to reach out to snatch the charcoal stick from him and snap it in two. How dare he! God damn him!

"Yes, yes," Mr. Starr said hurriedly, an odd, elated look on his face, as if, studying her so intently, he was not seeing her at all, "—yes, dear, like that. Any memory—any! So long as it's yours."

Sybil said, "Whose else would it be?" She laughed, and was surprised that her laughter sounded like sobbing.

"Why, many times innocent children are given memories by adults; contaminated by memories not their own," Mr. Starr said somberly. "In which case the memory is spurious. Inauthentic."

Sybil saw her likeness on the sheet of stiff white paper, upsidedown. There was something repulsive about it. Though she was wearing her usual jogging clothes (a shirt, running pants) Mr. Starr made it look as if she were wearing a clinging, flowing gown; or, maybe, nothing at all. Where her small breasts would have been were swirls and smudges of charcoal, as if she were on the brink of dissolution. Her face and head were vividly drawn, but rather raw, crude, and exposed.

She saw too that Mr. Starr's silver hair had a flat metallic sheen this afternoon; and his beard was faintly visible, metallic too, glinting on his jaws. He was stronger than she'd thought. He had knowledge far beyond hers.

Sybil resumed her position. She stared out at the ocean—the tall, cresting, splendidly white-capped waves. Why was she here, what did this man want out of her? She worried suddenly that, whatever it was, she could not provide it.

But Mr. Starr was saying, in his gentle, murmurous voice, "There are people—primarily women!—who are what I call 'conduits of emotion.' In their company, the half-dead can come alive. They need not be beautiful women or girls. It's a matter of blood-warmth. The integrity of the spirit." He turned the page of his sketch pad, and began anew, whistling thinly through his teeth. "Thus an icy-cold soul, in the presence of one so blessed, can regain something of his lost self. Sometimes!"

Sybil tried to summon forth a memory, an image at least, of her mother. *Melanie. Twenty-six at the time. Eyes . . . cheekbones . . . pale wavy hair.* A ghostly face appeared but faded almost at once. Sybil sobbed involuntarily. Her eyes stung with tears.

"—sensed that you, dear Blake—*is* your name Blake, really?—are one of these. A 'conduit of emotion'—of finer, higher things. Yes, yes! My intuition rarely misguides me!" Mr. Starr spoke as, hurriedly, excitedly, he sketched Sybil's likeness. He was squatting close beside her, on his haunches; his dark glasses winked in the sun. Sybil knew, should she glance at him, she would not be able to see his eyes.

Mr. Starr said, coaxingly, "Don't you remember anything—at all—about your mother?"

Sybil shook her head, meaning she didn't want to speak.

"Her name. Surely you know her name?"

Sybil whispered, "Mommy."

"Ah, yes: 'Mommy.' To you, that would have been her name."

"Mommy—went away. They told me—"

"Yes? Please continue!"

"—Mommy was gone. And Daddy. On the lake—"

"Lake? Where?"

"Lake Champlain. In Vermont, and New York, Aunt Lora says—"

" 'Aunt Lora'—?"

"Mommy's sister. She was older. Is older. She took me away. She adopted me. She—"

"And is 'Aunt Lora' married?"

"No. There's just her and me."

"What happened on the lake?"

"—it happened in the boat, on the lake. Daddy was driving the boat, they said. He came for me too but—I don't know if that was that time or some other time. I've been told, but I don't *know*."

Tears were streaming down Sybil's face now; she could not maintain her composure. But she managed to keep from hiding her face in her hands. She could hear Mr. Starr's quickened breath, and she could hear the rasping sound of the charcoal against the paper.

Mr. Starr said gently, "You must have been a little girl when—whatever it was—happened."

"I wasn't little to *myself*. I just *was*."

"A long time ago, was it?"

"Yes. No. It's always—there."

"Always where, dear child?"

"Where I, I—see it."

"See what?"

"I—don't *know*."

"Do you see your mommy? Was she a beautiful woman?—did she resemble you?"

"Leave me alone—I don't *know*."

Sybil began to cry. Mr. Starr, repentant, or wary, went immediately silent.

Someone—it must have been bicyclists—passed behind them, and Sybil was aware of being observed, no doubt quizzically: a girl leaning forward across a stone ledge, face wet with tears, and a middle-aged man on his haunches busily sketching her. An artist and his model. An amateur artist, an amateur model. But how strange, that the girl was crying! And the man so avidly recording her tears!

Sybil, eyes closed, felt herself indeed a conduit of emotion—she *was* emotion. She stood upon the ground but she floated free.

Mr. Starr was close beside her, anchoring her, but she floated free. A veil was drawn aside, and she saw a face—Mommy's face—a pretty heart-shaped face—something both affectionate and petulant in that face—how young Mommy was!—and her hair up, brown-blond lovely hair, tied back in a green silk scarf. Mommy hurried to the phone as it rang, Mommy lifted the receiver. Yes? yes? oh he*llo*—for the phone was always ringing, and Mommy was always hurrying to answer it, and there was always that expectant note to her voice, that sound of hope, surprise— Oh, he*llo*.

Sybil could no longer maintain her pose. She said, "Mr. Starr, I am through for the day, I am *sorry*." And, as the startled man looked after her, she walked away. He began to call after her, to remind her that he hadn't paid her, but, no, Sybil had had enough of modeling for the day. She broke into a run, she escaped.

8. A Long Time Ago . . .

A girl who'd married too young: was that it?

That heart-shaped face, the petulant pursed lips. The eyes widened in mock-surprise: Oh, Sybil, what have you *done*. . . ?

Stooping to kiss little Sybil, little Sybil giggling with pleasure and excitement, lifting her chubby baby arms to be raised in Mommy's and carried in to bed.

Oh honey, you're too big for that now. Too heavy!

Perfume wafting from her hair, loose to her shoulders, pale golden-brown, wavy. A rope of pearls around her neck. A low-cut summer dress, a bright floral print, like wallpaper. Mommy!

And Daddy, where *was* Daddy?

He was gone, then he was back. He'd come to her, little Sybil, to take her in the boat, the motor was loud, whining, angry as a bee buzzing and darting around her head, so Sybil was crying, and someone came, and Daddy went away again. She'd heard the motor rising, then fading. The churning of the water she couldn't see from where she stood, and it was night too, but she wasn't crying and no one scolded.

She could remember Mommy's face, though they never let her see it again. She couldn't remember Daddy's face.

Grandma said, You'll be all right, poor little darling, you'll be all right, and Aunt Lora too, hugging her tight, Forever now you'll be all right, Aunt Lora promised. It was scary to see Aunt Lora crying: Aunt Lora never cried, did she?

Lifting little Sybil in her strong arms to carry her in to bed but it wasn't the same. It would never be the same again.

9. The Gift

Sybil is standing at the edge of the ocean.

The surf crashes and pounds about her . . . water streams up the sand, nearly wetting her feet. What a tumult of cries, hidden within the waves! She feels like laughing, for no reason. *You know the reason: he has returned to you.*

The beach is wide, clean, stark, as if swept with a giant broom. A landscape of dreamlike simplicity. Sybil has seen it numberless times but today its beauty strikes her as new. *Your father: your father they told you was gone forever: he has returned to you.* The sun is a winter sun, but warm, dazzling. Poised in the sky as if about to rapidly descend. Dark comes early because, after all, it is winter here, despite the warmth. The temperature will drop twenty degrees in a half-hour. *He never died: he has been waiting for you all these years. And now he has returned.*

Sybil begins to cry. Hiding her face, her burning face, in her hands. She stands flatfooted as a little girl and the surf breaks and splashes around her and now her shoes are wet, her feet, she'll be shivering in the gathering chill. *Oh, Sybil!*

When Sybil turned, it was to see Mr. Starr sitting on the beach. He seemed to have lost his balance and fallen—his cane lay at his feet, he'd dropped the sketch pad, his sporty golfing cap sat crooked on his head. Sybil, concerned, asked what was wrong—she prayed he hadn't had a heart attack!—and Mr. Starr smiled weakly and told her quickly that he didn't know, he'd become dizzy, felt the strength go out of his legs, and had to sit. "I was overcome suddenly, I think, by your emotion!—whatever it was," he said. He made no effort to get to his feet but sat there awkwardly, damp sand on his trousers and shoes. Now Sybil

149

stood over him and he squinted up at her, and there passed between them a current of—was it understanding? sympathy? rec-
ognition?

Sybil laughed to dispel the moment and put out her hand for
Mr. Starr to take, so that she could help him stand. He laughed
too, though he was deeply moved, and embarrassed. "I'm afraid
I make too much of things, don't I?" he said. Sybil tugged at his
hand (how big his hand was! how strong the fingers, closing
about hers!) and, as he heaved himself to his feet, grunting, she
felt the startling weight of him—an adult man, and heavy.

Mr. Starr was standing close to Sybil, not yet relinquishing her
hand. He said, "The experiment was almost too successful, from
my perspective! I'm almost afraid to try again."

Sybil smiled uncertainly up at him. He was about the age her
own father would have been—wasn't he? It seemed to her that a
younger face was pushing out through Mr. Starr's coarse, sallow
face. The hooklike quizzical scar on his forehead glistened oddly
in the sun.

Sybil politely withdrew her hand from Mr. Starr's and
dropped her eyes. She was shivering—today, she had not been
running at all, had come to meet Mr. Starr for purposes of modeling, in a blouse and skirt, as he'd requested. She was bare-leg-
ged and her feet, in sandals, were wet from the surf.

Sybil said, softly, as if she didn't want to be heard, "I feel the
same way, Mr. Starr."

They climbed a flight of wooden steps to the top of the bluff,
and there was Mr. Starr's limousine, blackly gleaming, parked a
short distance away. At this hour of the afternoon the park was
well populated; there was a gay giggling bevy of high school girls
strolling by, but Sybil took no notice. She was agitated, still;
weak from crying, yet oddly strengthened, elated too. *You know
who he is. You always knew.* She was keenly aware of Mr. Starr
limping beside her, and impatient with his chatter. Why didn't
he speak directly to her, for once?

The uniformed chauffeur sat behind the wheel of the limousine, looking neither to the right nor the left, as if at attention.
His visored cap, his white gloves. His profile like a profile on an
ancient coin. Sybil wondered if the chauffeur knew about her—

if Mr. Starr talked to him about her. Suddenly she was filled with excitement, that someone else should *know*.

Mr. Starr was saying that, since Sybil had modeled so patiently that day, since she'd more than fulfilled his expectations, he had a gift for her—"In addition to your fee, that is."

He opened the rear door of the limousine, and took out a square white box, and, smiling shyly, presented it to Sybil. "Oh, what *is* it?" Sybil cried. She and Aunt Lora rarely exchanged presents any longer, it seemed like a ritual out of the deep past, delightful to rediscover. She lifted the cover of the box, and saw, inside, a beautiful purse; an over-the-shoulder bag; kidskin, the hue of rich dark honey. "Oh, Mr. Starr—thank you." Sybil said, taking the bag in her hands. "It's the most beautiful thing I've ever seen." "Why don't you open it, dear?" Mr. Starr urged, so Sybil opened the bag, and discovered money inside—fresh-minted bills—the denomination on top was twenty dollars. "I hope you didn't overpay me again," Sybil said, uneasily, "—I never have modeled for three hours yet. It isn't fair." Mr. Starr laughed, flushed with pleasure. "Fair to whom?" he asked. "What is 'fair'?—*we* do what *we* like."

Sybil raised her eyes shyly to Mr. Starr's and saw that he was looking at her intently—at least, the skin at the corners of his eyes was tightly puckered. "Today, dear, I insist upon driving you home," he said, smiling. There was a new authority in his voice that seemed to have something to do with the gift Sybil had received from him. "It will soon be getting chilly, and your feet are wet." Sybil hesitated. She had lifted the bag to her face, to inhale the pungent kidskin smell: the bag was of a quality she'd never owned before. Mr. Starr glanced swiftly about, as if to see if anyone was watching; he was still smiling. "Please do climb inside, Blake!—you can't consider me a stranger, now."

Still, Sybil hesitated. Half teasing, she said, *"You* know my name isn't Blake, don't you, Mr. Starr?—how do you know?"

Mr. Starr laughed, teasing too. *"Isn't* it? What is your name, then?"

"Don't you know?"

"Should I know?"

"Shouldn't you?"

There was a pause. Mr. Starr had taken hold of Sybil's wrist; lightly, yet firmly. His fingers circled her thin wrists with the subtle pressure of a watchband.

Mr. Starr leaned close, as if sharing a secret. "Well, I did hear you sing your solo, in your wonderful Christmas pageant at the high school! I must confess, I'd sneaked into a rehearsal too—no one questioned my presence. And I believe I heard the choir director call you—is it 'Sybil'?"

Hearing her name in Mr. Starr's mouth, Sybil felt a sensation of vertigo. She could only nod, mutely, yes.

"*Is* it?—I wasn't sure if I'd heard correctly. A lovely name, for a lovely girl. And 'Blake'—is 'Blake' your surname?"

Sybil murmured, "Yes."

"Your father's name?"

"No. Not my father's name."

"Oh, and why not? Usually, you know, that's the case."

"Because—" And here Sybil paused, confused, uncertain what to say. "It's my mother's name. Was."

"Ah, really! I see," Mr. Starr laughed. "Well, truly, I suppose I *don't,* but we can discuss it another time. Shall we—?"

He meant, shall we get into the car; he was exerting pressure on Sybil's wrist, and, though kindly as always, seemed on the edge of impatience. Sybil stood flatfooted on the sidewalk, wanting to acquiesce; yet, at the same time, uneasily thinking that, no, she should not. Not yet.

So Sybil pulled away, laughing nervously, and Mr. Starr had to release her, with a disappointed downturning of his mouth. Sybil thanked him, saying she preferred to walk. "I hope I will see you tomorrow, then?—'Sybil'?" Mr. Starr called after her. "Yes?"

But Sybil, hugging her new bag against her chest, as a small child might hug a stuffed animal, was walking quickly away.

Was the black limousine following her, at a discreet distance?

Sybil felt a powerful compulsion to look back, but did not.

She was trying to recall if, ever in her life, she'd ridden in such a vehicle. She supposed there had been hired, chauffeur-drawn limousines at her parents' funerals, but she had not attended those funerals; had no memory of anything connected with them, except the strange behavior of her grandmother, her Aunt Lora, and other adults—their grief, but, underlying that grief, their air of profound and speechless shock.

Where is Mommy, she'd asked, where is Daddy, and the replies were always the same: Gone away.

And crying did no good. And fury did no good. Nothing little Sybil could do, or say, or think did any good. That was the first lesson, maybe.

But Daddy isn't dead, you know he isn't. You know, and he knows, why he has returned.

10. "Possessed"

Aunt Lora was smoking again!—back to two packs a day. And Sybil understood guiltily that she was to blame.

For there was the matter of the kidskin bag. The secret gift. Which Sybil had hidden in the farthest corner of her closet, wrapped in plastic, so the smell of it would not permeate the room. (Still, you could smell it—couldn't you? A subtle pervasive smell, rich as any perfume?) Sybil lived in dread that her aunt would discover the purse, and the money; though Lora Dell Blake never entered her niece's room without an invitation, somehow, Sybil worried, it *might* happen. She had never kept any important secret from her aunt in her life, and this secret both filled her with a sense of excitement and power, and weakened her, in childish dread.

What most concerned Lora, however, was Sybil's renewed interest in *that*—as in, "Oh, honey, are you thinking about *that* again? *Why?*"

That was the abbreviated euphemism for what Lora might more fully call "the accident"—"the tragedy"—"your parents' deaths."

Sybil, who had never shown more than passing curiosity about *that* in the past, as far as Lora could remember, was now in the grip of what Lora called "morbid curiosity." That mute, perplexed look in her eyes! That tremulous, though sometimes a bit sullen, look to her mouth! One evening, lighting up a cigarette with shaking fingers, Lora said, bluntly, "Sybil, honey, this tears my heart out. What *is* it you want to know?"

Sybil said, as if she'd been waiting for just this question, "Is my father alive?"

"What?"

"My father. George Conte. *Is* he—maybe—alive?"

The question hovered between them, and, for a long pained moment, it seemed almost that Aunt Lora might snort in exasperation, jump up from the table, walk out of the room. But then she said, shaking her head adamantly, dropping her gaze from Sybil's, "Honey, no. The man is not alive." She paused. She smoked her cigarette, exhaled smoke vigorously through her nostrils; seemed about to say something further; changed her mind; then said, quietly, "You don't ask about your mother, Sybil. Why is that?"

"I—believe that my mother is dead. But—"

"But—?"

"My—my father—"

"—isn't?"

Sybil said, stammering, her cheeks growing hot, "I just want to *know*. I want to see a, a—grave! A death certificate!"

"I'll send to Wellington for a copy of the death certificate," Aunt Lora said slowly. "Will that do?"

"You don't have a copy here?"

"Honey, why would I have a copy here?"

Sybil saw that the older woman was regarding her with a look of pity, and something like dread. She said, stammering, her cheeks warm, "In your—legal things. Your papers. Locked away—"

"Honey, no."

There was a pause. Then Sybil said, half-sobbing, "I was too young to go to their funeral. So I never saw. Whatever it was—I never *saw*. Is that it? They say that's the reason for the ritual—for displaying the dead."

Aunt Lora reached over to take Sybil's hand. "It's one of the reasons, honey," she said. "We meet up with it all the time, at the medical center. People don't believe that loved ones are dead—they know, but can't accept it; the shock is just too much to absorb at once. And, yes, it's a theory, that if you don't see a person actually dead—if there isn't a public ceremony to define it—you may have difficulty accepting it. You may—" and here Aunt Lora paused, frowning, "—be susceptible to fantasy."

Fantasy! Sybil stared at her aunt, shocked. *But I've seen him, I know. I believe him and not you!*

The subject seemed to be concluded for the time being. Aunt Lora briskly stubbed out her cigarette and said, "I'm to blame—probably. I'd been in therapy for a couple of years after it happened and I just didn't want to talk about it any longer, so when you'd asked me questions, over the years, I cut you off; I realize that. But, you see, there's so little to say—Melanie is dead, and *he* is dead. And it all happened a long time ago."

That evening, Sybil was reading in a book on memory she'd taken out of the Glencoe Public Library: *It is known that human beings are "possessed" by an unfathomable number of dormant memory-traces, of which some can be activated under special conditions, including excitation by stimulating points in the cortex. Such traces are indelibly imprinted in the nervous system and are commonly activated by mnemonic stimuli—words, sights, sounds, and especially smells. The phenomenon of déjà vu is closely related to these experiences, in which a "doubling of consciousness" occurs, with the conviction that one has lived an experience before. Much of human memory, however, includes subsequent revision, selection, and fantasizing. . . .*

Sybil let the book shut. She contemplated, for the dozenth time, the faint red marks on her wrist, where Mr. Starr—the man who called himself Mr. Starr—had gripped her, without knowing his own strength.

Nor had Sybil been aware, at the time, that his fingers were so strong; and had clasped so tightly around her wrist.

11. "Mr. Starr"—or "Mr. Conte"

She saw him, and saw that he was waiting for her. And her impulse was to run immediately to him, and observe, with childish delight, how the sight of her would illuminate his face. *Here!*

155

Here I am! It was a profound power that seemed to reside in her, Sybil Blake, seventeen years old—the power to have such an effect upon a man whom she scarcely knew, and who did not know her.

Because he loves me. Because he's my father. That's why.

And if he isn't my father—

It was late afternoon of a dull, overcast day. Still, the park was populated at this end; joggers were running, some in colorful costumes. Sybil was not among them, she'd slept poorly the previous night, thinking of—what? Her dead mother who'd been so beautiful?—her father whose face she could not recall (though, yes surely, it was imprinted deep, deep in the cells of her memory)?—her Aunt Lora who was, or was not, telling her the truth, and who loved her more than anyone on earth? And Mr. Starr of course.

Or Mr. Conte.

Sybil was hidden from Mr. Starr's gaze as, with an air of smiling expectancy, he looked about. He was carrying his duffel bag and leaning on his cane. He wore his plain, dark clothes; he was bareheaded, and his silvery hair shone; if Sybil were closer, she would see light winking in his dark glasses. She had noticed the limousine, parked up on the Boulevard a block away.

A young woman jogger ran past Mr. Starr, long-legged, hair flying, and he looked at her, intently—watched her as she ran out of sight along the path. Then he turned back, glancing up toward the street, shifting his shoulders impatiently. Sybil saw him check his wristwatch.

Waiting for you. You know why.

And then, suddenly—Sybil decided not to go to Mr. Starr after all. The man who called himself Starr. She changed her mind at the last moment, unprepared for her decision except to understand that, as, quickly, she walked away, it must be the right decision: her heart was beating erratically, all her senses alert, as if she had narrowly escaped great danger.

12. The Fate of "George Conte"

On Mondays, Wednesdays, and Fridays Lora Dell Blake attended an aerobics class after work, and on these evenings she rarely returned home before seven o'clock. Today was a Friday, at four: Sybil calculated she had more than enough time to search out her aunt's private papers, and to put everything back in order, well before her aunt came home.

Aunt Lora's household keys were kept in a top drawer of her desk, and one of these keys, Sybil knew, was to a small aluminum filing cabinet beside the desk, where confidential records and papers were kept. There were perhaps a dozen keys, in a jumble, but Sybil had no difficulty finding the right one. "Aunt Lora, please forgive me," she whispered. It was a measure of her aunt's trust of her that the filing cabinet was so readily unlocked.

For never in her life had Sybil Blake done such a thing, in violation of the trust between herself and her aunt. She sensed that, unlocking the cabinet, opening the sliding drawers, she might be committing an irrevocable act.

The drawer was jammed tight with manila folders, most of them well-worn and dog-eared. Sybil's first response was disappointment—there were hundreds of household receipts, financial statements, Internal Revenue records dating back for years. Then she discovered a packet of letters dating back to the 1950s, when Aunt Lora would have been a young girl. There were a few snapshots, a few formally posed photographs—one of a strikingly beautiful, if immature-looking, girl in a high-school graduation cap and gown, smiling at the camera with glossy lips. On the rear was written "Melanie, 1969." Sybil stared at this likeness of her mother—her mother long before she'd become her mother—and felt both triumph and dismay; for, yes, here was the mysterious Melanie, and, yet, *was* this the Melanie the child knew?—or, simply, a high school girl, Sybil's own approximate age, the kind who, judging from her looks and self-absorbed expression, would never have been a friend of Sybil's?

Sybil put the photograph back, with trembling fingers. She was half grateful that Aunt Lora had kept so few mementos of the past—there could be fewer shocks, revelations.

No photographs of the wedding of Melanie Blake and George Conte. Not a one.

No photographs, so far as Sybil could see, of her father "George Conte" at all.

There was a single snapshot of Melanie with her baby daughter Sybil, and this Sybil studied for a long time. It had been taken in summer, at a lakeside cottage; Melanie was posing prettily, in a white dress, with her baby snug in the crook of her arm, and both were looking toward the camera, as if someone had just called out to them, to make them laugh—Melanie with a wide, glamorous, yet sweet smile, little Sybil gaping open-mouthed. Here Melanie looked only slightly more mature than in the graduation photograph: her pale brown hair, many shades of brown and blond, was shoulder-length, and upturned; her eyes were meticulously outlined in mascara, prominent in her heart-shaped face.

In the foreground, on the grass, was the shadow of a man's head and shoulders—George Conte, perhaps? The missing person.

Sybil stared at this snapshot, which was wrinkled and dog-eared. She did not know what to think, and, oddly, she felt very little: for was the infant in the picture really herself, Sybil Blake, if she could not remember?

Or did she in fact remember, somewhere deep in her brain, in memory-traces that were indelible?

From now on, she would "remember" her mother as the pretty, self-assured young woman in this snapshot. This image, in full color, would replace any other.

Reluctantly, Sybil slid the snapshot back in its packet. How she would have liked to keep it!—but Aunt Lora would discover the theft, eventually. And Aunt Lora must be protected against knowing that her own niece had broken into her things, violated the trust between them.

The folders containing personal material were few, and quickly searched. Nothing pertaining to the accident, the "tragedy"?—not even an obituary? Sybil looked in adjacent files, with increasing desperation. There was not only the question of who her father was, or had been, but the question, nearly as compelling, of why Aunt Lora had eradicated all trace of him, even in her own private files. For a moment Sybil wondered if there had ever been any "George Conte" at all: maybe her mother had not married, and that was part of the secret? Melanie had died in some terrible way, terrible at least in Lora Dell Blake's eyes, thus the very fact must be hidden from Sybil, after so many years? Sybil recalled Aunt Lora saying, earnestly, a few years ago, "The only thing you should know, Sybil, is that your mother—and your father—would not want you to grow up in the shadow of their deaths. They would have wanted you—your mother especially—to be *happy*."

Part of this legacy of happiness, Sybil gathered, had been for her to grow up as a perfectly normal American girl, in a sunny, shadowless place with no history, or, at any rate, no history that concerned her. "But I don't want to be *happy*, I want to *know*," Sybil said aloud.

But the rest of the manila files, jammed so tightly together they were almost inextricable, yielded nothing.

So, disappointed, Sybil shut the file drawer, and locked it.

But what of Aunt Lora's desk drawers? She had a memory of their being unlocked, thus surely containing nothing of significance; but now it occurred to her that, being unlocked, one of these drawers might in fact contain something Aunt Lora might want to keep safely hidden. So, quickly, with not much hope, Sybil looked through these drawers, messy, jammed with papers, clippings, further packets of household receipts, old programs from plays they'd seen in Los Angeles—and, in the largest drawer, at the very bottom, in a wrinkled manila envelope with "MEDICAL INSURANCE" carefully printed on its front, Sybil found what she was looking for.

Newspaper clippings, badly yellowed, some of them spliced together with aged cellophane tape—

WELLINGTON, VT. MAN SHOOTS WIFE, SELF
SUICIDE ATTEMPT FAILS

AREA MAN KILLS WIFE IN JULY 4 QUARREL
ATTEMPTS SUICIDE ON LAKE CHAMPLAIN

GEORGE CONTE, 31, ARRESTED FOR MURDER
WELLINGTON LAWYER HELD IN SHOOTING DEATH OF
WIFE, 26

CONTE TRIAL BEGINS
PROSECUTION CHARGES PREMEDITATION
Family Members Testify

So Sybil Blake learned, in the space of less than sixty seconds, the nature of the tragedy from which her Aunt Lora had shielded her for nearly fifteen years.

Her father was indeed a man named George Conte, and this man had shot her mother Melanie to death, in their speedboat on Lake Champlain, and pushed her body overboard. He had tried to kill himself too but had only critically wounded himself with a shot to the head. He'd undergone emergency neurosurgery, and recovered; he was arrested, tried, and convicted of second-degree murder; and sentenced to between twelve and nineteen years in prison, at the Hartshill State Prison in northern Vermont.

Sybil sifted through the clippings, her fingers numb. So this was it! This! Murder, attempted suicide! —not mere drunkenness and an "accident" on the lake.

Aunt Lora seemed to have stuffed the clippings in an envelope in haste, or in revulsion; with some, photographs had been torn off, leaving only their captions—"Melanie and George Conte, 1975," "Prosecution witness Lora Dell Blake leaving court-house." Those photographs of George Conte showed a man who surely did resemble "Mr. Starr": younger, dark-haired, with a face heavier in the jaws and an air of youthful self-assurance and expectation. *There. Your father. "Mr. Starr." The missing person.*

There were several photographs too of Melanie Conte, including one taken for her high-school yearbook, and one of her in a long, formal gown with her hair glamorously upswept—"Wellington woman killed by jealous husband." There was a wedding photograph of the couple looking very young, attractive, and happy; a photograph of the "Conte family at their summer home"; a photograph of "George Conte, lawyer, after second-degree murder verdict"—the convicted man, stunned, down-looking, being taken away handcuffed between two grim sheriff's men. Sybil understood that the terrible thing that had happened in her family had been of enormous public interest in Wellington, Vermont, and that this was part of its terribleness, its shame.

What had Aunt Lora said?—she'd been in therapy for some time afterward, thus did not want to relive those memories.

And she'd said, *It all happened a long time ago.*

But she'd lied, too. She had looked Sybil full in the face and lied, lied. Insisting that Sybil's father was dead when she knew he was alive.

When Sybil herself had reason to believe he was alive.

My name is Starr! Don't judge me too quickly!

Sybil read, and reread, the aged clippings. There were perhaps twenty of them. She gathered two general things: that her father George Conte was from a locally prominent family, and that he'd had a very capable attorney to defend him at his trial; and that the community had greatly enjoyed the scandal, though, no doubt, offering condolences to the grieving Blake family. The spectacle of a beautiful young wife murdered by her "jealous" young husband, her body pushed from an expensive speedboat to sink in Lake Champlain—who could resist? The media had surely exploited this tragedy to its fullest.

Now you see, don't you, why your name had to be changed. Not "Conte," the murderer, but "Blake," the victim, is your parent.

Sybil was filled with a child's rage, a child's inarticulate grief— Why, why! This man named George Conte had, by a violent act, ruined everything!

According to the testimony of witnesses, George Conte had been "irrationally" jealous of his wife's friendship with other men in their social circle; he'd quarreled publicly with her upon several occasions, and was known to have a drinking problem. On the afternoon of July Fourth, the day of the murder, the couple had been drinking with friends at the Lake Champlain Club for much of the afternoon, and had then set out in their boat for their summer home, three miles to the south. Midway, a quarrel erupted, and George Conte shot his wife several times with a .32 caliber revolver, which, he later confessed, he'd acquired for the purpose of "showing her I was serious." He then pushed her body overboard, and continued on to the cottage where, in a "distraught state," he tried to take his two-year-old daughter Sybil with him, back to the boat—saying that her mother was waiting for her. But the child's grandmother and aunt, both relatives of the murdered woman, prevented him from taking her, so he returned to the boat alone, took it out a considerable distance onto the lake, and shot himself in the head. He collapsed in the idling boat, and was rescued by an emergency medical team and taken to a hospital in Burlington where his life was saved.

Why, why did they save *his* life?—Sybil thought bitterly. She'd never felt such emotion, such outrage, as she felt for this person George Conte: "Mr. Starr." He'd wanted to kill her too, of course—that was the purpose of his coming home, wanting to get her, saying her mother wanted her. Had Sybil's grandmother and Aunt Lora not stopped him, he would have shot her too, and dumped her body into the lake, and ended it all by shooting himself—but not killing himself. A bungled suicide. And then, after recovering, a plea of "not guilty" to the charge of murder.

A charge of second-degree murder, and a sentence of only twelve to nineteen years. So, he was out. George Conte was out. As "Mr. Starr," the amateur artist, the lover of the beautiful and the pure, he'd found her out, and he'd come for her.

And you know why.

13. "Your Mother Is Waiting for You"

Sybil Blake returned the clippings to the envelope so conspicuously marked "MEDICAL INSURANCE," and returned the envelope to the very bottom of the unlocked drawer in her aunt's desk. She closed the drawer carefully, and, though she was in an agitated state, looked about the room to see if she'd left anything inadvertently out of place; any evidence that she'd been in here at all.

Yes, she'd violated the trust Aunt Lora had had in her. Yet Aunt Lora had lied to her too, these many years. And so convincingly.

Sybil understood that she could never again believe anyone fully. She understood that those who love us can, and will, lie to us; they may act out of a moral conviction that such lying is necessary, and this may in fact be true—but, still, they *lie*.

Even as they look into your eyes and insist they are telling the truth.

Of the reasonable steps Sybil Blake might have taken, this was the most reasonable: she might have confronted Lora Dell Blake with the evidence she'd found and with her knowledge of what the tragedy had been, and she might have told her about "Mr. Starr."

But she hated him so. And Aunt Lora hated him. And, hating him as they did, how could they protect themselves against him, if he chose to act? For Sybil had no doubt, now, her father had returned to her to do her harm.

If George Conte had served his prison term, and been released from prison, if he was free to move about the country like any other citizen, certainly he had every right to come to Glencoe, California. In approaching Sybil Blake, his daughter, he had committed no crime. He had not threatened her, he had not harassed her, he had behaved in a kindly, courteous, generous way; except for the fact (in Aunt Lora's eyes this would be an outrageous, unspeakable fact) that he had misrepresented himself.

"Mr. Starr" was a lie, an obscenity. But no one had forced Sybil to model for him, nor to accept an expensive gift from him. She had done so willingly. She had done so gratefully. After her initial timidity, she'd been rather eager to be so employed.

For "Mr. Starr" had seduced her—almost.

Sybil reasoned that if she told her aunt about "Mr. Starr," their lives would be irrevocably changed. Aunt Lora would be upset to the point of hysteria. She would insist upon going to the police. The police would rebuff her, or, worse yet, humor her. And what if Aunt Lora went to confront "Mr. Starr" herself?

No, Sybil was not going to involve her aunt. Nor implicate her in any way.

"I love you too much," Sybil whispered. "You are all I have."

To avoid seeing Aunt Lora that evening, or, rather, to avoid being seen by her, Sybil went to bed early, leaving a note on the kitchen table explaining that she had a mild case of the flu. Next morning, when Aunt Lora looked in Sybil's room, to ask her worriedly how she was, Sybil smiled wanly and said she'd improved; but, still, she thought she would stay home from school that day.

Aunt Lora, ever vigilant against illness, pressed her hand against Sybil's forehead, which did seem feverish. She looked into Sybil's eyes, which were dilated. She asked if Sybil had a sore throat, if she had a headache, if she'd had an upset stomach or diarrhea, and Sybil said no, no, she simply felt a little weak, she wanted to sleep. So Aunt Lora believed her, brought her Bufferin and fruit juice and toast with honey, and went off quietly to leave her alone.

Sybil wondered if she would ever see her aunt again.

But of course she would: she had no doubt, she could force herself to do what must be done.

Wasn't her mother waiting for her?

A windy, chilly afternoon. Sybil wore warm slacks and a wool pullover sweater and her jogging shoes. But she wasn't running today. She carried her kidskin bag, its strap looped over her shoulder.

Her handsome kidskin bag, with its distinctive smell.

Her bag, into which she'd slipped, before leaving home, the sharpest of her aunt's several finely honed steak knives.

Sybil Blake hadn't gone to school that day but she entered the park at approximately three-forty-five, her usual time. She'd sighted Mr. Starr's long elegantly gleaming black limousine parked on the street close by, and there was Mr. Starr himself, waiting for her.

How animated he became, seeing her!—exactly as he'd been in the past. It seemed strange to Sybil that, somehow, to him, things were unchanged.

He imagined her still ignorant, innocent. Easy prey.

Smiling at her. Waving. "Hello, Sybil!"

Daring to call her that—"Sybil."

He was hurrying in her direction, limping, using his cane. Sybil smiled. There was no reason not to smile, thus she smiled. She was thinking with what skill Mr. Starr used that cane of his, how practiced he'd become. Since the injury to his brain?—or had there been another injury, suffered in prison?

Those years in prison, when he'd had time to think. Not to repent—Sybil seemed to know he had not repented—but, simply, to think.

To consider the mistakes he'd made, and how to unmake them.

"Why, my dear, hello!—I've missed you, you know," Mr. Starr said. There was an edge of reproach to his voice but he smiled to show his delight. "I won't ask where *were* you, now you're *here*. And carrying your beautiful bag—"

Sybil peered up at Mr. Starr's pale, tense, smiling face. Her reactions were slow at first, as if numbed; as if she were, for all that she'd rehearsed this, not fully wakened—a kind of sleep-walker.

"And—you *will* model for me this afternoon? Under our new, improved terms?"

"Yes, Mr. Starr."

Mr. Starr had his duffel bag, his sketch pad, his charcoal sticks. He was bareheaded, and his fine silver hair blew in the wind. He wore a slightly soiled white shirt with a navy-blue silk necktie and his old tweed jacket; and his gleaming black shoes that put Sybil in mind of a funeral. She could not see his eyes behind the dark lenses of his glasses but she knew by the puckered skin at the corners of his eyes that he was staring at her intently, hungrily. She was his model, he was the artist, when could they begin? Already, his fingers were flexing in anticipation.

"I think, though, we've about exhausted the possibilities of this park, don't you, dear? It's charming, but rather common. And so *finite*," Mr. Starr was saying, expansively. "Even the beach, here in Glencoe. Somehow it lacks—amplitude. So I was thinking—I was hoping—we might today vary our routine just a bit, and drive up the coast. Not far—just a few miles. Away from so many people, and so many distractions." Seeing that Sybil was slow to respond, he added, warmly, "I'll pay you double, Sybil— of course. You know you can trust me by now, don't you? Yes?"

That curious, ugly little hook of a scar in Mr. Starr's fore-head—its soft pale tissue gleamed in the whitish light. Sybil wondered was that where the bullet had gone in.

Mr. Starr had been leading Sybil in the direction of the curb, where the limousine was waiting, its engine idling almost soundlessly. He opened the door. Sybil, clutching her kidskin bag, peered inside, at the cushioned, shadowy interior. For a moment, her mind was blank. She might have been on a high board, about to dive into the water, not knowing how she'd gotten to where she was, or why. Only that she could not turn back.

Mr. Starr was smiling eagerly, hopefully. "Shall we? Sybil?"

"Yes, Mr. Starr," Sybil said, and climbed inside.

NANCY PICKARD

SEX AND VIOLENCE

*Nancy Pickard, author of several award-winning novels about
sleuth Jenny Cain and a past president of Sisters in Crime,
makes her first appearance in this series with a story from*
Deadly Allies, *the joint anthology from Sisters in Crime and
the Private Eye Writers of America. It's a memorable tale of a
male-female relationship that existed over the years, in good
times and bad, far longer than it should have.*

The call came at 10:30 on a Saturday morning in January.

When her phone rang, Amy Giddens was still in her white chenille bathrobe, seated in her rocking chair in front of her gas
fireplace, her slippered feet up on a hassock. She was drinking
coffee and reading *The Kansas City Star;* the crumbs of a croissant lay on a plate on the floor beside her. A fragrance of
bayberry rose from a fat green candle on the hearth; a scent of
cinnamon drifted into the living room from a pot of apple cider
that simmered on the stove.

She picked up the phone and said hello.

"Oh, Amy, something awful has happened."

It was her friend, Kathy Weltner.

Amy sat straight up, sweeping the newspaper off her lap.

"Of all people," Kathy said. "I mean, I thought he'd live forever. Oh, Amy, Ross Powell is dead." Her voice broke. "I knew
you'd want to know. It's just so . . . unbelievable."

Inside her, Amy's voice cried, *No.*

As she listened to Kathy, she stared out her own picture window, noticing in some part of her consciousness that this was just
the kind of gray, bitterly cold day that would have inspired Ross

Powell to take off for some place like Portugal, where the sun was always shining. She felt a big, lonely emptiness begin to inflate her body, and into the emptiness there poured the huge, silent *No*.

She managed to inquire: how, where, what happened?

"He drove over a cliff." Kathy laughed a little wildly, but the sound got snagged on her tears. "In France. Above Monte Carlo. I mean, of course. Like Princess Grace. Oh God. It's not funny. But if he had to go, I'll bet this is how he'd want to do it, except maybe if he could have had a heart attack while he was fucking, that would have been even better. Maybe that's how he drove off the cliff." Again, she half laughed, half cried, "It would have been just like him, wouldn't it?"

At the word "France," Amy was jolted by a wave of nostalgia so strong that it shocked her. It was three years since she'd seen him, but at that moment she remembered Ross as clearly, as vibrantly, as if he were that moment leaning over her, just as he had towered over the Europeans in the train stations. He was so much taller than most of them that she'd always been able to spot him easily in crowds. She saw his shoulders, such all-American male shoulders, that strained the leather of the jacket he bought in Spain; and his arms, which were longer than normal, giving him a simian, disproportionate appearance that you couldn't detect face-on, but which you caught sometimes when you glanced at him out of the corner of your eye; and the curly brown hair that hadn't looked so rebellious in Europe where so many other men also wore ponytails; and his mustache that drooped to the corner of his mouth when he frowned; and his lips and nose that were too large for the rest of his face, giving him a lazy, sensuous look; and his hazel eyes that held a woman's for a promising, tantalizing moment before sliding away, as if he knew a sexy secret or had told her a lie. In that startling, vivid instant, Amy could even smell him, and the greatest shock was remembering that his after-shave had smelled like bayberry, just like her favorite kind of candles.

"Amy? Are you there . . . are you all right?"

The memory disappeared. Amy wanted to cry out: *No! Wait!*

"When did it happen?" she managed to say.

"Last week. I heard it from somebody who heard it from his mother. They say it was at night, and they think he was alone—"

"*Think?*"

"Well, the car just sailed off a cliff into the Mediterranean. They say he probably died on impact, instead of drowning, although they won't know for sure until they find, oh God, his body. So it was probably instantaneous. I hope. I can't bear to think how he felt on the way down, can you?"

"So there's no funeral?" Amy felt as if she had to pull her voice up from deep inside a great, hollow well.

"His mother will hold a memorial service of some kind, I guess, but we're having everybody over here tonight for a sort of party in his honor. I know you didn't care about him anymore. And I know he was such a jerk to you. But he was *Ross,* you know? And everybody from the old days will be here. And they'll all want to see you. So you'll come, won't you, Amy?"

She promised to.

After she put the receiver down, Amy stared into her real fire burning between her phony logs. And it was at that moment that her memories began, as if by some sort of romantic, nostalgic alchemy, to transform themselves from bitter into sweet. *He was in a good mood that last morning in Albufiera. And earlier, he had looked so sexy, so tempting, lying asleep in their room. What if she had slid back into bed with him? What if she had smiled back at him at the café, forgiven him, kept traveling with him? Would he still be alive?*

Five years ago . . .

Outside the drawn curtains of their hotel room in Albufiera, the morning sun struck the rough surfaces of the whitewashed buildings like a match, shooting fierce sparks into the cool air. A thin beam of light filtered through the muslin and lay like a warm dime on Amy's cheek. Her mind came reluctantly awake before her eyes opened; it took a few foggy moments for her to comprehend the nature of the unexpected heat on her face.

Sun? she thought, unbelieving.

She was afraid to open her eyes and look for fear this blessing might fade back to darkness in her dreams. She squeezed her eyelids tighter and prayed to whatever gods had been harassing her, Let that be the sun shining. Then she opened her eyes cautiously, only to snap them shut when the glare hurt them. Blessed pain.

"Thank you," she murmured into her pillow.

Amy lay still in the expanding pool of warmth, and listened for sounds from the other side of the bed. Ross was breathing deeply, but he wasn't snoring. He never snored. It was one of those qualities of his for which she had continued to try to feel grateful. He was funny, when he wasn't depressed, that was another one. He was tall. Charming to strangers. Kind to dogs. "Arf," she said softly, and stifled a giggle. God knew she'd wagged her tail for him. "Arf, arf."

And he was incredibly patient when she made major blunders—like the time she left her passport on a table in a cafeteria in Paris—even if almost everything else she did annoyed him. One memorable night, he'd been angry because she left food on her plate. Food on her plate, for God's sake, as if she were five years old!

"I'll order the child's plate next time," she'd snapped back.

"Well, that would be appropriate in more ways than one," he'd said coolly, so that she'd had to bite back the tears that would have seemed to him to prove his point.

In point of fact, she was twenty-six and he was thirty-one. His life was devoted to finding jobs that paid enough for nine months to allow him to escape to the south of Europe every winter; her life, for the past two years, had been devoted to saving enough money to join him this time. It had been, mostly, a disastrous idea, she had finally admitted to herself: she couldn't get close enough to him; he couldn't get far enough away from her.

But this is this morning, Amy thought, lying in bed, and the sun is shining. It was not a trivial thought, she knew; in long, cold, gray winters, the sun was never trivial, and its promises were not to be taken lightly.

Amy still had not opened her eyes again, but at least she knew where she was. No small accomplishment that, considering the rate they'd been traveling. "I am on the Algarve," she recited reassuringly to herself, "in the south of Portugal, on the Iberian

Peninsula, on the continent of Europe, northern and western hemispheres, third planet from the sun." She smiled. "No wonder it took so long to get here."

Then she discovered another miracle.

She put a doubting hand to her abdomen just to be sure; she pushed in, then out. No cramps, no nausea. Her stomach had unclenched itself in the night.

She'd been the sickest two nights before, in Lisbon.

"Maybe I'll die," she'd told Ross, and had imagined a flicker of hope in his eyes. "For heaven's sake, go to dinner without me."

"I'll bring you back something," he'd offered, looking resentful. Then without waiting for a reply, he had rendered the offer meaningless. "I'll probably stop for a drink, so don't wait up for me."

"I'm not likely to do that," she'd said, dryly.

It seemed to her that everything she said lately was dry, as if to compensate for the eternal rain. Or, possibly, because she herself had condensed. When she met strangers on the road, she wondered if they could tell she had turned into a block of dry ice, expelling lifeless steam instead of air.

Ross had returned to their room after midnight when she was aching with fever and wretched from hours of diarrhea and vomiting.

He had not inquired about her health.

"I found a wonderful bar," he'd exclaimed, full of the energy of his evening. Rapidly, he'd stripped down to naked, talking all the while. "In the old part of town, down this wonderful windy street, all cobblestones. And there was a Fado singer you would have been crazy about, all melancholy and kind of haunting. I met this old guy there—"

He'd jabbered on while she'd huddled in a fetal position, resenting the hell out of him, yet glad that he was talking to her again, and smiling. She was worn down by the mercurial changes in his temperament, depressed one week, manic the next. And he accused her of being emotional! Was he crazy? she wondered as she lay aching, or just selfish? If he was crazy, as in truly mentally ill, did she have to feel sorry for him and keep loving him? If he was just selfish, *could* she stop loving him?

171

And then he'd crawled into the bed and pressed himself against her burning back. He'd wanted sex. She was too sick and weak to fight about it, and so she'd let him do it. And hated him.

Finally, she'd hated him.

Months later, she confided to a friend about that night in Lisbon, and was surprised and embarrassed when the friend called it "shocking," and said he had "raped" her. "Oh no," Amy protested, "I could have said no, and he wouldn't have done it, it isn't the same thing at all, I'm sorry I ever said anything about it, and please don't tell anybody else, okay?" After that, she didn't confide to anybody certain things about her relationship with Ross. Like the time they were screaming at each other in their room, after too much beer, in a hotel in Germany, and the manager intervened because she said that Ross was so much bigger than Amy that the manager was afraid "the little American girl" might get hurt. He never would have done that, Amy, thoroughly mortified, told the woman; he would never lay a hand on her in violence. And he certainly never had, except for that time in Florence when he slapped her when she cried hysterically because he hadn't spoken to her in five days. But that didn't count, and besides, it worked. She stopped weeping and he started talking. They'd been cooped up together too much, that was all. And that German manager, she was just overreacting out of some sort of guilt left over from World War II, Amy figured out, that was all, like maybe she hadn't protested when the Nazis took her Jewish neighbors away, or something like that. Anyway, that was her problem, not Amy's or Ross's.

Maybe it's the weather that makes us crazy, she thought as she lay in bed, in Albufiera, as the sun radiated into her vital organs.

They'd been weeks in search of the sun, or was it years? They'd chased its winter shadow from London down to the Atlantic. But even on the road from Lisbon, it had rained and they'd despaired of ever feeling warm again. Amy had wrapped herself in a blanket that Ross had stolen from their hotel and she had huddled in the passenger seat of the rented car and shivered with the flu. All the way along the two-lane blacktop, through green fields of black olive trees, she'd shivered. Past square, one-room houses painted brilliant pastel colors that shone fluorescent in the rain, she had shivered and sweated into the scratchy wool. Halfway, they got stuck behind a funeral cortege. The coffin, a simple wooden affair loaded onto the flatbed of a clean truck, was trailed by somber men on motorcycles and squat, walking women in black. Amy had gotten the feeling she was the corpse and the world was mourning. Knowing better, but playing for sympathy, she'd confided her hallucination to Ross. He'd suggested it was time for her to take another Tylenol. . . .

She slipped out from under her covers and stood beside him, staring down at him in bed. One or two people had told her he reminded them of the actor James Coburn. In the sunlight, Amy examined the long, lean body that gave him that look, and the high cheekbones and the wide mouth, and the creases around his eyes that hinted at intelligence and cruel wit.

"I've known you to be gentle," she whispered. "I've even known you to be kind."

But not lately.

He slept snorelessly on.

She padded barefoot across the rug to her suitcase to scoop up underwear, slacks, and a shirt. Then she went quietly into the bathroom to shower and dress, anxious to avoid the heat of his glance on her nakedness. She didn't want him to want her this morning. Most of all, she didn't want to want him.

A few minutes later, before she left their room, she looked back at it. It appeared so elegant to Amy, and it was cheap, to boot. God, she loved Europe. She had yearned to come here almost as much as she had desired to be with Ross this winter. And now here she was, existing on two different planes—still thrilled by the journey, but miserable with loneliness and resentment. She knew she would never have taken this trip without him; basically, she was a sedentary person, not an adventurer like Ross. Loving him had freed her to do this extraordinary thing— to quit her job and to travel for three months in Europe. Without him, she wouldn't have had the nerve. If she left him, she wouldn't have the courage to continue traveling by herself, she'd probably fly straight home, and even the thought of managing *that* by herself made her feel sick with nervousness. They were both free, and yet he felt imprisoned by her presence and she felt imprisoned by her own fear. Weird. In the bed, Ross moved an arm. Amy quickly, quietly, closed the door.

Ross found her two hours later on the veranda of the big luxury hotel on the beach. The sun was just coming over the building, and there was a slight breeze, so the morning wasn't really all that warm yet; Amy was glad that she'd slipped a sweater on over her shirt and jeans. The Atlantic Ocean, looking gray and restless, was only a strip of beach away from her table. She had known that Ross would have to wander in this direction to find breakfast.

"Hi," he said, and smiled down at her.

"Hi."

He leaned down to kiss her, lingering a moment on her lips, so she knew this day he would honor her with the privilege of one of his good moods.

He dragged a chair up to her table in a rectangle of sun, put an exuberant arm around her shoulders, and hugged her with every evidence of fondness.

"Café au lait," he said to the waiter. "I mean, *con leche.*" He laughed, as if the waiter and Amy would enjoy his predicament, and threw up his hands. "Christ, what country is this? Which language this morning?"

The waiter didn't appear to get the joke.

"Can you believe this glorious day?" Ross squinted into the sunshine, looking as pleased as if the day had been especially arranged for him.

She put a finger in her mystery novel, and closed it.

"Yes, it's wonderful."

"How're you feeling?"

"Okay. Good."

"Thought you were going to die on me."

"I felt like it, I guess."

He gazed at her appraisingly, but in a friendly way, over his steaming coffee cup. "You look better," he said finally, and then he grinned. "Good enough to eat."

"Try a croissant, instead," she said, and felt the steam come off the dry ice again.

He leaned back in his chair, and laughed.

"Listen," he said suddenly, eagerly, like a small boy with a big plan. He grabbed her free hand and squeezed it. "How about if we take the car and drive on down the coast for the day? Maybe have lunch on the beach somewhere, get some wine and cheese, what do you say?"

"Ross," she said, then bit her lip.

"All right!" He released her hand, then leaned back again, appearing satisfied with the state of things. "All right."

No! Amy's voice cried inside her head: *It isn't all right!*

"Ross?"

"What?" Was there a hint of awareness, a suspicion at the back of his eyes? Then he smiled again, and whatever she thought she read in his glance was gone. "What, honey?"

"I can't stand—" *to ride your roller coaster again! Stop it! Or let me off!* But for a moment, she lost her nerve.

"What can't you stand? You don't want to go to the beach? It'll be gorgeous. What?"

"Nothing."

"Oh, that!" he teased. "Well, that's nothing."

"Ross?"

"What?" He laughed. "What, *what?*"

"Nothing." Suddenly she was furious, at him, at herself. *I'm getting off, damn you!* "I'm leaving, I'm getting off!"

He looked utterly surprised, and the beginning of angry. How could she ruin their day? he'd demand to know. How could she throw a stupid, goddamned tantrum on a gorgeous day like this? What in the hell was the matter with her?

"*Nothing!*" she said, and other customers turned to look. "*Nothing!*" As Ross stared at her, Amy pushed back from the table, threw down her napkin, and ran from the veranda.

She slowed to a walk near their hotel.

There would be buses returning to Lisbon that very day. And from Lisbon there would be planes to carry her home. She hadn't meant to do it this way, but it was better than . . . nothing. Yes, she was frightened, but a smile was growing on her face. *It is,* she thought, *so good to leave on a sunny day when the world is bright and clear and sharp.* The winter sun was strong and hot on her back, like a warm, moist hand, pushing her. . . .

* * *

It was the last time she saw Ross.

She thought she had left him forever. She thought she had left herself with only a healthy residue of bitter memories of a selfish man. She had married somebody else, and divorced that man. Dated other men, broken a couple of hearts, and suffered her own being broken again.

But five years later, upon hearing that Ross Powell was dead, Amy was awash in a passionate, sentimental longing for him. He'd been so much fun, she'd loved him so much, and she felt sure that he'd cared about her too, in his own strange way, that maybe he'd even loved her more than he'd ever loved any other woman, and that he'd missed her terribly when she was gone, and that he was sorry for all the times . . .

Oh, God, if only she could love him one more time.

He couldn't be dead. No!

Although she hated the idea of what the party represented—that he was really dead—she couldn't stay away.

Kathy Weltner and Sam DeLucca had married in the old days when the whole gang, including Ross and Amy, worked as copywriters or artists in the advertising department of Macy's, back when there was a Macy's in Kansas City. There'd been many pairings back then, but Sam and Kathy were the only two who were still a couple.

"It's your three kids that keep you together," proclaimed Steve Allison, as he set down his contribution to the evening: a case of Budweiser, which was Ross Powell's favorite back in the good old days. "You can't either of you bear the thought of being left alone with the kids."

"Not a problem Ross ever had," Sam DeLucca observed, his dry wit still intact after all those years. "God love him."

"At least not that we ever knew," his wife, Kathy Weltner, added in her own tartly distinctive style, which had also distinguished her writing. "It's difficult for me to believe, however, that there aren't a few little Rosses—or Rossettes—scattered about the globe, you know?"

"God, what a terrifying thought," said Lara Eisenstein, who

was still an advertising illustrator in town. "I loved him, too, but . . . clones of Ross? Mothers, hide your daughters."

"My theory," Steve said, as he popped the tops on Budweisers for each of them, "is that he didn't accidentally go over that cliff at all. He was too good a driver. So I figure a woman killed him. It's only logical—"

"Inevitable, you mean," Sam said, and they all laughed.

"Not to mention justifiable," Kathy interjected.

"Okay," Steve said, "so maybe it was that one who went after him with a knife that time, remember her? What was her name? Or the other one—the accountant—who rammed her car into the back of his. And then into the front. On purpose. And there was that lady, God, poor thing, who tried to kill herself when Ross left her." He took a swig of Bud, wiped his mouth, and smiled. "I think one of them pushed him over the cliff, and who could blame them?"

"Maybe they all got together and did it," somebody called in from the living room. "All the women he ever dumped. You know, like that Agatha Christie mystery, what was it called? *Murder on the Orient Express?* Where they all took a stab, pardon the pun, at the victim?"

"They never called *me,*" Amy said.

Sam DeLucca laughed loud enough for his amusement to carry in to the gang in the living room. "Ross, as victim? You expect us to buy that? No way! Ross was a penetrator . . . excuse me . . . perpetrator if there ever was one!"

"Very funny," his wife said. "You're all wrong, anyway. It was a jealous husband or boyfriend."

"Couldn't be," Lara Eisenstein objected. "Ross never dated married women. Remember? It was a principle of his—"

"Principle!" Sam and Kathy hooted at the same time, and Kathy added, "The man hadn't seen a principal since he left high school."

Lara laughed, and made a face at them. "No, really, I mean it was a prin-ci-ple of his never to date married women because . . ." She looked around at each of them, smiling, and shaking her head. "Why should he mess with that kind of trouble, when there were so many other women who were so utterly available to him?"

Kathy suddenly turned toward Amy. "Oops. Listen, guys, maybe this is not tactful. I mean, obviously, it's tasteless, which is only fitting considering the subject, but maybe it's also tactless? You want we should shut up about Ross and his other women, Amy?"

"Don't be silly," Amy said, "it's history."

"I don't get it," Steve said. "How could a man who wouldn't hurt a flea inspire so much violence in so many women? I always thought he was kind of a gentle guy, you know? I mean, he was a good friend, loyal, do anything for you, give you the shirt off his back—"

"Big deal," Sam laughed. "K mart special, all polyester."

Steve laughed, too, but he said, insistently, "All right, but you know what I mean. He was a hell of a lot of fun to be around. I thought he was a nice guy." He took another drink of Bud. "So there, asshole."

"He was nice if you were his friend," Kathy said, in a reflective tone of voice. "That's true. Although he could drive you crazy, the way he used to just drop by any time of day or night, like just when we would be trying to get the kids to sleep. But for his girlfriends"—she glanced at Amy with a smile full of sympathy—"I think there was a lot of wear and tear."

Lara Eisenstein laughed. "You make him sound like a Laundromat."

"I'll tell you what I could never understand." Sam affected a woebegone expression that made him look like his own golden retriever. "What was it about him that attracted women like flies? Begging your pardon, ladies. But I mean it was like they were the flies and he was the screen door. Or they were the flies and he was the garbage . . . no, no, I didn't mean that, that can't be right. Do you understand it, Stevie? Hell, he wasn't even good-looking. What did he have that we don't have?"

The women in both rooms smirked, with the exception of Amy, and one of the men in the living room called out, "You had to ask, dummy!"

"He had glamour," Kathy said. "And style. All of those trips to Europe. Those sports cars he drove, because he didn't have to pay for a mortgage or for preschool like the rest of us. What was attractive about Ross was the life he led, which consisted of periods of compulsive responsibility interspersed with total abandon and adventure. Like a Yuppie Indiana Jones." Her smile was self-deprecating. "I guess it's obvious that I've been thinking about it a lot since he died." Suddenly there were tears in her eyes and in the eyes of several other people there, as well. "Ross was bigger than life. Shouldn't that mean that he wasn't supposed to die?"

Sam slapped his beer can angrily down on his kitchen counter. "What the hell was he doing there, anyway? Wasn't he getting a little old for that stuff?"

"He'd been working for one of those Texas savings and loan companies," Steve said. "One of the ones that went belly up. I think he took his last paycheck and said, adios, guys, have a good time in court, I'm off to Europe."

There was a moment of silence in both the kitchen and the living room. Finally, somebody said, "Let's pretend he's not dead, he's just late to the party."

"Okay then, here," said Steve, holding high a Budweiser, "this is to the late Ross Powell, who's going to walk in that door any minute now and tell us it was all a joke on us. Ha." He drained his beer and then set the can quietly on the counter. "Ha." In a choked voice, he said, "Well, he hated winter, and now he'll never have to see it again. It'll always be summer on the Riviera for Ross."

"We agreed that he wasn't really dead," Sam snapped at him. "He's merely late to the party, probably out picking up a woman somewhere. So cut the sentimental crap. Shut up and drink."

Later, when they had a moment alone in the bathroom, Kathy said to Amy, "You're so quiet. Are you feeling just too sad? Are you okay?"

"I'm not sad," Amy said, and it was true, she wasn't. What she was, was excited. She didn't have to pretend, as the rest of them did. In her heart, she was beginning to feel it was true: Ross couldn't be dead, because he *wasn't* dead. It really *was* unbelievable that he could be dead . . . because it literally . . . wasn't . . . true. They might play around with the idea of what had "really" happened to him, but she had known him better, more intimately, than any of them ever had, and she knew that only she was able to put the facts together to fit the only possible conclusion. *Fact one: they'd found a car, but no body. Fact two: he'd walked off with money from the failed savings and loan company in Texas, probably more than they knew, possibly even a lot of it, and he may have even stolen it. Fact three: if that were so, it would have been just like him to stage his ultimate escape.*

It was all she could do to restrain herself from grabbing Kathy and hugging her and exclaiming, "I think he's alive! And I can find him!"

Once she had the notion, she couldn't shake it.

Driving to work, eating lunch with her friends, talking on the phone to her mother, going to the bathroom, taking a shower, putting on makeup—at all times, a part of her mind was doubting. That he was dead. Hoping. That he was alive. Figuring out. How it could be possible. Dreaming. What she might do about it.

Amy didn't say a word about what she was thinking to anybody, not even to Kathy. She knew that anybody she might confide in would think she was nuts; worse, they'd say she was still in love with him, and they'd feel sorry for her.

Well, maybe she was still in love with him.

But they didn't need to pity her.

They should envy me, Amy thought when she had it all figured out, *because I'm the only one of them—of his friends, of his family, of all of the people who ever knew him—who may get one more chance to see him again.*

Deep down, she wondered—she fantasized—about how he might, by now, be desperately hungry to connect with somebody who really knew him, about how glad he'd be to see her again, about how he might invite her to slip inside his new life, to start all over again with him now that they were older and wiser, about how he might beg her to share his last, best escape.

But most of the time she told herself she only wanted to see him. One more time. One last time. It would be a sort of triumph, a sort of victory, a trick on the trickster, but one that would surely make him laugh the hardest of all. It amused Amy so much to think: I escaped from you, lover, but you can't escape from me.

At work, they only knew that Amy Giddens took her regular two-week vacation and flew off for a glamorous fortnight to Europe. Cyprus. Torremolinos. The Canary Islands. The Algarve. They looked at her travel folders and envied her exotic, sunstroked itinerary, marveling at the stamina it would take to visit so many wonderful places in so short a time, and at the adventurous spirit that propelled her to make this trip by herself. A few bluenoses at the office sniffed at her spendthrift manner of throwing money away on an outrageously expensive vacation. Amy stared at those same travel folders and saw Ross Powell's favorite destinations in his search for never-ending summer.

On the airplane, she kept thinking: there are so many places he could be, places she remembered that he had liked, places where the sun always shone, like almost anyplace along the Riviera, Morocco, Tunisia, Majorca. But the most likely place was Albufiera, because nobody Ross ever knew was ever likely to go there, and because Portugal was still cheap compared with the rest of Europe. Amy remembered Albufiera as a town where the only noticeable foreigners were German and British; Americans preferred the resorts north of Lisbon instead of the Algarve to the south.

And, she had to admit to herself, she *wanted* it to be Albufiera. Because it was beautiful, and because its beauty and her melancholy had made her heart ache, and because she had left him sitting there, and it would be so natural to walk back into the café, at the hotel on the ocean, and to find him sitting there again, to go up to his table, to smile as he had smiled at her and to say, "Hi. Can you believe this gorgeous day? Let's take the car and drive on down the beach. We can stop for a bottle of wine, some bread and cheese, what do you say?"

When she thought of how Albufiera looked, she remembered a

particular arch that separated the street from the luxury hotel. In her memory, the street was cobblestones; the hotel had no remembered shape at all. But the arch was vivid in its particularity in her memory: lovely in its simplicity, thick as a man's arm from wrist to shoulder, rounded like the innermost curve of a woman's neck; the sun cast half of it in shadow, the other half in light so bright the whiteness of the arch made her eyes hurt when she remembered it; and what she remembered most of all—whether or not it had actually been true—was that when you stepped through the arch you moved out of cool, sad shadow into the light.

Amy's plane landed in Lisbon on a Monday morning. She drove, in a rented car, all the way to Albufiera that afternoon, arriving at dusk.

Leaving her bags in the car, she walked first to the beach where she and Ross had hung out to watch the sun set over the Atlantic Ocean. Just as she had remembered, the Portuguese fishermen were pulling in their nets from their brilliantly painted little boats. Women sold glittering silver fish out of buckets set up on wooden tables in the sand. There were tourists there with lighter skin and hair, and men who were taller and thinner than the Portuguese, but none of them was Ross Powell.

As the sunset grew ever more violently pink and orange, Amy abandoned the beach and walked toward a little dinner restaurant that still lived in her memory. It had been frequented by foreigners, and the tables had been so close together that you couldn't help but get to know your neighbors. But when she thought she found the right location, she saw only a gift store selling knickknacks.

It was dark by the time she found the hotel where they'd stayed, and she wasn't surprised when the clerk told her that no Mr. Powell was registered there. Of course, Ross wouldn't use his real name, she realized. She was expecting that problem. But the clerk also volunteered that there were no Americans at the hotel at all. "Australians?" she asked. No, none of those. "English, Scottish . . ." She began to feel foolish, inquiring of various nationalities under which Ross might be hiding. The clerk grew impatient, and resorted to claiming that she didn't speak English, which of course she had been, if haltingly, until that very moment.

"Oh God," Amy said to herself as she left the hotel. "If I'm wrong . . ."

It would be an expensive mistake, not only in terms of her limited funds but also in the amount of time she had in which to look for him. There were so many places he could be, all of them hot and sunny, except . . .

She remembered a bar—long and cool and dim, even in the daytime—manned by a British expatriate who called out your name the second time you came in, and who paid you the compliment of talking to you in a humorous, cynical way about tourists, as if you weren't one. It was a bar where at any time you could find Germans, Scandinavians, British, and Americans, and always somebody who spoke English. Foreigners stuck together in Portugal, she believed, because they felt like time travelers in an earlier century. The natives either didn't or wouldn't speak English, and the English didn't speak Portuguese, which was so different, so separate from Spanish; everybody stuck to their own kind, staring at the others, and wondering, but rarely pushing through the door from one culture into the other. It was such a good place to hide, she knew it was, and she knew that Ross would think so, too. Here, everybody seemed to be hiding something, some secret—the Portuguese, most of all, hiding their glances, their language, and their souls from the foreign tourists, and most of all, hiding their curiosity. They asked no questions, they gave nothing away in their dark faces: perfect people to hide among, because they appeared to take no interest at all in their visitors.

She was willing to bet the English bar owner would still be mixing drinks behind the counter and welcoming strangers as if they were regulars. So what if Ross wasn't at the beach, and so what if that restaurant was gone now? There were cafés where Ross might be eating dinner this very evening.

But first she would try to find that old bar.

* * *

Amy stepped into the cool, dim interior of the bar and scanned the length of the room. She didn't see the Englishman. That depressed her so that she was ready to give up and go find a room for the night. Then her heart lurched and she nearly cried out when she noticed the man seated on the last stool at the end. He was tall, too thin, with a full beard and a mustache; he'd brushed his hair back off his forehead and it fell, curly and unbound to his shoulders—which looked too wide in proportion to the rest of his body. His profile, as he raised a glass of beer to his mouth, displayed a wide nose and full lips. He was wearing a battered brown leather jacket over a black turtleneck sweater and well-worn blue jeans.

Amy ducked, so that she could observe the man at the end of the bar without being seen. Was it Ross? It couldn't really be! Suddenly, for the first time, Amy was struck by the absurdity, the absolute unlikelihood of her quest. Ross Powell was dead. He was supposed to be dead, he wasn't supposed to be sitting here, in the same bar where they'd sat together five years before. And even if he was still alive, it wasn't possible that she had really found him. Out of an entire world of places to hide, she couldn't have picked the one. It wasn't possible, this wasn't the man, she was out of her mind, and she ought to face that truth, have a quick drink, go back and pack her bags and go home, clear-eyed and sane once more.

He turned his face in her direction.

It was undeniably Ross Powell.

And he saw her, looking at him.

After the first instant of surprise, he smiled.

His lips moved as if he were saying something to her, and he pushed his weight forward on the palm of his left hand, as if he were going to push himself off of the bar stool and come toward her.

"Wine!" A woman shoved her way to the bar directly in front of Ross, and she was followed by two other women. "We'd like a carafe of red wine, please."

Amy couldn't see Ross behind the women.

And then the women were joined by three men, and all of them

bunched up jovially at the bar, arguing loudly and good-na-
turedly over whether to order wine or beer.

Rooted to the floor by the shock of actually seeing him, Amy
waited for him to get off his bar stool and walk around the
crowd and come over to her. When he didn't appear, she took a
couple of tentative steps in his direction.

But then the party of six separated enough for her to see that
the bar stool behind them was empty. One of the women noticed,
and sat down on it.

"Ross?"

A man at the bar turned to stare at her.

Amy hurried forward.

He was gone. Nowhere in the bar. There were some Portuguese
coins thrown down on the counter beside his half-finished drink.

Amy started to hurry out the door, to chase him into the night,
to find him and grab him.

But was it really Ross she had seen?

Leaving the bar, she wasn't sure any longer.

Such a quick glimpse, after so many years . . .

But that *smile* . . .

Amy stumbled out of the cool, dim bar into the even colder,
even darker Portuguese night. And suddenly, she was also aware
of how alone she was: a woman alone outside of a bar in a
strange country. She suddenly wanted to get back safely to her
car, and to find a hotel room quickly.

That smile. *It* was *him. She knew it.*

She'd look for Ross again tomorrow.

Amy slowed down. Or maybe she wouldn't. If he'd stolen
money from the savings and loan, if he'd faked his own death,
he wouldn't want to be found, not even by her. How could she
have been so foolish as to think he would?

She walked into the dark, narrow street that led in the direction of her car. She felt desolate, stupid. And suddenly, frighten-
ingly, she felt as if she were being followed. Amy picked up her
pace until she was nearly running.

She heard footsteps running behind her, drawing nearer.

If she screamed, in this foreign country, where everybody ignored her, would anybody help her?

Amy felt a hand land roughly on her back. It pushed her off balance, shoved her into an alley beside the bar. She cried out as it grasped her shoulder and whirled her around.

"Ross!"

She was staring into his face as he grabbed her hair and pulled her head back. Her eyes were still open as he leaned down and kissed her, forcing her mouth open, pushing his tongue between her teeth, shoving her body against the brick wall.

Her eyes closed as she felt his hands meet in a circle around her neck.

RUTH RENDELL

THE MAN WHO WAS
THE GOD OF LOVE

*One of the major mystery events in England this past year was
the celebration of Julian Symons's eightieth birthday. The occasion brought forth two commemorative anthologies of new
stories by leading writers, some of which are being published
in the United States by EQMM. For the Detection Club anthology, edited by H. R. F. Keating, story titles began with the
words "The Man Who . . ." in keeping with the title of the
book. Ruth Rendell is no stranger to this series, and I was
especially attracted to her contribution to* The Man Who . . .
*because it's so different from her usual tales of dark psycho-
logical suspense. It shows a new side to one of our best and
most dependable writers. (This story also appears in the
March 1993 issue of EQMM.)*

"Have you got *The Times* there?" Henry would say, usually
at about eight, when she had cleared the dinner table and put the
things in the dishwasher.

The Times was on the coffee table with the two other dailies
they took, but it was part of the ritual to ask her. Fiona liked to
be asked. She liked to watch Henry do the crossword puzzle, the
real one of course, not the quick crossword, and watch him
frown a little, his handsome brow clear as the answer to a clue
came to him. She could not have done a crossword puzzle to save
her life (as she was fond of saying), she could not even have done
the simple ones in the tabloids.

While she watched him, before he carried the newspaper off into his study as he often did, Fiona told herself how lucky she was to be married to Henry. Her luck had been almost miraculous. There she was, a temp who had come into his office to work for him while his secretary had a baby, an ordinary, not particularly good-looking girl, who had no credentials but a tidy mind and a proficient way with a word processor. She had nothing but her admiration for him, which she had felt from the first and was quite unable to hide.

He was not appreciated in that company as he should have been. It had often seemed to her that only she saw him for what he was. After she had been there a week she told him he had a first-class mind.

Henry had said modestly, "As a matter of fact, I have got rather a high IQ, but it doesn't exactly get stretched round here."

"I suppose they haven't the brains to recognize it," she said. "It must be marvelous to be really intelligent. Did you win scholarships and get a double first and all that?"

He only smiled. Instead of answering he asked her to have dinner with him. One afternoon, half an hour before they were due to pack up and go, she came upon him doing *The Times* crossword.

"In the firm's time, I'm afraid, Fiona," he said with one of his wonderful, half-rueful smiles.

He hadn't finished the puzzle but at least half of it was already filled in and when she asked him he said he had started it ten minutes before. She was lost in admiration. Henry said he would finish the puzzle later and in the meantime would she have a drink with him on the way home?

That was three years ago. The firm, which deserved bankruptcy it was so mismanaged, got into difficulties and Henry was among those made redundant. Of course he soon got another job, though the salary was pitiful for someone of his intellectual grasp. He was earning very little more than she was, as she told him indignantly. Soon afterward he asked her to marry him. Fiona was overcome. She told him humbly that she would have gladly lived with him without marriage, there was no one else she had ever known to compare with him in intellectual terms, it would have been enough to be allowed to share his life. But he said no, marriage or nothing, it would be unfair on her not to marry her.

She kept on with her temping job, making sure she stopped in time to be home before Henry and get his dinner. It was ridiculous to waste money on a cleaner, so she cleaned the house on Sundays. Henry played golf on Saturday mornings and he liked her to go with him, though she was hopeless when she tried to learn. He said it was an inspiration to have her there and praise his swing. On Saturday afternoons they went out in the car and Henry had begun teaching her to drive.

They had quite a big garden—they had bought the house on an enormous mortgage—and she did her best to keep it trim because Henry obviously didn't have the time. He was engaged on a big project for his new company which he worked on in his study for most of the evenings. Fiona did the shopping in her lunchtime, she did all the cooking and all the washing and ironing. It was her privilege to care for someone as brilliant as Henry. Besides, his job was so much more demanding than hers, it took more out of him and by bedtime he was sometimes white with exhaustion.

But Henry was first up in the mornings. He was an early riser, getting up at six-thirty, and he always brought her a cup of tea and the morning papers in bed. Fiona had nothing to do before she went off to take first a bus and then the tube but put the breakfast things in the dishwasher and stack yesterday's newspapers in the cupboard outside the front door for recycling.

The Times would usually be on top, folded with the lower left-hand quarter of the back page uppermost. Fiona soon came to understand it was no accident that the section of the paper where the crossword was, the *completed* crossword, should be exposed in this way. It was deliberate, it was evidence of Henry's pride in his achievement, and she was deeply moved that he should want her to see it. She was touched by his need for her admiration. A sign of weakness on his part it might be, but she loved him all the more for that.

A smile, half-admiring, half-tender, came to her lips, as she looked at the neatly printed answers to all those incomprehensible clues. She could have counted on the fingers of one hand the number of times he had failed to finish the crossword. The evening before his father died, for instance. Then it was anxiety which must have been the cause. They had sent for him at four in the morning and when she looked at the paper before putting it outside with the others, she saw that poor Henry had only been able to fill in the answers to four clues. Another time he had flu and had been unable to get out of bed in the morning. It must have been coming on the night before to judge by his attempt at the crossword, abandoned after two answers feebly penciled in.

His father left him a house that was worth a lot of money. Henry had always said that when he got promotion, she would be able to give up work and have a baby. Promotion seemed less and less likely in time of recession and the fact that the new company appreciated Henry no more than had his previous employers. The proceeds of the sale of Henry's father's house would compensate for that and Fiona was imagining paying off the mortgage and perhaps handing in her notice when Henry said he was going to spend it on having a swimming pool built. All his life he had wanted a swimming pool of his own, it had been a childhood dream and a teenage ideal and now he was going to realize it.

Fiona came nearer than she ever had to seeing a flaw in her husband's perfection.

"You only want a baby because you think he might be a genius," he teased her.

"*She* might be," said Fiona, greatly daring.

"He, she, it's just a manner of speaking. Suppose he had my beauty and your brains. That would be a fine turn-up for the books."

Fiona was not hurt because she had never had any illusions about being brighter than she was. In any case, he was implying, wasn't he, that she was good-looking? She managed to laugh. She understood that Henry could not always help being rather difficult. It was the penalty someone like him paid for his gifts of brilliance. In some ways intellectual prowess was a burden to carry through life.

"We'll have a heated pool, a decent-size one with a deep end," Henry said, "and I'll teach you to swim."

The driving lessons had ended in failure. If it had been anyone else but Henry instructing her, Fiona would have said he was a harsh and intolerant teacher. Of course she knew how inept she was. She could not learn how to manage the gears and she was afraid of the traffic.

"I'm afraid of the water," she confessed.

"It's a disgrace," he said as if she had not spoken, "a woman of thirty being unable to swim." And then, when she only nodded doubtfully, "Have you got *The Times* there?"

Building the pool took all the money the sale of Henry's father's house realized. It took rather more and Henry had to borrow from the bank. The pool had a roof over it and walls round, which were what cost the money. That and the sophisticated purifying system. It was eight feet deep at the deep end with a diving board and a chute.

Happily for Fiona, her swimming lessons were indefinitely postponed. Henry enjoyed his new pool so much that he would very much have grudged taking time off from swimming his lengths or practicing his dives in order to teach his wife the basics.

Fiona guessed that Henry would be a brilliant swimmer. He was the perfect all-rounder. There was an expression in Latin which he had uttered and then translated for her which might have been, she thought, a description of himself: *mens sana in corpore sano*. Only for "sana" or "healthy" she substituted "wonderful." She would have liked to sit by the pool and watch him and she was rather sorry that his preferred swimming time was six-thirty in the morning, long before she was up.

One evening, while doing the crossword puzzle, he consulted her about a clue, as he sometimes did. "Consulted" was not perhaps the word. It was more a matter of expressing his thoughts aloud and waiting for her comment. Fiona found these remarks, full of references to unknown classical or literary personages, nearly incomprehensible. She had heard, for instance, of Psyche but only in connection with "psychological," "psychiatric," and so on. Cupid to her was a fat baby with wings and she did not know this was another name for Eros, which to her was the statue.

"I'm afraid I don't understand at all," she said humbly.

Henry loved elucidating. With a rare gesture of affection, he reached out and squeezed her hand. "Psyche was married to Cupid who was, of course, a god, the god of love. He always came to her by night and she never saw his face. Suppose her husband was a terrible monster of ugliness and deformity? Against his express wishes"—here Henry fixed a look of some severity on his wife—"she rose up one night in the dark and, taking a lighted candle, approached the bed where Cupid lay. Scarcely had she caught a glimpse of his peerless beauty, when a drop of hot wax fell from the candle onto the god's naked skin. With a cry he sprang up and fled from the house. She never saw him again."

"How awful for her," said Fiona, quite taken aback.

"Yes, well, she shouldn't have disobeyed him. Still, I don't see how that quite fits in here—wait a minute, yes, I do. Of course, that second syllable is an anagram of Eros . . ."

Henry inserted the letters in his neat print. A covert glance told her he had completed nearly half the puzzle. She did her best to suppress a yawn. By this time of the evening she was always so tired she could scarcely keep awake while Henry could stay up for hours yet. People like him needed no more than four or five hours sleep.

"I think I'll go up," she said.

"Good night." He added a kindly, "Darling."

For some reason, Henry never did the crossword puzzle on a Saturday. Fiona thought this a pity because, as she said, that was the day they gave prizes for the first correct entries received. But Henry only smiled and said he did the puzzle for the pure intellectual pleasure of it, not for gain. Of course you might not know your entry was correct because the solution to Saturday's puzzle did not appear next day but not until a week later. Her saying this, perhaps naïvely, made Henry unexpectedly angry. Everyone knew that with this kind of puzzle, he said, there could only be one correct solution, even people who never did crosswords knew that.

It was still dark when Henry got up in the mornings. Sometimes she was aware of his departure and his empty half of the bed. Occasionally, half an hour later, she heard the boy come with the papers, the tap-tap of the letterbox and even the soft thump of *The Times* falling onto the mat. But most days she was aware of nothing until Henry reappeared with her tea and the papers.

Henry did nothing to make her feel guilty about lying in, yet she was ashamed of her inability to get up. It was somehow unlike him, it was out of character, this waiting on her. He never did anything of the kind at any other time of the day and it sometimes seemed to her that the unselfish effort he made must be almost intolerable to someone with his needle-sharp mind and— yes, it must be admitted—his undoubted lack of patience. That he never complained or even teased her about oversleeping only added to her guilt.

Shopping in her lunch hour, she bought an alarm clock. They had never possessed such a thing, had never needed to, for Henry, as he often said, could direct himself to wake up at any hour he chose. Fiona put the alarm clock inside her bedside cabinet where it was invisible. It occurred to her, although she had as yet done nothing, she had not set the clock, in failing to tell Henry about her purchase of the alarm she was deceiving him. This was the first time she had ever deceived him in anything and perhaps, as she reflected on this, it was inevitable that her thoughts should revert to Cupid and Psyche and the outcome of Psyche's equally innocent stratagem.

The alarm remained inside the cabinet. Every evening she thought of setting it, though she never did so. But the effect on her of this daily speculation and doubt was to wake her without benefit of mechanical aid. Thinking about it did the trick and Henry, in swimming trunks and toweling robe, had no sooner left their bedroom than she was wide awake. On the third morning this happened, instead of dozing off again until seven-thirty, she lay there for ten minutes and then got up.

Henry would be swimming his lengths. She heard the paper boy come, the letterbox make its double tap-tap and the newspapers fall onto the mat with a soft thump. Should she put on her own swimming costume or go down fully dressed? Finally, she compromised and got into the tracksuit that had never seen a track and scarcely the light of day before.

This morning it would be she who made Henry tea and took *him* the papers. However, when she reached the foot of the stairs there was no paper on the mat, only a brown envelope with a bill on it. She must have been mistaken and it was the postman she had heard. The time was just on seven, rather too soon perhaps for the papers to have arrived.

Fiona made her way to the swimming pool. When she saw Henry she would just wave airily to him. She might call out in a cheerful way, "Carry on swimming!" or make some other humorous remark.

The glass door to the pool was slightly ajar. Fiona was barefoot. She pushed the door and entered silently. The cold chemical smell of chlorine irritated her nostrils. It was still dark outside, though dawn was coming, and the dark purplish-blue of a presunrise sky shimmered through the glass panel in the ceiling. Henry was not in the pool but sitting in one of the cane chairs at the glass-topped table not two yards from her. Light from a ceiling spotlight fell directly onto the two newspapers in front of him, both folded with their back pages uppermost.

Fiona saw at once what he was doing. That was not the difficulty. From today's *Times* he was copying into yesterday's *Times* the answers to the crossword puzzle. She could see quite clearly that he was doing this but she could not for a moment believe. It must be a joke or there must be some other purpose behind it.

When he turned round, swiftly covering both newspapers with the *Radio Times,* she knew from his face that it was neither a joke nor the consequence of some mysterious purpose. He had turned quite white. He seemed unable to speak and she flinched from the panic that leapt in his eyes.

"I'll make us a cup of tea," she said. The wisest and kindest thing would be to forget what she had seen. She could not. In that split second she stood in the doorway of the pool watching him he had been changed forever in her eyes. She thought about it on and off all day. It was impossible for her to concentrate on her work.

She never once thought he had deceived her, only that she had caught him out. Like Psyche, she had held the candle over him and seen his true face. His was not the brilliant intellect she had thought. He could not even finish *The Times* crossword. Now she understood why he never attempted it on a Saturday, knowing there would be no opportunity next morning or on the Monday morning to fill in the answers from that day's paper. There were a lot of other truths that she saw about Henry. No one recognized his mind as first class because it wasn't first class. He had lost that excellent well-paid job because he was not intellectually up to it.

She knew all that and she loved him the more for it. Just as she had felt an almost maternal tenderness for him when he left the newspaper with its completed puzzle exposed for her to see, now she was overwhelmed with compassion for his weakness and his childlike vulnerability. She loved him more deeply than ever and if admiration and respect had gone, what did those things matter, after all, in the tender intimacy of a good marriage?

That evening he did not touch the crossword puzzle. She had known he wouldn't and, of course, she said nothing. Neither of them had said a word about what she had seen that morning and neither of them ever would. Her feelings for him were completely changed, yet she believed her attitude could remain unaltered. But when, a few days later, he said something more about its being disgraceful that a woman of her age was unable to swim, instead of agreeing ruefully, she laughed and said, really, he shouldn't be so intolerant and censorious, no one was perfect.

He gave her a complicated explanation of some monetary question that was raised on the television news. It sounded wrong, he was confusing dollars with pounds, and she said so.

"Since when have you been an expert on the stock market?" he said.

Once she would have apologized. "I'm no more an expert than you are, Henry," she said, "but I can use my eyes and that was plain to see. Don't you think we should both admit we don't know a thing about it?"

She no longer believed in the accuracy of his translations from the Latin nor the authenticity of his tales from the classics. When some friends who came for dinner were regaled with his favorite story about how she had been unable to learn to drive, she jumped up laughing and put her arm round his shoulder.

"Poor Henry gets into a rage so easily I was afraid he'd give himself a heart attack, so I stopped our lessons," she said.

He never told that story again.

"Isn't it funny?" she said one Saturday on the golf course. "I used to think it was wonderful you having a handicap of twenty-five. I didn't know any better."

He made no answer.

"It's not really the best thing in a marriage for one partner to look up to the other too much, is it? Equality is best. I suppose it's natural to idolize the other one when you're first married. It just went on rather a long time for me, that's all."

She was no longer in the least nervous about learning to swim. If he bullied her she would laugh at him. As a matter of fact, he wasn't all that good a swimmer himself. He couldn't do the crawl at all and a good many of his dives turned into belly flops. She lay on the side of the pool, leaning on her elbows, watching him as he climbed out of the deep end up the steps.

"D'you know, Henry," she said, "you'll lose your marvelous figure if you aren't careful. You've got quite a spare tire round your waist."

His face was such a mask of tragedy, there was so much naked misery there, the eyes full of pain, that she checked the laughter that was bubbling up in her and said quickly, "Oh, don't look so sad, poor darling. I'd still love you if you were as fat as a pudding and weighed twenty stone."

He took two steps backward down the steps, put up his hands and pulled her down into the pool. It happened so quickly and unexpectedly that she didn't resist. She gasped when the water hit her. It was eight feet deep here, she couldn't swim more than two or three strokes, and she made a grab for him, clutching at his upper arms.

He pried her fingers open and pushed her under the water. She tried to scream but the water came in and filled her throat. Desperately she thrashed about in the blue-greenness, the sickeningly chlorinated water, fighting, sinking, feeling for something to catch hold of, the bar round the pool rim, his arms, his feet on the steps. A foot kicked out at her, a foot stamped on her head. She stopped holding her breath, she had to, and the water poured into her lungs until the light behind her eyes turned red and her head was black inside. A great drum beat, boom, boom, boom, in the blackness, and then it stopped.

Henry waited to see if the body would float to the surface. He waited a long time but she remained, starfish-like, face-downward, on the blue tiles eight feet down, so he left her and, wrapping himself in his toweling robe, went into the house. Whatever happened, whatever steps if any he decided to take next, he would do *The Times* crossword that evening. Or as much of it as he could ever do.

STEVEN SAYLOR

A WILL IS A WAY

Steven Saylor burst upon the mystery scene last year with two novels, Roman Blood *(published late in 1991) and* Arms of Nemesis, *and three short stories in EQMM—all featuring Gordianus the Finder, a citizen of ancient Rome and Cicero's hired investigator. Gordianus's first short case is based upon a crime recounted in one of Cicero's orations. It presents us with a classic mystery situation involving a murder and a will, set against a colorful, well-researched background that comes amazingly to life. The Mystery Writers of America chose it as the winner of the Robert L. Fish Memorial Award for the best first mystery short story of 1992.*

Lucius Claudius was a sausage-fingered, plum-cheeked, cherry-nosed nobleman with a fuzzy wreath of thinning red hair on his florid pate and a tiny, pouting mouth.

The name Claudius marked him not only as a nobleman, but a patrician, hailing from that small group of old families who first made Rome great (or who at least fooled the rest of the Romans into thinking so). Not all patricians are rich; even the best families can go to seed over the centuries. But from the gold seal ring that Lucius wore, and from the other rings that kept it company—one of silver set with lapis, another of white gold with a bauble of flawless green glass—I suspected he was quite rich indeed. The rings were complemented by a gold necklace, from which more glittering glass baubles dangled amid the frazzled red hair that sprouted from his fleshy red chest. His toga was of the finest wool, and his shoes were of exquisitely tooled leather.

He was the very image of a wealthy patrician, not handsome and not very bright-looking either, but impeccably groomed and dressed. His green eyes twinkled and his pouting lips pursed easily into a smile, betraying a man with a naturally pleasant personality. Wealthy, wellborn, and with a cheerful disposition, he struck me as a man who shouldn't have a worry in the world—except that he obviously did, or else he would never have come to see me.

We sat in the little garden of my house on the Esquiline Hill. Once upon a time a man of Lucius's social standing would never have been seen entering the house of Gordianus the Finder, but in recent years I seem to have acquired a certain respectability. I think the change began after my first case for the young advocate Cicero. Apparently Cicero has been saying nice things about me behind my back to his colleagues in the law courts, telling them that he actually put me up in his house once and it turned out that Gordianus, consorter with assassins and professional ferret notwithstanding, knew how to use a bowl and spoon and an indoor privy after all, and could even tell the difference between them. Lucius Claudius filled the chair I had pulled up for him almost to overflowing. He shifted a bit nervously and toyed with his rings, then smiled sheepishly and held up his cup. "A bit more?" he said, making an ingratiatingly silly face.

"Of course." I clapped my hands. "Bethesda! More wine for my guest. The best, from the green clay bottle."

Bethesda rather sullenly obeyed, taking her time to rise from where she had been sitting cross-legged beside a pillar. She disappeared into the house. Her movements were as graceful as the unfolding of a flower. Lucius watched her with a lump in his throat. He swallowed hard.

"A very beautiful slave," he whispered.

"Thank you, Lucius Claudius." I hoped he wouldn't offer to buy her, as so many of my wealthier clients do. I hoped in vain.

"I don't suppose you'd consider—" he began.

"Alas, no, Lucius Claudius."

"But I was going to say—"

"I would sooner sell my thirteenth rib."

"Ah." He nodded sagely, then wrinkled his fleshy brow. "*What* did you say?"

"Oh, an expression I picked up from Bethesda. According to her ancestors on her father's side, the first woman was fashioned from a rib bone taken from the first man, by a god called Jehovah. That is why all men are lacking a thirteenth rib."

"Are they?" Lucius poked at his rib cage, but I think he was much too well-padded to actually feel a rib.

I took a sip of wine and smiled. Bethesda has told me the Hebrew tale of the first man and woman many times. Each time she tells it I clutch my side and pretend to bleat from pain, until she starts to pout and we both end up laughing. It seems to me a most peculiar tale, but no stranger than the stories her Egyptian mother told her about jackal-headed gods and crocodiles who walk upright. If it is true, this Hebrew god is worthy of respect. Not even Jupiter could claim to have created anything half as exquisite as Bethesda.

I had spent enough time putting my guest at ease. "Tell me, Lucius Claudius, what is it that troubles you?"

"You will think me very foolish . . ." he began.

"No, I will not," I assured him, thinking I probably would.

"Well, it was only the day before yesterday—or was it the day before that? It was the day after the Ides of May, of that I'm sure, whichever day that was—"

"I believe that was the day before yesterday," I said. Bethesda reappeared and stood in the shadows of the portico, awaiting a nod from me. I shook my head, telling her to wait. Another cup of wine might serve to loosen Lucius's tongue, but he was befuddled enough already. "And what transpired on the day before yesterday?"

"I happened to be in this very neighborhood—well, not up here on the Esquiline Hill, but down in the valley, in the Subura—"

"The Subura is a fascinating neighborhood," I said, trying to imagine what attraction its tawdry streets might hold for a man who probably lived in a mansion on the Palatine Hill. Gaming houses, brothels, taverns, and criminals for hire—these came to mind.

He sighed. "You see, my days are very idle. I've never had a head for politics or finance, like others in my family; I feel useless in the Forum. I've tried living in the country, but I'm not much of a farmer; cows bore me. I don't like entertaining, either—strangers coming to dinner, all of them twice as clever as I am, and me obliged to think up some way to amuse them—such a bother. I get bored rather easily, you see. So very, very bored."

"Yes?" I prompted, suppressing a yawn.

"So I go wandering about the city. Over to Tarentum to see the old people easing their joints in the hot springs. To the Field of Mars to see the chariot racers train their horses. All up and down the Tiber, to the fish markets and the cattle markets and the markets with foreign goods. I like seeing other people at work; I relish the way they go about their business with such determination. I like watching women haggle with vendors, or seeing a builder argue with his masons, or noticing how the women who hang from brothel windows slam their shutters when a troupe of rowdy gladiators come brawling down the street. All these people seem so alive, so full of purpose, so—so very opposite of *bored*. Do you understand, Gordianus?"

"I think I do, Lucius Claudius."

"Then you'll understand why I love the Subura. What a neighborhood! One can almost smell the passion! The crowded tenements, the strange odors, the spectacle of humanity! The winding, narrow little streets, the dark, dank alleys, the sounds that drift down from the upper-story windows of strangers arguing, laughing, making love—what a mysterious and vital place the Subura is!"

"There's nothing so very mysterious about squalor," I suggested.

"Ah, but there is," insisted Lucius; and to him, I suppose, there was.

"Tell me about your adventure two days ago, on the day after the Ides."

"Certainly. But I thought you sent the girl for more wine?"

I clapped my hands. Bethesda stepped from the shadows. The sunlight glinted on her long, blue-black tresses. As she filled Lucius's cup he seemed unable to look up at her. He swallowed, smiled shyly, and nodded vigorously at the quality of my best wine, which was probably not good enough to give to his slaves. He continued.

"That morning, quite early, I happened to be strolling down one of the side streets off the main Subura Way, whistling a tune, noticing how spring had brought out all sorts of tiny flowers and shoots between the paving stones. Beauty asserts itself even here amid such squalor, I thought to myself, and I considered composing a poem, except that I'm not very good at poems—"

"And then something *happened?*" I prompted.

"Oh, yes. A man shouted down to me from a second-story window. He said, 'Please, Citizen, come quick! A man is dying!' I hesitated. After all, he might have been trying to lure me into the building to rob me, or worse, and I didn't even have a slave with me for protection—I like going out alone, you see. Then another man appeared at the window beside the first, and said, 'Please, Citizen, we need your help. The young man is dying and he's made out a will—he needs seven citizens to witness it and we already have six. Won't you come up?"

"Well, I did go up. It's not very often that anybody needs me for anything. How could I refuse? The apartment turned out to be a rather nicely furnished set of rooms, not at all shabby and certainly not menacing. In one of the rooms a man lay wrapped in a blanket upon a couch, moaning and shivering. An older man was attending to him, daubing his brow with a damp cloth. There were six others crowded into the room. No one seemed to know anyone else—it seemed we each had been summoned off the street, one by one."

"To witness the will of the dying man?"

"Yes. His name was Asuvius, from the town of Larinum. He was visiting the city when he was struck by a terrible malady. He lay on the bed, wet with sweat and trembling with fever. The illness had aged him terribly—according to his friend he wasn't yet twenty, yet his face was haggard and lined. Doctors had been summoned but had been of no use. Young Asuvius feared that he would die at any moment. Never having made a will—such a young man, after all—he had sent his friend to procure a wax tablet and a stylus. I didn't read the document as it was passed

among us, of course, but I saw that it had been written by two
different hands. He must have written the first few lines himself,
in a faltering, unsteady hand; I suppose his friend finished the
document for him. Seven witnesses were required, so to expedite
matters the older man had simply called for citizens to come up
from the street. While we watched, the poor lad scrawled his
name with the stylus and pressed his seal ring into the wax."

"After which you signed and sealed it yourself?"

"Yes, along with the others. Then the older man thanked us
and urged us to leave the room so that young Asuvius could rest
quietly before the end came. I don't mind telling you that I was
weeping like a fountain as I stepped onto the street, and I wasn't
the only one. I strolled about the Subura in a melancholy mood,
thinking about that young man's fate, about his poor family
back in Larinum and how they would take the news. I remember
walking by a brothel situated at the end of the block, hardly a
hundred paces from the dying man's room, and being struck by
the contrast, the irony, that within those walls there lurked such
pleasure and relief, while only a few doors down, the mouth of
Pluto was opening to swallow a dying country lad. I remember
thinking what a lovely poem such an irony might inspire—"

"No doubt it would, in the hands of a truly great poet," I
acknowledged quickly. "So, did you ever learn what became of
the youth?"

"A few hours later, after strolling about the city in a sad haze,
I found myself back on that very street, as if the invisible hand of
a god had guided me there. It was shortly after noon. The landlord told me that young Asuvius had died not long after I left.
The older man—Oppianicus his name was, also of Larinum—
had summoned the landlord to the room, weeping and lament-
ing, and had shown the landlord the body all wrapped up in a
sheet. Later the landlord saw Oppianicus and another man from
Larinum carry the body down the stairs and load it into a cart to
take it to the embalmers outside the Esquiline Gate." Lucius
sighed. "I tossed and turned all night, thinking about the fickle-
ness of the Fates and the way that Fortune can turn her back even
on a young man starting out in life. It made me think of all the
days I've wasted, all the hours of boredom . . ."

Before he could contemplate the birth of another poem, I nod-ded to Bethesda to refill his cup and my own." A sad tale, Lucius Claudius, but not uncommon. Life in the city is full of tragedies. Strangers die around us every day. We persevere."

"But that's just the point—young Asuvius *isn't* dead! I saw him just this morning, strolling down the Subura Way, smiling and happy! Oh, he still appeared a bit haggard, but he was certainly up and walking."

"Perhaps you were mistaken."

"Impossible. He was with the older man, Oppianicus. I called to them across the street. Oppianicus saw me—or at least I thought he did—but he took the younger man's arm and they disappeared into a shop on the corner. I followed after them, but a cart was passing in the street and the stupid driver almost ran me down. When I finally stepped into the shop they were gone. They must have passed through the shop into the cross street beyond."

He sat back and sipped his wine. "I sat down in a shady spot by the public fountain and tried to think it through, then I re-membered your name. I think it was Cicero who mentioned you to me, that young advocate who did a bit of legal work for me last year. I can't imagine who else might help me. What do you say, Gordianus? Am I mad? Or is it true that the shades of the dead walk abroad in the noonday sun?"

"The answer to both questions may be yes, Lucius Claudius, but that doesn't explain what's occurred. From what you've told me, I should think that something quite devious and all too hu-man is afoot. But tell me, what is your concern? You don't know either of these men. What is your interest in this mystery?"

"Don't you understand, Gordianus, after all I've told you? I spend my days in idle boredom, peeking into the windows of other people's lives. Now something has happened that actually titillates me. I would investigate the circumstances by myself, only—" the great bulk of his body shrank a bit "—I'm not ex-actly brave."

I glanced at the glittering jewelry about his fingers and throat. "I should tell you, then, that I'm not exactly cheap."

"And I am not exactly poor."

* * *

Lucius insisted on accompanying me, though I warned him that if he feared boredom, my initial inquiries were likely to prove more excruciating than he could bear. Searching through the Subura for a pair of strangers from out of town was hardly my idea of excitement, but Lucius wanted to follow my every step. I could only shrug and allow it; if he wanted to follow me like a dog, he was certainly paying well enough for the privilege.

I began at the house where the young man had supposedly died and where Lucius had witnessed the signing of his will. The landlord had nothing more to say than what he had already said to Lucius—until I nudged my client and indicated that he should rattle his coin purse. The musical jingling induced the landlord to sing.

The older man, Oppianicus, had been renting the room for more than a month. He and his younger friends from Larinum were much given to debauchery—the landlord could deduce that much from the sour smell of spilled wine that wafted from their room, from the raucous gambling parties they held, and from the steady parade of prostitutes who visited them from the brothel down the street.

"And the younger man, Asuvius, the one who died?" I asked.

"Yes, what of him?"

"He was equally debauched?"

The landlord shrugged. "You know how it is, these young men from small towns, especially the lads who have a bit of money, they come to Rome and they want to live a little."

"Sad, that this one should die, instead."

"That has nothing to do with me," the landlord protested. "I keep a safe house. It wasn't as if the boy was murdered in one of my rooms. He took sick and died."

"Did he look particularly frail?"

"Not at all, but debauchery can ruin any man's health."

"Not in a month's time."

"When illness strikes, it strikes; neither man nor god can lengthen a man's time once the Fates have measured out the thread of his life."

"Wise words," I agreed. I pulled a few copper coins from Lucius's purse and slapped them into the man's waiting palm.

The brothel down the street was one of the Subura's more respectable, which is to say more expensive, houses of entertainment. Several well-dressed slaves lingered outside the door, waiting for their masters to come out. Inside, the floor of the little foyer was decorated with a black and white mosaic of Priapus pursuing a wood nymph. Rich tapestries of red and green covered the walls.

The clientele was not shoddy, either. While we waited for the master of the house, a customer passed us on his way to the door. He was at least a minor magistrate, to judge from his gold seal ring, and he seemed to know Lucius, at whom he cast a puzzled gaze.

"You—Lucius Claudius—here in Priapus's Palace?"

"Yes, and what of it, Gaius Fabius?"

"But I'd never have dreamed you had a lustful bone in your body!"

Lucius sniffed at the ceiling. "I happen to be here on important business, if you don't mind."

"Oh, I see. But of course. Don't let me interrupt you!" The man suppressed a laugh until he was out the door. I heard him braying in the street.

"Harrumph! Let him laugh and gossip about me behind my back," said Lucius. "I shall compose a satirical poem for my revenge, so witheringly spiteful that it shall render that buffoon too limp to visit this—what did he call this place?"

"Priapus's Palace," piped an unctuously friendly voice. Our host suddenly appeared between us and slid his arms around our shoulders. "And what pleasures may I offer to amuse two such fine specimens of Roman manhood?" The man smiled blandly at me, then at Lucius, then at the baubles that decorated Lucius's neck and fingers. He licked his lips and slithered to the center of the room, turned, and clapped his hands. A file of scantily clad women began to enter the room.

"Actually," I said hurriedly, "we've come on behalf of a friend."

"Oh?"

"A regular client of your establishment in recent days, I believe. A young visitor to Rome, named Asuvius."

From the corner of my eye I saw a sudden movement among the girls. One of them, a honey blond, tripped and thrust out her hands for balance. She turned a pair of startled blue eyes in my direction.

"Oh yes, that handsome lad from Larinum," gushed our host. "We haven't seen him for at least a day and a half—I was beginning to wonder what had become of him!"

"We're here on his behalf," I said, thinking it might not be a lie, when all was said and done. "He sent us to fetch his favorite girl—but I can't seem to remember her name. Can you remember it, Lucius?"

Lucius gave a start and blinked his eyes, which were trained on the girls and threatened to pop from their sockets. "Me? Oh no, I can't remember a thing."

A look of pure avarice crossed our host's face. "His favorite? Ah, let me think . . . yes, that would be Merula, most definitely Merula!" Another clap of his hands fetched a slave who put an ear to his master's whispering lips, then ran from the room. A moment later Merula appeared, a stunning Ethiopian so tall that she had to bow her head to pass through the doorway. Her skin was the color of midnight and her eyes flashed like shooting stars.

Lucius was visibly impressed and reached for his purse, but I stayed his hand. It occurred to me that our host was offering us his most expensive property, not the one which had necessarily been the favorite of young Asuvius.

"No, no," I said, "I'm sure I would have remembered a name like Merula."

"Ah, and she sings like a blackbird, as well," interjected our host.

"Nevertheless, I think we were meant to fetch *that* one." I nodded at the honey blond, who gazed back at me with apprehensive blue eyes.

*   *   *

The tavern across the street was pleasantly cool and dark, and almost deserted. Columba sat within the cloak Lucius had thrown over her transparent gown, looking pensive.

"The day before yesterday?" She frowned.

"Yes, the day after the Ides of May," offered Lucius, certain at last that he had his chronology straight, and eager to help.

"And you say that you saw Asuvius in his room, deathly ill?" She continued to frown.

"So it appeared when this man Oppianicus called me up to the room." Lucius leaned on one elbow, gazing at her raptly and ignoring his cup of wine. He was not used to being so near such a beautiful girl, I could tell.

"And this was in the morning?" Columba asked.

"Yes, quite early in the morning."

"But Asuvius was with me!"

"Can you be sure of that?"

"Certainly, because he had slept the whole night with me, in my room at the Palace, and we didn't wake until quite late that morning. Even then, we didn't leave the room . . ."

"Ah, youth!" I sighed.

She blushed faintly. "And we stayed in our room to eat our midday meal. So you see, you must have the days mixed up, or else—"

"Yes?"

"Well, it's the oddest thing. Some of Asuvius's freedmen were by the Palace only yesterday, asking for him. They seemed not to know where he was. They seemed rather worried." She looked at me, suddenly suspicious. "What is your interest in Asuvius?"

"I'm not really sure," I said truthfully. "Does it matter?" I slid a copper coin from Lucius's purse and pushed it across the table to her. She looked at it coolly, then slipped her tiny white hand over it.

"I should hate it if anything has really happened to Asuvius," she said quietly. "He really is a sweet boy. Do you know, he said it was his very first time, when he came to the Palace a month ago? I could believe it, too . . ." She broke off with a wistful sigh, laughed sadly, then sighed again. "I shall hate it if it's true that he's taken sick and died so suddenly."

"Oh, but he hasn't," said Lucius. "That's why we're here; that's what we don't understand. I saw him alive and well with my own eyes, this very morning!"

"But then, how can you say he was deathly ill two days ago, and that the landlord saw his body taken away in a cart?" Columba frowned. "I tell you, he was with me the whole morning. Asuvius was never sick at all; you must be confused."

"Then you last saw him on the day before yesterday, the same day that Lucius Claudius was called up to witness the lad's will," I said. "Tell me, Columba, and this might be very important: was he wearing his seal ring? All citizens possess one."

"He was wearing very little at all," she said frankly.

"Columba, that is not an answer."

"Well, of course, he wears his ring always. I'm sure he was wearing it that morning."

"You seem awfully certain. Surely he wasn't signing documents there in your room?"

She looked at me coolly, then spoke very slowly. "Sometimes, when a man and woman are being intimate, there is cause to notice that one of them happens to be wearing a ring . . . perhaps one feels a certain discomfort . . . Yes, I'm sure he was wearing his ring."

I nodded, satisfied. "When did he leave you?"

"After we ate our midday meal. His friends from Larinum came to collect him."

"Not his freedmen?"

"No, Asuvius doesn't have much use for servants, he says they only get in his way. He's always sending them off on silly errands to keep them away from him. He says they'll carry gossip back to his sisters in Larinum."

"And to his parents, as well, I suppose?"

"Alas, Asuvius has no parents. His mother and father died in a fire only a year ago. It was a hard year that followed, having to take on his father's duties in such a hurry, and after such a terrible tragedy. All the big farms he owns, and all the slaves! All the paperwork, counting up figures so he'll know what he's worth. To hear him talk, you'd think a rich man has more work to do than a poor one!"

"So it may seem, to a young lad who'd rather be carefree and reckless," I noted.

"This trip to Rome was to be his holiday, after so much grieving and labor. It was his friends who suggested the trip."

"Ah, the same friends who came for him the day before yesterday."

"Yes, crusty old Oppianicus and his young friend, Vulpinus on account of his foxy disposition. Always nosing into things, never seems to be completely honest, even when there's no point in lying. Quite a charmer, really, and not bad looking."

"I know the sort," I said.

"He plays a sort of older brother to Asuvius, since Asuvius has no brothers—brought him to the city, arranged for a place to stay, showed him how to have a good time."

"I see. And two days ago, as they were leaving Priapus's Palace, did Oppianicus and the Fox give any hint as to where they were taking young Asuvius?"

"More than a hint. They said they were off to the Gardens."

"What Gardens?"

"Why, the ones outside the Esquiline Gate. Oppianicus and Vulpinus had been telling Asuvius how splendid they are, with splashing fountains and flowers in full bloom—May is a perfect month to visit them. Asuvius was very eager to go. There are so many sights here in the city that he hasn't yet seen, having spent so much of his time, well, enjoying indoor pleasures." Columba smiled a bit crookedly. "He's hardly stepped outside the Subura. I don't think he's even been down to see the Forum!"

"Ah yes, and of course a young visitor from Larinum would hardly want to miss seeing the famous Gardens outside the Esquiline Gate."

"I suppose not, from the way Oppianicus and Vulpinus described them—leafy green tunnels and beautiful pools, meadows of blossoms and lovely statues. I wish I could see them myself, but the master hardly ever lets me out of the house except for business. Would you believe that I've been in Rome for almost two years and I'd never even heard of the Gardens?"

"I can believe that," I said gravely.

"But Asuvius said if the place turned out to be as special as his friends claimed, he might take me there himself in a few days, as a treat." She brightened a bit. I sighed.

We escorted her back to the Palace of Priapus. Her owner was surprised to see her back so soon, but he made no complaint about the fee.

Outside, the street darkened for a moment as a cloud obscured the sun. "No matter whose account is accurate, young Asuvius most assuredly did not die in his bed the day before yesterday," I said. "Either he was with Columba, very much alive and well, or, if indeed you saw him lying feverish in his apartment, he recovered and you saw him on the street this morning. Still, I begin to fear for the lad. I fear for him most desperately."

"Why?" asked Lucius.

"You know as well as I, Lucius Claudius, that there are no gardens outside the Esquiline Gate!"

One passes through the Esquiline Gate from the city of the living into the city of the dead. On the left hand is the public necropolis of Rome, where the modest tombs of the Roman masses are crowded together like spectators in a mob. Long ago, when Rome was young, the lime pits were discovered nearby. Just as the city of the living sprang up around the river and the Forum and the markets, so the city of the dead sprang up around the lime pits and the crematoria and the parlors where corpses are beautified. On the right hand are the public refuse pits, where the residents of the Subura and surrounding neighborhoods dump their trash. All manner of waste lies heaped in the sandpits— broken bits of crockery and furniture, rotting scraps of food, discarded garments soiled and torn beyond even a beggar's use. Here and there the custodians light small fires to consume the debris, then rake fresh sand over the smoldering embers.

No matter in which direction one looks, there are certainly no gardens outside the Esquiline Gate, unless one counts the isolated flowers that spring up among the moldering debris of the trash heaps, or the scraggly vines which wind their way about the old, neglected tombs of the forgotten dead. I began to suspect that Oppianicus and the Fox had a cruel sense of humor indeed.

A glance at Lucius told me that he was having second thoughts about accompanying me on this part of my investigation. The Subura and its vices might seem colorful or quaint, but even Lucius could find no charm in the necropolis and the rubbish pits. He wrinkled his nose and batted a swarm of flies from his face, but he did not turn back.

We passed back and forth between the right side of the road and the left, questioning the few people we met about three strangers they might have seen two days before—an older man, a foxy young rogue, and a mere lad. The tenders of the dead waved us aside, having no patience to deal with the living; the custodians of the trash heaps shrugged and shook their heads.

We stood at the edge of the sandpits, surveying a prospect that might have looked like Hades, if there were a sun to shine through the hazy smoke of Hades onto its smoldering wastes. Suddenly, there was a low hissing noise behind us. Lucius started. My hand jumped to my dagger.

The maker of the noise was a shuffling, stooped derelict who had been watching us from behind a heap of smoldering rubbish.

"What do you want?" I asked, keeping my hand close to the dagger.

The lump of filthy hair and rags swayed a bit, and two milky eyes stared up at me. "I hear you're looking for someone," the man finally said.

"Perhaps."

"Then perhaps I can help you."

"Speak plainly."

"I know where you'll find the young man!"

"What young man are you talking about?"

The figure stooped and looked up at me sidelong. "I heard you asking one of the workers a moment ago. You didn't see me, but I saw you, and I listened. I heard you asking about the three men who were by here two days ago, the older man and the boy and the one between. I know where the boy is!"

"Show us."

The creature held out a hand so stained and weathered it

looked like a stump of wood. Lucius drew back, appalled, but reached for his purse. I stayed his hand.

"After you show us," I said.

The thing hissed at me. It stamped its foot and growled. Finally it turned and waved for us to follow.

I grabbed Lucius's arm and whispered in his ear. "You mustn't come. Such a creature is likely to lure us into a trap. Look at the jewels you wear, the purse you carry. Go to the crematoria, where you'll be safe. I'll follow the man alone."

Lucius looked at me, his lips pursed, his eyes open wide. "Gordianus, you must be joking. No power of man or god will stop me from seeing whatever this man has to show us!"

The creature shambled and lurched over the rubbish heaps and drifts of dirty sand. We strode deeper and deeper into the wastes. The heaps of ash rose higher around us, hiding us from the road. The creature led us around the flank of a low sandy hill. An orange haze engulfed us. An acrid cloud of smoke swirled around us. I choked. Lucius reached for his throat and began to cough. The hot breath of an open flame blew against my face.

Through the murk I saw the derelict silhouetted against the fire. He bobbed his head up and down and pointed at something in the flames.

"What is it?" I wheezed. "I see nothing."

Lucius gave a start. He seized my arm and pointed. There, within the inferno, amid the indiscriminate heap of fiery rubbish, I glimpsed the remains of a human body.

The flaming heap collapsed upon itself, sending out a spray of orange cinders. I covered my face with my sleeve and put my arm around Lucius's shoulder. Together we fled from the blazing heat and smoke. The decrepit creature scampered after us, his long brown arm extended, palm up.

"There is no proof that the body the derelict showed us was that of Asuvius. It might have been another of his kind, for all we know. The truth is beyond proving. That is the crux of the matter."

I took a long sip of wine. Night had descended on Rome. Crickets chirred in my garden. Bethesda sat beneath the portico nearby, beside a softly glowing lamp. She pretended to stitch a torn tunic, but listened to every word. Lucius Claudius sat beside me, staring at the moon's reflection in his cup.

"Tell me, Gordianus, how exactly do you explain the discrepancies between what I saw and the tale that Columba told us? What really happened the day after the Ides of May?"

"I should think that the sequence of events is clear."

"Even so—"

"Very well, this is how I would tell the story. There was once a wealthy young orphan in a town called Larinum who chose his friends very poorly. Two of those friends, an old rogue and a young predator with a long snout and pointed ears, talked him into going to Rome for a long holiday. The three of them took up residence in one of the seedier parts of town and proceeded to indulge in just the sorts of vices that are likely to lull a green country lad into a vulnerable stupor. Away from the boy's watchful sisters and the town gossips in Larinum, the Fox and old Oppianicus were free to hatch their scheme.

"On a morning when Asuvius was dallying with his favorite prostitute, the Fox pretended to be the boy and took to his bed, feigning a mortal illness. Oppianicus summoned strangers off the street to act as witnesses to a will—people who wouldn't know Asuvius from Alexander. Oppianicus made at least one mistake, but he got away with it."

"What was that?"

"Someone must have asked the dying man's age. Oppianicus, without thinking, said he was not yet twenty; you told me so. True enough, if he meant Asuvius, and I gather that the Fox is well beyond twenty. Even so, you yourself ascribed the discrepancy to illness—'haggard and lined,' you said he looked, as if terribly aged from his sickness. The other witnesses probably thought the same thing. People will go to great lengths to make the evidence of their own eyes conform to whatever someone tells them is the truth."

Lucius frowned. "Why was the will in two different handwritings?"

"Yes, I remember you mentioning that. The Fox began it, feigning such a weak hand that he couldn't finish it; such a ploy would help to explain why his signature would not be recognizable as the hand of Asuvius—anyone would think it was the scrawl of a man nearly dead."

"But the Fox pressed his own seal ring into the wax," protested Lucius. "I saw him do it. It couldn't have been the true seal of Asuvius, who was with Columba, wearing his ring."

"I'll come to that. Now, once the will was witnessed all around, you and the others were shunted from the room. Oppianicus wound the Fox up in a sheet, tore his hair and worked tears into his eyes, then called for the landlord."

"Who saw a corpse!"

"Who *thought* he saw a corpse. All he saw was a body in a sheet. He thought Asuvius had died of a sudden illness; he took no pains to examine the corpse."

"But later he saw the two men taking the body away in a cart."

"He saw Oppianicus and the Fox, who had changed back into his clothes, carrying out something wrapped up in a sheet—a sack of corn meal, for all we know."

"Ah, and once they were out of sight they got rid of the cart and the corn meal and went to fetch Asuvius from the brothel."

"Yes, for their appointed stroll through the 'Gardens.' The derelict told us the rest, how they ushered the confused boy to a secluded spot where the Fox strangled him to death, how they stripped his body and hid his corpse amid the rubbish. That was when they stole the seal ring from his finger. Later they must have rubbed the Fox's seal from the wax and applied the true seal of Asuvius to the will."

"There's a law against that," said Lucius, without much conviction.

"Yes, the Cornelian law, enacted by our esteemed Senate just three years ago. Why do you think they passed such a law? Because falsifying wills has become as commonplace as senators picking their noses in public!"

Lucius nodded. "And so the scheme is complete; the false will cheats Asuvius's sisters and other relatives, no doubt, and leaves a tidy fortune to his dear friends Oppianicus and Marcus Avillius—also known as the Fox, for good reason."

I nodded.

"We must do something!"

"Yes, but what? I suppose you could bring a suit against the culprits and attempt to prove that the will is fraudulent. That should take up a great deal of your time and money; if you think you suffer from boredom now, wait until after you've spent a month or two bustling from clerk to clerk filing actions down in the Forum. And if Oppianicus and the Fox find a lawyer half as crafty as they are, you'll likely as not be laughed out of court."

"Forget the fraudulent will. These men are guilty of cold-blooded murder!"

"But will you be able to prove it, without a corpse and with no reliable witness? Even if you could find him, our derelict friend is not the sort of man whose testimony would impress a Roman jury."

"You're telling me that we've come to the end of it?"

"I'm telling you that if you wish to proceed any further, what you need is an advocate, not Gordianus the Finder."

Ten days later, Lucius Claudius came knocking at my door again.

I was more than a little surprised to see him. Having set me on the trail of young Asuvius and having followed me to its end, I expected him to quickly lose interest and lapse into his customary boredom. Instead he informed me that he had been doing a bit of legwork on his own.

He invited me for a stroll. While we walked he talked of nothing in particular, but I noticed that we were drawing near to the street where the whole story had begun. Lucius remarked that he was thirsty. We stepped into the tavern across from Priapus's Palace.

"I have been thinking a great deal about what you said, Gordianus, about Roman justice. You're right; we can't trust the courts anymore. Advocates twist words and laws to their own purposes, pervert the sentiments of jurors, resort to intimidation and outright bribery. Still, true justice must be worth pursuing. I keep thinking of the flames . . . the sight of that young man's body, thrown into a rubbish pit and burned to ashes. By the way, Oppianicus and the Fox are back in town."

"Oh? Did they ever leave?"

"They were on their way back to Larinum when I saw them that day, before I came to you. Oppianicus made a great production of showing Asuvius's will to anyone who cared to look and filing it with the clerks in the Forum at Larinum. So my messengers to Larinum tell me."

"Messengers?"

"Yes, I thought I would get in touch with Asuvius's sisters. A band of his freedmen arrived in Rome just this morning."

"I see. And Oppianicus and the Fox are here already."

"Yes. Oppianicus is staying with friends in a house over on the Aventine Hill. But the Fox is just across the street, in the apartment where they played their little charade."

I turned and looked out the window. From where we sat, I could see the ground-floor door of the tenement and the window above, the same window from which Lucius had been summoned to witness the will. The shutters were drawn.

"What a neighborhood," said Lucius. "Some days I think that almost anything could happen in the Subura." He craned his neck and looked over my shoulder. From up the street I heard the noise of an approaching mob.

There were twenty of them or more, brandishing knives and clubs. They gathered outside the tenement, where they banged their clubs against the door and demanded entrance. When the door did not open, they broke it down and streamed inside.

The shutters were thrown back and a face appeared at the window above. If the Fox was handsome and charming, as Columba had told us, it was impossible to tell at that moment. His eyes were bulging in panic and all the blood had drained from his cheeks. He stared down at the street and swallowed hard, as if working up his courage to jump. He hesitated a moment too long; hands gripped his shoulders and yanked him back into the room.

A moment later he was thrust stumbling from the doorway. The mob surrounded him and hounded him up the street. Street vendors and idlers scattered and disappeared into doorways. Windows flew open and curious faces peered down.

"Hurry," said Lucius, throwing back the last of his wine, "or we'll miss the fun. The Fox has been run out of his hole, and the hounds shall pursue him all the way to the Forum."

We hurried into the street. As we passed Priapus's Palace I looked up. Columba stood at a window, gazing down in confusion and excitement. Lucius waved to her, flashing an enormous grin. She gave a start and smiled back at him.

He cupped his hands and shouted, "Come with us!" When she bit her lip in hesitation, he waved with both hands.

Columba vanished from the window and a moment later was running up the street to join us. Her master appeared at the door, gesticulating and stamping his foot. Lucius turned and shook his purse at the man.

Asuvius's freedmen roared all the way to the Forum. The outer circle banged their clubs against walls and passing wagons; the inner circle kept the Fox hemmed in with a ring of daggers. They took up a chant: "Jus-tice! Jus-tice! Jus-tice!" By the time we reached the Forum, the Fox was looking hounded indeed.

The gang of freedmen put away their weapons and used their open hands to shove the Fox around and around in a dizzying circle. At last we came to the tribunal of the commissioners, whose most neglected duty is keeping order in the streets, and who also, incidentally, conduct investigations preliminary to bringing charges for crimes of violence. Beneath the shade of a portico, the unsuspecting commissioner for the Subura, Quintus Manilius, sat squinting at a stack of parchments. He looked up in alarm when the Fox came staggering before him. The freedmen, excited to fever pitch by their parade through the streets, all began speaking at once, creating an indecipherable roar.

Manilius wrinkled his brow. He banged his fist against the table and raised his hand. All voices fell silent except for one.

Even then I thought that the Fox would get the best of his accusers. He had only to stand up to his rights as a citizen and to keep his mouth shut. But the wicked are often cowards, even the coldest heart may be haunted by crime, and human foxes as often as not step into traps of their own devising.

The Fox rushed up to the bench, weeping, "Yes! Yes, I murdered him, it's true! Oppianicus made me do it! I would never have come up with such a plot on my own. It was Oppianicus's idea from the start, to create the false will and then murder Asuvius! If you don't believe me, call Oppianicus before this bench and force him to tell you the truth!"

I turned and gazed at Lucius Claudius, who looked just the same as he had always looked—sausage-fingered, plum-cheeked, cherry-nosed—but who no longer appeared to me the least bit foolish or dim-witted. His eyes glinted oddly. He looked a bit frightening, in fact, and terribly sure of himself, which is to say that he looked like what he was, a Roman noble. On his face was a smile such as great poets must smile when they have finished a magnum opus.

The rest of the tale is both good and bad mixed together.

I wish that I could report that Oppianicus and the Fox received their just desserts, but alas, Roman justice prevailed—which is to say that the honorable commissioner Quintus Manilius proved not too honorable to take a bribe from Oppianicus; that at least is what the Forum gossips say. Manilius first announced he would bring a charge of murder against the Fox and Oppianicus, then suddenly dropped the case. Lucius Claudius was bitterly disappointed. I advised him to take heart; from my own experience, villains like Oppianicus and the Fox eventually come to a bad end, though many others may suffer before they reach it.

Perhaps not coincidentally, at about the same time that the murder charges were dropped, the fraudulent will went missing in Larinum. In consequence, the property of the late Asuvius was divided among his surviving blood relations. Oppianicus and the Fox did not profit from his death.

The owner of Priapus's Palace was furious with Columba for leaving the establishment without his permission, and threatened to chastise her by putting hot coals on her feet, whereupon Lucius Claudius offered to buy her on the spot. I have no doubt that she is well treated in her new household. Lucius may not be the endlessly virile young man that Asuvius was, but that has not kept him from acting like a young man in love.

These days, I see Lucius Claudius quite often in the Forum, in the company of reasonably honest advocates like Cicero and Hortensius. Rome can always use another honest man in the Forum. He tells me that he recently completed a book of love poems and is thinking of running for office. He holds occasional dinner parties and spends his quiet time in the country, overseeing his farms and vineyards.

As the Etruscans used to say, it is an ill will that doesn't bring someone good fortune. The unfortunate Asuvius may not have left a will, after all, but I think that Lucius Claudius was a beneficiary nonetheless.

BENJAMIN M. SCHUTZ

MARY, MARY, SHUT THE DOOR

*Winner of the Shamus Award for Best Novel for his Leo Hag-
gerty novel* A Tax in Blood, *Ben Schutz is another author new
to this series. His private eye Leo Haggerty, who starred in the
novel and the story that follows, is not your usual one-man
operation. His office is large and well-staffed—a private detective for today. In this story Schutz ably demonstrates that his
skill with a novel works just as well in the shorter form.
"Mary, Mary, Shut the Door" won the MWA Edgar as the best
short story of 1992.*

Enzo Scolari motored into my office and motioned me to sit.
What the hell, I sat. He pulled around to the side of my desk,
laced his fingers in his lap, and sized me up.

"I want to hire you, Mr. Haggerty," he announced.

"To do what, Mr. Scolari?"

"I want you to stop my niece's wedding."

"I see. And why is that?"

"She is making a terrible mistake, and I will not sit by and let
her do it."

"Exactly what kind of mistake is she making?"

"She knows nothing about him. They just met. She is infatu-
ated, nothing more. She knows nothing about men. Nothing.
The first one to pay any attention to her and she wants to get
married."

"You said they just met. How long ago, exactly?" Just a little
reality check.

"Two weeks. Can you believe it? Two weeks. And I just found out about it yesterday. She brought him to the house last night. There was a party and she introduced him to everyone and told us she was gong to marry him. How can you marry someone you've known for two weeks? That's ridiculous. It's a guarantee of failure and it'll break her heart. I can't let that happen."

"Mr. Scolari, I'm not sure we can help you with this. Your niece may be doing something foolish, but she has a right to do it. I understand your concern for her well-being, but I don't think you need a detective, maybe a priest or a therapist. We don't do premarital background checks. Our investigations are primarily criminal."

"The crime just hasn't happened yet, Mr. Haggerty. My niece may be a foolish girl, but he isn't. He knows exactly what he's doing."

"And what is that?"

"He's taking advantage of her naïveté, her innocence, her fears, her loneliness, so he can get her money. That's a crime, Mr. Haggerty."

And a damn hard one to prove. "What are you afraid of, Mr. Scolari? That he'll kill her for her money? That's quite a leap from an impulsive decision to marry. Do you have any reason to think that this guy is a killer?"

He straightened up and gave that one some thought. Enzo Scolari was wide and thick with shoulders so square and a head so flat he could have been a candelabra. His snow-white eyebrows and mustache hung like awnings for his eyes and lips.

"No. Not for that. But I can tell he doesn't love Gina. Last night I watched him. Every time Gina left his side his eyes went somewhere else. A man in love, his eyes follow his woman everywhere. No, he's following the maid or Gina's best friend. Gina comes back and he smiles like she's the sunrise. And she believes it.

"He spent more time touching the tapestries than he did holding her hand. He went through the house like a creditor, not a guest. No, he doesn't want Gina, he wants her money. You're right, murder is quite a step from that, but there are easier ways to steal. Gina is a shy, quiet woman who has never had to make any decisions for herself. I don't blame her for that. My sister, God rest her soul, was terrified that something awful would happen to Gina and she tried to protect her from everything. It didn't work. My sister was the one who died and it devastated the girl. Now Gina has to live in the world and she doesn't know how. If this guy can talk her into marrying him so quickly, he'll have no trouble talking her into letting him handle her money."

"How much money are we talking about here?"

"Ten million dollars, Mr. Haggerty." Scolari smiled, having made his point. People have murdered or married for lots less.

"How did she get all this money?"

"It's in a trust for her. A trust set up by my father. My sister and I each inherited half of Scolari Enterprises. When she died, her share went to Gina as her only child."

"This trust, who manages it?"

"I do, of course."

Of course. Motive number two just came up for air. "So, where's the problem? If you control the money, this guy can't do anything."

"I control the money as trustee for my sister. I began that when Gina was still a little girl. Now she is of age and can control the money herself if she wants to."

"So you stand to lose the use of ten million dollars. Have I got that right?"

Scolari didn't even bother to debate that one with me. I liked that. I'll take naked self-interest over the delusions of altruism any day.

"If they've just met, how do you know that this guy even knows that your niece has all this money?"

Scolari stared at me, then spat out his bitter reply. "Why else would he have pursued her? She is a mousy little woman, dull and plain. She's afraid of men. She spent her life in those fancy girls' schools where they taught her how to set the table. She huddled with her mother in that house, afraid of everything. Well, now she is alone and I think she's latched onto the first person who will rescue her from that."

"Does she know how you feel?"

He nodded. "Yes, she does. I made it very clear to her last night."

"How did she take it?"

"She told me to mind my own business." Scolari snorted. "She doesn't even know that that's what I'm doing. She said she loved him and she was going to marry him, no matter what."

"Doesn't sound so mousy to me. She ever stand up to you before?"

"No, never. On anything else, I'd applaud it. But getting married shouldn't be the first decision you ever make."

"Anyone else that might talk to her that she'd listen to?"

"No. She's an only child. Her father died when she was two in the same explosion that killed my father and took my legs. Her mother died in an automobile accident a little over a year ago. I am a widower myself and Gina was never close to my sons. They frightened her as a little girl. They were loud and rough. They teased her and made her cry." Scolari shrugged as if boys would be boys. "I did not like that and would stop it whenever I caught them, but she was such a timid child, their cruelty sprouted whenever she was around. There is no other family."

I picked up the pipe from my desk, stuck it in my mouth, and chewed on it. A glorified pacifier. Kept me from chewing up the inside of my mouth, though. Wouldn't be much of a stretch to take this one on. What the hell, work is work.

"Okay, Mr. Scolari, we'll take the case. I want you to understand that we can't and we won't stop her wedding. There are guys who will do that, and I know who they are, but I wouldn't give you their names. We'll do a background check on this guy and see if we can find something that'll change her mind or your mind. Maybe they really love each other. That happens, you know. This may be a crazy start, but I'm not sure that's a handicap. What's the best way to run a race when you don't know where the finish is?" I sure didn't have an answer and Scolari offered none.

"Mr. Haggerty, I am not averse to taking a risk, but not a blind one. If there's information out there that will help me calculate the odds, then I want it. That's what I want you to get for me. I appreciate your open mind, Mr. Haggerty. Perhaps you will change my mind, but I doubt it."

"Okay, Mr. Scolari. I need a description of this guy, his name and anything else you know about him. First thing Monday morning, I'll assign an investigator and we'll get on this."

"That won't do, Mr. Haggerty, You need to start on this immediately, this minute."

"Why is that?"

"Because they flew to St. Mary's this morning to get married."

"Aren't we a little late, then?"

"No. You can't apply for a marriage license on St. Mary's until you've been on the island for two days."

"How long to get the application approved?"

"I called the embassy. They say it takes three days to process the application. I'm looking into delaying that, if possible. Once it's issued they say most people get married that day or the next."

"So we've got what, five or six days? Mr. Scolari, we can't run a complete background check in that period of time. Hell, no one can. There just isn't enough time."

"What if you put everyone you've got on this, round the clock?"

"That gets you a maybe and just barely that. He'd have to have a pimple on his backside the size of Mount Rushmore for us to find it that fast. If this guy's the sneaky, cunning, opportunist that you think he is, then he's hidden that, maybe not perfectly, but deep enough that six days won't turn it up. Besides, I can't put everyone on this, we've got lots of other cases that need attention."

"So hire more staff, give them the other cases, and put everyone else on this. Money is no object, Mr. Haggerty. I want you to use all your resources on this."

My jaw hurt from clamping on the dead pipe. Scolari was old enough to make a foolish mistake. I told him it was a long shot at best. What more could I tell him? When did I become clairvoyant, and know how things would turn out? Suppose we did find something, like three dead ex-wives? Right! Let's not kid ourselves—all the staff for six days—round the clock—that's serious money. What was it Rocky said? When you run a business, money's always necessary but it's never sufficient. Don't confuse the two and what you do at the office won't keep you up at night.

I sorted everything into piles and then decided. "All right, Mr. Scolari, we'll do it. I can't even tell you what it'll cost. We'll bill you at our hourly rates plus all the expenses. I think a reasonable retainer would be thirty thousand dollars."

He didn't even blink. It probably wasn't a week's interest on ten million dollars.

"There's no guarantee that we'll find anything, Mr. Scolari, not under these circumstances. You'll know that you did everything you could, but that's all you'll know for sure."

"That's all you ever know for sure, Mr. Haggerty."

I pulled out a pad to make some notes. "Do you know where they went on St. Mary's?"

"Yes. A resort called the Banana Bay Beach Hotel. I have taken the liberty of registering you there."

"Excuse me." I felt like something under his front wheel.

"The resort is quite remote and perched on the side of a cliff. I have been assured that I would not be able to make my way around. I need you to be my legs, my eyes. If your agents learn anything back here, someone has to be able to get that information to my niece. Someone has to be there. I want that someone to be you, Mr. Haggerty. That's what I'm paying for. Your brains, your eyes, your legs, to be there because I can't."

I stared at Scolari's withered legs and the motorized wheelchair he got around in. More than that he had money, lots of money. And money's the ultimate prosthetic.

"Let's start at the top. What's his name?"

The island of St. Mary's is one of lush green mountains that drop straight into the sea. What little flat land there is, is on the west coast, and that's where almost all the people live. The central highlands and peaks are still wild and pristine.

My plane banked around the southern tip of the island and headed toward one of those flat spots, the international airport. I flipped through the file accumulated in those few hours between Enzo Scolari's visit and my plane's departure. While Kelly, my secretary, made travel arrangements I called everyone into the conference room and handed out jobs. Clancy Hopper was to rearrange caseloads and hire temporary staff to keep the other cases moving. Del Winslow was to start investigating our man Derek Marshall. We had a name, real or otherwise, an address, and phone number. Del would do the house-to-house with the drawing we made from Scolari's description. Larry Burdette would be smilin' and dialin'. Calling every computerized data base we could access to get more information. Every time Marshall's name appeared he'd take the information and hand it to another investigator to verify every fact and then backtrack each one by phone or in person until we could re-create the life of Derek Marshall. Our best chance was with the St. Mary's Department of Licenses. To apply for a marriage license Marshall had to file a copy of his passport, birth certificate, decrees of divorce if previously married, death certificate if widowed, and proof of legal name change, if any. If the records were open to the public, we'd get faxed copies or I'd go to the offices myself and look at them personally. I took one last look at the picture of Gina Dalesandro and then the sketch of Derek Marshall, closed the file, and slipped it into my bag as the runway appeared outside my window.

I climbed out of the plane and into the heat. A dry wind moved the heat around me as I walked into the airport. I showed my passport and had nothing to declare. They were delighted to have me on their island. I stepped out of the airport and the cabmaster introduced me to my driver. I followed him to a battered Toyota, climbed into the front seat, and stowed my bag between my feet. He slammed the door and asked where to.

"Banana Bay Beach Hotel," I said as he turned the engine on and pulled out.

"No problem."

"How much?" We bounced over a sleeping policeman.

"Eighty ecee."

Thirty-five dollars American. "How far is it?"

"Miles or time?"

"Both."

"Fifteen miles. An hour and a half."

I should have gotten out then. If the road to hell is paved at all, then it doesn't pass through St. Mary's. The coast road was a lattice of potholes winding around the sides of the mountains. There were no lanes, no lights, no signs, and no guardrails. The sea was a thousand feet below and we were never more than a few inches from visiting it.

Up and down the hills, there were blue bags on the trees.

"What are those bags?" I asked.

"Bananas. The bags keep the insects away while they ripen."

I scanned the slopes and tried to imagine going out there to put those bags on. Whoever did it, they couldn't possibly be paying him enough. Ninety minutes of bobbing and weaving on those roads like a fighter on the ropes and I was exhausted from defying gravity. I half expected to hear a bell to end the trip as we pulled up to the resort.

I checked in, put my valuables in a safe-deposit box, took my key and information packet, and headed up the hill to my room. Dinner was served in about an hour. Enough time to get oriented, unpack, and shower.

My room overlooked the upstairs bar and dining area and below that the beach, the bay, and the surrounding cliffs. I had a thatched-roof verandah with a hammock and clusters of flamboyant and chenille red-hot cattails close enough to pluck. The bathroom was clean and functional. The bedroom large and sparsely furnished. Clearly, this was a place where the attractions were outdoors and rooms were for sleeping in. The mosquito netting over the bed and the coils on the dresser were not good signs. It was the rainy season and Caribbean mosquitoes can get pretty cheeky. In Antigua one caught me in the bathroom and pulled back the shower curtain like he was Norman Bates.

I unpacked quickly and read my information packet. It had a map of the resort, a list of services, operating hours, and tips on how to avoid common problems in the Caribbean such as sunburn, being swept out to sea, and a variety of bites, stings, and inedible fruits. I familiarized myself with the layout and took out the pictures of Gina and Derek. Job one was to find them and then tag along unobtrusively until the home office gave me something to work with.

I showered, changed, and lay down on the bed to wait for dinner. The best time to make an appearance was midway through the meal. Catch the early birds leaving and the stragglers on their way in.

Around 8:30, I sprayed myself with insect repellent, slipped my keys into my pocket, and headed down to dinner. The schedule said that it would be a barbecue on the beach.

At the reception area I stopped and looked over the low wall to the beach below. Scolari was right, he wouldn't be able to get around here. The rooms jutted out from the bluff and were connected by a steep roadway. However, from this point on, the hillside was a precipice. A staircase wound its way down to the beach. One hundred and twenty-six steps, the maid said.

I started down, stopping periodically to check the railing. There were no lights on the trail. Late at night, a little drunk on champagne, a new bride could have a terrible accident. I peered over the side at the concrete roadway below. She wouldn't bounce and she wouldn't survive.

I finished the zigzagging descent and noted that the return trip would be worse.

Kerosene lamps led the way to the beach restaurant and bar. I sat on a stool, ordered a Yellowbird, and turned to look at the dining area. Almost everyone was in couples, the rest were families. All white, mostly Americans, Canadians, British, and German. At least that's what the brochure said.

I sipped my drink and scanned the room. No sign of them. No problem, the night was young even if I wasn't. I had downed a second drink when they came in out of the darkness. Our drawing of Marshall was pretty good. He was slight, pale, with brown hair parted down the middle, round-rimmed tortoiseshell glasses, and a deep dimpled smile he aimed at the woman he gripped by the elbow. He steered her between the tables as if she had a tiller.

They took a table and I looked about to position myself. I wanted to be able to watch Marshall's face and be close enough to overhear them without looking like it. One row over and two up a table was coming free. I took my drink from the bar and ambled over. The busboy cleared the table and I took a long sip from my drink and set it down.

Gina Dalesandro wore a long flower-print dress. Strapless, she had tan lines where her bathing suit had been. She ran a finger over her ear and flipped back her hair. In profile she was thin-lipped, hook-nosed, and high-browed. Her hand held Marshall's, and then, eyes on his, she pulled one to her and kissed it. She moved from one knuckle to the next, and when she was done she took a finger and slowly slid it into her mouth.

"Gina, please, people will look," he whispered.

"Let them," she said, smiling around his finger.

Marshall pulled back and flicked his eyes around. My waitress had arrived and I was ordering when he passed over me. I had the fish chowder, the grilled dolphin with stuffed christophene, and another drink.

Gina picked up Marshall's hand and held it to her cheek and said something soothing because he smiled and blew her a kiss. They ordered and talked in hushed tones punctuated with laughter and smiles. I sat nearby, watching, waiting, her uncle's gargoyle in residence.

When dessert arrived, Gina excused herself and went toward the ladies' room. Marshall watched her go. I read nothing in his face or eyes. When she disappeared into the bathroom, his eyes wandered around the room, but settled on no one. He locked in on her when she reappeared and led her back to the table with his eyes. All in all it proved nothing.

We all enjoyed the banana cake and coffee and after a discreet pause I followed them back toward the rooms. We trudged silently up the stairs, past the bar and the reception desk, and back into darkness. I kept them in view as I went toward my room and saw that they were in Room 7, two levels up and one over from me. When their door clicked closed, I turned around and went back to the activities board outside the bar. I scanned the list of trips for tomorrow to see if they had signed up for any of them. They were down for the morning trip to the local volcano. I signed aboard and went to arrange a wake-up call for the morning.

After a quick shower, I lit the mosquito coils, dialed the lights way down, and crawled under the netting. I pulled the phone and my book inside, propped up the pillows, and called the office. For his money, Scolari should get an answer. He did.

"Franklin Investigations."

"Evening, Del. What do we have on Derek Marshall?"

"Precious little, boss, that's what."

"Well, give it to me."

"Okay, I canvassed his neighborhood. He's the invisible man. Rented apartment. Manager says he's always on time with the rent. Nothing else. I missed the mailman, but I'll catch him tomorrow. See if he can tell me anything. Neighbors know him by sight. That's about it. No wild parties. Haven't seen him with lots of girls. One thought he was seeing this one particular woman but hasn't seen her around in quite a while."

"How long has he been in the apartment?"

"Three years."

"Manager let you look at the rent application?"

"Leo, you know that's confidential. I couldn't even ask for that information."

"We prosper on the carelessness of others, Del. Did you ask?"

"Yes, and he was offended and indignant."

"Tough shit."

"Monday morning we'll go through court records and permits and licenses for the last three years, see if anything shakes out."

"Neighbors tell you anything else?"

"No, like I said, they knew him by sight, period."

"You find his car?"

"Yeah. Now that was a gold mine. Thing had stickers all over it."

"Such as?"

"Bush-Quayle. We'll check him out with Young Republican organizations. Also, Georgetown Law School."

"You run him through our directories?"

"Yeah, nothing. He's either a drone or modest."

"Call Walter O'Neil, tonight. Give him the name, see if he can get a law firm for the guy, maybe even someone who'll talk about him."

"Okay. I'm also going over to the school tomorrow, use the

library, look up yearbooks, et cetera. See if we can locate a classmate. Alumni affairs will have to wait until Monday."

"How about NCIC?"

"Clean. No warrants or arrests. He's good or he's tidy."

"Anything else on the car?"

"Yeah, a sticker for something called Ultimate Frisbee. Nobody here knows anything about it. We're trying to track down an association for it, find out where it's played, then we'll interview people."

"Okay. We've still got three, maybe four days. How's the office doing? Are the other cases being covered?"

"Yeah, we spread them around. Clancy hired a couple of freelancers to start next week. Right now, me, Clancy, and Larry are pulling double shifts on this. Monday when the offices are open and the data bases are up, we'll probably put the two new guys on it."

"Good. Any word from the St. Mary's registrar's office?"

"No. Same problem there. Closed for the weekend. Won't know anything until Monday."

"All right. Good work, Del." I gave him my number. "Call here day or night with anything. If you can't get me directly, have me paged. I'll be out tomorrow morning on a field trip with Marshall and Gina, but I should be around the rest of the day."

"All right. Talk to you tomorrow."

I slipped the phone under the netting. Plumped the pillows and opened my book. Living alone had made me a voracious reader, as if all my other appetites had mutated into a hunger for the words that would make me someone else, put me somewhere else, or at least help me to sleep. The more I read, the harder it was to keep my interest. Boredom crept over me like the slow death it was. I was an old jaded john needing ever kinkier tricks just to get it up, or over with. Pretty soon nothing would move me at all. Until then, I was grateful for Michael Malone and the jolts and length of *Time's Witness*.

I woke up to the telephone's insistent ring, crawled out of bed, and thanked the front desk for the call. A chameleon darted out from under the bed and headed out the door. "Nice seeing you,"

I called out, and hoped he'd had a bountiful evening keeping my room an insect-free zone. I dressed and hurried down to breakfast.

After a glass of soursop, I ordered saltfish and onions with bakes and lots of coffee. Derek and Gina were not in the dining room. Maybe they'd ordered room service, maybe they were sleeping in and wouldn't make it. I ate quickly and kept checking my watch while I had my second cup of coffee. Our driver had arrived and was looking at the activities board. Another couple came up to him and introduced themselves. I wiped my mouth and left to join the group. Derek and Gina came down the hill as I checked in.

Our driver told us that his name was Wellington Bramble and that he was also a registered tour guide with the Department of the Interior. The other couple climbed into the back of the van, then Derek and Gina in the middle row. I hopped in up front, next to Wellington, turned, and introduced myself.

"Hi, my name is Leo Haggerty."

"Hello, I'm Derek Marshall and this is my fiancée, Gina Dalesandro."

"Pleasure to meet you."

Derek and Gina turned and we were all introduced to Tom and Dorothy Needham of Chicago, Illinois.

Wellington stuck his head out the window and spoke to one of the maids. They spoke rapidly in the local patois until the woman slapped him across the forearm and waved a scolding finger at him.

He engaged the gears, pulled away from the reception area, and told us that we would be visiting the tropical rain forests that surround the island's active volcano. All this in perfect English, the language of strangers and for strangers.

Dorothy Needham asked the question on all of our minds. "How long will we be on this road to the volcano?"

Wellington laughed. "Twenty minutes, ma'am, then we go inland to the volcano."

We left the coast road and passed through a gate marked ST. MARY'S ISLAND CONSERVANCY—DEVIL'S CAULDRON VOLCANO AND TROPICAL RAIN FOREST. I was first out and helped the women step down into the muddy path. Wellington lined us up and began to lead us through the jungle, calling out the names of plants and flowers and answering questions.

There were soursop trees, lime trees, nutmeg, guava, bananas, coconuts, cocoa trees, ginger lilies, lobster-claw plants, flamboyant and hibiscus, impression fern, and chenille red-hot cattails. We stopped on the path at a large fern. Wellington turned and pointed to it.

"Here, you touch the plant, right here," he said, pointing at Derek, who eyed him suspiciously. "It won't hurt you."

Derek reached out a finger and touched the fern. Instantly the leaves retracted and curled in on themselves.

"That's Mary, Mary, Shut the Door. As you can see, a delicate and shy plant indeed."

He waved us on and we followed. Gina slipped an arm through Derek's and put her head on his shoulder She squeezed him once.

"Derek, you know I used to be like that plant. Before you came along. All closed up and frightened if anybody got too close. But not anymore. I am so happy," she said, and squeezed him again.

Other than a mild self-loathing, I was having a good time, too. We came out of the forest and were on the volcano. Wellington turned to face us.

"Ladies and gentlemen, please listen very carefully. We are on top of an active volcano. There is no danger of an eruption, because there is no crust, so there is no pressure buildup. The last eruption was over two hundred years ago. That does not mean that there is no danger here. You must stay on the marked path at all times and be very careful on the sections that have no guardrail. The water in the volcano is well over three hundred degrees Fahrenheit; should you stumble and fall in, you would be burned alive. I do not wish to alarm you unreasonably, but a couple of years ago we did lose a visitor, so please be very careful. Now follow me."

We moved along, single file and well spaced through a setting unlike any other I'd ever encountered. The circular top of the volcano looked like a wound on the earth. The ground steamed and smoked and nothing grew anywhere. Here and there black water leaked out of crusty patches like blood seeping from under a scab. The smell of sulfur was everywhere.

I followed Derek and Gina and watched him stop a couple of times and test the railings before he let her proceed. Caution, Derek? Or a trial run?

We circled the volcano and retraced our path back to the van. As promised, we were back at the hotel twenty minutes later. Gina was flushed with excitement and asked Derek if they could go back again. He thought that was possible, but there weren't any other guided tours this week, so they'd have to rent a car and go themselves. I closed my eyes and imagined her by the side of the road, taking a picture perhaps, and him ushering her through the foliage and on her way to eternity.

We all went in for lunch and ate separately. I followed them back to their room and then down to the beach. They moved to the far end of the beach and sat facing away from everyone else. I went into the bar and worked my way through a pair of long necks.

A couple in the dining room was having a spat, or maybe it was a tiff. Whatever, she called him a *schwein* and really tagged him with an open forehand to the chops. His face lit up redder than a baboon's ass.

She pushed back her chair, swung her long blond hair in an about-face, and stormed off. I watched her go, taking each step like she was grinding out a cigarette under her foot. Made her hips and butt do terrible things.

I pulled my eyes away when I realized I had company. He was leering at me enthusiastically.

I swung around slowly. "Yes?"

It was one of the local hustlers who patrolled the beach, as ubiquitous and resourceful as the coconuts that littered the sand.

"I seen you around, man. Y'all alone. That's not a good thin', man. I was thinkin' maybe you could use some company. Someone to share paradise wit'. Watcha say, man?"

I shook my head. "I don't think so."

He frowned. "I know you ain't that way, man. I seen you watch that blond with the big ones. What'sa matter? What you afraid of?" He stopped and tried to answer that one for me. "She be clean, man. No problem."

When I didn't say anything, he got pissed. "What is it then? You don't fuck strange, man?"

"Watch my lips, bucko. I'm not interested. Don't make more of it than there is."

He sized me up and decided I wasn't worth the aggravation. Spinning off his stool, he called me something in patois. I was sure it wasn't "sir."

I found a free lounge under a bohio and kept an eye on Derek and Gina. No sooner had I settled in than Gina got up and headed across the cocoa-colored volcanic sands to the beach bar. She was a little pink around the edges. Probably wouldn't be out too long today. Derek had his back to me, so I swiveled my head to keep her in sight. She sat down and one of the female staff came over and began to run a comb through her hair. Cornrowing. She'd be there for at least an hour. I ordered a drink from a wandering waiter, closed my eyes, and relaxed.

Gina strolled back, her hair in tight little braids, each one tipped with a series of colored beads. She was smiling and kicking up little sprays of water. I watched her take Derek by the hands and pull him up out of his chair. She twirled around and shook her head back and forth, just to watch the braids fly by. They picked up their snorkels and fins and headed for the water. I watched to see which way they'd go. The left side of the bay had numerous warning signs about the strong current including one on the point that said TURN BACK—NEXT STOP PANAMA.

They went right and so did I. Maybe it was a little fear, maybe it was love, but she held on to his hand while they hovered over the reef. I went farther out and then turned back so I could keep them in sight. The reef was one of the richest I'd ever been on and worthy of its reputation as one of the best in the Caribbean.

I kept my position near the couple, moving when they did, just like the school of squid I was above. They were in formation, tentacles tucked in, holding their position by undulating the fins on each lateral axis. When the school moved, they all went at once and kept the same distance from each other. I drifted off the coral to a bed of sea grass. Two creatures were walking through the grass. Gray green, with knobs and lumps everywhere, they had legs and wings! They weren't toxic-waste mutants, just the flying gurnards. I dived down on them and they spread their violet wings and took off.

When I surfaced, Derek and Gina were heading in. I swam downstream from them and came ashore as they did. Gina was holding her side and peeking behind her palm. Derek steadied her and helped get her flippers off.

"I don't know what it was, Derek. It just brushed me and then it felt like a bee sting. It really burns," Gina said.

I wandered by and said, "Looks like a jellyfish sting. When did it happen?"

"Just a second ago." They answered in unison.

"Best thing for that is papaya skins. Has an enzyme that neutralizes the toxin. The beach restaurant has plenty of them. They keep it just for things like this. You better get right over, though. It only works if you apply it right away."

"Thanks. Thanks a lot," Derek said, then turned to help Gina down the beach. "Yes, thank you," she said over his shoulder.

"You're welcome," I said to myself, and went to dry off.

I sat at the bar, waiting for dinner and playing backgammon with myself. Derek and Gina came in and went to the bar to order. Her dress was a swirl of purple, black, and white and matched the color of the beads in her hair. Derek wore lime-green shorts and a white short-sleeved shirt. Drinks in hand, they walked over to me. I stood up, shook hands, and invited them to join me.

"That tip of yours was a lifesaver. We went over to the bar and got some papaya on it right away. I think the pain was gone in maybe five minutes. How did you know about it?" Gina asked.

"I've been stung myself before. Somebody told me about it. Now I tell you. Word of mouth."

"Well, we're very grateful. We're getting married here on the island and I didn't want anything to mess this time up for us," Derek said.

I raised my glass in a toast. "Congratulations to you. This is a lovely place to get married. When is the ceremony?" I asked, sipping my drink.

"Tomorrow," Gina said, running her arm through Derek's. "I'm so excited."

I nearly drowned her in rerouted rum punch but managed to turn away and choke myself instead. I pounded my chest and waved off any assistance.

"Are you okay?" Derek asked.

"Yes, yes, I'm fine," I said as I got myself under control. Tomorrow? How the hell could it be tomorrow? "Sorry. I was trying to talk when I was drinking. Just doesn't work that way."

Derek asked if he could buy me another drink and I let him take my glass to the bar.

"I read the tourist brochure about getting married on the island. How long does it take for them to approve an application? They only said that you have to be on the island for two days before you can submit an application."

Gina leaned forward and touched my knee. "It usually takes two or three days, but Derek found a way to hurry things up. He sent the papers down early to the manager here and he agreed to file them for us as if we were on the island. It'll be ready tomorrow morning and we'll get married right after noon."

"That's wonderful. Where will the ceremony be?" My head was spinning.

"Here at the hotel. Down on the beach. They provide a cake, champagne, photographs, flowers. Would you join us afterward to celebrate?"

"Thank you, that's very kind. I'm not sure that I'll still be here, though. My plane leaves in the afternoon, and you know with that ride back to the airport, I might be gone. If I'm still here, I'd be delighted."

Derek returned with drinks and sat close to Gina and looped an arm around her.

"Honey, I hope you don't mind, but I invited Mr. Haggerty to join us after the ceremony." She smiled anxiously.

"No, that sounds great, love to have you. By the way, it sounded like you've been to the islands before. This is our first

time. Have you ever gone scuba diving?" Derek was all gracious-
ness.

"Yeah, are you thinking of trying it?"

"Maybe, they have a course for beginners tomorrow. We were
talking about taking the course and seeing if we liked it," he said.

"I'm a little scared. Is it really dangerous?" Gina asked.

Absolutely lethal. Russian roulette with one empty chamber.
Don't do it. Wouldn't recommend it to my worst enemy.

"No, not really. There are dangers if you're careless, and
they're pretty serious ones. The sea is not very forgiving of our
mistakes. But if you're well trained and maintain some respect
for what you're doing, it's not all that dangerous."

"I don't know. Maybe I'll just watch you do it, Derek."

"Come on, honey. You really liked snorkeling. Can you imagine how much fun it would be if you didn't have to worry about
coming up for air all the time?" Derek gave Gina a squeeze.
"And besides, I love the way you look in that new suit."

I saw others heading to the dining room and began to clean up
the tiles from the board.

"Mr. Haggerty, would you—" Gina began.

"I'm sure we'll see Mr. Haggerty again, Gina. Thanks for your
help this afternoon," Derek said, and led her to the dining room.

I finished my drink and took myself to dinner. After that, I sat
and watched them dance to the shak-shak band. She put her head
on his shoulder and molded her body to his. They swayed together in the perfect harmony only lovers and mothers and babies
have.

They left that way, her head on his shoulder, a peaceful smile
on her lips. I could not drink enough to cut the ache I felt and
went to bed when I gave up trying.

Del was in when I called and gave me the brief bad news.

"The mailman was a dead end. I went over to the school library and talked to teachers and students. So far, nobody's had
anything useful to tell us. I've got a class list and we're working
our way through it. Walt did get a lead on him, though. He's a
junior partner in a small law firm, a 'boutique' he called it."

"What kind of law?" Come on, say tax and estate.

"Immigration and naturalization."

"Shit. Anything else?"

"Yeah, he's new there. Still don't know where he came from. We'll try to get some information from the partners first thing in the morning."

"It better be first thing. Our timetable just went out the window. They're getting married tomorrow at noon."

"Jesus Christ, that puts the screws to us. We'll only have a couple of hours to work with."

"Don't remind me. Is that it?"

"For right now. Clancy is hitting bars looking for people that play this 'Ultimate Frisbee' thing. He's got a sketch with him. Hasn't called in yet."

"Well, if he finds anything, call me no matter what time it is. I'll be around all morning tomorrow. If you don't get me direct, have me paged, as an emergency. Right now we don't have shit."

"Hey, boss, we just ran out of time. I'm sure in a couple of days we'd have turned something up."

"Maybe so, Del, but tomorrow around noon somebody's gonna look out over their heads and ask if anybody has anything to say or forever hold your peace. I don't see myself raising my hand and asking for a couple of more days, 'cause we're bound to turn something up."

"We did our best. We just weren't holding very good cards is all."

"Del, we were holding shit." I should have folded when Scolari dealt them.

I hung up and readied my bedroom to repel all boarders. Under the netting, I sat and mulled over my options. I had no reason to stick my nose into Gina's life. No reason at all to think that Derek was anything but the man she'd waited her whole life for. Her happiness was real, though. She was blossoming under his touch. I had seen it. And happiness is a fragile thing. Who was I to cast a shadow on hers? And without any reason. Tomorrow was a special day for her. How would she remember it? How would I?

I woke early from a restless night and called the office. Nothing new. I tried Scolari's number and spoke briefly to him. I told him we were out of time and had nothing of substance. I asked him a couple of questions and he gave me some good news and some bad. There was nothing else to do, so I went down to see the betrothed.

They were in the dining room holding hands and finishing their coffee. I approached and asked if I could join them.

"Good morning, Mr. Haggerty. Lovely day, isn't it?" Gina said, her face aglow.

I settled into the chair and decided to smack them in the face with it. "Before you proceed with your wedding, I have some news for you."

They sat upright and took their hands, still joined, off the table.

"Gina's uncle, Enzo Scolari, wishes me to inform you that he has had his attorneys activate the trustee's discretionary powers over Miss Dalesandro's portion of the estate so that she cannot take possession of the money or use it in any fashion without his consent. He regrets having to take this action, but your insistence on this marriage leaves him no choice."

"You son of a bitch. You've been spying on us for that bastard," Derek shouted, and threw his glass of water at me. I sat there dripping while I counted to ten. Gina had gone pale and was on the verge of tears. Marshall stood up, "Come on, Gina, let's go. I don't want this man anywhere near me." He leaned forward and stabbed a finger at me. "I intend to call your employer, Mr. Scolari, and let him know what a despicable piece of shit I think he is, and that goes double for you." He turned away. "Gina, are you coming?"

"Just a second, honey," she whispered. "I'll be along in just a second." Marshall crashed out of the room, assaulting chairs and tables that got in his way.

"Why did you do this to me? I've waited my whole life for this day. To find someone who loves me and wants to live with me and to celebrate that. We came here to get away from my uncle and his obsessions. You know what hurts the most? You reminded me that my uncle doesn't believe that anyone could love me for myself. It has to be my money. What's so wrong with *me?* Can you tell me that?" She was starting to cry and wiped at her tears with her palms. "Hell of a question to be asking on your wedding day, huh? You do good work, Mr. Haggerty. I hope you're proud of yourself."

I'd rather Marshall had thrown acid in my face than the words she hurled at me. "Think about one thing, Miss Dalesandro. This way you can't lose. If he doesn't marry you now, you've avoided a lot of heartache and maybe worse. If he does, knowing this, then you can relax knowing it's you and not your money. The way I see it, either way you can't lose. But I'm sorry. If there had been any other way, I'd have done it."

"Yes, well, I have to go, Mr. Haggerty." She rose, dropped her napkin on the table, and walked slowly through the room, using every bit of dignity she could muster.

I spent the rest of the morning in the bar waiting for the last act to unfold.

At noon, Gina appeared in a long white dress. She had a bouquet of flowers in her hands and was trying hard to smile. I sipped some anesthetic and looked away. No need to make it any harder now. I wasn't sure whether I wanted Marshall to show up or not.

Derek appeared at her side in khaki slacks and an embroidered white shirt. What will be, will be. They moved slowly down the stairs. I went to my room, packed, and checked out. By three o'clock I was off the island and on my way home.

It was almost a year later when Kelly buzzed me on the intercom to say that a Mr. Derek Marshall was here to see me.

"Show him in."

He hadn't changed a bit. Neither one of us moved to shake hands. When I didn't invite him to sit down, he did anyway.

"What do you want, Marshall?"

"You know, I'll never forget that moment when you told me that Scolari had altered the trust. Right there in public. I was so angry that you'd try to make me look bad like that in front of Gina and everyone else. It really has stayed with me. And here I am, leaving the area. I thought I'd come by and return the favor before I left."

"How's Gina?" I asked with a veneer of nonchalance over trepidation.

"Funny you should ask. I'm a widower, you know. She had a terrible accident about six months ago. We were scuba diving. It was her first time. I'd already had some courses. I guess she misunderstood what I'd told her and she held her breath coming up. Ruptured a lung. She was dead before I could get her to shore."

I almost bit through my pipe stem. "You're a real piece of work, aren't you? Pretty slick, death by misinformation. Got away with it, didn't you?"

"The official verdict was accidental death. Scolari was beside himself, as you can imagine. There I was, sole inheritor of Gina's estate, and according to the terms of the trust her half of the grandfather's money was mine. It was all in Scolari stock, so I made a deal with the old man. He got rid of me and I got paid fifty percent more than the shares were worth."

"You should be careful, Derek, that old man hasn't got long to live. He might decide to take you with him."

"That thought has crossed my mind. So I'm going to take my money and put some space between him and me."

Marshall stood up to leave. "By the way, your bluff wasn't half-bad. It actually threw me there for a second. That's why I tossed the water on you. I had to get away and do some thinking, make sure I hadn't overlooked anything. But I hadn't."

"How did you know it was a bluff?" You cocky little shit.

Marshall pondered that a moment. "It doesn't matter. You'll never be able to prove this. It's not on paper anywhere. While I was in law school I worked one year as an unpaid intern at the law firm handling the estate of old man Scolari, the grandfather. This was when Gina's mother died. I did a turn in lots of different departments. I read the documents when I was Xeroxing them. That's how I knew the setup. Her mother's share went to Gina. Anything happens to her and the estate is transferred according to the terms of Gina's will. An orphan, with no siblings. That made me sole inheritor, even if she died intestate. Scolari couldn't change the trust or its terms. Your little stunt actually convinced Gina of my sincerity. I wasn't in any hurry to get her

243

to write a will and she absolutely refused to do it when Scolari pushed her on it.

"Like I said, for a bluff it wasn't half-bad. Gina believed you, but I think she was the only one who didn't know anything about her money. Well, I've got to be going, got a plane to catch." He smiled at me like he was a dog and I was his favorite tree.

It was hard to resist the impulse to threaten him, but a threat is also a warning and I had no intention of playing fair. I consoled myself with the fact that last time I only had two days to work with. Now I had a lifetime. When I heard the outer door close, I buzzed Kelly on the intercom.

"Yes, Mr. Haggerty?"

"Reopen the file on Derek Marshall."

Acknowledgments

I'd like to thank the following people for their contributions to this story: Joyce Huxley of Scuba St. Lucia for her information on hyperbaric accidents; Michael and Alison Weber of Charlottesville for the title and good company; and John Cort and Rebecca Barbetti for including us in their wedding celebration and tales of "the spork" among other things.

DONALD E. WESTLAKE

LOVE IN THE LEAN YEARS

Donald E. Westlake, who has just been honored by the Mystery Writers of America with its Grand Master Award, is an author whose long and distinguished career has ranged from the hard-boiled to the humorous. We don't know exactly where you'd place this little gem about love and marriage, as seen from both sides.

Charles Dickens knew his stuff, you know. Listen to this: "Annual income twenty pounds, annual expenditure nineteen nineteen six, result happiness. Annual income twenty pounds, annual expenditure twenty pounds ought and six, result misery."

Right on. You adjust the numbers for inflation and what you've got right there is the history of Wall Street. At least, so much of the history of Wall Street as includes me: seven years. We had the good times and we lived high on that extra jolly sixpence, and now we live day by day the long decline of shortfall. Result misery.

Where did they all go, the sixpences of yesteryear? Oh, pshaw, we know where they went. You in Gstaad, him in Aruba, her in Paris and me in the men's room with a sanitary straw in my nose. We know where it went, all right.

My name's Kimball, by the way; here's my card. Bruce Kimball, with Rendall/LeBeau. Account exec. May I say I'm still making money for my clients? There's a lot of good stuff undervalued out there, my friend. You can still make money on the Street. Of course you can. I admit it's harder now; it's much harder when I have only thruppence and it's sixpence I need to keep my nose filled, build up that confidence, face the world with that winner's smile. Man, I'm only hitting on one nostril, you know? I'm *hurtin'*.

Nearly three years a widow; time to remarry. I need a true heart to share my penthouse apartment (unfurnished terrace, unfortunately) with its grand view of the city, my cottage (14 rooms) in Amagansett, the income of my portfolio of stocks.

An income—ah, me—which is less than it once was. One or two iffy margin calls, a few dividends undistributed; bad news can mount up, somehow. Or dismount and move right in. Income could become a worry.

But first, romance. Where is there a husband for my middle years? I am Stephanie Morwell, 42, the end product of good breeding, good nutrition, a fine workout program and amazingly skilled cosmetic surgeons. Since my parents died as my graduation present from Bryn Mawr, I've more or less taken care of myself, though of course, at times, one does need a man around the house. To insert light bulbs and suchlike. The point is, except for a slight flabbiness in my stock portfolio, I am a fine catch for just the right fellow.

I don't blame my broker, please let me make that clear. Bruce Kimball is his name and he's unfailingly optimistic and cheerful. A bit of a blade, I suspect. (One can't say *gay* blade anymore, not without the risk of being misunderstood.) In any event, Bruce did very well for me when everybody's stock was going up, and now that there's a—oh, what are the pornographic euphemisms of finance? A shakeout, a mid-term correction, a market adjustment, all of that—now that times are tougher, Bruce has lost me less than most and has even found a victory or two amid the wreckage. No, I can't fault Bruce for a general worsening of the climate of money.

In fact, Bruce . . . hmmm. He flirts with me at times, but only in a professional way, as his employers would expect him to flirt with a moneyed woman. He's handsome enough, if a bit thin. (Thinner this year than last, in fact.) Still, those wiry fellows. . . .

Three or four years younger than I? Would Bruce Kimball be

the answer to my prayers? I do already know him and I'd rather not spend *too* much time on the project.

Stephanie Kimball. Like a schoolgirl, I write the name on the notepad beside the telephone on the Louis XIV writing table next to my view of the East River. The rest of that page is filled with hastily jotted numbers: income, outgo, estimated expenses, overdue bills. *Stephanie Kimball.* I gaze upon my view and whisper the name. It's a blustery, changeable, threatening day. *Stephanie Kimball.* I like the sound.

"There is a tide in the affairs of men, which, taken at the flood, leads on to fortune." Agatha Christie said that. Oh, but she was quoting, wasn't she? Shakespeare! Got it.

There was certainly a flood tide in my affair with Stephanie Morwell. Five years ago, she was merely one more rich wife among my clients, if one who took more of an interest than most in the day-to-day handling of the portfolio. In fact, I never did meet her husband before his death. Three years ago, that was; some ash blonds really come into their own in black, have you noticed?

I respected Mrs. Morwell's widowhood for a month or two, then began a little harmless flirtation. I mean, why not? She was a widow, after all. With a few of my other female clients, an occasional expression of male interest had eventually led to extremely pleasant afternoon financial seminars in midtown hotels. And now, Mrs. Morwell; to peel the layers of black from that lithe and supple body. . . .

Well. For three years, all that was merely a pale fantasy. Not even a consummation devoutly to be wished—now, who said that? No matter—it was more of a daydream while the computer's down.

From black to autumnal colors to a more normal range. A good-looking woman, friendly, rich, but never at the forefront of my mind unless she was actually in my presence, across the desk. And now it has all changed.

Mrs. Morwell was in my office once more, hearing mostly bad news, I'm afraid, and in an effort to distract her from the grimness of the occasion, I made some light remark, "There are better things we could do than sit here with all these depressing numbers." Something like that; and she said, in a kind of swollen voice I'd never heard before, "There certainly are."

I looked at her, surprised, and she was arching her back, stretching like a cat. I said, "Mrs. Morwell, you're giving me ideas."

She smiled. "Which ideas are those?" she asked, and 40 minutes later we were in bed in her apartment on Sutton Place.

Aaah. Extended widowhood had certainly sharpened *her* palate. What an afternoon. Between times, she put together a cold snack of salmon and champagne while I roved naked through the sunny golden rooms, delicately furnished with antiques. What a view she had, out over the East River. To live such a life. . . .

Well. Not until this little glitch in the economy corrects itself.

"Champagne?"

I turned and her body was as beautiful as the bubbly. Smiling, she handed me a glass and said, "I've never had such a wonderful afternoon in my entire life."

We drank to that.

We were married, my golden stockbroker and I, seven weeks after I first took him to bed. Not quite a whirlwind romance, but close. Of course, I had to meet his parents, just the once, a chore we all handled reasonably well.

We honeymooned in Caneel Bay and had such a lovely time we stayed an extra week. Bruce was so attentive, so charming, so—how shall I put it?—ever ready. And he got along amazingly well with the natives; they were eating out of his hand. In no time at all, he was joking on a first-name basis with half a dozen fellows I would have thought of as nothing more than dangerous layabouts, but Bruce could find a way to put almost anyone at ease. (Once or twice, one of these fellows even came to chat with Bruce at the cottage. I know he lent one of them money—it was changing hands as I glanced out the louvered window—and I'm sure he never even anticipated repayment.)

I found myself, in those first weeks, growing actually fond of Bruce. What an unexpected bonus! And my warm feeling toward this new husband only increased when, on our return to New

York, he insisted on continuing with his job at Rendall/LeBeau. "I won't sponge on you," he said, so firm and manly that I dropped to my knees that instant. *Such* a contrast with my previous marital experience!

Still, romance isn't everything. One must live as well; or, that is, some must live. And so, in the second week after our return, I taxied downtown for a discussion with Oliver Swerdluff, my new insurance agent. (New since Robert's demise, I mean.) "Congratulations on your new marriage, Mrs. Kimball," he said, this red-faced, portly man who was so transparently delighted with himself for having remembered my new name.

"Thank you, Mr. Swerdluff." I took my seat across the desk from him. "The new situation, of course," I pointed out, "will require some changes in my insurance package."

"Certainly, certainly."

"Bruce is now co-owner of the apartment in the city and the house on Long Island."

He looked impressed. "Very generous of you, Mrs., uh, Kimball."

"Yes, isn't it? Bruce is so important to me now, I can't imagine how I got along all those years without him. Oh, but that brings up a depressing subject. I suppose I must really insure Bruce's life, mustn't I?"

"The more important your husband is to you," he said, with his salesman's instant comprehension, "the more you must consider every eventuality."

"But he's priceless to me," I said. "How could I choose any amount of insurance? How could I put a dollar value on *Bruce?*"

"Let me help you with that decision," Mr. Swerdluff said, leaning that moist red face toward me over the desk.

We settled on an even million. Double indemnity.

"Strike while the widow is hot." Unattributed, I guess.

It did all seem to go very smoothly. At first, I was merely enjoying Stephanie for her own sake, expecting no more than our frequent encounters, and then somehow the idea arose that we might get married. I couldn't see a thing wrong with the proposition. Stephanie was terrific in bed, she was rich, she was beautiful and she obviously loved me. Surely, I could find some fondness in myself for a package like that.

And what she could also do, though I had to be very careful she never found out about it, was take up that shortfall, those pennies between me and the white medicine that makes me such a winning fellow. A generous woman, certainly generous enough for that modest need. And I understood from the beginning that if I were to keep her love and respect and my access to her piggy bank, I must never be too greedy. Independent, self-sufficient, self-respecting, only dipping into her funds for those odd sixpences which would bring me, in Mr. Dickens' phrase, "result happiness."

The appearance of independence was one reason why I kept on at Rendall/LeBeau, but I had other reasons as well. In the first place, I didn't want one of those second-rate account churners to take over the Morwell—now Kimball—account and bleed it to death with percentages of unnecessary sales. In the second place, I needed time away from Stephanie, private time that was reasonably accounted for and during which I could go on medicating myself. I would never be able to maintain my proper dosages at home without my bride sooner or later stumbling across the truth. And beyond all that, I've always enjoyed the work, playing with other people's money as if it were merely counters in a game, because that's all it is when it's other people's money.

Four lovely months we had of that life, with Stephanie never suspecting a thing. With neither of us, in fact, ever suspecting a thing. And if I weren't such a workaholic, particularly when topped with my little white friend, I wonder what eventually might have happened. No, I don't wonder; I know what would have happened.

But here's what happened instead. I couldn't keep my hands off Stephanie's financial records. It wasn't prying, it wasn't suspicion, it wasn't for my own advantage, it was merely a continuation of the work ethic on another front. And I wanted to do something nice for Stephanie because my fondness had grown— no, truly, it had. Did I love her? I believe I did. Surely, she was lovable. Surely, I had reason. Every day, I was made happy by her existence; if that isn't love, what is?

And Stephanie's tax records and household accounts were a mess. I first became aware of this when I came home one evening to find Stephanie, furrow-browed, huddled at the dining-room table with Serge Ostogoth, her—our—accountant. It was tax time and the table was a snowdrift of papers in no discernible order. Serge, a harmless drudge with leather elbow patches and a pathetic small mustache, was patiently taking Stephanie through the year just past, trying to match the paperwork to the history, a task that was clearly going to take several days. Serge had been Stephanie's accountant for three years, I later learned, and every year they had to go through this.

So I rolled up my sleeves to pitch in. Serge was grateful for my help. Stephanie, with shining eyes, kept telling me I was her savior, and eventually we managed to make sense of it all.

It was then I decided to put Stephanie's house in order. There was no point mentioning my plan; Stephanie was truly ashamed of her record-keeping inabilities, so why rub her nose in it? Evenings and weekends, if we weren't doing anything else, not flying out to the cottage or off to visit friends or out to theater and dinner, I'd spend half an hour or so working through her fiscal accounts.

Yes, and her previous husband, Robert, had been no help. When I got back that far, there was no improvement at all. In fact, Robert had been at least as bad as Stephanie about keeping records, and much worse when it came to throwing money around. A real wastrel. Outgo exceeded income all through that marriage. His life insurance, at the end, had been a real help.

And so had Frank's.

It was a week or two after I'd finished rationalizing the Robert years—two of them, though in three tax years—that my work brought me to my first encounter with Frank. Another husband, last name Bullock. Frank Bullock died three and a half years before Stephanie's marriage to Robert Morwell. Oh, yes, and he, too, had been well-insured. And with him, too, insurance paid double indemnity for accidental death.

Robert had been drowned at sea while on a cruise with Stephanie. Frank had fallen from the terrace of this very apartment while leaning out too far with his binoculars to observe the passage of an unusual breed of sea gull; Frank had been an amateur ornithologist.

And Leslie Hanford had fallen off a mountain in the Laurentians while on a Canadian ski holiday. Hanford was the husband before Bullock. Apparently, the first husband. Leslie's insurance, in fact, had been the basis for the fortune Stephanie now enjoyed, supplemented when necessary or convenient by the insurance of her later husbands. After each accidental death, Stephanie changed insurance agents and accountants. And each husband had died just over a year after the policy had been taken out.

Just over a year. So that's how long my bride expected to share my company, was it? Well, she was right about that, though not in the way she expected. I, too, could be decisive when called upon.

Whenever the weather was good, Stephanie took the sun on our terrace. Although it would be plagiarizing a bit from my bride, I could one day, having established an alibi at the office. . . .

The current insurance agent was named Oliver Swerdluff. I went to see him. "I just wanted to be sure," I said, "that the new policy on my life went through without a hitch. In case anything happened to me, I'd want to be certain Stephanie was cared for."

"An admirable sentiment," Swerdluff said. He was a puffy, sweaty man with tiny eyes, a man who would never let suspicion get between himself and a commission. Stephanie had chosen well.

I said, "Let me see, that was—half a million?"

"Oh, we felt a million would be better," Swerdluff said with a well-fed smile. "Double indemnity."

"Of course!" I exclaimed. "Excuse me, I get confused about these numbers. A million, of course. Double indemnity. And that's exactly the amount we want for the new policy, to insure Stephanie's life. If that's what I'm worth to her, she's certainly that valuable to me."

Call me a fool, but I fell in love. Bruce was so different from the others, so confident, so self-reliant. And it was so clear he loved me, loved *me*, not my money, not the advantages I brought him.

I tried to be practical, but my heart ruled my head. This was a husband I was going to have to keep.

Many's the afternoon I spent sunbathing and brooding on the terrace while Bruce was downtown at the firm. On one hand, I would have financial security for at least a little while. On the other hand, I would have Bruce.

Ah, what this terrace could be! Duckboarded, with wrought-iron furniture, a few potted hemlocks, a gaily striped awning. . . .

Well, what of it? What was a row of hemlocks in the face of true love? Bruce and I could discuss our future together, our finances. A plan, shared with another person.

We would have to economize, of course, and the first place to do so was with that million-dollar policy. I wouldn't be needing it now, so that was the first expense that could go. I went back to see Mr. Swerdluff. "I want to cancel that policy," I said.

"If you wish," he said. "Will you be canceling both of them?"

APPENDIX

THE YEARBOOK OF THE MYSTERY AND SUSPENSE STORY

THE YEAR'S BEST MYSTERY AND SUSPENSE NOVELS

Lawrence Block, *A Walk Among the Tombstones* (Morrow)
Rosellen Brown, *Before and After* (Farrar, Straus & Giroux)
Mary Higgins Clark, *All Around the Town* (Simon & Schuster)
Patricia D. Cornwell, *All That Remains* (Scribner's)
Michael Crichton, *Rising Sun* (Knopf)
Nelson DeMille, *The General's Daughter* (Warner Books)
Colin Dexter, *The Way Through the Woods* (Macmillan, London)
John Dunning, *Booked to Die* (Scribner's)
Dick Francis, *Driving Force* (Putnam)
Elizabeth George, *For the Sake of Elena* (Bantam)
Sue Grafton, *"I" Is for Innocent* (Henry Holt)
John Grisham, *The Pelican Brief* (Doubleday)
Jack Kelly, *Mad Dog* (Atheneum)
Elmore Leonard, *Rum Punch* (Delacorte)
Steve Martini, *Compelling Evidence* (Putnam)

APPENDIX

Ed McBain, *Mary, Mary* (Heinemann, London)

Sharyn McCrumb, *The Hangman's Beautiful Daughter* (Scribner's)

Mariam Grace Monfredo, *Seneca Falls Inheritance* (St. Martin's Press)

John Mortimer, *Dunster* (Viking)

Walter Mosley, *White Butterfly* (Norton)

Marcia Muller, *Pennies on a Dead Woman's Eyes* (Mysterious Press)

Bill Pronzini, *Epitaphs* (Delacorte)

Ruth Rendell, *Kissing the Gunner's Daughter* (Mysterious Press)

Craig Smith, *Ladystinger* (Crown)

Donna Tartt, *The Secret History* (Knopf)

BIBLIOGRAPHY

I. COLLECTIONS AND SINGLE STORIES

1. Brooks, Clive. *The Memoirs of Professor Moriarty, Volume One.* Bitterne, Southampton, England: SpyGlass Crime/ Brooks Books. Four new stories about Sherlock Holmes's foe. (1990)
2. ———. *Sherlock Holmes Revisited, Volume One.* Bitterne, Southampton, England: SpyGlass Crime/Brooks Books. Seven new pastiches. (1990)
3. ———. *Sherlock Holmes Revisited, Volume Two.* Bitterne, Southampton, England: SpyGlass Crime/Brooks Books. Five new pastiches. (1990)
4. Collins, Max Allan. *The Perfect Crime.* Eugene, OR: Mystery Scene/Pulphouse. Revised version of a 1988 short story.
5. Collins, Michael. *Crime, Punishment and Resurrection.* New York: Donald I. Fine. Eight Dan Fortune stories, one new, and a new Fortune novella. Introduction by Sue Grafton.
6. Crider, Bill. *My Heart Cries for You.* Eugene, OR: Mystery Scene/Pulphouse. Reprint of a single 1988 short story.
7. Fischer, Bruno. *A Mate for Murder, and Other Tales from the Pulps.* Brooklyn: Gryphon Books. Six stories written in 1940–41 for the mystery pulps but unpublished until now. Introduction by Gary Lovisi.
8. Geason, Susan. *Shaved Fish.* North Sydney, Australia: Allen &

Unwin. Ten stories about Australian private eye Syd Fish, half of them from the Australian *Penthouse*. (1990)

9. Gores, Joe. *Mostly Murder*. Eugene, OR: Mystery Scene/ Pulphouse. Eight stories, 1958–87. Introduction by the author.

10. Gorman, Ed. *Prisoners and Other Stories*. Baltimore: CD Publications. Twenty-two stories, two new. Afterword by Dean R. Koontz.

11. ———. *The Reason Why*. Eugene, OR: Mystery Scene/Pulphouse. Reprint of a single 1988 short story.

12. Grafton, Sue. *Kinsey and Me*. Santa Barbara, CA: Bench Press. Eight Kinsey Millhone stories plus eight brief autobiographical stories, in a limited edition. Introduction by the author. (1991)

13. Hodgson, William Hope. *Demons of the Sea*. West Warwick, RI: Necronomic Press. Ten weird stories and essays, some criminous. Edited by Sam Gafford.

14. Ikenami, Shotaro. *Master Assassin: Tales of Murder from the Shogun's City*. New York and Tokyo: Kodansha International. Six novelettes about a hired killer. (1991)

15. Mortimer, John. *Rumpole on Trial*. New York: Viking. Seven new stories about the British barrister.

16. Pickard, Nancy. *Afraid All the Time*. Eugene, OR: Mystery Scene/Pulphouse. Reprints of two stories, 1989–90.

17. Rankin, Ian. *A Good Hanging and Other Stories*. London: Century. Twelve stories about Edinburgh's Inspector Rebus.

18. Rowe, Jennifer. *Death in Store*. New York: Doubleday. Seven stories and a novelette about Australian sleuth Verity Birdwood, five previously published in Australian magazines and anthologies. (1/93)

19. Thomson, June. *The Secret Chronicles of Sherlock Holmes*. London: Constable. Seven new Holmes pastiches.

20. White, Teri. *Outlaw Blues*. Eugene, OR: Mystery Scene/ Pulphouse. Reprint of a single 1990 short story.

II. ANTHOLOGIES

1. Adams Round Table. *Missing in Manhattan*. Stamford, CT: Longmeadow Press. Ten new stories, one also published in

The Armchair Detective, in a continuing anthology series from a group of New York area mystery writers. Introduction by Dorothy Salisbury Davis.

2. Bailey, Don and Daile Unruh, eds. *Great Canadian Murder and Mystery Stories.* Kingston, Ontario, Canada: Quarry Press. Twenty-four stories, at least two new. (1991)

3. Baldick, Chris, ed. *The Oxford Book of Gothic Tales.* Oxford and New York: Oxford University Press. Thirty-seven stories, 1773–1991, mainly fantasy but some criminous.

4. Beals, Stephen, ed. *Mysteries from the Finger Lakes, Volume 2.* Seneca Falls, NY: Chapel Street Publishing. Six new stories in the second volume of a series. (1991)

5. Carper, Steve, ed. *The Defective Detective: Mystery Parodies by the Great Humorists.* New York: Citadel Press/Carol Publishing. Twenty-one parodies from various sources, 1902–86.

6. Cody, Liza and Michael Z. Lewin, eds. *1st Culprit.* London: Chatto & Windus. Twenty-four stories, fifteen new, in the first of an annual anthology series from the Crime Writers Association.

7. Cox, Michael, ed. *Victorian Tales of Mystery & Detection.* Oxford and New York: Oxford University Press. Thirty-one stories, 1845–1904.

8. Craig, Patricia, ed. *Julian Symons at 80: A Tribute.* Helsinki: Eurographica. Fourteen new stories, essays, and poems honoring Symons. For another tribute see no. 24.

9. Crawley, Michael, ed. *Murder, Mayhem and the Macabre.* Mississauga, Ontario, Canada: Mississauga Arts Council Library System. Thirteen new stories.

10. Dean, Christopher, ed. *Encounters with Lord Peter.* Hurstpierpoint, West Sussex, England: The Dorothy L. Sayers Society. Two new stories and nine essays about Lord Peter Wimsey. (1991)

11. Dolphin, Jack, *The Vig* & Ted Fitzgerald, *Wild Card.* Brooklyn: Gryphon Books. Two new novelettes in a paperbound booklet. (1991)

12. Edwards, Martin, ed. *Northern Blood.* Manchester, England: Didsbury Press. Five nonfiction pieces and ten stories, nine new, by crime writers living and working in the north of England.

13. Gorman, Ed, ed. *Dark Crimes 2: Modern Masters of Noir.* New York: Carroll & Graf. Twenty-one stories, one new, plus Teri White's Edgar-winning 1982 novel *Triangle.* Second in a continuing series. (1/93)

14. Greenberg, Martin H., ed. *The Further Adventures of Batman #2: Featuring the Penguin.* New York: Bantam Books. Eleven new stories.

15. ———. *Women on the Edge.* New York: Donald I. Fine. Fourteen stories, one new, by male and female mystery writers, 1952–92.

16. ——— and Ed Gorman, eds. *Cat Crimes II.* New York: Donald I. Fine. Nineteen new stories, some fantasy.

17. ———. *Cat Crimes III.* New York: Donald I. Fine. Eighteen new stories.

18. Haining, Peter, ed. *Murder on the Menu.* New York: Carroll & Graf. Twenty-seven stories about food, a few fantasy, from various sources.

19. ———. *The Television Detectives' Omnibus: Great Tales of Crime and Detection.* London: Orion Books. Thirty-two stories featuring famous sleuths who have starred in television series over the past fifty years.

20. Hale, Hilary, ed. *Midwinter Mysteries 2.* London: Little Brown. Ten new stories by British crime writers, one also published in *EQMM.*

21. Hoch, Edward D., ed. *The Year's Best Mystery and Suspense Stories 1992.* New York: Walker and Company. Twelve of the best stories from 1991, with bibliography, necrology and awards lists.

22. Jakubowski, Maxim, ed. *Constable New Crimes I.* London: Constable. Nineteen stories from England and America in the first of an annual series.

23. ———. *Murders for the Fireside.* London: Pan. Twenty-four stories from the first twenty-three years of the *Winter's Crimes* series. See also no. 38.

24. Keating, H. R. F., ed. *The Man Who . . .* London: Macmillan. Thirteen new stories by members of London's Detection Club, written in honor of Julian Symons's eightieth birthday. A few of the stories also appeared in *EQMM* following their British publication. See also no. 8.

25. Manson, Cynthia, ed. *Murder Takes a Holiday*. New York: Barnes & Noble Books. Forty-three stories with foreign settings, from *EQMM* and *AHMM*.
26. ———. *Murder Under the Mistletoe*. New York: Signet. Fifteen Christmas mysteries that have appeared in *EQMM* and *AHMM*.
27. ———. *Thou Shalt Not Kill*. New York: Signet. Ten stories, mainly from *EQMM* and *AHMM*, featuring ecclesiastical sleuths.
28. ———. *Women of Mystery*. New York: Carroll & Graf. Fifteen stories by women writers, from *EQMM* and *AHMM*.
29. ——— and Charles Ardai, eds. *FutureCrime: An Anthology of the Shape of Crime to Come*. New York: Donald I. Fine. Fifteen stories, three new.
30. ———. *Kingpins: Tales from Inside the Mob*. New York: Carroll & Graf. Seventeen stories from *EQMM* and *AHMM*.
31. ———. *New England Crime Chowder*. New York: International Polygonics. Fourteen stories with New England settings, from *EQMM* and *AHMM*.
32. Mortimer, John, ed. *Great Law and Order Stories*. New York: Norton. Fourteen detective and crime stories, from Poe to the present. (The 1990 British edition contains an additional story by Damon Runyon.)
33. ———. *The Oxford Book of Villains*. Oxford and New York: Oxford University Press. Nearly three hundred brief selections from fiction and nonfiction, dealing with villains of all sorts.
34. Mystery Scene, Staff of, eds. *The Year's 25 Finest Crime and Mystery Stories*. New York: Carroll & Graf. Twenty-five of the best stories from 1990, in the first of a planned annual series. Introduction by Jon L. Breen.
35. Peters, Elizabeth, presented by *Malice Domestic I*. New York: Pocket Books. Thirteen new "traditional" mysteries in the first of a planned annual series. Martin H. Greenberg is the uncredited editor. Introduction by Elizabeth Peters.
36. Queen, Ellery, ed. *Ellery Queen's Edgar Award Winners*. London: Robert Hale. Fourteen Edgar-winning stories from *EQMM*, 1954–83.
37. Randisi, Robert J. and Marilyn Wallace, eds. *Deadly Allies: Private Eye Writers of America/Sisters in Crime Collaborative*

Anthology. New York: Doubleday/Perfect Crime. Twenty new stories, one also published in a limited edition.

38. Rejt, Maria, ed. *Winter's Crimes 24*. London: Macmillan. Ten new stories by British writers, three also published in *EQMM*. See also no. 22.

39. Resnick, Mike, ed. *Whatdunits*. New York: DAW Books. Eighteen new science fiction mysteries, in which the editor challenged individual writers to create solutions for the brief problems he posed. Many involve alien creatures and physical problems different from those on earth.

40. Sellers, Peter, ed. *Cold Blood IV*. Oakville, Ontario, Canada: Mosaic Press. Thirteen new stories by Canadian writers in the latest volume of an anthology series.

41. Smith, Marie, ed. *Nobel Crimes*. New York: Carroll & Graf. Seventeen stories of mystery and detection by winners of the Nobel Prize for Literature.

42. Wallace, Marilyn, ed. *Sisters in Crime 5*. New York: Berkley. Seventeen new stories and two reprints from *AHMM* in the latest volume of a continuing series by women writers.

43. Weinberg, Robert, Stefan R. Dziemianowicz, and Martin H. Greenberg, eds. *Hard-Boiled Detectives: 23 Great Stories from Dime Detective Magazine*. New York and Avenel, NJ: Gramercy Books. Stories and novelettes from each year of the pulp magazine's existence, 1931–53.

44. Wishingrad, Jay, ed. *Legal Fictions: Short Stories about Lawyers and the Law*. New York: Overlook Press. Thirty-five stories, some criminous.

45. Wright, Eric and Howard Engel, eds. *Criminal Shorts*. Toronto: Macmillan Canada. Sixteen stories, twelve new, by members of the Crime Writers of Canada.

III. NONFICTION

1. Caprio, Betsy. *The Mystery of Nancy Drew*. Trabuco Canyon, CA: Source Books. A study of the long-running mystery series for girls.

2. Carr, Nick. *The Other Detective Pulp Heroes*. Chicago: Tattered Pages Press. Brief notes on forty series detectives who

appeared in American pulp magazines, with a checklist of their cases.

3. Coomes, David. *Dorothy L. Sayers: A Careless Rage for Life.* Batavia, IL: Lion Publishing. A biography of the famed British mystery writer, concentrating on her religious writing after 1937.

4. Dale, Alzina Stone. *Mystery Reader's Walking Guide: New York.* Lincolnwood (Chicago), IL: Passport Books. A walking guide to sites around Manhattan mentioned in various mystery novels. Third in a series.

5. Deeck, William F. and Steven A. Stilwell, compilers. *The Armchair Detective Index: Volumes 1–20, 1967–1987.* New York: The Armchair Detective. A complete index to the first twenty years of the leading mystery fan magazine.

6. Friedland, Martin L., ed. *Rough Justice: Essays on Crime in Literature.* Toronto: University of Toronto Press. A nominee for the Genre Criticism/Reference Award from Crime Writers of Canada. (1991)

7. Grafton, Sue, ed. *Writing Mysteries: A Handbook by the Mystery Writers of America.* Cincinnati: Writer's Digest Books. Twenty-seven authors, agents, and editors contribute chapters on various aspects of mystery writing. Introduction by Gregory Mcdonald.

8. Greenberg, Martin H., ed. *The Tom Clancy Companion.* New York: Berkley. Essays on the author, his characters, and the military hardware featured in his books, plus an interview with Clancy. Introduction by Larry Bond.

9. Harmon, Jim. *Radio Mystery and Adventure and Its Appearance in Film, Television and Other Media.* Jefferson, NC: McFarland & Co. A study of fourteen of the leading radio mystery and adventure series.

10. Lellenberg, Jon L., ed. *Irregular Memories of the Early Forties: An Archival History of the Baker Street Irregulars, January 1941–March 1944.* Bronx, NY: Fordham University Press. Correspondence and memoirs of early Baker Street Irregulars.

11. Loughery, John. *Alias S. S. Van Dine: The Man Who Created Philo Vance.* New York: Scribners. A biography of Willard Huntington Wright, who used the "S. S. Van Dine" pseud-

onym for his best-selling mystery novels of the 1920s and 1930s.

12. Mackler, Tasha. *Murder by Category: A Subject Guide to Mystery Fiction*. Metuchen, NJ: Scarecrow Press. A sampling of titles under various subject headings. (1991)

13. Marnham, Patrick. *The Man Who Wasn't Maigret: A Portrait of Georges Simenon*. London: Bloomsbury. A new biography of Maigret's creator.

14. Meyers, Jeffrey. *Edgar Allan Poe: His Life and Legacy*. New York: Scribner's. A biography of Poe, with chapters on his reputation and his influence on modern writers.

15. Nehr, Ellen. *Doubleday Crime Club Compendium 1928– 1991*. Martinez, CA: Offspring Press. A study of Doubleday's Crime Club imprint with binding and jacket descriptions, jacket blurbs, etc., of all 2,485 books published during the imprint's lifetime. Includes twenty-four pages of color photos of Crime Club jackets.

16. Payne, David S. *Myth and Modern Man in Sherlock Holmes: Sir Arthur Conan Doyle and the Uses of Nostalgia*. Blooming- ton, IN: Gaslight Press. A study of Holmes's instant and enduring popularity.

17. Sampson, Robert. *Yesterday's Faces, Volume V: Dangerous Horizons*. Bowling Green, OH: Bowling Green State Univer- sity Popular Press. Fifth in a planned six-volume study of series characters in the early pulp magazines, concentrating on adventure heroes, some from the mystery pulps. (1991)

18. Sander, Gordon F. *Serling: The Rise and Twilight of Televi- sion's Last Angry Man*. New York: Dutton. Biography of television and film writer and host Rod Serling, who worked mainly in the fantasy field but wrote a few criminous screen- plays.

19. Shallcross, Martyn. *The Private World of Daphne du Maurier*. New York: St. Martin's Press. Biography of the author of *Rebecca* and other popular novels of romantic suspense, many of which were filmed.

20. Van Dover, J. Kenneth. *At Wolfe's Door: The Nero Wolfe Novels of Rex Stout*. San Bernardino, CA: Borgo Press. A guide to the seventy-four Wolfe novels and novelettes, plus eleven novels and stories about other characters, with brief

plot synopsis and critical comment. Volume 52 of *The Milford Series: Popular Writers of Today.* (1991)

21. Wark, Wesley K., ed. *Spy Fiction, Spy Films and Real Intelligence.* London: Frank Cass. Winner of the Genre Criticism/Reference Award from Crime Writers of Canada. (1991)
22. Weller, Philip and Christopher Roden. *The Life and Times of Sherlock Holmes.* Avenel, NJ: Crescent/Outlet Books. Illustrated study of Conan Doyle's sleuth, with complete summaries of each story.
23. Wilson, Keith D. *Cause of Death.* Cincinnati: Writer's Digest Books. Mystery writer's guide to death, murder, and forensic medicine.
24. Wingate, Anne. *Scene of the Crime.* Cincinnati: Writer's Digest Books. Mystery writer's guide to crime scene investigation.

AWARDS

MYSTERY WRITERS OF AMERICA EDGAR AWARDS

Best Novel: Margaret Maron, *Bootlegger's Daughter* (Mysterious Press)

Best First Novel: Michael Connely, *The Black Echo* (Little, Brown)

Best Original Paperback: Dana Stabenon, *A Cold Day for Murder* (Berkley)

Best Fact Crime: Harry Farrell, *Swift Justice* (St. Martin's)

Best Critical/Biographical: John Loughery, *Alias S. S. Van Dine* (Scribner's)

Best Short Story: Benjamin M. Schutz, "Mary, Mary, Shut the Door" (*Deadly Allies*)

Best Young Adult: Chap Reaver, *A Little Bit Dead* (Delacorte)

Best Juvenile: Eve Bunting, *Coffin on a Case* (HarperCollins)

Best Episode in a Television Series: Michael S. Chernuchin and Rene Balcer, "Conspiracy" (*Law and Order*, Universal)

Best Television Feature or Miniseries: Lynda LaPlant: "Prime Suspect" (*Mystery!*, PBS)

Best Motion Picture: Peter Tolkin, *The Player* (Fineline)

Grandmaster: Donald E. Westlake

Robert L. Fish Memorial Award: Steven Saylor, "A Will Is a Way." (*EQMM*, March)

CRIME WRITERS ASSOCIATION (BRITAIN)

Gold Dagger: Colin Dexter, *The Way Through the Woods* (Macmillan)
Silver Dagger: Liza Cody, *Bucket Nut* (Chatto)
John Creasey Memorial Award: Minette Walters, *The Ice House* (Macmillan)
Last Laugh Award: Carl Hiaasen, *Native Tongue* (Macmillan)
'92 Award: Timothy Williams: *Black August* (Gollancz)
Rumpole Award: Peter Rawlinson, *Hatred and Contempt* (Chapmans)
Golden Handcuffs Award: Catherine Aird
Diamond Dagger: Leslie Charteris

CRIME WRITERS OF CANADA ARTHUR ELLIS AWARDS (FOR 1991)

Best Crime Novel: Peter Robinson, *Past Reason Hated* (Viking Penguin)
Best First Novel: Paul Grescoe, *Flesh Wound* (Douglas & McIntyre)
Best Short Story: Eric Wright, "Two in the Bush" (*Christmas Stalkings,* Mysterious Press)
Best True Crime: William Lowther, *Arms and the Man: Dr. Gerald Bull, Iraq and the Supergun* (Doubleday Canada)
Best Genre Criticism/Reference: Wesley K. Wark, ed., *Spy Fiction, Spy Films and Real Intelligence* (Frank Cass)
Derrick Murdoch Award: William Bankier, James Powell, Peter Sellers

PRIVATE EYE WRITERS OF AMERICA SHAMUS AWARDS (FOR 1991)

Best Novel: Max Allan Collins, *Stolen Away* (Bantam)
Best Paperback Original: Paul Kemprecos, *Cool Blue Tomb* (Bantam)
Best First Novel: Thomas D. Davis, *Suffer Little Children* (Walker)

Best Short Story: Nancy Pickard, "Dust Devil" (*The Armchair Detective*)
Lifetime Achievement: Joseph Hanson

BOUCHERCON ANTHONY AWARDS (FOR 1991)

Best Novel: Peter Lovesey, *The Last Detective* (Doubleday)
Best First Novel: Sue Henry, *Murder on the Iditarod Trail* (Atlantic)
Best True Crime: David Simon, *Homicide: A Year on the Killing Streets* (Houghton Mifflin)
Best Short Story: Liza Cody, "Lucky Dip" (*A Woman's Eye*)
Best Short Story Anthology: Sara Paretsky, *A Woman's Eye* (Delacorte)
Best Critical Work: Maxim Jakubowski, ed., *100 Great Detectives* (Carroll & Graf)
Lifetime Achievement: Charlotte MacLeod

MYSTERY READERS INTERNATIONAL MACAVITY AWARDS (FOR 1991)

Best Novel: Nancy Pickard, *I.O.U.* (Pocket Books)
Best First Novel (tie): Sue Henry, *Murder on the Iditarod Trail* (Atlantic); Mary Willis Walker, *Zero at the Bone* (St. Martin's)
Best Short Story: Margaret Maron, "Deborah's Judgement" (*A Woman's Eye*)
Best Biographical/Critical: Tony Hillerman and E. Bulow, *Talking Mysteries: A Conversation with Tony Hillerman* (University of New Mexico Press)

MALICE DOMESTIC AGATHA AWARDS (FOR 1991)

Best Novel: Nancy Pickard, *I.O.U.* (Pocket Books)
Best First Novel: Mary Willis Walker, *Zero at the Bone* (St. Martin's)

Best Short Story: Margaret Maron, "Deborah's Judgement" (*A Woman's Eye*)

INTERNATIONAL ASSOCIATION OF CRIME WRITERS HAMMETT PRIZE

Elmore Leonard, *Maximum Bob* (Delacorte)

NECROLOGY

1. Isaac Asimov (1920–1992). Famed science fiction author who published two mystery novels and combined both genres into novels like *The Caves of Steel* (1954) and *The Naked Sun* (1957). He also published more than a hundred detective short stories, notably his Black Widowers series for *EQMM*.
2. Reginald Bretnor (1911–1992). Science fiction writer and critic who authored five *EQMM* stories and one novel, *A Killing in Swords* (1978), about sleuth Alastair Timuroff.
3. J. F. (Jackson Frederick) Burke (1915–1993). Author of five mystery novels, three about black house detective Samuel Moses Kelly, as well as short stories in *AHMM* and elsewhere.
4. Joseph Commings (1913–1992). Short story writer, creator of impossible-crime expert Senator Banner. His work appeared in *The Saint Magazine, Mike Shayne,* and numerous pulp magazines and anthologies, sometimes as by "Monte Craven."
5. William J. Coughlin (1924–1992). Author of about a dozen thrillers and courtroom novels, notably *Shadow of a Doubt* (1991) and *Death Penalty* (1992). Two paperbacks were published as by "Sean A. Key."
6. John Crosby (1912–1991). Television critic who published more than a half-dozen suspense and espionage novels, notably *Men in Arms* (1983).
7. Monica Dickens (1915–1992). British author, great-granddaughter of Charles Dickens, who published a single suspense novel, *The Room Upstairs* (1966).

8. Mel Dinelli (1912?–1991). Hollywood scriptwriter whose stories appeared in *EQMM* and *The Saint Magazine*.
9. Dorothy Cameron Disney (1903–1992). Author of nine mystery novels, notably *The 17th Letter* (1945). With her husband, Milton Mackaye, she published a 1948 biography and checklist of Mary Roberts Rinehart.
10. Bruno Fischer (1908–1992). Author of some 165 pulp detective stories and 25 novels, notably *The Dead Men Grin* (1945) and *The Paper Circle* (1951).
11. Steve Frazee (1909–1992). Western writer who published three crime novels, notably *The Sky Block* (1953). He won first prize in the 1953 *EQMM* contest with his story "My Brother Down There."
12. Roy Fuller (1912–1991). British lawyer and poet who authored three mystery novels, notably *The Second Curtain* (1953).
13. Ernest K. Gann (1910–1991). Well-known novelist whose work included one crime novel, *Of Good and Evil* (1963).
14. Peter Godfrey (1917–1992). South African-British journalist who authored dozens of detective short stories and a single book, *Death Under the Table* (1954). Contributor to *EQMM* and numerous anthologies.
15. Cyril Joyce (?–1992). British author of twenty-three suspense novels, unpublished in America, beginning with *A Web to Catch a Spider* (1975).
16. Carlton Keith (1914–1991). Author of children's books who also published six mystery novels starting with *The Diamond-Studded Typewriter* (1956). His real name was Keith Carlton Robertson.
17. Fritz Leiber (1910–1992). Famed fantasy novelist who contributed occasional stories to *EQMM*, *Mike Shayne*, and other mystery magazines.
18. Seicho Matsumoto (1909–1992). Prolific Japanese mystery writer, only two of whose novels have been translated into English. A collection, *The Voice and Other Stories*, appeared in English in 1989.
19. Sidney Meredith (1919?–1992). New York literary agent who, along with his brother, founded the Scott Meredith Literary Agency and edited a single anthology, *The Best from Man-*

hunt (1958). Both brothers played an active part in the magazine's early days.

20. Lenore Glen Offord (1905–1991). Novelist and longtime mystery critic for the *San Francisco Chronicle*, author of eight detective novels, notably *The Smiling Tiger* (1949).
21. Theodore Roscoe (1906–1992). Pulp writer who authored six mystery novels, notably *Only in New England* (1959).
22. Jack Sharkey (1931–1992). Author of two detective novels in the 1960s as well as numerous plays and science fiction stories.
23. Roy Sparkia (1924–1992). Author of four paperback mysteries, 1954–74.
24. Grace Zaring Stone (1891–1991). Author of four mystery thrillers, three as by "Ethel Vance," notably *Escape* (1939).
25. Dwight V. Swain (1915–1992). Mystery and science fiction pulp writer whose works included a novel under the "Nick Carter" house name and several books on writing.
26. Michael Underwood (1916–1992). Pseudonym of John Michael Evelyn, British crime novelist and short story writer who published nearly fifty novels, more than a dozen about female investigator Rosa Epton.
27. W. J. (William John) Weatherby (1930–1992). British journalist who published five crime novels, four as by "Will Perry," notably *Death of an Informer* (1973), an MWA Edgar winner for best paperback.
28. Ted Willis (1918–1992). Well-known British scriptwriter who published nearly a dozen crime novels beginning with *The Blue Lamp* (1950), based on a film that became a long-running BBC police series, *Dixon of Dock Green*.

HONOR ROLL

ABBREVIATIONS

AHMM—Alfred Hitchcock's Mystery Magazine
EQMM—Ellery Queen's Mystery Magazine
(Starred stories are included in this volume. All dates are 1992.)

Akagawa, Jiro, "Beat Your Neighbor Out of Doors," *EQMM*,
    March
Allyn, Doug, "Icewater Mansions," *EQMM*, January
———, "The Ten-Pound Parrott," *EQMM*, February
*———, "Candles in the Rain," *EQMM*, November
Ambler Eric, "The One Who Did For Blagden Cole," *The Man
    Who . . .*
Anders, K. T., "A Simple Matter of Training," *Sisters in Crime 5*
Andrews, Sarah, "Invitation," *Deadly Allies*
Bannister, Jo, "The Garden Party," *EQMM*, April
*———, "A Poisoned Chalice," *EQMM*, May
———, "Howler," *EQMM*, October
Barnard, Robert, "A Hotel in Bucharest," *EQMM*, mid-December
Beck, K. K., "Seascape," *Sisters in Crime 5*
Beechcroft, William, "Turkey Durkin and the Catfish," *EQMM*,
    October
Boshinski, Blanche, "Games," *EQMM*, January
Butler, Gwendoline, "The Child Cannot Speak," *Midwinter Mys-
    teries 2*

*Butler, Jacklyn, "A Bit of Flotsam," *AHMM*, January

Campbell, Robert, "The Journeyer," *EQMM*, May

Carlson, P. M., "The Dirty Little Coward That Shot Mr. Howard;
   or, Such Stuff As Dreams Are Made On," *Sisters in Crime 5*

Carroll, William J., Jr., "Mixed Agenda," *AHMM*, October

Cash-Domingo, Lea, "The Disintegrating Man," *EQMM*, June

Cenedella, Robert, "Flies With Honey," EQMM, April

Collins, Barbara and Max Allan Collins, "Cat Got Your Tongue,"
   Cat Crimes III

*Collins, Max Allan, "Louise," *Deadly Allies*

Curtis, Ashley, "Anomalies of the Heart," *AHMM*, July

Delman, David, "The Conspiracy," *EQMM*, November

DuBois, Brendan, "Grave on a Hill," *EQMM*, October

Elkins, Charlotte and Aaron, "Nice Gorilla," *Malice Domestic*

Engel, Howard, "Custom Killing," *Criminal Shorts*

Ferrars, Elizabeth, "Stop Thief!" *EQMM*, November

Frankel, Valerie, "Angel on the Loose," *Malice Domestic*

Fraser, Antonia, "The Man Who Wiped the Smile Off Her Face,"
   EQMM, July

———, "The Bottle Dungeon," *EQMM*, September

Gilbert, Michael, "The Man Who Was Reconstituted," *The Man
   Who . . .*

*Gorman, Ed, "Mother Darkness," *Prisoners and Other Stories*

Grape, Jan, "Whatever Has To Be Done," *Deadly Allies*

Green, Christine, "Drummond Street," *EQMM*, mid-December

Hansen, Joseph, "An Excuse for Shooting Earl," *AHMM*, September

———, "Storm Damage," *AHMM*, November

Hart, Carolyn G., "Nothing Ventured," *Deadly Allies*

Heald, Tim, "A Winter Break," *EQMM*, September

Healy, Jeremiah, "Georgie Boy," *EQMM*, July

Hill, Reginald, "Strangers on a Bus," *Midwinter Mysteries 2*

Hoch, Edward D., "Saratoga Cat," *Cat Crimes II*

———, "The Summer of Our Discontent," *EQMM*, November

*———, "The Problem of the Leather Man," *EQMM*, December

Howard, Clark, "The Last High Mountain," *EQMM*, February

Keating, H. R. F., "Scrabble Babble Dabble," *EQMM*, February

Kellerman, Jonathan, "His Victory Garden," *The Armchair Detective*, Spring

*Kelly, Susan B., "The Last Sara," *1st Culprit*
Kijewski, Karen, "Alley Kat," *Sisters in Crime 5*
Kilpatrick, Nancy, "Mantrap," *Murder, Mayhem and the Macabre*
Kraft, Gabrielle, "One Hit Wonder," *Sisters in Crime 5*
Krich, Rochelle Majer, "A Golden Opportunity," *Sisters in Crime 5*
LaPierre, Janet, "Take Care of Yourself," *Malice Domestic*
——, "The Woman Who Knew What She Wanted," *Sisters in Crime 5*
Limón, Martin, "Seoul Story," *AHMM*, January
——, "Ascom City," *AHMM*, mid-December
Lovesey, Peter, "The Man Who Ate People," *EQMM*, October
*——, "You May See a Strangler," *Midwinter Mysteries 2*
Lutz, John, "Before You Leap," *Deadly Allies*
MacGregor, T. J., "Wild Card," *Sisters in Crime 5*
Mayberry, Florence V., "Miz Sammy's Honor," *EQMM*, June
McCarry, Charles, "The Hand of Carlos," *The Armchair Detective*, Fall
McCrumb, Sharyn, "Nine Lives to Live," *Cat Crimes II*
Monfredo, Mariam Grace, "Gather Not Thy Rose," *EQMM*, July
Mullins, Terry, "The Threat to the Cathedral," *EQMM*, March
——, "Topaz," *EQMM*, mid-December
Murray, Stephen, "A Quiet Evening at Fountains," *Northern Blood*
Naparsteck, Marton, "The 9:13," *EQMM*, February
Natsuki, Shizuko, "A Midnight Coincidence," *EQMM*, May
*Oates, Joyce Carol, "The Model," *EQMM*, October
——, "The Premonition," *Playboy*, December
Obermayr, Erich, "Murder in the Passage Vendome," *AHMM*, January
Olson, Donald, "Somewither Cold and Strange," *EQMM*, March
——, "Period of Mourning," *EQMM*, October
Owens, Barbara, "Mercy's Killing," *EQMM*, January
——, "Teeny Ann," *EQMM*, mid-December
Peverell, Anne, "Pritt the Twit," *AHMM*, January
*Pickard, Nancy, "Sex and Violence," *Deadly Allies*
Powell, James, "Unquiet Graves," *EQMM*, June
——, "Ruby Laughter, Tears of Pearl," *EQMM*, mid-December
Randisi, Robert J., "Turnabout," *Deadly Allies*

*Rendell, Ruth, "The Man Who Was the God of Love," *The Man Who . . .*

— — —, "The Mouse in the Corner," *1st Culprit*

Roberts, Les, "The Scent of Spiced Oranges," *Cat Crimes II*

Robinson, Peter, "Anna Said. . . ," *Cold Blood IV*

— — —, "Not Safe After Dark," *Criminal Shorts*

Sale, Medora, "The Mouse in the Mattress," *Criminal Shorts*

*Saylor, Steven, "A Will Is a Way," *EQMM*, March

— — —, "The Lemures," *EQMM*, October

Schossau, P. K., "Where Angels Fear," *AHMM*, March

*Schutz, Benjamin M., "Mary, Mary, Shut the Door," *Deadly Allies*

Scott, Jeffry, "The Poisoning of Mr. Paisley," *AHMM*, February

— — —, "Curse of the Irish King," *EQMM*, September

Sellers, Peter, "Last Resort," *Cold Blood IV*

Slesar, Henry, "A Letter Too Late," *EQMM*, July

Stevens, B. K., "True Adventure," *AHMM*, April

Thomson, June, "Secrets," *EQMM*, March

Waskin, David, "Heroes Never Say Goodbye," *AHMM*, August

Wasylyk, Stephen, "Floater," *AHMM*, December

*Westlake, Donald E., "Love in the Lean Season," *Playboy*, February

— — —, "Party Animal," *Playboy*, December

Whitehead, J. W., "The White Mansion," *EQMM*, June

Wood, Ted, "Murder at Louisburg," *Cold Blood IV*

Woodward, Ann F., "The Education of the Kamo Virgin," *AHMM*, February